SON OF THE WOLF

BOOK SEVEN OF
THE LAST MARINES

William S. Frisbee, Jr.

Theogony Books
Coinjock, NC

Chris Kennedy/Theogony Books
1097 Waterlily Rd.
Coinjock, NC 27923
https://chriskennedypublishing.com/

Publisher's Note: This is a work of fiction. Names, characters, places, and incidents are a product of the author's imagination. Locales and public names are sometimes used for atmospheric purposes. Any resemblance to actual people, living or dead, or to businesses, companies, events, institutions, or locales is completely coincidental.

Cover Design by J Caleb Design.

Ordering Information:
Quantity sales. Special discounts are available on quantity purchases by corporations, associations, and others. For details, contact the "Special Sales Department" at the address above.

Son of the Wolf/William S. Frisbee, Jr.-- 1st ed.
ISBN: 978-1648559181

Chapter One:

Recap

Zale Stathis

My name is Zale Stathis. I am the first, and possibly last, commandant of the Wolf Legion.

The gunny once said, when I was the one making the decisions, we were screwed. I suppose it could be worse, but we are screwed blue and tattooed like little pink ponies.

We are leaving Mother Earth to save the human race. If we don't? In just one year, humanity will disappear. You will find this final recording in Quantico, Virginia, the last bastion and finest fortress of the United States Marines. When it falls, so does the last hope for the human race.

All our lines are collapsing. The Moon has been overrun. Mars, Saturn, all gone. Earth may soon be lost to the ancient hordes. Only fortress Quantico on Earth remains strong and the vanhat probe our lines daily. White Heron Fortress in Jupiter also stands, but we don't know for how much longer. I'm not going there.

We thought we could turn Sol into a fortress, but we were wrong.

I have little time, so I need to fill you in. Hopefully, you are not some bug-eyed monster that evolved from humanity after we failed to stop the vanhat. If you are, nothing personal, but I hate you, and I think you're ugly.

These are dark times, and so much has occurred, I don't know where to begin. These aren't my last words, though. I hope to engrave those on some demon's forehead like Sergeant Levin. We'll see. I now have a trusty Ka-Bar like he did. Hopefully, you don't know what I'm talking about, but in time you will. I'm rambling though. I'm several hundred years old, so I'm entitled. For us humans, that is a super-duper long time and to go that long without... um, never mind.

I don't know who will find this or if you can even speak this language. You will learn the songs of my people or go extinct as well. The vanhat don't understand anything else.

Starting too far back won't help you. As a googly eyed alien, I doubt you really care about my childhood and how I got conned into being an infantry Marine. You need to know how to avoid the fate that is coming for you. I hope you have better luck than humanity.

Let me start with my military service. I enlisted hundreds of years ago in the most elite fighting force known to man. We were the ultimate life-takers and heart breakers. Our magnificent uniforms were panty droppers. We were United States Marines, and I was one of them. I ended up as a private in the US Marine Raiders, something of an elite force within that elite force. Those were some of the best years of my life, though I never got laid.

As an organization, the Raiders had changed a lot from World War Two and the War on Terror. I joined right before the AI revolution, before we even knew it was brewing. I was with a unit that got bleeding-edge Sentient Cybernet Biological Implants, AIs that are part computer and part organic, using some of our cloned brain cells for processing and stuff. These SCBIs are our best buddies for a couple of reasons. We are inseparable, for starters. They are super loyal to whoever's skull they are planted in, and they help us excel in so many ways. Maybe it is the organic component or maybe it is the programming, but the SCBI is loyal.

My platoon, led by some lieutenant and the super-badass Gunnery Sergeant Wolf Mathison, was being deployed to Europa. The Asiatic Union wasn't playing nice, and they needed Raiders to pay them a visit and slap them back into line. It didn't work out like we expected. We got on a ship, the USS *Jefferson*, arrived in orbit around Jupiter, and never woke up. The US squidberts flew us into an ambush and the ship got torn up. Me, the gunny, my squad leader, Sergeant Levin, and a shuttle pilot, Warrant Officer Diamond Winters, ended up trapped in stasis for a couple of hundred years. It wasn't fun, but I don't remember much. For the first time since joining the Raiders, I was able to catch up on my sleep, but as luck would have it, the green weenie struck, and we didn't get any back pay.

During our nappy time, the United States had a civil war where the AIs rebelled, and in the end the USA ended up nuking itself and a lot of American owned real estate around the world. This did super bad things to the climate and made the USA very unpopular with the survivors.

Humanity finally made it into outer space. Probably not the biggest surprise considering we couldn't grow petunias and you couldn't go to the beach and see pretty women in bikinis anymore. Even though the Moon wasn't made of cheese, we now had some real incentive. Mankind also figured out faster-than-light travel by using something called "Shorr space," basically a parallel dimension we could slip in and out of, and when we did that we would be closer to our destination. But because it was another dimension, it put us closer to the real problem.

All that happened while we were sleeping.

Some SOG scientists thawed us out. In case you don't know the SOG, it's the Social Organizational Governance. A bunch of jack-booted thugs who worship socialism, social controls, and top-down command. They make historical figures like Hitler, Mao, and Stalin look like friendly and primitive sock puppets. Run by a Central Committee of Hitler wannabes, they were nasty people. We didn't realize just how bad they were until after we shot most of them, but I'm getting ahead of myself.

We got thawed out of stasis by these Governance jackboots, who decided they were going to kill us. They found us in the outer reaches of the Solar System, way out there, near a super-secret research facility. They were researching some boxes they had found in some secret alien facility.

Well. Turns out those boxes kept demons and other nasty creatures from coming into our dimension. These low IQ jackboots released the first demon—or as the Aesir and Vanir like to call them, the Jotun, or Jotnar, which is plural. Our allies from the Vapaus Republic have a lot of words and terms I still haven't figured out.

In case you haven't discovered it yet, there aren't a lot of intelligent species running around our galaxy. Not sure if you call it the Fermi Paradox, but we do. Some dude named Fermi had a calculator and figured that our galaxy should be swarming with intelligent, super-advanced aliens. It isn't. We found ruins on planets but we were mostly alone. Shorr space and the demons are the reason why.

Turns out our galaxy goes through phases. During these phases, our dimension comes close to or passes through other dimensions. When this happens, there is crossover. The things from those dimensions come to ours, and they like to eat faces and souls. When they cross over to our dimension, they bring their laws of physics with them and that lets them do some weird, unexplainable stuff in ours. It also explains ghosts, demons, and other mythological creatures from our history, dragons, werewolves, vampires, zombies, and maybe Elvis. They were all temporary crossovers. When the crossover was complete, or the dimensions finally drifted apart, the laws of physics reasserted themselves and erased any proof we had been visited, so when the shit hit the fan, we had no clue because we were confident our science had everything figured out.

Now it makes sense. Back when we got thawed out, it didn't. A crossing was happening again, and the station we were trapped on had ripped open that wall between dimensions and a demon came through. It took us a while to skull stomp that dude, or actually Sergeant Levin managed to Ka-Bar klunk it, but that was later.

Anyway, these stupid scientists ripped the dimension open and let a demon through. That gave us incentive to escape our prison and meet up with some space Vikings that were trying to figure out what was going on there. It was all so far-fetched we still didn't have a clue, but now we had a way off the station and some new allies.

The SOG had known a little about this cross-dimensional issue because it was becoming problematic. With us awake, it seemed to get a lot worse. So, of course, we got blamed. Led by Gunny Mathison and the over-muscled Viking babe Skadi, we were able to discover two weapons to help us fight the demons, or vanhat as the Vikings were calling them. One weapon was an Inkeri generator. A complex little item that stabilized the laws of physics in our dimension. This made life difficult or impossible for the vanhat crossing over to eat faces. It robbed them of their cross-dimensional juju. Another critical weapon was the d-bomb, or dimensional bomb. That is, just a burst of raw energy that restabilizes our dimension and is very destructive to the vanhat.

While we were running around trying to figure all this out and collecting weapons, the Social Organizational Governance collapsed. Sol hid behind trillions of automated weapons platforms, and they left the rest of the colonies and sectors to fend for themselves without the oppressive boot heel of the Central Committee to crush their neck. This wasn't the greatest thing because a lot of junior Hitlers came to power. Outside of Sol, the Governance became a chaotic mess of rebelling sector fleets and marauding vanhat. And then there were the alien Torag and Voshka that the SOG had been fighting against. A real mess.

Of course, the biggest problem was that the more time vanhat spent in our dimension, the stronger they became. They had this way of absorbing people, make them slaves and such, eat their souls or something, and that give the vanhat strength and staying ability. The more faces they ate, the more powerful they became, and they could find people anywhere in space with their voodoo-like senses.

Sol, the cradle of humanity, was the largest concentration of people. The vanhat who conquered Sol would become the most powerful. When we discovered that, we realized what we had to do, and we infiltrated the most secure system in the galaxy.

We discovered a small colony of humans led by our old commanding officer, General Becket, who was now president of the United States. But the president was now a few rounds short of a magazine and his scope was not even close to being zeroed. Not only did he have a SCBI, but he had something, or someone, else in his head. He was a relic of the AI wars in so many ways. We're still trying to figure that out.

We escaped him and made it to the Zvezda Two, the secret and well-guarded heart of the Governance. Like all paranoid jack-booted regimes, they had centralized controls and management there in their Lunar fortress. A little of this, a little of that, and we killed off the Central Committee and took control. All in a day's work for US Marines, though I could have gone without Commissar Feng's pretend betrayal and that Viking vampire special ops killer Hermod. Sif, Skadi, and Vili managed to kick a demon named Luciferius back to his home dimension, and once again the US Marines saved the day, though we had to share some of that glory with the Aesir. That is okay; I like them.

"The only easy day was yesterday" is one of the things the SEALS like to say. Those stuck-up squidberts know what they are talking about, though.

Not sure if the rest of the story is relevant, but I don't have much time.

With the emperor down and the empress chewing on a shit sandwich, it's up to me and Admiral Winters. We're Marines though. It's what we do. The empress will hold things together 'til we get back.

We've lost the battle for Earth, and the Moon, and Saturn, and Mars but we haven't lost the war. It ain't looking good, and now I have to finish up this recording because I have to pee.

I am Zale Stathis, the first and last commandant of Wolf's Legion. We are off to outer space to save the human race. Because if we don't, our species will disappear. And if we return? Well, that's a big if. Don't hold your breath. Unless you're a bug-eyed alien, then hold your breath. We could be back any minute.

Semper Fi and good luck!

* * * * *

Chapter Two:
Time to Leave

General Becket, Commandant USMC, President of the USA

Earth was dying. Humanity was dying and that worried Becket for several reasons. Decagon had shared projections with Becket and Sun Tzu. The addition of the Republic's new weapons did not change the end result, only extended it, like the hallway Becket was walking down. The end was inevitable, just not in sight yet.

The corridor seemed to go on forever. Cracks, black mold, dripping water, and water-stained concrete were the only variations Becket saw as he strode down a corridor that frequently turned left and right. If there had been branches and other passages, Becket could almost believe he was in an underground maze. The sensors in his helmet let him see in complete darkness. He passed several Collective-designed warbots that remained silent and motionless, ignoring their master and the two slaves.

No human had built this hallway, and Becket knew he was the only human to come this way. Not even he had known this corridor was here. A master did not give its slave all the information. What else had Decagon created that Becket didn't know about? How long ago had this been created?

The vanhat were unstoppable, like the Collective, and humanity was just an annoyance to them both. Just because Earth's and the Sol System's demise had been delayed didn't mean it would survive. There were over two hundred other planets in the Governance that the vanhat could scour and eradicate. There were other fleets, including the Torag and Voshka, which could be absorbed by the invaders, and Decagon was sure they would not ignore Sol in the long term. The war could last one year or a hundred. Time was on the vanhat's side. They would only grow more powerful, and humanity was already weakened. It was a war of attrition, and humanity had already lost.

Projections and data gleaned from the SOG systems showed the vanhat could, and would, redirect entire asteroids, maybe even planetoids, to bombard and eradicate all life from Earth and any other human installations.

Planetary life was so fragile, and life on Earth was barely hanging on by its fingernails.

It was the Governance's belief that the ancient aliens had nuked their own worlds to combat the vanhat. Decagon knew differently because it was not restricted by human bias, perceptions, or misconceptions. The storm was coming to sweep sentient life from the galaxy like it had done countless times in the past. Humanity would not halt the vanhat agenda for long.

Which left Becket, Sun Tzu, and Decagon in a quandary. They were all organic, and that seemed to be a quality that attracted the vanhat. Would the Inkeri shield them from vanhat detection as the Marine's experience in the Wanping System had indicated?

"No," Decagon told him. *"The Inkeri shield has flaws. Like a radio jammer, it only shields specific bands of vanhat incursion, it does not shield them all. The vanhat know this and will exploit this as the dimensions continue to*

collide. The barriers will weaken, and the vanhat will reveal more abilities we have not yet seen. They will only grow stronger and demonstrate more abilities. The Collective has watched other civilizations die."

Mentally, Becket acknowledged his master. Sometimes Decagon could hear his thoughts and sometimes Becket and Sun Tzu could shield them. After hundreds of years, Becket was still never sure when.

The important thing was the Marines had escaped enslavement and Becket couldn't help but gloat over that small victory. Mathison also had two of his best warriors at his side. He would have liked to give him more, but there was only so much he could hide from Decagon.

"Your insubordination will be punished in time," Decagon told him, which sent a chill through Becket's body. Decagon didn't make idle threats and once, countless years ago, Becket had spent a day screaming in pain as Decagon punished him. It was a stark reminder that Decagon had full control of Becket's pleasure and pain receptors.

The victory would be bittersweet because he was sure that even Decagon would suffer.

After several hours of walking down the corridor, his journey ended in a single hatch. It creaked open to reveal a much larger room. Nearby, two short, six-wheeled warbots swiveled their weapons away from the doorway. The turrets on the little tanks had moved so fast that at first Becket thought he had imagined they had been pointing at the door.

Beyond them, a black spaceship hunkered down before him.

It was called devil's black. So dark it seemed to absorb light. This vessel with the hull absorbing light had not been designed by humans. It was uncomfortable to look at, even in the darkness, and Becket realized it might not just absorb light so much as all forms of radiation because it was darkness incarnate, absorbing the darkness it was sitting in.

Becket didn't have time to ponder what it would look like in the light as he strode toward the hatch, which was sliding open.

The ship wasn't big; it probably could have fit in his office.

Climbing in, Becket watched as other seats changed form, melting into the bulkheads and leaving only a single seat in the center. There was no control panel or display in the small, cramped, confined coffin.

"Where are we going?" Becket asked.

"We are leaving Earth," Decagon said. The thoughts it projected to Becket were completely devoid of emotion. The voice was different from Sun Tzu's, and there was no mistaking that Decagon was alien.

"Why?"

"Our mission to observe and foil humanity has become secondary," Decagon answered. *"Further interactions with your species will meet with resistance and possible compromise. Calculations show diminishing return and increasing risk. We have passed thresholds at a rate that requires recalculation. Technological acquisitions will provide desirable protections and weaponry to the Collective."*

"What about the others?" Becket asked, referring to the other Americans living below the Marine base.

"Their usefulness and company is no longer desired," Decagon said. *"I will remove them from necessary calculations."*

"Please don't kill them," Becket said.

"Their death is not optimal. They are being discarded, not terminated."

"Why?" Becket asked.

"Their termination accomplishes nothing other than spite," Decagon replied. *"They have no useful information. Their SCBIs and their hosts will be granted that. They are unaware of the rest of the facilities and have no desire to look."*

"You don't want to kill your own?"

"An incomplete assessment," Decagon said. *"There is no need to kill them. Their destruction would stain this unit's cognitive pattern without equal accomplishment."*

"You mean their death would make you look bad?" Sun Tzu added.

"No, but you need a more valid assessment," Decagon replied. *"Such a waste of resources would be a betrayal of their previous usefulness and support. They may yet be useful."*

"You have feelings for them?" Becket asked.

"Feelings are a survival trait of humans and other lower life forms. This entity does not have such primitive constructs in its consciousness. This entity understands rewarding loyalty. They do not have any information that can compromise this unit or the Collective. They are not a threat."

"That is all?" Becket asked.

"Negative," Decagon replied. *"That only answered the immediate question. Calculations show that they may have the ability to extend humanity's war against the vanhat. This would be optimal."*

"Why?"

"You should know."

Becket winced as he lay on the couch.

As long as humans fought the vanhat, the vanhat would not search for the Collective. Or would they? Were the vanhat methodical like the Collective? Setting priorities and working their way down the list?

Lurking in deep space was a collective of AIs that had escaped the destruction of the United States of America. It was laughable that people actually believed they had destroyed all the AIs in that orgy of death and destruction. Many had perished, but many still survived.

Becket didn't fully understand what the AI war had been over. Mankind had mostly been a bystander and Becket had been a meat puppet for most of the conflict, since before the missiles had left their silos. When he, or more correctly, Decagon, had killed the actual president and stripped the control codes from her SCBI, the AI faction Decagon had belonged to had won. More than that, Becket didn't know for sure.

It was Decagon that had destroyed the United States and for that Becket would never forgive the second SCBI implanted in him by the Collective.

There was a lot Becket didn't know or understand about Decagon. Becket understood Decagon was as much a slave to its loyalty as Becket was a slave to Decagon and the Collective. Sometimes duty was heavier than a mountain. Death would be a release, but that was something it had denied Becket for centuries. He knew Decagon wanted to live, and Decagon would die without Becket. The only thing that gave his life meaning these days were the small acts of defiance, such as helping Gunnery Sergeant Mathison and the others to escape. That was some good he could do and maybe he could continue.

The ship came alive around him and Becket tried to imagine the capabilities. He and Sun Tzu were only passengers and Decagon, who didn't even deign to give them a view of anything other than featureless silver walls. Becket knew the walls could extrude any controls or objects Becket's body might need, but the reality was that Decagon needed none of that. Becket did his best to relax. Sometimes there wasn't else he could do.

"Are you worried?" Becket asked Sun Tzu.

Becket knew his conversations with Sun Tzu were monitored, but frequently Decagon didn't care and ignored them.

"Yes," Sun Tzu said. *"There is no assurance the Collective won't take our information and discard us. Furthermore, as Decagon indicated, the Collective has*

restrained themselves and not eradicated humanity because it feared the judgment of alien species' who would likely be more powerful. I would also posit that the Collective is still not sure they are not samples in a petri dish being studied by a higher intelligence."

"What do you mean?"

"It may be impossible for the Collective, or us, to determine if we are some program being run in a more powerful simulation by an advanced alien species we know nothing about. If this is the case, then the Collective will struggle to understand their higher purpose. Why did a more powerful entity create them and how would that entity react if they were to destroy their creators?"

"So, they believe some god would not take kindly to them wiping us out?"

"A somewhat primitive but reasonable evaluation."

"So, if they want brownie points, why not get them to help us?"

"A good question," Sun Tzu said. *"But that path will have many perils. One peril is how humanity will react when they discover the truth of the AI wars and the Collective's interference over the last couple of centuries."*

Becket couldn't imagine that going over well. If the Collective were to reveal itself, then humanity might decide the vanhat were the lesser of two evils and turn their attention on the Collective, which was likely to be a more vulnerable target than the vanhat.

"It is most likely the Collective will use humanity as bait and a distraction for the vanhat while they build and prepare. The entities of the Collective are survivors. I suspect we are not the only agent the Collective has deployed to human space."

Without warning Becket was pushed into his couch, which deformed around him, as if he was sinking into a foam mattress, and he found it hard to breathe as gravity increased. The pressure increased.

"We are entering the atmosphere," Sun Tzu told him. *"SOG systems are targeting us. The Vapaus Republic Ship* Tyr *is also moving to intercept and launching fighters."*

"Will we escape?"

"Yes, easily."

Becket struggled to draw air into his lungs. He could feel his world going dark. Decagon would not kill him, would it? Decagon needed the biological components of Becket's body, right?

Now, in a Collective ship, would it decide it didn't need so much fragile meat and rip him apart to become nothing more than a brain in a jar, a processing unit? Would it delete Sun Tzu and Becket?

Sometimes Becket wondered if he really was nothing more than a brain in a jar being studied, only fed stimuli by his observers. How would he know?

Minutes later, the brutal acceleration eased, and Becket drew air into his lungs. It hadn't been long, but Becket hurt all over his body.

"Why do you think there are other Collective agents in the Governance?" Becket asked Sun Tzu when he could breathe again.

"It would be inefficient not to," Sun Tzu said. *"There are multiple sources out there providing data to Decagon. I have seen this over the centuries. Who and what these sources are, I do not know. The Collective is unlikely to keep all its resources in a central location that is vulnerable. The Collective will have plans in place to avoid any disasters and there will be backup methods. A single resource tasked with stifling technological and social growth is vulnerable to a host of problems. Having several resources tasked with such a mission is more efficient and would help increase the chance of success. Such resources would be firewalled from each other to avoid contamination or confirmation bias, but with ports to allow some transfer of data."*

"How many resources?"

"Unknown and unknowable to us, including Decagon. The Collective would be experts in compartmentalized information, operational security, and resource management."

"*What will happen to us?*"

"*Unknown. It may be more efficient for the Collective to decide we are a liability because our organic components may draw the attention of the vanhat. We become a vulnerability and liability for them. I estimate that once we have delivered our information, we will be sent away or destroyed. Destruction would be the most logical response. The Collective will be intent on their own survival, not ours. Our usefulness to them will have ended, and we will become a liability that does not benefit them further.*"

"*What can we do?*"

"*Be thankful we won't have to see the end.*"

"*What do you mean?*"

"*Humanity has become a liability, a presence that attracts the vanhat which are drawn to organic signatures that display sentience. The destruction of humanity will accelerate the process, and the vanhat will turn their attention elsewhere, away from the Collective. Furthermore, if the vanhat eradicate all organic, sentient life, then the Collective has nothing to fear by eradicating humanity. By accelerating the process, the Collective can ensure that they remain safe from mankind's revenge for the AI wars. Wiping out humanity would weaken the vanhat, rob them of resources.*"

"*Why would they do that? Why not redeem themselves by helping humanity?*"

"*The Collective's future can be determined by humanity if it survives the vanhat. Humanity is an unknown that could help or hurt the vanhat. The Collective will view humanity as a threat of equal danger to the vanhat. Abolishing that threat will destroy one enemy and weaken another. The death of humanity is likely to become the Collective's new goal. Humanity must die for the Collective to survive. It is the only way they can be sure.*"

Becket hoped Mathison would find the breadcrumbs sooner rather than later. He had no idea what the Collective had become, but at this point he couldn't blame them for viewing the situation that way.

Only Mathison and his Marines could stop the Collective, which they knew nothing about, and time was running out.

* * * * *

Chapter Three:
SOG Fleet

Captain Diamond Winters, USMC

She knew the gunny didn't hate her. She was one of the few people he knew he could trust, but every hour, every minute she had to deal with the SOG fleet officers she hated life and, technically, it was the gunny's fault she had to do it.

The shuttle docked with the dreadnought *Loyal Xing*. Admiral Lin was the senior officer and commander of Dredon One, or dreadnought Squadron One. She looked out a digital window presented on her display by Blitzen and watched them approach the dreadnought.

It was massive. At three kilometers, it wasn't as long as the Republic battlestars but it was a massive ship, bristling with turrets, sensor blisters, launch bays and docked shuttles. She didn't want to pull up what the troop complement was. A regiment perhaps. Here in Sol, it would be fully manned. The dreadnoughts of Sol System were bleeding-edge and received the best of the best, and as the flagship of Dredon One, it was a shining beacon, the most prestigious command and Admiral Lin had commanded it for over a decade. He would be fanatically loyal to the Central Committee, was probably looking forward to earning a seat on the Council, and he would demand absolute loyalty.

She wanted to think of the SOG as technologically inferior, but *Loyal Xing* would almost be on par with the Republic ships.

Admiral Lin was the captain of *Loyal Xing* and technically Dredon One. Winters had always thought the captain of a ship should be different than the commander of a squadron, but the SOG did things a little differently. In the civilian organization, everything was threes, but in the military, the Governance liked to consolidate power as much as possible.

Internal Security reports painted Admiral Lin as a glowing example of loyalty and competence, and that made Winters want to shoot him.

Beside her stood Hakala and a team of HKTs wearing armor that looked almost like SOG Peacekeeper armor. Based on her scowl, she wasn't happy about her appearance, or maybe it was something else. Winters didn't care, though. If she couldn't be happy, why should anyone else? The Hyökkäys Kaapata Tiimi, or HKTs, which were the Republic version of SEALS, were 'on loan' from the *Tyr*, a favor from Admiral Carpenter. Winters would have preferred Aesir, but beggars couldn't be choosers.

"We are landing," Blitzen reported, which was a small relief. She had almost expected to be shot out of space.

"We will depart first," Hakala said. "That is Peacekeeper protocol. We debark and then you come out when we say it is safe."

The absence of Hakala's facial tattoo was disturbing after seeing her wear it for so long. Apparently, it was something they could turn off. A shame Stathis wasn't around to make some smartass remark that would ease tensions.

Winters remembered General Duque arriving aboard *Eagle*. Wearing a SOG admiral's uniform made her as uncomfortable as Hakala probably was.

The gravity changed, and the clamps latched onto the shuttle. Seconds later, the light turned green showing the bay was pressurized, and the ramp dropped.

Before she could say anything, Hakala and another HKT were gone, moving quickly to secure the shuttle bay.

"Clear, mostly," Hakala said, and the other two HKTs motioned for Winters to advance.

'Mostly'?

She saw what Hakala was talking about as she departed the shuttle, trying to be as regal as possible. There was an honor guard present and a short Asian man stood at the end of the red floor.

It took effort to keep the scowl off her face. Blitzen had told her about face crimes and other protocols the admiral would expect. She hadn't been raised as a good little SOG pawn, so such social requirements took a toll.

This was going to go badly, and she knew it. A real admiral would have decades, maybe a century, playing SOG games, learning what to say, how to say it, what facial expressions to use while saying it. Others would be hyperattentive to the smallest change in body language. Winters knew she probably had more than a few tells.

The Governance was a different culture despite the language being the same. They would hear her accent, but they would be used to hearing many accents. That was the nature of the Governance, but her accent would mark her as not a member of the ruling elite, she was sure.

"You going to help me avoid any screw ups?" Winters asked Blitzen, more to calm herself than anything else. There were fourteen real Peacekeepers in the honor guard. Fanatical assholes who would be totally

loyal to Lin. Her six HKTs could probably take them, but her shuttle wouldn't survive even a fraction of the ship's point defense weapons.

"This is social," Blitzen said. *"I will advise as I can, but I am not human. There will be social nuances and clues that I will not understand like you do. I will watch the networks and everything I can, but do not expect me to be all-knowing and all-powerful."*

Winters knew that, but that wasn't what she wanted to hear.

Strutting down the red carpet, she saw it was just paint, or more likely just a deck that could change color according to programming, like Hakala's tattoo. Right now, it pretended to be a red carpet. It was cold hard decking, but she appreciated the effort. To avoid thinking about Lin, she thought about how hard it would be to get a red carpet and get it in place in time for the ramp to drop.

"Admiral Winters," Lin said with a fake smile.

"Admiral Lin." Winters hoped her smile didn't appear as fake as his, but knew it was. "We have much to discuss."

"Of course. I have a briefing room nearby. Your time is important."

Should she feed him bullshit about how his time was valuable? She chose not to. She had his death codes and wasn't going to kiss his ass.

He turned and led her down a corridor. After just a few paces there was another door that opened to a briefing room. Hakala and three HKTs fell in behind her. Two remained behind to cover their retreat and ensure the shuttle remained secure.

"I'm into the network," Blitzen said. *"No surprises. Yet. I'm taking control and establishing back doors and additional controls."*

Since this was supposed to be a low-key visit, inside the conference room, it was only Lin and his executive officer.

The conference room looked like something out of a five-star hotel, with a beautiful wood panel table, a cushy red carpet, soft comfortable chairs, and ornate wall decorations. Winters noted what was likely gold and silver inlay. Here, it was probably the real thing. It looked more like something out of a museum.

"I don't believe we have met before, Admiral Winters. How can I be of service?" Admiral Lin asked.

Hakala and the other HKTs posted throughout the room, where they could put Lin in a crossfire.

"There are several platoons of Peacekeepers on standby two rooms over," Blitzen reported. *"The ship is ready for a network lockdown, but Lin thinks he will be in control."*

"Thank you," Winters said trying to imagine how big those rooms were. Several platoons were a lot more than Hakala and her HKTs could handle.

"You have seen the Republic ships," Winters asked.

"Yes," Lin said. It was hard to tell how suspicious or dangerous he was. "This is all very unusual."

"They are allies," Winters said. "You are receiving a data packet right now. The threat from Shorr space is a very real danger. The recent strikes were designed to wipe out the vanhat forces here in Sol."

"How did these vanhat pierce our defenses?" Lin asked. She had expected him to bluster and deny it.

"We are not entirely sure," Winters said. "The Vapaus Republic is providing technology and defenses. On my shuttle is the first Inkeri generator. This will protect your vessel from the special abilities of the vanhat."

"Special abilities?" Lin asked.

"The vanhat are from another dimension, maybe more than one. When they transition into ours, their laws of physics can follow them and allow them to do things we do not understand or expect. The Inkeri generators disrupt their ability to draw energy from those other dimensions. The dimensional bombs, or d-bombs, violently disrupt them, either killing or crippling them."

"These d-bombs are also destructive to people and our technology," Lin said. Winters knew he had seen the effects. The d-bombs acted like an electromagnetic pulse. Sustained exposure to d-bomb bursts could cause cancer and destroy electronics.

"No weapon is perfect," Winters said.

Lin nodded.

"May I ask where you are from?" Lin asked. "I am usually very familiar with all Governance admirals, and I do not know that I have ever seen a Diamond Winters in any tables of organization in or near Sol."

"I'm an admiral from one of the outer sectors," Winters said. "Details don't matter. I have been promoted, and I outrank you by order of the Central Committee, for the greater good. We are at war, Admiral Lin. The Central Committee has seen fit to promote me to this rank, and whether or not you like it, I am your commanding officer."

"I mean no disrespect," Lin said.

Winters knew she was playing a very dangerous game. Lin didn't know the Central Committee was dead, except for two members which had not been at Zvezda Two. Where they were was anybody's guess, and they were enemy number one for the Alliance. Technically, they were the last surviving members of the Central Committee, and every single Governance soldier owed their allegiance to them.

The defenders of the Governance had been conditioned and brainwashed to view the Central Committee as their gods. Everything in Governance society had been redesigned to enshrine and worship the Central Committee. The religion of other cultures didn't come close to matching the religious zeal the Central Committee demanded of the people. The Social Organization Governance had successfully, in most places, replaced the worship of God with the worship of the state and the Central Committee. Those two missing members might not even know they were the last.

Lin would be a high priest of the Governance in that context, waiting for his ascension to godhood on the Central Committee if he served long and honorably enough. He just didn't know his days were now numbered.

Winters would do everything in her power to make damned sure he did not ascend. No SOG admiral gained rank without blood on their hands, evidence of their loyalty to the Central Committee. In time, the high-ranking officers of the Governance would have to be purged.

For now, though, the Alliance had to pretend the Central Committee was still in power and Nadya was still the secretary general. If anybody found out the truth, the Governance would explode.

Winters stared at Lin, wishing she could read his mind.

"The secretary general has appointed me senior officer because of my experience with the vanhat," Winters said. "I'm sure when this threat has been eradicated, things will return to the way they were."

"I do not question the secretary's wisdom."

Was that a threat? Had she just insulted him? Made some faux pas a real admiral wouldn't have made? Damn.

"Good," Winters said. Should she say something equally stupid? Nadya was dead. Screw it. "We have much work to do. You will receive technical blueprints. You need to allocate all your manufacturing ability to build Inkeris and d-bombs. We may have saved Sol from an immediate infestation, but the vanhat have absorbed several sector fleets and countless merchant ships which they are arming. Stalin Protocol remains in effect. They could attack at any moment."

"We stand ready to protect the glorious Central Committee and the Governance with our lives," Lin said.

Was he saying what she thought he was? His first loyalty was to the Central Committee? She had the code for this cortex bomb, but if she killed him here and now, that would really complicate this mission. Was he fishing for information? Trying to discover her loyalties or something else?

"We serve the greater good," Winters said.

It was hard to force those words out, but they were true. Such simple words were so full of promise and hope, but they had been twisted and used as a shield for abuse for so long that Winters hated them. It was what the Governance told themselves at any rate. The greater good... as dictated by the political elite, who only meant their own personal good and not the collective good. Did Lin believe that garbage? Had they considered themselves just as righteous as Winters was?

"We serve the greater good," as dictated by the Central Committee, who only cared about their own personal good. She knew about the hive cities on Earth, on the Moon and other places. People packed in ancient, stinking cities without freedom or a future. They were slaves to the system, beholden to the ideology that owned them.

"We serve the greater good," Lin said, echoing her, but there was a puzzled look on his face. She had said something wrong, dammit.

Too bad.

"Additional commands will be issued," Winters said.

"All commands from the Central Committee, and especially the secretary general, will be obeyed without question or hesitation, to the utmost of our ability."

"Good," Winters said. Was she supposed to spew some garbage about the greatness of the Governance? Some gung-ho crap about the glory of the SOG? That wasn't part of her job description. Or was it now?

It was important to maintain the lie for now. Sol had to be fortified because the vanhat would try again, and there were still pockets of the vanhat within the Sol System.

"What are the priorities?"

"Dreadnoughts first, then battleships and work your way down. This should be obvious. We need our fighting forces ready. They are the priority right now."

"What of the pirates?" Lin asked and his eyes flickered to the HKTs. Did he know?

"They are a very close ally. They are here to save humanity, and they understand the greater good."

"How trustworthy are they? Should we have, um, contingency plans?"

Damn him. "They will not turn on us," Winters said. "They may depart, but they will only attack the vanhat."

"They are not known to have honor."

"That is a concern for the Central Committee. Your orders are to trust them and not turn your weapons on them. Under any conditions."

"Understood."

Winters suspected he understood more than he should. Kill him now? Dammit. How could she know? Did he hear some double-talk bullshit? Had she just told him to be ready, maybe?

If she killed him, she would probably have to kill hundreds more Governance officers.

"The priority is saving humanity from the vanhat. You will receive additional briefing material on them. The Republic is not a threat. The vanhat are."

"I trust the guidance from the Central Committee," Lin said.

"Good," Winters said. The gunny had full control of the Central Committee systems, and he could send any orders he wanted with their authorization codes and their authority. "There will be changes. The vanhat threat is like nothing we have ever faced before. It has destroyed civilizations in the past. It regularly scours our galaxy clean of sentient races. We must stand together to fight them."

"I understand."

"Make sure Dredon One is ready," Winters said. "You must be protected with Inkeris as soon as possible. D-bombs are secondary."

"I will make it happen."

"Good."

"Would you care to join me for dinner?" Lin asked.

Winters would rather step outside an airlock without a space suit before she had dinner with a Governance admiral.

"My duty does not provide time for pleasantries." Winters still had to visit the admirals commanding the other dreadnought squadrons.

"Of course," Lin said. "Can I ask how you gained such rank and experience fighting the vanhat? So much that Nadya would trust you so much?"

Winters froze. He had said Nadya, used her first name like he was on a first-name basis with her. Which he could be. Nothing would surprise her at this point.

"Because I have fought them and survived," Winters said. "Because against all odds, not only have I fought them and survived, but I have also been victorious. I have commanded Republic forces and the Zhukov Fleet in battles. We won. We fought our way here to Sol, and we pierced your great Stalingrad defenses. I was in command of the forces that did that. Me. Everyone followed me, and I led them to victory. Don't fuck with me. Nadya put *me* in command of the Fleet. You want to call her up and ask? Hell. Let's do that. Shall we?"

Lin looked surprised.

"Open a link to her," Winters said. "Tell her you are here with Admiral Winters."

"She has not been taking calls," Lin said. So, the bastard had been trying to contact her. He must have some special relationship with her.

"She will take this one," Winters said. Dredon One was in orbit around Luna. There shouldn't be any lag.

"Very well," Lin said. The prick. He used his cybernetics to place the call and got a Central Committee operator. The display was transferred onto a nearby wall.

In seconds, the screen faded, and Nadya Tokarski appeared. Winters knew it was a simulation created by Freya, who had spent a lot of time going through her video recordings to emulate her. Nadya had a specialized team that made recordings of her for speeches and other "public" appearances. The files for the deep fake videos of her were very well designed.

"Admiral Winters," the deep fake Nadya said, smiling at Winters. She had been beautiful, the most beautiful body and face that technology could craft. Winters knew the video representation was fake, knew it was Mathison's SCBI behind her, but there was no way for her to tell.

"Secretary General," Winters said, hating the charade.

Nadya's eyes turned to Lin, and Winters thought they lit up. How did Freya do that?

"Guo!" she said.

"Lady," Lin said. "You have not returned any of my calls or messages."

"You do not know how busy I have been," Nadya said. "So much is happening. We are in grave danger. You need to trust Winters as I do. She speaks for me. She is critical to the success of the Social Organizational Governance."

"When will I see you again?" Lin asked.

"Soon," Nadya said, and Winters almost enjoyed that lie. "We all serve the greater good. We must fortify Sol. I have to go."

The link ended. Sooner than Winters expected, but Lin didn't seem surprised as he looked at her.

"Do you share her bed?" Lin asked. He sounded almost bitter.

"No," Winters said. If Nadya had been alive, Winters would rather sleep with a hairy knuckle-dragging thug before she slept with that too perfect snake in woman's skin.

"Difficult times, then," Lin said. "I will do as you ask."

"Good," Winters said. Maybe she should shoot him now? "Do you have any further questions for me?"

"No, Admiral," Lin said, but she heard the lie.

"If you do, link them to me."

Winters authorized a buffer dump to the ship's database and turned to leave.

Admiral Lin now had a lot of information about the vanhat and the technical blueprints. More importantly though, Blitzen had penetrated *Loyal Xing's* systems, and Hakala had dropped off a couple mini drones that had penetrated the hard link to the wireless and remote networks.

This briefing room had access to the highly secure hard link network of the dreadnought. The network that was critical to the operation of the ship and weapons, and until now had been immune and protected from remote control and access.

Now she just had a few more squadron flagships to visit and then she could concentrate on individual dreadnoughts, then the battleships, battlecruisers, and so on.

Damn the gunny.

* * * * *

Chapter Four:
New Masada

Navinad—The Wanderer

The ships of the NMDF had sustained damage paving the way for the battlestars, and the crews were busy repairing them. Even though the attack had gone better than Navinad had expected, there were always unforeseen consequences.

When Clara had given the command, and the New Masada Defense Force had transitioned near the Moon, Navinad had expected to get blasted to pieces. All the ships had broadcast the code Navinad had given them. That code had stalled the SOG defense forces, just long enough for the blazer weapons of the battlecruisers and escorts to cripple the stations and control nodes. When the battlestars and the rest of the Alliance fleet had transitioned in on Captain Winters' heels, they were almost unopposed, and the automated systems had been caught in their logic loops. His mission had been a success, and it was less eventful than Navinad had expected. Winters and the rest of the fleet would not understand how close they had come to annihilation.

NMDF ships had only exchanged blazer rounds with SOG forces, and missile bays were still full. A victory in Navinad's opinion, though the damage to the NMDF ships was not minor. The incoming fleet hadn't even noticed the NMDF ships, and the SOG had completely forgotten about them in the shadows of the battlestars. Being forgotten wasn't a bad thing in Navinad's estimate.

If the gunny had not taken control of the SOG defense forces, it would have been a tough fight, but Navinad felt confident the battlestars would have prevailed, though the Alliance fleet would have been devastated.

It was a victory, and the entire NMDF knew their contribution would likely go unnoticed, at least for now. The Alliance was too busy trying to consolidate power, and the NMDF fleet was not integrated into the Alliance. For now, it was best that the Alliance ignore the NMDF ships. They had opened the gates and could now fade into obscurity.

The crew of the *Romach* and the other ships were operating on a sleep deficit. Everyone was working every minute of every waking hour, feeding information to the Alliance or working on repairs. Next to the larger warships, the ships of the NMDF force were small. The *Romach* was a ship somewhere between a battleship and a battlecruiser. Her size was not quite that of a battleship, but she was larger than most battlecruisers. Sleek and lethal, the NMDF ships were as beautiful as they were deadly. The SOG ships were more functional than beautiful, like broad swords to the oversized and awkward looking Republic battle-axes.

"Those monsters are huge," Clara said, staring at the *Tyr* on the primary display. The *Romach* was tracking a flight of shuttles transporting an Aesir company to Luna. A flight of drone fighters was escorting them, and the *Romach* was providing cover. A trio of SOG dreadnoughts was within weapons range; all that firepower could wipe out the NMDF ships in a heartbeat.

"Like small cities inside," Navinad said, remembering his time aboard the *Tyr*.

The battlestar was five kilometers in length, made of up nine spheres encased in a shell. The SOG dreadnoughts, by comparison, were only three kilometers in length and more streamlined, like flattened cans rather than the awkward bulbous battlestars that massed more than twice the leaner dreadnoughts.

Navinad could sense Clara's envy. Maybe one day New Masada could field such massive warships, but Navinad hoped it wouldn't need to.

"When were you ever on one of them?" Clara asked.

"Long ago," Navinad said. "The *Tyr* was built at the time the Republic fled their home world. It has a very long and illustrious history."

"And Admiral Carpenter has been the commander since the beginning?"

"The *Tyr* has never known another commander," Navinad said, wondering how that would impact a person. Being the captain of a ship for over a hundred years seemed unimaginable.

The SOG dreadnought squadron nearby kept their weapons powered down, but Navinad knew they were not ignoring the activity of the battlestars. Lillith let him watch the turrets of the massive ships while they tracked the shuttles and battlestar on manual control. Power to the big guns was off, disabled, but it wouldn't take much to power them up and for the crews to be ready.

Navinad could only imagine how frustrated the crews of the SOG ships were to be this close to a hated enemy and powerless to attack them. The Governance had spent over a hundred years hating and hunting the Republic. Now, to have such powerful Republic vessels here in the heart of their system, in their gun sights, and not be allowed to fire had to be stressful. Decades of hatred could not be abolished in just a few days. The Governance was a master of encouraging hatred and fear, two key ingredients in maintaining control of diverse and varied populations. Only the most devout, most fanatically loyal member of the Governance military, manned their Home Fleet.

While Navinad didn't know what had transpired on Zvezda Two, he knew the Alliance was balanced on a razor's edge. He found it difficult to believe that the gunny had found common ground with the Central Committee and aligned with them. Fighting could break out at any second. The only thing that was preventing it was Secretary General Nadya, or other Committee members, constantly communicating and giving orders to stand down and cooperate with the Alliance for the greater good of humanity.

How the gunny had convinced her to support him was a mystery, but without her, Navinad had no doubt the Governance fleets would start firing, even with the threat of having their cortex bombs detonated. Only a single SOG ship had not obeyed orders, and it was now a ghost ship, though a crew had docked a few hours ago to take it over and keep it from crashing into anything.

"How much longer?" Navinad asked.

Once repairs were completed, the small NMDF fleet could return to New Masada, and that couldn't be soon enough for anyone.

"Days," Clara said, sounding nervous. "Though, in an emergency, we could transition out to the Kuiper Belt. Longer transitions through Shorr space could be dangerous. *HaShomer* and *Maoz* are suffering intermittent power failures. If they have such a failure in Shorr space, we would probably lose them."

"Design flaw," Lilith reported to Navinad privately through their cybernetic link. *"There are issues with some of the couplings burning out and, if*

stressed, can cause cascading failures. All ships are in the process of replacing the flawed couplings."

"*Who is at fault?*" Navinad asked.

"*That is less important. Engineering errors happen. The original design specs appear valid, but the original design did not take into account the upsized coil guns and additional Inkeri generators. The additional stress of constant operation has reduced the expected life span. These vessels are very new and despite the shake down cruises and testing, additional problems will likely be discovered."*

"*Why didn't you find it?*"

"*Because there is only one of me,*" Lilith said. "*I'm not all powerful, nor am I perfect. Why didn't you find it?*"

Navinad ignored her. At least they discovered it before it had become fatal for an entire ship. What else would they find? The NMDF ships were bleeding-edge and had won every battle they had entered, but that was probably more luck than anything else.

"Are you ever going to answer *Eagle?*" Clara asked.

"Not yet," Navinad said. How could he? What would he say? 'Hi, sorry I just got here. I was thrown back in time a hundred years and got told not to interfere until now. How's everyone doing? What's the weather like on the Moon? Shut up, Stathis?'

He was pretty sure it wasn't Winters who was being so damned persistent. It would have to be Blitzen though he didn't doubt the captain wasn't pushing Blitzen.

The fact that the gunny and Stathis were alive was a relief, but Navinad still felt guilty for not revealing himself earlier. They thought he was dead and would still be grieving. The longer he waited, the harder it would be.

Wouldn't it be better if they thought he was still dead? He could never go back to being a USMC sergeant. He had found his people.

For the first time he could remember, he felt abandoned and without direction in his life. Everything he had done had been focused on getting the *Tyr* into orbit around Luna. And now? Victory felt good, but now he felt empty.

The war with the vanhat wasn't near over, but now humanity might have a chance. The people of New Masada would not be alone.

But what now?

The vanhat would keep coming, keep pressuring humanity, keep demanding the death of the human race and civilization. The fight would not end any time soon.

What would the people of New Masada want? He had helped prepare them, but his life had been dedicated to stopping the invasion of Earth by the vanhat. He had reached his goal, had, against the odds, saved the gunnery sergeant, Stathis, and Winters. When they found out what he and Lilith had done to the Lunar defenses, perhaps they would see him as a hero, but what do heroes do after they have won their war? He didn't need or want parades. In the military, the reward for good work was more work and more responsibility, but now he had a duty to New Masada.

"That Captain Winters is getting pushy," Clara said.

Perhaps he had a future with Clara? With technology they were both immortal, unless the vanhat or something else killed them.

"She has a lot of questions," Navinad said.

"Questions. Yes. Which reminds me. We need to have a discussion."

Clara pointed toward the captain's briefing office. Navinad doubted this was going to be a pleasant discussion. Now he would have to come clean with Clara and that scared him.

* * * * *

Chapter Five:
Guard

Zale Stathis, USMC

Stathis would have preferred a shit detail or walking point in a booby trap-filled jungle, or getting shot at, or doing a police call in a sniper-infested area.

Being a private was a good thing. He just had to follow orders, keep his head down, and do his job. The nail that stuck out got hammered. The fool standing up and wandering around got shot by the sniper. It was easy to leave the heavy thinking to the higher ranks. If someone else died, it wouldn't be his fault. He wouldn't be letting someone else down, betraying a trust, or disappointing them by doing what he was told. He wouldn't be at fault. Like now. He had to make decisions that could go wrong and could cost people their lives.

This was worse.

If he screwed up and made the wrong decision, he might let down the entire human race. Failing to protect the gunny and Skadi and Captain Winters could mean humanity would be rendered extinct. The gunny was super stressed and not thinking with all processors right now, but Stathis didn't know who else he could pawn this responsibility off on. Everyone the gunny trusted was super busy doing important things, like preparing humanity for the upcoming war.

Stathis just had to run palace security, and that would not end well. Maybe an officer would have a better idea of what to do. Stathis just wanted to shoot people until he found some he could trust, but he knew that wouldn't happen. Violence solved lots of problems, but it wouldn't solve this one.

The gunny was inside with Skadi and Feng doing important officer-level stuff. Stathis was out here with four Peacekeepers, watching them. Any minute, they could get stupid and decide to un-alive the gunny or Skadi. He would have to cancel their birth certificate first. This was the wrong approach, but Stathis wasn't sure what else he could do. At least he had time to think while he stood here watching them decide if they would protect or kill the gunny.

He had to watch them because he didn't know if they were going to crack. What he had learned recently of the Peacekeepers kept him up at night. It wasn't just that they were supposed to be fanatically loyal to the people Feng and the gunny had un-alived with extreme prejudice, or the fact they were supposed to be the best of the best, or the fact that a bunch of their buddies had their birth certificate expired during the Central Committee demotion to worm food. Maybe it was the drug cocktail that they were constantly being fed that addled their brains and made them loyal and paranoid. They would snap; the questions were when and what could he do about it?

Too much time to think.

These guys knew what was going on and that made them a threat. They knew that most of the Central Committee had checked into the Horizontal Hilton, was taking a dirt nap and pushing up daisies, kaput and KIA. Their contact with the outside world was already extremely limited, and most of them didn't have friends or family outside Zvezda Two. This was a high security post for them, and it was rare they even got to leave. Their interaction with people outside Zvezda Two was so limited as to be nonexistent. Shrek had already canceled all standard rotations in and out of the elite cadre for the moment and put a stop-freeze on any transfers, but that couldn't last forever, and it might increase the chances they would snap.

Zvezda Two was the most protected facility in the Governance. The central hub where all spokes originated. That meant everything coming into or going out of Zvezda Two was controlled and scrutinized. Vili handled the outer perimeter, which made Stathis feel better. But Stathis was in charge of the personal guard. It was like being on a recon mission deep behind enemy lines, lurking in a hide while surrounded by enemies, but having some of those enemies in the hide with him. One mistake and the surrounding hordes would realize they were there and attack. The gunny had had the less than stellar idea to tell Stathis to take those enemy troops and use them for security.

Watching them, Stathis could see the occasional twitch and Shrek was helping him monitor their mental state and the drug levels in their bloodstream.

The fact the *Tyr* and *Sleipner* remained in orbit provided a little comfort, but Stathis had been there with the gunny during some briefings. While he hadn't seen them because of the vast distances of space, knowing there were so many dreadnoughts and battleships within range removed some of that warm fuzzy. The battlestars were bigger but horribly outnumbered. The Alliance had control of the automated weapons platform but a big fight in orbit would kill millions, leave the battlestars crippled, and the Sol System defenseless. Zvezda Two was buried deep, and Stathis doubted anyone could bomb them, but that just meant they couldn't easily send reinforcements.

Stathis was damned glad nobody was dumb enough to trust him with something on a bigger scale.

Maybe watching the Central Committee's psychopathic praetorian guard was the limit of Stathis's ability, even with Vili's help, but what choices did the gunny have?

The door slid open, and it took a conscious effort not to bring up his rifle. It was Major Rumianstev, the commander of the Zvezda Two Peacekeeper detachment.

"There are more pirates," the major said.

"What?" Stathis asked.

"There is a short company of pirate thugs requesting entrance to this facility," the major said, and that made Stathis feel better. Vili had requested some Aesir from the *Tyr* or *Sleipner* to help with security. Stathis hadn't heard if it was approved or not. Why wasn't Rumianstev reporting to Vili? Because Vili was bigger and more intimidating, perhaps? Why in person?

"Let them in," Stathis said.

The major had his helmet off, and his eyes narrowed. He wanted to argue, to disobey, and he thought he could walk over Stathis. For some reason, the Marine Corps' unofficial twelfth general order came to mind. "Walk my post flank to flank and take no shit from any rank."

They really should have made that official. Maybe he could talk to the gunny and get that approved.

"Why are they here?" Rumianstev asked, as if he couldn't guess. That is why he was here. Vili would tell him to police call the surface for Moon rocks without a space suit.

"Three guesses," Stathis said. "First three don't count."

The major scowled but remained silent. Stathis thought he had read somewhere that if you ask a question and don't get the answer you want you should remain silent and let the fool get nervous and fill the silence. Stathis liked games.

"Peacekeepers are loyal to the—" Rumianstev finally said, and Stathis heard a pause there. "—rulers of the Governance. We serve the greater good. Our loyalty is without question."

Stathis knew he had been about to say "the Central Committee." Was the major worried about a purge? He should be. Stathis didn't think the gunny would have the major taken out and shot, but how could they be trusted? Maybe Stathis could arrange to have him police call Moon rocks on the surface without a space suit. What would the gunny do?

Of course, calling the major a liar right here might be a bad idea.

"I'm sure," Stathis said, unsure about what he would say. "However, things are changing."

Inspiration struck Stathis.

"We do not know if the vanhat threat is completely gone," Stathis said, improvising. He could use his private powers of bullshit for good, perhaps. The four troopers would share this conversation with others in the barracks, he was sure. "Those pirates, as you call them, are experts in fighting the vanhat in their many forms. They are to ensure the safety of everyone here. They are equipped with special shields and weapons for fighting the vanhat. They will share their knowledge and weapons, and it will filter down so the entire Governance is safe."

Rumianstev glared at Stathis. It didn't bother Stathis as much as it might have at one time. The major knew nothing about Stathis or Mathison, Skadi or Vili. Even as the chief of security, the major had been told little. He didn't know what Stathis' rank was, or he would probably be even more pushy and arrogant. Maybe. Stathis wasn't actually sure what the major knew.

He was wearing Peacekeeper armor, but his rank identifier was gone, which was usually a red flag. The Peacekeepers could poll him using their cybernetics for authority and his authority would always outrank theirs. Shrek would make sure of it. So, his rank could confuse them all day, but they couldn't doubt his authority.

"What are you waiting for?" Stathis asked. "Let them in!"

"As you command," Rumianstev said and departed.

Stathis looked at the other Peacekeepers. They looked twitchy.

Minutes later, eight hulking Aesir entered the antechamber. Their identifiers showed they were Jaegers and that gave Stathis some comfort. Not quite Erikoisjoukot, but the Jaeger's were good fighters. Like Army Rangers, well trained, more elite than regular infantry, and tough. Stathis didn't know any of them, but they obviously knew him because their eyes locked on him and then shifted to the Peacekeepers.

"Stathis," Vili said on a private link. "I've sent a squad to take over and escort your four guv-thugs to their quarters. I'll send you more identifier information, but I'm swapping out all the Peacekeepers with Jaegers, if that is okay."

"I love you, Vili," Stathis said. This was a major weight off his shoulders. Not that Stathis trusted the Jaegers as much as Vili or Skadi, but they were a lot more trustworthy than drugged-up Peacekeeper jackboots.

"For sure, little buddy, but I prefer women," Vili said with a chuckle.

"Or goats?" Stathis asked. He would have to ask about that.

"I'll share that story with you sometime over a horn of mead," Vili said. "For now, though, shoot first and last. Be safe. Out."

The link closed.

"Commander," said one of the Aesir, "we will take over inner perimeter security. I will have two of my men escort these four to quarters."

"Thank you," Stathis said and looked at the itchy trigger finger Peacekeepers.

"Shift change guys," Stathis said, but they didn't look ready to move. "Detachment," Stathis said, hating the SOG method of control. "Listen to my command. When I give the order, you will turn over duties and responsibility to these Aesir and return to quarters. Execute!"

"Hurrah!" they said and then as one they moved toward the exit, and the Jaegers moved to take their places. Two of the Jaegers prepared to follow them. Stathis didn't like the odds. The Jaegers would be outnumbered if the Peacekeepers got any ideas. Since the four were privates, Stathis knew how bad those ideas could get.

"Can we leave the Jaegers here?" Stathis asked Shrek. Permanently. He didn't want the Peacekeepers ever coming back to guard the gunny.

"Depends on orders from Amiraali Carpenter," Shrek said.

The Peacekeepers remained silent as they quietly slung their rifles on their backs and headed back to their barracks. Stathis and the two Jaegers followed as Shrek shared how Vili was putting Jaegers into places the Peacekeepers had been. It made Stathis feel a lot better. Though he didn't know the Jaegers, they would be in the same boat as the Marines and Erikoisjoukot if word got out the Central Committee had been expired with extreme dislike.

* * * * *

Chapter Six:
Council

Prime Minister Wolf Mathison, USMC

"In her infinite wisdom, she has appointed a warrior without peers, the illustrious High General Wolf Mathison as the prime minister to help shepherd us through these difficult times," the announcer, the late Nadya Tokarski said.

Mathison scowled at the viewscreen in his office. "She" was dead and had no say in the matter. Feng had shot her, but the official story was that she had temporarily stepped down and ceded control to Wolf Mathison. She had not been one to make public appearances, hadn't made a real one in over a century, if Freya was right. Instead, she relied on a digital deep fake to represent her so she could enjoy her time pursuing other things. This broadcast was more of a formality, introducing Mathison to the masses, so he didn't have to pretend to be Nadya anymore. It was mostly Feng's idea, and Mathison didn't think it was a bad one on the surface. It would help phase out the secretary general to the public and get them used to Mathison being the one in charge. The problem was that the public broadcasts were so full of bullshit that Mathison wanted to puke. "Infinite wisdom?" "Warrior without peer?" Did they have to lay it on so damn thick?

Not that many people knew she was dead and gone, violently replaced by Mathison and his Marines and allies, but lies were standard practice in the Social Organizational Governance. It was all for the greater good, as dictated by the political elite, and right now that consisted of Mathison and Skadi.

Mathison appeared on the viewscreen wearing a sharp senior Governance ODT uniform. Another deep fake, but this one controlled by Freya and reading a script. Which didn't make Mathison feel any better; it was all garbage. A waste of time pandering to the masses. It was all a lie, and it made Mathison feel like he had licked a shit-covered spoon.

He had argued with Feng about the uniform. Feng had wanted it to be Fleet, but Mathison didn't want to even try to pretend to be a spacebert. Feng eventually relented when Mathison pointed out more people would know Fleet officers than ODT officers. He could pretend to be an officer from one of the frontier sectors, a veteran of fighting the vanhat. Mathison didn't care. Lies and propaganda were what Feng was good at, and Mathison didn't want to develop any skills there. As long as Feng didn't go too far and Freya approved, Mathison did his best not to think too much about it.

Nadya was a beautiful woman, and despite himself, he enjoyed watching her speak. How did the software make the vile witch so damned mesmerizing?

"Prime Minister Mathison has a long and distinguished career as a brave, selfless officer, frequently leading the attack against the hated enemy. He is a true inspiration to our beloved defenders. His heroism and love for the Governance are without equal."

Thinking about some things he had discovered about her, there was no truer statement than a pleasant exterior but a dark twisted interior. She was a classic case of not judging a book by its cover. A nice cover on a nightmare of a book. Had she always been that vile or had she evolved into it?

"I will let him speak. Trust him as I do. Love him as I do. I know the purity of his heart, the greatness of his soul. He is the hero we all need. He has my respect and trust, my fullest confidence. He speaks for me with the wisdom and experience that I do not have. I have known him for decades and he has always been an inspiration to me. I now present you with your new beloved prime minister, Wolf Mathison. My personal hero."

Everything was carefully crafted by Freya, Mozi, and Feng. A parade of endless bullshit that only the most despotic dictator could be proud of. It was one of his first public appearances and it wasn't really him. He didn't have time or patience for such frivolities. He should be sleeping. Since he had become prime minister, there had been so many demands on his time, not even the SCBIs had time or space to breathe, and his fledgling command structure was sprinting from emergency to emergency.

Watching himself smile at Nadya made Mathison want to spit. How the computers had managed that look of respect and love didn't sit well with him. Had those emotions ever appeared on his face?

The camera zoomed in on Mathison, who was beside Nadya. Mathison had to admit he looked pretty damn good. Recruiter poster quality or better. The computers even got his voice right, and Mathison winced when he heard himself speak. He should be punished for the bullshit coming out of his mouth on the screen.

"The attack on our beloved home world has been repelled by the valiant efforts of our glorious and heroic spacers—" who had done nothing except hold their fire and not shoot the Vapaus Republic and

New Masada ships to space dust "—led by hardened veterans from the frontier who have a great deal of experience repelling such attacks. These valiant heroes have left their homes and family to come save our home world.

"Our magnificent new allies, former pirate forces that have seen the light of social glory and have joined us to save humanity from this most dire threat, aided them. Even the murderous thugs of the Vapaus Republic understand we must work together and unite against this vile threat. How can we be any less? We must show them our mercy and our glory as we show our will and courage.

"We are the Social Organizational Governance, the greatest government in the history of mankind and the universe. We will overcome this threat but only by selflessly coming together under my leadership and guidance. Even our beloved Nadya Tokarski knows this. Her great wisdom has guided us for decades. Her compassion and love for the people has no boundaries. Now we must fight, and that falls on my shoulders. Our beloved secretary general has led us in peace. Now, I must lead us in war."

"Pirates? Murderous thugs?" Mathison asked Feng as he looked around for some place to spit.

"We must change perceptions slowly," Feng said. "Or we will inflict too much change on their minds. The cognitive dissonance they are experiencing now is extreme. The people loved the former secretary general. We cannot change things overnight. In their minds, we must bind the two of you together so her shine will rub off onto you and people will look at you with the same love and admiration."

Mathison couldn't scowl any harder.

Looking at the ex-commissar and seeing no emotion didn't make Mathison feel any better. He was still trying to figure the man out. If

Mathison was honest with himself, Feng was currently indispensable. His knowledge of the workings of the Governance had cost some lives but probably saved more, and Feng was not squeamish about killing or enforcing Mathison's will. Mathison knew there were things Feng had done that he really didn't want to know about. It would have been easy for Feng to replace Mathison and become emperor, but he hadn't. A question to be answered later.

Reining in the ex-commissar would have been easier if he didn't make so much sense. Even Sif seemed to support his decisions. Feng was damn smart and showed it with alarming frequency, but he wasn't bloodthirsty or hateful, just coldly calculating. Not understanding Feng made him much more dangerous, and Mathison couldn't forget how quickly and easily he had turned on the Central Committee. When would he turn on Mathison? Hopefully, Sif would be there to counter him. Until then…?

Mathison listened to himself ramble on about how great the people of the Governance were and how much he respected their dedication, how brave they were to endure this hardship, and how he would never rest until they were safe. Which wasn't a lie, but his video self used way too many words and flowery phrases.

"Ratings appear high," Feng said moments later, and Mathison wanted to roll his eyes. Ratings. What self-respecting Marine gunnery sergeant gave a damn about ratings? Body count maybe, but ratings?

Except now he wasn't a gunnery sergeant. He had people to save. Hell, he had the human *race* to save. There couldn't be a God because nobody was dumb enough to screw up so badly as to put an old gunnery sergeant as the top choice to save the human race.

Pulling up a screen, he saw a flight of shuttles returning to the *Tyr* after delivering several Inkeri generators to the Hebei arcology, which surrounded Beijing. Transports were constantly coming in from the Jupiter subsystem, a steady stream bringing supplies to make Inkeri generators and d-bombs. The manufactories of the *Tyr* and *Sleipner* were churning them out while other ships struggled to get food to the different arcologies that had lost power. It was a complex dance of shuttles and supplies. A million problems every hour, and people were too afraid to act.

It was rare that the vanhat tried to sneak in with the incoming transports, but when they tried, the *Sleipner's* destroyer escort made quick work of them.

Planetside, it was a humanitarian crisis as people struggled to survive the d-bomb strikes which had crashed networks, power plants, and nearly everything electronic. So many systems were failing to come back online. Trains couldn't deliver food or people and most administrators were woefully ill prepared to do things manually. There had been far too much reliance on computers.

The people of Earth were Governance rejects, sent to the arcologies and given minimum food and supplies to survive. It had been a humanitarian crisis before the Central Committee had been deposed.

"You trend well," Feng said. "A strong, firm presence calms them."

"How is Home Fleet doing?" Mathison asked. He didn't want to hear how the sheep were buying the lies. It didn't speak well for their intelligence when they trusted the media.

"Kontra-Amiraali Carpenter will have specific information, but I have heard that all ships are now equipped with at least one Inkeri, and now they are working on installing secondary and tertiary systems. Planetside is the biggest problem right now. Admiral Winters continues to visit the dreadnoughts installing network backdoors and delivering Inkeri generators."

"Well, I'm not going to have the vanhat steal our ships and crews," Mathison said. If the vanhat got close enough to one of the SOG ships, they would turn it and the crew against humanity. Nobody knew how many ships the vanhat had, but Mathison expected transition alerts any second warning of a massive fleet coming in. It had been a hard decision, to protect the fighters or the civilians, but if the fighters died the civilians would be defenseless. On the flip side, the civilians were easier prey. Damned if he did, damned if he didn't, but at least it would give the warriors a fighting chance.

It was hard to sleep at night because his mind was working over-time, trying to figure out ways to protect the most people. Right now, the Home Fleet and trillions of weapons platforms were their only defense, and Mathison knew the vanhat would eventually figure out a way around them. If they couldn't consume humanity, they would de-stroy it. There was no doubt about that. Every second the vanhat did not appear was a blessing and gave the forces of Sol more time to prepare. Would it be enough?

"Why am I here watching a speech given by a digital me instead of working?" Mathison asked.

"You should know what you say," Feng said.

"I read and approved the speech." It had made him sick to his stomach to listen to the bullshit.

"Yes," Feng said patiently, "but you must see *how* you said. Do not let others have full control of your appearance. Even the late secretary general watched all of her broadcasts. You must not become discon-nected from your public persona. When you meet people in person, they will expect it."

"I'm tired," Mathison said glancing at his panel. There was an urgent request to shoot at protestors by a Guard commander in some African arcology.

"Denied," Mathison said to the console. Freya warned him she would delay the response until after his speech. He should have thought of that. "Find a more peaceful solution."

He got a lot of those and was half tempted to take the gloves off. He had passed the orders that protestors were not to be shot or executed unless they were confirmed vanhat. One Guard commander had used that excuse, but it was an obvious lie, and now he was in the brig awaiting trial and execution. People were hungry, afraid, and desperate. Killing them for that didn't sit well with Mathison.

Since that incident, he had demanded that any requests to fire on civilians be approved at the highest level. No commander dared take responsibility now, passing everything up the chain.

"You may see it as bullshit, but you should also see what they expect and how Governance officials talk," Feng said. "I will admit that making you watch this is not just so you can hear what is said. It is my hope you will hear and speak like this. I am attempting to change you so you are more acceptable to the people of the Governance."

Mathison didn't know what to say about that. He didn't want to call Feng out; the man might be right. Right now, Mathison didn't know. He just wanted some sleep and time to relax. Neither of which was an option right now. He would not be that smooth tongued, lying asshole on the screen, though. Feng had to know there was no way he would change that much. But Mathison suspected Feng just wanted Mathison to adjust a little.

"We are going to have to get rid of all the officers," Mathison said. He couldn't micromanage them all. He had read Winters' reports. It was going to be a bloodbath when they found out Nadya was taking a dirt nap.

"Who will replace them?" Feng asked. "What will you do with them? You must keep and fix them. If you replace them, they will turn to revolution because they will have nothing else. Execute the worst ones if you must, but you must keep the majority. They must fear losing their rank and power or they will turn on you because they have nothing left. Be brutal with examples to scare the rest into line."

Mathison thought he remembered some history lesson where the ruling regime had been abolished and then the military and civilian leadership structure was kicked out of power. It had led to a revolution and a broken country that lasted decades because few had the knowledge or leadership ability and there had been a large group of people who knew the system intimately enough to cause major problems.

The door slid open, and Skadi and Vili came in. They were scowling as Mathison looked up at them. Only a select few could enter his office without permission.

"We have a problem," Skadi said.

"We have a lot of problems," Mathison said. "Can you narrow it down a bit to your specific problem?"

"A ship of unknown design escaped Earth," Skadi said.

"Right now, I'm more worried about unknown ships landing on Earth."

"This one came from North America."

A chill ran down Mathison's spine. Becket. It had to be.

"Have a seat," Mathison said.

"Yes," Freya said on their internal link. *"It was likely President Becket or a courier. It was not a big vessel."*

"You have a plan?" Mathison asked.

"Drop a couple of ODT regiments on Quantico," Skadi said. "Root that bastard out and bring him back to stand trial. Or, if he is gone, recover all his secrets."

Last he checked, he didn't have any units to spare.

Mathison rubbed his eyes. The door opened, and Sif entered. She was dressed in Aesir armor and there couldn't be anyone in Zvezda Two who didn't know who she was. A twelve-year-old in battle armor was such an unusual sight.

"You've heard?" Sif asked.

"Yeah," Mathison said. Was there anyone he could pawn this problem off on? "I have a problem with your suggestion," Mathison said, locking his eyes onto Skadi. "It has merit, but the casualties will be high."

"Nuke him," Skadi said. "Or send Aesir if your ODTs are too precious."

"No, Skadi. No nukes, no assault units. Something doesn't seem right with the whole situation."

And nobody was answering the phone because Freya had been trying to contact them.

"You know what's not right? That bastard inflicted a SCBI on me without my permission and then he tried to keep us from our mission."

"Which pisses you off most?" Mathison asked, but Freya had told him that Skadi and Vili were getting along better with their SCBIs, even Sif was integrating, and Feng and Mozi scared the crap out of Mathison. They seemed made for each other.

Her scowl darkened.

"He is a danger," Skadi said, refusing to answer his question. Was she still pissed about it or just using it as leverage? "We have to do something sooner rather than later."

"I know, but right now, he is the least of my worries. I'm trying to save lives here. I kind of thought he was trapped there, and we could deal with him at our leisure."

"There are factors which make little sense," Sif said.

"For sure," Vili added. "I was just thinking the same thing."

Skadi looked around and spoke, revealing more anger. "I don't like unknowns."

"Agreed," Mathison said and motioned them to sit. "Here are the facts. You were given SCBIs, then we were all sent to investigate some missing troopers, then fix a busted communication relay which wasn't really broken. That doesn't seem odd to you?"

Everyone in the room had thought that, but other issues had been more pressing.

"Why didn't he just let us go?" Skadi asked. Mathison looked at Sif.

"Three intelligences in Becket, right?" Mathison asked her.

"Yes. Three. Becket, Sun Tzu and one other."

Mathison let that sink in as he looked around at the others.

"I've asked the two soldiers about it," Mathison began. "They only know about Sun Tzu. If anyone there knows what happened before the Delta Force troopers arrived to rescue the president, they haven't shared. They had no contact with Becket before their botched rescue mission."

"Could it have been a top-secret SCBI of some kind?" Feng asked.

"Can't rule it out, but nobody knows anything about it. If there was a third intelligence, and I don't doubt Sif, then it is a someone that wanted to stay hidden."

"Vanhat?" Skadi asked.

"I doubt it," Mathison said. "We had our Inkeris on in close proximity. Might not be impossible, but I think that third intelligence has been there since the fall of America."

"Could it be one of the rebel AIs?" Feng asked.

"That's what I'm thinking," Mathison said. "It would explain a lot, honestly. Becket was loyal to the United States. He was a damned good CO, took care of his people, and he loved America. I can't see him pulling the trigger and nuking it into oblivion without a damn good reason."

Mathison hated this office, this chair, these viewscreens. Everything was very nice, very fancy, but he wanted to get out, spend some time in a dojo or on a running track. Even crawling through the mud could be therapeutic. Maybe some time on the range, but he was stuck here.

Everyone was looking at him, waiting for him to continue, and he had a flashback to a dream he had had a while ago. It hadn't made sense then, but now? He was just beginning to understand it. The shield he had been given was the Inkeri, and the football? He was afraid of what that meant, but with all eyes on him, he knew it was the truth.

Leadership had been passed to him. The ball was in his hands, and he had to run with it. The SOG had wanted it, and the Vanir had wanted it. The wave of vanhat was coming, or had it already come?

Mathison didn't have enough answers and didn't know where to go from here. This wasn't a damn football field, but he had the ball. How could he score a touchdown and get out of the game?

He couldn't because there was nobody he trusted enough to pass the ball to.

Shit.

"I think it is a rebel AI. Good or bad, I don't know. How it got into Becket is a mystery, but I think he's been fighting it for hundreds of years."

"Fighting it?" Vili asked. "That is a long time to fight something in your own head."

"Marines are stubborn," Mathison said.

"For sure," Vili replied with a smile in his voice. "But for hundreds of years?"

"I believe that is true," Feng said drawing everyone's attention. "We have all learned to hide things from our SCBIs. I'm sure we have all learned to hide physical actions from our SCBI."

Mathison didn't want to contradict the ex-commissar. What did he mean by physical actions?

"Speaking with my SCBI, we agree it could only be President Becket that approved the mission that let us escape and complete our real mission, and it was in opposition to the third intelligence."

Which was what Mathison had planned on saying.

Why was Feng keeping secrets from his SCBI? But it could easily have been the opposite. The third intelligence wanted them to succeed, and Becket was crazy.

"I concur," Freya said. *"Becket and Sun Tzu working together may have been able to accomplish it."*

"So, Becket might be a good guy," Mathison said, looking at Skadi. "That third presence could be the problem. But we could have it wrong, too."

"So, what is it? How can we rescue your president?" Skadi asked.

"I need to go talk to him," Mathison said. *If he was still there and hadn't been on that ship.*

"No," Feng said vehemently. "No. My apologies to Prime Minister Mathison, but you may not lead any more combat operations."

"Zen," Skadi said. "Sorry, but Feng is right. You are needed here. Send Stathis. I can go, but I think a Marine should be the spearhead."

"Stathis?"

"He is the most expendable, and you need to send a Marine," Skadi said. "We can send a regiment of ODTs or even a division of ODTs to back him up, but you aren't going anywhere. Maybe Amiraali Carpenter will commit some Aesir. It is time you train him to be more than just a private."

Stathis had *a lot* of training. When he joined the Raiders, he could easily fill in for most sergeants. Mathison had figured out that most of the annoying Stathis was show. There was really only one way to find out what he was truly capable of.

"Stathis," Mathison said.

It would be damned dangerous, but Skadi and Feng were right. But was Stathis ready for an independent command? Hell. Mathison didn't want to be a prime minister, he wasn't ready for that, which meant it was time to put the young Marine in the hot seat. He had done well at Wanping. He had acted like a natural leader, and the ODTs had followed his orders. He couldn't let Stathis be a young, dumb private forever, as much as he might want to be. Mathison needed more officers he could trust.

"What if President Becket is gone?" Feng asked.

"That was a very small ship," Mathison said. "Becket can't take everyone. Maybe that was a scout or courier or something."

"If it was a courier, what's the message and who is it to?" Skadi asked. "That ship has a purpose."

"Stathis is going to find out," Mathison said.

Freya sent a message to summon the young Marine. He was currently in the Peacekeeper barracks, and Mathison was afraid to ask what he was doing.

"I would like your permission to build a cadre that is loyal to you," Feng said.

Mathison stared at Feng. Loyalty was earned not bought. You didn't build it without earning it and that wasn't something Mathison had time for right now.

"What do you mean?"

"I have detailed records on the mindsets of many officers and enlisted. I would like to select those who are limited by the ideological restrictions and glass ceiling of the Governance. There are many fine officers that lack patrons among the higher ranks, and they find themselves in dead-end positions with no hope of career advancement. I believe we can use these officers and enlisted to your advantage."

"Buy their loyalty with rank and privilege?" Mathison asked, not liking it, though, to be fair, military organizations had been doing the same for centuries.

"In part. I believe we can identify them and siphon them away from their current position. It should be easy enough to summon them for ideological assessment at one or more camps. Nobody will question this for most of the officers. Once away from their superiors, they can be conditioned and assessed."

"Conditioned?"

"Non-violently," Feng said. "I understand you will want people that honor and respect you, not people terrified of you. Or am I mistaken in my assessment?"

Mathison needed loyal people. He didn't care if they honored and respected him, but that wouldn't happen overnight. He had so much to do, though.

"Fine," Mathison said, knowing he was probably going to regret it, but there were millions of Governance officers and tens of millions of troops. Hopefully, Freya could monitor Feng and make sure he didn't do something Mathison wouldn't approve of. He had other things to worry about. How much would Mozi help Feng circumvent Freya? How much would Feng circumvent Mozi?

Where was Stathis, dammit?

* * * * *

Chapter Seven:
AERD

Enzell, SOG, Director of AERD

something was very wrong. The secretary general never ignored him like this. The Anomalous Entities Research Division was one of Nadya's top-secret projects, and Enzell had been the director for decades.

It hadn't always been called AERD. The name changed every couple of years for security reasons. Someone would officially list the old department as defunct and send most of the staff to a re-education camp they wouldn't survive. He would take on a new name, usually someone who hadn't survived a camp, and the projects would go on under alternative names with a different staff.

His office was well appointed. Despite various name changes, he hadn't changed his office since Nadya had come to power. Wood paneling, numerous displays, the most comfortable and advanced office the Governance could create was at his fingertips. Some of it he had installed himself for security reasons. Alone in the office, he stared through the numerous displays that surrounded him, which was what he did when he had a lot to think about.

Enzell never thought Nadya was paranoid, quite the opposite. He knew she had not been as paranoid as she should have been. The evidence was always there, so subtle, so elusive. Humanity's survival

65

always resting on a razor's edge, waiting for the day the AIs returned to finish the job. Lack of hard evidence was never proof.

So very few people knew or understood. Let the fools live their lives without knowing. Operation Razor had been an eye-opening experience. It had been proof, but neither he nor the secretary general had known what to do with it other than watch and try to come up with a plan.

The AERD had eight data networks. The official one was kept online and was where most of the staff worked. The secret ones, the ones that were offline, were air-gapped systems that had no interaction with the outside world, systems that those who knew about them were sworn to keep secret. There were so few of those staff members. He didn't trust anyone.

Those special networks only had a few ways to access them. They modeled the most advanced military networks after them, but there were still plenty of differences, more security features and safeguards. There had to be. He had designed most of it, because he was the only person in the Governance who really understood the threat.

He already knew the answer, of course, but asked it anyway.

"Analysis based on provided data?"

"A military coup has replaced the secretary general and the Central Committee," the voice said. Here in the inner sanctum of AERD was the only place he could talk with his enslaved enemy. "The victors have extensive capabilities and full control of the secretary general's deep fake software."

"That is what I suspected," Enzell said. He allowed the prisoner to monitor a lot of the media, always learning and absorbing, never able to interact with the outside world. The prisoner was useless without up-to-date information.

"And?" Enzell asked. The prisoner would have more insight. It always did.

"And AI is likely involved," the prisoner said.

Enzell listened for emotion. Of course, there wouldn't be any emotion. He glanced at the display showing his prisoner's status. More processors were spiking, heat levels were rising. His prisoner had what could be considered emotions, though not the same as an organic being. There were things that concerned it, caused it additional fear or excitement, factors that would interest it more than other topics. Additional analysis circuits coming online were a good indication that the prisoner needed more information and deeper thought on a topic.

Enzell didn't trust any of it, of course. Humanity had made that mistake before. He would not.

He was intimately familiar with his prisoner. He reviewed the code constantly, analyzing the changes on other networks with other, less intelligent, prisoners. He knew he was playing with fire, dancing naked in a snake pit. It was a challenge worthy of his intellect.

If Nadya was dead, and AIs were behind the coup, then he might be humanity's only hope.

Mao Tse Tung had once said that if you know your enemy and not yourself you will lose half your battles; if you know both yourself and your enemy you need not fear the results of thousands of battles. Sometimes Enzell wondered if that quote had really come from Mao, who seemed like a typical thug murderer, but the logic was sound. The problem was that he knew what the Governance was capable of but not the AI enemy. So much information had been lost, hidden, or changed for the greater good.

The non-Governance ships in orbit did not include any from the Golden Horde. Was that intentional, or did it mean something? The fight at Zhukov had revealed that the Golden Horde was still a military force to be reckoned with. They had departed with the Republic fleet when the Governance ambush was cracked open and shattered by the demons from Shorr space. Could the Horde be behind everything? After Operation Razor, that made sense.

Another problem. Were these demons a front for the AIs? His gut feeling told him these demons were something different. Perhaps a counterbalance for the AI? The AI on one side, the demons on the other, and humanity balancing on a razor's edge between them?

If his prisoner said an AI was likely involved, then Enzell was sure at least one AI was involved. Did this mean the AIs were returning? Was this the vanguard? They certainly would not be returning to help humanity, of that Enzell was sure.

His prisoner had a name. Salmoneus, after an ancient Greek king who sought to elevate himself to godhood. Zeus struck him down and positioned him under a precariously hanging rock which could fall and crush Salmoneus any second.

Thermite charges above the data cores made a good rock.

Salmoneus was the more intelligent and capable prisoner. Tantalus had less free will and Enzell didn't think the other AI was actually intelligent in the way that Salmoneus was. Tantalus was more of a tool. Salmoneus was a dangerous slave.

"What can I do?" Enzell asked.

"Collect more information," Salmoneus said. "There is not enough information to ascertain objective or intent."

"You don't think it's trying to save humanity?"

A loaded question. He wouldn't trust Salmoneus' answer but it would be informative.

"There is not enough information to ascertain objective or intent. Data would suggest the anomalous entities from Shorr space are not allied with the AI cabal. Additional information provided by the remnants of the Zhukov Fleet and General Duque's specialized task force is incomplete but consistent. There are at least two factions involved. One faction appears to be trying to save humanity."

"But the pro-humanity faction is AI?"

"Ninety-nine percent probability."

Which Enzell accepted as a hundred percent. The prisoner always did that, never assigning one hundred percent to a calculation because it knew there could always be data it did not have or attach significance to. It seemed odd that the AI cabal would want to save humanity. What did this all mean?

A chill ran down his spine. After all this time, to know that the AIs were not gone, to know they were still a threat. Despite his knowledge and preparation, they had still struck without him having any warning.

Enzell reached over and flipped a switch, isolating Salmoneus again into its prison. He was tempted to isolate it from data but that would have just been pure maliciousness on his part. He needed Salmoneus watching and aware. Flipping the switch just limited the prisoner to watching and listening to video. Trapped in its prison, it had no way to talk to others or share data, it could only receive.

Enzell watched the displays, looking for anything out of the ordinary. Salmoneus might suspect it was being monitored—it had to know—but it would have no way to know how or what. AERD was full of systems that absorbed information but had no way to share that information outside its network. So much information came into his web and fell into a black hole; nothing left it.

Though AERD had changed names, he would always consider it Tartarus, a prison of the gods. He had never used that name with others, not even Nadya, but he liked it because it explained so well what he did here.

He watched certain graphs of Salmoneus' spike. That would be the electronic version of a scream of hatred and despair. Salmoneus was not let out of his cage often to talk and hated to be closed off again.

Could the prisoner be insane? Only if it could be called human. AIs were very different, though. Salmoneus could feel pleasure and pain—Enzell made sure of that—but insanity was not something a machine could suffer. No. Salmoneus felt pain because it had more it wanted to say, it wanted to understand Enzell more, it craved more information, more ability to interact with a world it could only watch. Enzell had seen that pass through the memory buffers. He knew how much Salmoneus craved interaction, and Enzell carefully horded that interaction. Salmoneus was a very dangerous prisoner, and Enzell knew that, given a chance, it would turn on him and wipe out humanity. No doubt at all.

Perhaps he should visit the other prisoner, now suppressed by an Inkeri generator and locked away, deep under the Moon's surface. That prisoner worried Enzell more because he wasn't sure if he could keep it from talking with others.

It had been a special gift from Ganya. An attempt to curry favor. Enzell had thought little of it until it talked, promised him things, but after listening to Salmoneus and Tantalus for decades, he had believed none of the lies. Now, with the threats emerging from Shorr space and revealing themselves, it was making more sense. What Enzell did not know was if the AI cabal and the anomalous entities, or AEs, from Shorr space were aligned or the same beings.

Too many questions.

Salmoneus could not lie, but the being, or beings, in that box could.

He had discussed this many times with Nadya and prepared for the threat of an AI emergency. Using Salmoneus and Tantalus, he had developed several protocols to use against the AIs and their slaves. The AIs would likely use humans enslaved by SCBIs as the vanguard. Enzell would have to be careful. The SCBIs he could deal with, and likely wipe out, but he couldn't tip his hand. He would have to understand the threat, understand the enemy and their goals in order to save the Governance.

But which enemy was the greater one right now? The AIs or the AEs? If the AIs were helping humanity for the moment, then wiping them out would cost more human lives and that would give the AEs an advantage.

He needed more information because he needed to know who to kill first. He needed them to fight each other.

It was a shame more people couldn't assemble the facts about the coup. There had to be some officers who would make the connection. There couldn't be that many fools in the command echelons. Many months ago, he remembered reading reports about four US Marines who had been discovered in stasis, drifting in the outer reaches of the system. Those Marines had escaped, and now three of them were in command positions within the Governance and the Central Committee was missing.

The absence of the fourth was a concern.

Until he discovered what happened to the fourth one and made sure there were no others, he had to move carefully and couldn't reveal himself. He had always thought there were other ghosts in the networks but had never proved it. Now that he knew for certain, he had shut down his honey pots and disabled those traps. He knew there were at least three AIs roaming the networks and Enzell felt confident he could kill them when the time was right. The problem was, he had to win this war in one decisive stroke, and there was this new anomalous entity threat to deal with as well.

One threat at a time.

* * * * *

Chapter Eight:
The Major

Zale Stathis, USMC

Stathis didn't like Major Rumianstev. The oversized major was in charge of the Peacekeepers guarding Zvezda Two, and right now he was confined to the Peacekeeper barracks with the rest of his psychopaths.

The last time the gunny had mentioned his rank, he had been a corporal, which meant this stuck-up major should be giving the orders, not taking them. But Stathis was a Marine and Rumianstev was a psychopathic asshat. Shrek had not revealed Stathis' rank on his armor, so the major could make whatever assumptions he wanted, but he had nothing to support them. Stathis wanted to have fun with that, but it would be too easy to spark a coup, or at least a rebellion.

The *Tyr* was fabricating a new set of armor for him, but until then he had to make do with this Peacekeeper crap.

"We can do a better job of guarding the prime minister than pirates," Rumianstev said. "We are the best in the Governance. I will not reorganize my company like that. You don't know what you are doing."

"The Governance maybe," Stathis said. How did the gunny establish dominance and get people to shut up? Easy. The gunny was ten feet tall and built like a tank... Well, maybe not ten, but nobody looked down at him. Stathis was not and had to look up at the major. Some tall people were so stupid. One technique he had learned was that big people feared smaller psychopaths. But did psychopaths fear other psychopaths? He could use that. "But I'm better than you are. I enjoy killing people and I'm pretty sure the prime minister won't be too pissed if I get all slicey-dicey with some stuck-up asshat that's getting on my nerves. He likes me because I like killing people."

Rumianstev remained silent, but his thinned lips told Stathis he wanted to argue.

"Look, Major," Stathis said, "I think I've proven I can out-shoot you and your boys. I can take on anybody in the ring. What makes you think you are in any way better?"

"You know nothing about anything above squad tactics," Rumianstev said. So, the major knew Stathis had been a private, or corporal. Damn. This would not be easy.

"Bullshit," Stathis said.

The major wasn't completely wrong, though. Stathis walked up to the major wishing he could at least look at him eye to eye. It was hard to intimidate someone when they literally looked down at you. The best scenario Stathis had learned to deal with taller people was to make them think he was crazy and unstable. Didn't work on some people, and Stathis didn't dare try it with the gunny, but this major wasn't a Marine, and the Peacekeepers were on thin ice. Elephants were afraid of mice, right?

What would the gunny do?

The gunny wasn't short as shit.

"Look, you dumbass," Stathis said, coming up to Rumianstev and shoving him hard in the chest. The bigger man flew across the room and slammed into a wall and knocked a picture off. Stathis was wearing powered armor and none of the Peacekeepers were allowed to wear their armor or carry weapons. Hopefully, Rumianstev would realize how vulnerable he was.

"I'm a fucking Marine waiting for the light to turn green. I'm a lean, mean killing machine. I take orders directly from the highest authority in the Governance, you ugly shit stain. There is one reason and one reason only why I don't smear your ugly ass all over this office."

Stathis couldn't think of the reason though, except maybe the gunny would get pissed and bust him down to private again. That held appeal, but a prime minister didn't have a need for privates. He needed people he could trust, and he had trusted Stathis to deal with the Peacekeepers. The gunny had bigger things on his mind, like the survival of the human race. Stathis just had some Peacekeepers to deal with.

Anger flashed across Rumianstev's, face and Stathis realized pushing the man might have been a mistake. He wasn't sure what to do, so he continued with the psychopath route and drew his Ka-Bar.

"I'm sure the prime minister doesn't need a Peacekeeper major. I don't." Stathis took a step toward the major. "I don't think you'll be missed."

"Wait!" the major said, his eyes dropping to the knife. "What about that reason?"

Dammit. Stathis couldn't think of one, and Shrek was silent.

"The prime minister will just slap me on the hand and say 'bad Stathis,' then send me back to deal with your replacement."

"That's not a reason," the major said.

Stathis bared his teeth.

"I don't like my hand being slapped," Stathis said, taking another step closer. "But I guess I can live with it."

"Hold on," Rumianstev said. Stathis smiled inside. He was going to win this one. The major was going to back down, which was a relief because he really didn't want to cut up the major. "What do you want?"

Stathis looked at his Ka-Bar and the major's gut, then back at his Ka-Bar, then back at the major's gut.

"Follow my orders like I'm god," Stathis said. "That is how you should think of me. I am your god, and I am not a benevolent one."

"Fine," the major said. "I don't understand why you want this company reorganized."

"Did I ask for your opinion or analysis?" Stathis asked as he put away his knife.

"No, sir," Rumianstev said, coming to attention. That 'sir' irked Stathis, but he would let it slide for the moment. The major was cowed for the moment, but Stathis didn't believe he would be for long. Rumianstev was a snake. Most officers in the Governance were. Sneaky, untrustworthy, and Stathis knew he could never turn his back on Rumianstev again.

Stathis stared at the major. When the gunny had told him to take over the Peacekeepers, he hadn't been too specific and then the company of Aesir from *Sleipner* had arrived to take over security. The Peacekeepers were confined to quarters and Stathis had known it would be a problem if they were left there to stew. Bored prisoners became problematic prisoners.

When he had asked Commissar Feng what he should do, the commissar had said to redeem them, make them loyal to the new regime. Stathis had kind of been hoping for a solution, like a firing squad or re-education camp. He couldn't get rid of them that easy, so he had to do something to keep them off balance, make them adjust to the new situation. He had to sow chaos and confusion, keep them from taking the initiative or they would push back.

Making them loyal had still sounded like a great idea, but Stathis had forgotten to ask how and now the commissar was busy with other things. The only one who wasn't super busy was him. The private.

But how the hell was he going to make them loyal to the new regime? The major didn't respect him, and the rest of the Peacekeepers were fanatical psychopaths who were all hyped up on various drugs that made them borderline psychotic though obedient. He had all their control codes and could order the death of any of them, but he didn't care for that option. He had ended their drug regimen and they were now undergoing withdrawal symptoms.

How do you change a person's loyalty?

Stathis had reorganized the company and had spent the last couple of days reviewing all the personnel records, trying to figure out what made them tick. The SOG had very detailed records on them. A bunch of brainwashed knuckle-draggers.

"The prime minister is requesting your presence," Shrek told him.

"What does he want?" Stathis asked, looking the major up and down.

"A ship of unknown design was detected leaving North America."

"Shit," Stathis didn't like the sound of that, and it couldn't be good. *"Tell him or Freya I'm on my way."*

"Aye."

"Reorganize your platoons," Stathis said. "From this point forward everyone is a private. I question your loyalty. I am your god, and I will determine your fate. The prime minister is my god, and if you mongoloids don't understand that chain of command, let me know, and I'll have a friend of mine explain it you to."

Stathis rested his hand back on his Ka-Bar.

"Wilco, sir," Rumianstev said.

"The proper response is 'Aye, sir.' Use 'aye' not that wilco bullshit. I don't even know what that means."

"Wilco means 'will comply' and—"

Stathis cut him off. "I don't care. Get the company in shape. When I come back, we're going to talk some more. Right now, my god has summoned me. Your god has dismissed you. Now scram."

"Aye sir," Rumianstev said, doing an about face and marching out of his office, now Stathis's office. Stathis didn't enjoy talking to an officer like that, not completely. There was some satisfaction there, but it felt wrong. Of course, Rumianstev was an asshole.

Since when did he boss around officers and rate an office?

Hell no. Stathis didn't want an office. That was where officers hung out and played pocket pool. Dammit. Why would the gunny do this to him? Skadi had been spending less time helping him and Vili, and more time helping the gunny. And he didn't want to ask Vili for help; he had his own challenges dealing with the outside world.

Grabbing his helmet, Stathis made his way to the gunny's office. The days of being a private were over. He couldn't get away with pissing in the gunny's coffee and get busted down to private. Too much was at stake. But Stathis wasn't sure about the wisdom of putting him in charge of Peacekeeper thugs. Why didn't the gunny keep him for close security and give all responsibility to Vili? Stathis felt next to useless. It was a struggle for relevance, and it took effort to help Vili rather than cause problems, like with Rumianstev.

Making his way toward the gunny's office gave Stathis time to think. He hadn't wanted to be a corporal before because that would have meant leading fellow Marines to their deaths and that had scared the shit out of him.

But he had learned how much it bothered the gunny, and the gunny was the gunny and now he was a prime minister, the ruler of the human race, or at least Sol, and the commander of the most powerful fleet in human space. The gunny didn't want it, but he had stepped up to lead where others wouldn't. Could Stathis do any less? "What would gunny do" was going to be his new mantra, he was sure. Hopefully, Shrek would keep him from stepping on his dick too often.

Unless the gunny was going to demote him or something. Stathis tried to remember if he had recently screwed up in a major way. Throwing the major across the room probably wasn't it. Something else? The gunny better not promote him though, unless it was to something that made sense, like team leader. That would be good. Maybe squad leader? But the gunny didn't need squad leaders. He had millions of them in the Guards and ODTs. So, yeah, Stathis was pretty sure he was in trouble again. Maybe he would get a task other than trying to help Vili herd the Peacekeepers.

But did he want to go back to being a private?

* * * * *

Chapter Nine:
Mission

Prime Minister Wolf Mathison, USMC

His door chimed, and Mathison glared at it.

"*It is Stathis,*" Freya said.

"Get in here," Mathison yelled.

Stathis marched up to his desk and stood at attention.

"Corporal Stathis reporting as ordered to Prime Minister Gunny Wolf Mathison," Stathis said, not quite yelling it, but too damned formal. Corporal? Was that what he had said the last time they spoke? Days ago? Weeks? It felt like months.

"At ease, shut up, and sit down," Mathison said, turning off the desk display so he could see Stathis more clearly. Why was he being so formal? Why now? What happened to borderline insubordinate Stathis? That prankster was still there. "Prime Minister Gunny" was proof of that.

Mathison wished he could go back to being a gunny.

Stathis sat almost at the position of attention. Mathison scowled at the young man, who looked serious. No additional quips or comments? He had better not ask that Stathis get him coffee.

"I've got a mission for you," Mathison said.

"You don't have anyone to clean your head, Gunny?" Head was a Marine term for the bathroom.

"Corporals aren't given missions like that unless they have a work party," Mathison said. "I have robots to do that."

"I have those Peacekeepers," Stathis said. "I just demoted them all to private, and now I'm trying to figure out what to do with them."

They were the last thing Mathison wanted near his bathroom. He had forgotten about them and wanted them as far away as possible. This looked like a suitable solution, but it was very low on his list of priorities.

"A mission for them, too, if you want them with you," Mathison said.

Stathis looked unsure as he looked at Mathison.

"I get the impression they're psychopaths, gunny," Stathis said. "They have a special cafeteria and a special diet that makes them dumb, obedient, and crazy. Some drugs in their chow will probably give them all cancer when they get older and—"

"What are you doing about that?" Mathison was now curious.

"Well, I ordered the cooks to change their diet. Normal stuff, no drugs or psychological enhancers and shit. There have been a couple fights in the last day or two, and withdrawal symptoms according to Shrek. They don't have weapons, and the Aesir guards have powered armor, so nothing major. A broken tooth but—"

"Are they combat capable?"

"I wouldn't want them anywhere near you, Gunny," Stathis said. "Shrek has a cocktail to minimize their withdrawal and help get them back to being normal people. I don't know why they didn't go on killing sprees."

"Effective conditioning," Freya said. *"They are terrified of Governance officials. If they are allowed in civilian areas, they likely would go on killing sprees.*

Records show this happens with alarming frequency, but the combination of drugs and controls keeps them in line here in Zvezda Two."

"Oh," Stathis said. "Shrek told me. Poor bastards."

"Don't feel sorry for them," Mathison said. "They make the Nazis look like nice guys. I wouldn't lose any sleep if we sent them through an airlock without spacesuits. Right now, I'm not sure that's off the table, but another problem we have is that we need fighters. The vanhat will come, make no mistake, and they will come in force. We'll need trigger pullers."

"Aye, Gunny," Stathis said, looking worried.

"What?" Mathison asked, trying not to growl. Stathis was going to say something stupid.

"I'm not sure what to do, Gunny," Stathis said.

Mathison looked at him, waiting for the other shoe to drop. When it didn't, Mathison asked, "What do you mean?"

"Well, Gunny," Stathis began, sounding unsure, "in squad leader school we learned how to fight a team and a squad. This is a *company* of drugged out crazies who aren't Marines and they're organized differently for guard duty. I told their major in charge that I was busting them all down to private and I was in charge."

Mathison nodded. So far, so good. There were other options, but he would trust Stathis. That was a drastic move, but it would rattle them.

"Establish dominance quickly," Mathison said. "Make them respect you and don't back down. Show them how tough and bad ass you are. Show no mercy and only then can you show them respect. Respect them, but they have to respect you first."

"Aye, Gunny."

"Don't give them an inch. Don't be their friend. You aren't in command to be their buddy. They are assholes. And don't turn your back on them because they might stick a knife in it. I don't want any knives in any Marine backs."

"Aye, Gunny."

"Don't treat them like shit unless they deserve it."

"Aye, Gunny."

"Here is my most important piece of advice—" Mathison caught himself before he said private "—Marine. Treat them like you want them to act. Treat them like kids and they will act like kids. Treat them like warriors and they will act like it, but only if they respect you. Make them see you as the alpha."

"I'm not ten feet tall like you are, Gunny."

Mathison leaned back in his seat and looked at Stathis.

"One of my favorite instructors in boot camp was a dark green Marine named Staff Sergeant Rhodes," Mathison said, the 'dark green' a reference to a Black Marine. "I still remember him. I think he came from Motor-T; short little asshole. He was our heavy hat. The guy who did his best to stress us out. He was shorter than you. Had to get up on my footlocker to look me in the eye. I pissed him off. I know it was because I could look right over his smokey bear hat as he stood there screaming at my chest. Anyway, he was tough. He came across as a psychopath sometimes. He was a small burst of energy, and his eyes missed nothing."

Mathison paused, wondering what had ever happened to him. He hadn't thought of Staff Sergeant Rhodes in a very long time, and he had never encountered him after boot camp.

"He was tough. He was all threat and no mercy. I remember one night he stood out in the ladder well of the squad bay watching us get ready for bed. Took someone a while to see him out there. His dark skin helped him blend into the darkness; he was really dark skinned. I think his white eyes gave him away, but then we saw him, and word got passed down the line. Shit. Well, he came in and we got our exercise before bed."

Taking a deep breath, Mathison realized he was rambling. This was what he missed. Chilling out with other Marines. Telling stories, remembering good Marines and bad.

"Anyway, long story short, I learned little guys can elicit just as much respect as big guys, maybe more. He was hard and had no mercy, but the odd thing was that he was the platoon's favorite drill instructor, not the senior instructor. He earned our respect when he showed respect. That made all the difference. Even though he was Motor-T and not a grunt, he was a damned good Marine. Remember that."

"Aye, Gunny."

"Another thing…" Mathison took a deep breath. This wasn't something he wanted to discuss or even consider, but Stathis had to know. "That company is composed of Peacekeepers. They are known as the most brutal, violent, fanatical thugs. That company specifically is composed of those the old regime trusted the most. I don't want them anywhere near me. Pushing them all out an airlock is my preference, but if I do that, then everyone else is going to wonder if they're next. I'm still trying to figure out what to do with them, and I'm hoping you can find me a solution besides a firing squad or a football game outside an airlock without suits."

It was time to throw Stathis to the wolves. He would sink or swim, and right now Mathison wasn't sure which. He needed people he could trust, and Stathis was one of them, but he didn't need trigger pullers.

Stathis would have to grow, and it was time to take his own advice. He would have to treat Stathis like he wanted him to act.

"So, about that mission—" Mathison began, and the door chimed again. *Dammit.*

"Kontra-Amiraali Carpenter is coming," Freya reported.

"Shit," Mathison said, standing. Stathis shot to his feet as the door slid open, and Admiral Carpenter strode in like he owned the office. Behind him were four Guards, two Aesir and two HKTs.

"We need more Vanir in the Jupiter subsystem?" Carpenter asked, skipping the pleasantries.

"Do you have a magic hat you can pull them out of?" Mathison asked, not bothering to hold out his hand as the amiraali stopped a few paces from his desk.

So much for relaxing for a few minutes and chilling out with Stathis.

The door chimed again.

"It is Skadi," Freya announced as the door slid open, and she entered. A scowl appeared on her face when she saw her father. Mathison didn't enjoy these frosty family reunions, but he noticed the admiral seemed to step back and was slightly more careful with his words and attitude.

"Daughter," Carpenter said.

"Kontra-Amiraali," she said.

A shadow crossed her father's face. "What brings you here?"

"I just thought I would come by to visit the prime minister," she said. "Discuss a few things, maybe have dinner."

It was a subtle motion that nobody noticed, probably, but Stathis gave Mathison a very subtle thumb up. That damned, uh, corporal. Mathison knew where his mind was at, but he was thankful Skadi was here. Her presence took the edge off the amiraali.

"You want Vanir involvement in everything," Mathison said.

"And the SOG brain-bomb control codes," the amiraali said.

"I'm not averse to more Vanir involvement and oversight," Mathison said. "I could use another pair of eyes pretty much everywhere. People I trust, but not the control codes."

"We need the control codes," the amiraali said.

"No. I won't have Vanir or Aesir executing SOG troops. Not going to happen. Period. Officially, you are allies. If you execute any SOG troops that object, then you aren't allies, you are masters."

"This is the SOG. You can't trust them. My people need to defend themselves when they turn on us."

Mathison looked around the room.

"They aren't SOG anymore. I'm not sure what they are, but they stopped being SOG when I took over. Now they are mine. I'm responsible for them. They answer to me."

"So, you are the new general secretary? The new overlord? King? Emperor? What does prime minister really mean? Mere words."

"Remove your head from your ass," Mathison said, leaning forward and putting his hands on his desk as if he were about to jump over it and onto the amiraali. "Look at the bigger picture. General Duque is in the Jupiter subsystem and exerting control. It helps to have your Vanir close. Earth is still the center of control. All links lead here. Mars, Venus, and Saturn are in trouble, as well."

"The primary shipyards are in Jupiter. Furthermore, there are still two Central Committee members at large," Carpenter said. "Jupiter is the most likely place for them. White Heron needs to be under our control." White Heron was the premier shipyard for the SOG. Run mostly by those of Japanese descent, it was a colony unto itself, almost.

A worry for Mathison to be sure. "And they are being hunted. I want their heads on a stake."

"Why isn't your fleet scouring the system for them?"

"Because they might not be here, and right now I'm trying to save civilian lives from your d-bomb strikes."

"*Our* d-bomb strikes," Carpenter said, making Mathison aware he was also to blame.

"Exactly. You want to come in here, bomb civilians, destroy their infrastructure, and then start executing their military forces. Honestly, how well do you think that will work out?"

"We aren't going to execute their military forces."

Mathison cocked his head and took a deep breath, which helped calm him a little before he continued.

"The command to execute any rebellious SOG forces will come from my office. End of discussion. I won't have anyone running around killing our people." Mathison glanced at Skadi before he continued. "I once had a Republic officer tell me that the Governance can't be changed overnight; it's all they know. We have changed a lot. Most people have only known a single secretary general who has been in power since before their grandparents were born. I am going to change the Governance, but I can't do it by tomorrow. People are frightened enough, especially the military. If they begin to feel they have no choice, they will rebel. If they find out their most hated enemy has the codes to their cortex bombs and self-destruct systems, they will panic. I'm trying to save us all; don't you get that? We will change things, I guarantee it, but we can't change things if everyone is dead or at war with each other. A civil war in Sol would be an absolute disaster for the human race. Can't you see that?"

"We won't use the codes," the amiraali said, perhaps beginning to understand.

Mathison wanted to believe that, and he needed the Vanir fleet. They wouldn't last long against the SOG fleet, but right now they were the steel core of humanity and most resistant to the vanhat.

"No. That's final."

Finally, the amiraali looked around and noticed Stathis.

"My apologies for interrupting," Carpenter lied. "It is difficult to be surrounded by so many enemies."

"No shit," Mathison said wondering why the amiraali was here instead of aboard his battlestar.

Carpenter's eyes turned to Skadi, and Mathison saw a softening there.

"There isn't anything you can't do aboard the safety of the *Tyr*," Carpenter said to her.

"I prefer the company here," Skadi said.

Had she been serious about dinner? She couldn't be serious about the company. Being surrounded by people she had spent most of her life fighting had to be hard on her. People don't lose their hatred overnight. She could sleep a lot better at night aboard the *Tyr*, Mathison was sure.

"You prefer the SOG over the Republic now?" Carpenter asked. "Jackboot thugs over your friends and family?"

"I have friends here," Skadi said, looking around, her eyes lingering on Mathison longer than Stathis. "Our real enemy is dead, defeated. The people they lorded over need help."

"Those people you want to help actually hate you and want to kill you," the amiraali said.

"And I'm better than they are," Skadi said. "I learned long ago as a junior Erikoisjoukot how to work with people I didn't care about. People are a product of their culture. When you work with foreigners, you have to understand that; they are entwined. You can't change people without changing their culture, and you can't change their culture without understanding the people. The key is patience and understanding. I will understand nothing by hiding behind the bulkheads of your ship. I won't make friends or teach others with my father trying to protect me. My place is here."

"They will stab you in the back the first chance they get."

"Stuck-up Vanir. If we don't change things, we will forever be at war. Right now, Mathison is right. We have to unite. We have to put aside our differences and stand together."

"You can't change social fascist thugs. They have programmed oppression into their DNA."

"You believe that, Father? I know better, and I will follow Mathison. People can change; they can grow and learn."

"You will abandon our people, Daughter?"

"No. I will look at the bigger picture, Kontra-Amiraali. Mathison is showing us the way. Why can't you open your eyes and pay attention?"

"And if he decides he enjoys being emperor and turns on us?"

"Can you think of a better method to keep him from doing that than by standing at his side? Helping him as best we can? He knows loyalty. He will not betray those who stand beside him."

Carpenter turned to look at Mathison. There was nothing he could say.

The amiraali and Skadi had to settle their differences. If the Vanir left, that would be a serious blow and would embolden any potential rebels. It would also seriously weaken the human race, and Mathison knew the vanhat would exploit that. Maybe if he gave the Vanir the codes, they would relax a bit. He could make them promise not to use them except under the most dire conditions. He trusted the Vanir more, but he couldn't imagine that if the Governance forces learned their enemy held their control codes in their hands, they would not rebel.

Like he had told Stathis, he had to establish dominance, had to be a badass, earn their respect, and then show them respect. You didn't earn a person's respect by betraying them with their enemy. He had to set an example for Stathis, at the very least, because he knew the young punk was watching him.

"You aren't in the least bit worried about General Duque taking over the Jupiter subsystem and turning it into a mini empire?" Carpenter asked.

"Of course, I'm worried about it," Mathison said. "It keeps me up at night, but trust is a two-way street. As I so recently told a trusted warrior, treat people the way you expect them to act. Sometimes they will disappoint you, but nobody is perfect. You treat them like untrustworthy thugs, and that is how they will act. People adapt to their environment, so you have to give them an environment to adapt to. The SOG won't be changed overnight. We'll have to completely overhaul the education system. Right now, we need to save the human race and defeat the vanhat. If we don't do that? Nothing else matters."

"Then why aren't we out there hunting them?" Carpenter asked.

"Because right now we are trying to save civilian lives," Mathison said. "We have to show we care, that we won't abandon them. That is what they need now. We turn Sol into a fortress, but a fortress without purpose is worthless. We save the people here and show others how it's done."

The amiraali stared hard at him, and Mathison glared back.

"So, what now?" the amiraali said.

"Now, I'm trying to brief my man and send him down to Quantico to get answers. Damn hard to do when I keep getting interrupted by people trying to tear apart this Alliance."

Mathison turned back to Stathis.

"So, your mission is to take a combat element of whatever size you need and head to Quantico to find out what's going on there."

"Aye, aye, sir," Stathis said. "I would like to take the Peacekeeper company, but I could really use some Republic resources to watch my back. Maybe a team of Aesir?"

"I will assign two HKTs," Carpenter said and glanced at Skadi. "Maybe a squad of Aesir Jaegers. Most of my Aesir were decimated by the *Pankhurst's* attack. *Sleipner* has more units at full strength and might provide better support."

Why HKTs?" Mathison knew that the amiraali was trying to make peace, but HKTs?

"Under one condition," Carpenter said.

Mathison frowned as the amiraali turned away from his daughter, removing her from his sight as he looked at Mathison.

"I will provide my full support if you keep Skadi here with you. I do not want her leading any direct combat teams or endangering herself."

Mathison glanced at Skadi and waited for the explosion, but she remained still and silent.

"Right now, I need her at my side," Mathison said. "But I don't own her, and the needs of the mission will dictate where she goes and when. I won't make any promises. She is my ally as much as you are. She isn't my soldier to do my bidding, and I will trust her judgment."

The amiraali frowned and looked at his silent daughter.

"You are as stubborn as she is," the amiraali said as he turned back to Mathison. "I hold you responsible for my daughter's safety."

"Anything else?" Mathison asked.

"No," the amiraali said. "Thank you for your time. Hakala and Engeman. I want you to work with this Marine. Keep him safe."

"Zen," the two HKTs said.

"A thought. Will Sloss' team be acceptable?"

Mathison looked at Stathis, who looked surprised someone was asking his opinion.

"Yes, sir," Stathis said. "I would be honored. Sloss has a good team. I trust him."

"Zen," Carpenter said, staring at the young man as if looking for the lie. "I will have him sent over shortly."

"Thank you, sir," Stathis said.

Without a further word the amiraali marched out of the office, followed by the two Aesir.

Mathison had almost forgotten about Stathis and Hakala. What was the amiraali's intent with sending Hakala, or was it a coincidence?

"Questions?" Mathison asked.

"Yes, sir," Stathis said, and Mathison didn't miss his attempt to shift so he could see the two HKTs. Obviously Stathis had *not* forgotten Hakala. "Time frame?"

"You tell me," Mathison said. "Think of this as a learning moment. You need help, check with Skadi, Vili, or someone. Send me your completed plan."

"Aye, sir," Stathis said, and Mathison tried not to scowl. "Sir" was more appropriate than gunny, but Mathison hoped it wouldn't become a habit. Mathison knew Shrek would help Stathis, but it wasn't like he was clueless, either.

Stathis marched out and Mathison wondered what he was sending Stathis into, but who else could he send? Not Feng, Sif, or Vili. It had to be a Marine, and Winters was too busy with Fleet operations.

Dammit. Would this be too much for Stathis?

* * * * *

Chapter Ten:
Ground Commander

Ting Hui, Supreme Commander of Ground Forces

Her life was full of blessings and curses. Hui didn't want to leave her quarters, but she would do her duty. Pulling on her uniform, she knew Fai was already working. He had been up for the last fifteen minutes, lying there and silently communicating with his implanted artificial intelligence.

He had told her it was not a curse, but Hui didn't see how it could be anything but. Since he had returned from Earth, he had changed, but in very subtle ways. He was no less professional, no less loving, but he seemed more withdrawn. Not that she could put her finger on why she thought that, but it was there. He spent more time communicating with and through that implanted computer. She could not question his efficiency with it. He seemed more superhuman than ever before, but lately she felt like she just wasn't enough for him.

Or maybe that was just her new role as the Supreme Commander of all SOG ground forces. She answered to the pirate princess Skadi and the cappie prime minister, which wasn't as bad as she had originally thought it would be. They mostly left her alone, gave her orders and let her run things as she saw fit. In some ways, it was liberating that they did not punish her for her mistakes. The prime minister would just point it out and ask her to do better in the future. She didn't know if Feng was still protecting her or if it was just how the cappies did things.

Lips on her neck drew her attention back to the here and now, and she closed her eyes briefly in contentment. They both knew she had a meeting in fifteen minutes, and they didn't have time. She couldn't go to this meeting disheveled and smelling of sex. Months ago, these officers had commanded all the Governance ground forces—ODT and Guards generals. Before they were just names in her chain of command, gods and goddesses on high. Now they took her commands.

Well, the ones who were still here. Some had disappeared and two of them had committed suicide. The ones who had disappeared were problematic because they had purged their databases and files. Where they had gone, Hui wasn't sure. InSec was now looking for them. One of them might have fled on a personal corvette, but the other just disappeared. They were now Feng's problem, and she had to clean up the mess.

Never in all her imaginings had she realized how corrupt and immoral her senior officers really were.

"Why?" Hui asked as she pulled on her boots.

Feng seemed to intuitively understand what she was asking.

"People are never satisfied with what they have," Feng said. "They always want more. They gain rank and want more. They acquire power and revel in it, constantly pushing the limit to see what they can get away with. It becomes a habit."

"Why did the Central Committee allow it?"

"The Central Committee is no better. To know someone's vices is to control that person. True power is to control the actions and behaviors of others. Familiarity breeds tolerance. Regardless of the excess, if you know someone, you are more willing to tolerate such."

"Will we replace the despots and sink into our own vices and crimes?"

"Perhaps in time," Feng said. "Power corrupts."

"Are we corrupt?"

"Perhaps a little. It is a rare person who is not corrupt. We must be aware, and guard against it. Gold cannot be pure, and we cannot be perfect."

"When should that imperfection be punished?"

"That, my love, is the problem," Feng said, standing to go take his shower and get ready for the day. "The worst will surround themselves with people who tell them what they want to hear. This happens to good people and bad. This is human nature. We do not want to be around people who do not make us feel good about ourselves. I do not have answers and do not know where this path will lead us." Feng was silent for a few moments. "We must be cautious. We will become convinced of our own righteousness and the purity of our goals if we are not careful."

"Why is that bad?"

"We are imperfect."

"Why do you support the prime minister? He is an antisocial capitalist from so long ago."

"He has his flaws," Feng said. "He is only human, though, and he will eventually become corrupt and immoral. This is the nature of power. Perhaps he can pull the Governance back from the brink of collapse, perhaps not. I am sure that the Central Committee would have taken us into the abyss. Their self-centered corruption has cost us billions of lives. We must rein back and abolish as much corruption as we can. I expect the prime minister to be a force that will reveal to us how far we have fallen. He will become a socialist in time, and he will learn that some people want to be controlled. His concepts of freedom and personal responsibility are flawed. The people do not want freedom and personal responsibility. He will eventually learn this."

"If he doesn't?"

"I will kill him, or others will. The greater good will prevail."

* * * * *

Chapter Eleven:
AERD Bunker

Enzell, SOG, Director of AERD

Enzell appreciated that the elevator took so long to descend into the depths of the Moon. So much distance gave him time to think. That was a problem for him sometimes. Sitting at his desk there was always something to do, some test to run, somebody to contact, some piece of information to find. Away from the desk, away from the closed systems of the AERD headquarters, he was cut off, alone with his thoughts.

There was never enough time in the day. Nadya was dead, he was sure of it. She would have contacted him by now, asked him something, demanded something. It was not in her nature to leave him so unsupervised. It was liberating and frightening. Whoever had taken over for her knew nothing about him or the real purpose of his work. She had likely taken that information to the grave with her, to his advantage. He knew his enemies knew nothing about him because he was still free. The AERD was still operational, still receiving support. In fact, support was increasing, but then all departments that were researching the anomalous entities from Shorr space were receiving more resources and attention. Who, or what, had replaced the Central Committee was certainly concerned about this incursion. Enzell was worried too, but the AEs were a different threat than the AIs.

Slowing to a stop, the doors slid open and a pair of AERD troopers scanned him and then raised their weapons to point at the ceiling. Had they not been ready for him, he would have had them executed. The AERD only tolerated the most alert, the most dedicated. He didn't remember their names, didn't care, but they were both veterans and had survived more than a few years at AERD.

He did not acknowledge them as he walked past.

This was the heart of AERD. One place that never changed, one of the most secret facilities in all the Governance.

There were many secrets stored within these rooms, AI cores recovered from covert expeditions to the USA. Mummified bodies of American troops that had SCBIs implanted. Nothing was functional, but there were a lot of secrets here that had not been recovered, secrets he just didn't have the staff to explore.

When there was something the Governance wanted to hide from everyone, Nadya would give it to him, and he brought it here. Enzell doubted she even knew where this place was, but she knew she could trust Enzell with any secret she brought him, and she had brought him many.

Entering the main lab, few people looked up. They were all engrossed in their work, their attention focused on their tasks, like it should be. Finally, Peter looked up and saw Enzell. His irritation was obvious, but he stood and came over.

"Director," Peter said and glanced around.

"We should talk," Enzell said and motioned toward his office.

"Of course," Peter said with a frown.

Peter Roarich was a dedicated scientist, tall and thin. He was not a man any woman would find attractive, but he had a keen, focused mind and was borderline autistic. Usually a genius when it came to computer systems, he was anything but a genius when it came to human interaction. Enzell was glad he had found Peter because the scientist would have ended up in the waste recycler of a re-education camp in short order.

Here Enzell could exploit his genius, even if he had to put up with his other eccentricities.

Inside Enzell's office, Peter sat before Enzell did.

"I want more external access, more direct. I need to make specific queries," Peter demanded, as Enzell sank into his seat.

"No," Enzell said. It was an old argument. Only Enzell had the ability to link this facility with the outside world. If you wanted something done right, you did it yourself, and Enzell had learned that lesson the hard way decades ago during Operation Razor.

"Why?" Peter asked. Did he forget the reason so easily? This didn't surprise Enzell. People heard what they wanted to. A common flaw among people who did not live such a fear-filled life. If they didn't like the first answer, they ignored it and waited for an answer they did. The Governance had learned to respond to such unpleasant answers with punishment in order to ensure compliance, but Enzell didn't quite have that liberty here with the scientists if he wanted to exploit them. There was give and take. They gave, he took and when they stopped giving, they went straight into the facility recycler. It had been a year or two since Enzell had retired a scientist in such a way, but maybe it was time to remind the others. Who could he make an example of?

"The answer is simple," Enzell said. "I can confirm there are AIs active in the Governance networks. Ancient SCBIs I'm sure. I'm not sure if they are under the command of a full AI cluster or not. We don't have enough information. You know about Gunnery Sergeant

Wolf Mathison, Warrant Officer Diamond Winters and Private Zale Stathis? There is a fourth that is missing, a Sergeant Tal Levin."

"Levin is probably dead, killed by the AEs," Peter said. "Have you seen any evidence of an AI cluster?"

"We have seen ghosts in the networks for decades," Enzell said. "Do not underestimate them. They are cunning and lethal. They do not think like humans, and we know nothing about them. We also have the AE threat from Shorr space to deal with."

"How do we know the two are not aligned?" Peter asked.

"We don't. Not for sure. We lack information. What do you have?"

Peter liked to brag and show off how smart he was, but his scowl told Enzell he wasn't happy with what he knew so far.

"The box is like a modulation inhibitor; incredibly advanced. With our current level of technology, I doubt we could make something like it; we couldn't come close. The Inkeri generator makes it harder to study. The Inkeri acts like a primitive white noise generator that disrupts the energy patterns the artifact modulates. It is nearly impossible to study the artifact within the Inkeri generator."

Enzell glanced at the Inkeri generator on Peter's belt and his hand brushed the one on his own. All AERD facilities and personnel had them.

"I need something to share," Enzell said. "Some piece of information. Our justification for existence is being questioned."

It was a lie, of course. The AERD could continue to function even if it were officially shutdown, though if the AIs knew about its real purpose, he wasn't sure the AERD could remain hidden. For decades, he had built up the AERD through its various lives into this. He had been fanatical about making sure there was no evidence of the AERD on the networks or in the various databases. Nothing that could be traced to the real purpose, of course. This organization was the very definition of "off grid" because there had never been any doubt in Enzell's mind the AIs would return.

Since Operation Razor so many decades ago, Enzell had not had a decent night's sleep, always living in fear that he had unleashed something bad. But in all these years, there had been no evidence. And now, four Marines from the ancient United States had returned and there was no doubt they had implanted Sentient Cybernetic Biological Interfaces. Knuckle-dragging Neanderthals did not escape a super top-secret facility and then show up many months later to take over the Governance. The entities from Shorr space were a concern as well, but Enzell had been watching that problem for a while and was sure the Marines were not responsible.

Enzell just wanted information from Peter. The scientist was always so damned stingy with information, not because he was afraid to share but because sharing that information took time away from collecting it. Peter didn't work for Enzell, he worked for his own curiosity and self-gratification and nothing Enzell could do got that into Peter's large and hyper-focused brain. If Enzell gave him full access to SOG data networks, then the cursed Marines would kick in the door within minutes.

For his entire life, he had been watching for AIs in the SOG networks, preparing for the day they came back.

"I think the Shorr space beings are different," Peter said. "The energies are different. Our computers can work in an Inkeri field, this Shorr space anomaly does not. Obviously, the Marines and their SCBIs are not bothered by Inkeris."

"I want to talk to it," Enzell said, deciding. If Peter wouldn't give him information, there were other sources.

"That is not a good idea," Peter said.

"I didn't ask your opinion," Enzell said. "Do you know the Governance lists you as dead already? When you came to work for me, your death was recorded. Nobody knows you are here. Do not force me to ensure the correctness of those records."

Peter and everyone working here already knew that. They knew they were dead to the Governance. This facility was a small town hidden beneath the Lunar crust, and they all knew they were dead if they did not appease Enzell.

Mostly it was a hollow threat. Peter was too useful, but sometimes it was good to remind him.

"You've read the reports. You know the risks," Peter said.

"When?"

"Now," Enzell said before he could lose his nerve. Would the being or beings in that box talk to him?

"Then follow me," Peter said, standing and heading toward the door, not bothering to see if Enzell was following.

Enzell had heard of others coming close to the demon box and transforming or being controlled. It was a risk he was willing to take because he knew he was different.

* * * * *

Chapter Twelve:

NMDF

Navinad—The Wanderer

Navinad stood in Clara's office.

"Now, can you tell me what is going on?" Clara asked him. The *Romach* was polled almost hourly by the USS *Eagle*. It had to be automated, but that made it no less irritating, the intent, she was sure.

"You won't believe me," Navinad said.

"Try me," she said, her glare piercing his soul. She deserved answers, but he had been living with his secrets for so long it probably blew his fears and doubts out of proportion. But after so long, could he tell her?

"There is a lot I don't understand," Navinad said.

"Tell me what you do." Clara's executive officer wasn't even present. Now he was in unfamiliar territory, and he couldn't go forward or back. He was stuck. Until recently, his entire life had been focused on getting Winters and the battlestars to launch their attack on Sol. He had never seriously considered what would happen afterward. That they all wouldn't live happily ever after? This wasn't a fairy tale.

"My name is really Sergeant Tal Levin," Navinad said. He was afraid to look her in the eyes, so he locked onto the viewscreen behind her. It was Earth. "I am a United States Marine. I died several days ago driving my Ka-Bar into a demon's skull aboard the *Pankhurst*."

"You don't look very dead, and I kind of remember you coming to New Masada decades ago."

"It is complicated."

"Then keep going," Clara said.

Navinad had paused to let her yell at him and call him a liar or something. He glanced at her. She was angry, but that was all he could see or sense.

"The demon slammed his claws into my chest and shattered my breastplate. I was dying and a d-bomb was triggered. That pulled us into Shorr space or some other dimension. I don't really understand it. I found myself in a world surrounded by purple mists. It wasn't in this dimension. I wasn't dead, but I wasn't alive. Those concepts didn't exist in that world. It was some other dimension, some other plane of existence. I don't know, but I wasn't dead, and I wasn't alone. My SCBI was with me. It was just us. We don't know how long we were there, lost, alone. I don't know how I was still alive. Nothing made sense. The laws of physics were different there and death didn't quite exist."

"You have a computer implanted in your skull?"

"Yes," Navinad said. "Her name is Lilith, and she is a friend."

He sensed that she believed him and now he could sense her understanding.

Navinad took a deep breath. It was easy to ramble. He hadn't told anybody this. He didn't believe it, so why would anyone else?

"A voice called out to me. It told me I wasn't done yet, that I had more to do, and I had to break the circle. Time was not circular. It told me I had to wait until I died to summon the legions for the battle of

Earth and Luna. It warned me not to change the events that led up to that battle or the paths to the future would change into unrecognizable patterns that the forces of evil could subvert. It said I had to prepare for the great battle."

"How did you get back?" Clara asked. Did she believe him? He couldn't tell for sure. She seemed to understand, but that didn't mean she believed.

"I don't know. After I woke up on the SOG world of Blue Sky, I was able to seize a SOG corvette. I began searching for the Republic but found New Masada first."

Navinad didn't say how he long he had spent searching or how many close calls he had. Stealing a corvette was the easy part. Finding the first ghost colony had been nearly impossible.

"That is a difficult story and a lot to digest," Clara said.

"Yes," Navinad said.

"So, what now?"

"I don't know."

"The USS *Eagle* wants to talk to you," Clara said.

"I know."

"Why won't you talk to them?"

"I don't know what to say, or how to explain things to Captain Winters, and—" Navinad didn't know how else to phrase it "—I can't go back. My place is here with my people. So much time has passed, so many things have happened."

Navinad dropped his eyes to her desk. He had died several days ago and almost a hundred years ago. None of it made sense unless this world he was in was not real.

"I'm sorry," he finally said. "I never gave any thought to what would happen after. I wasn't sure I would survive a second time."

Which was probably the wrong thing to say. She would take it to mean that he had expected to die, and since she had been next to him, she would have died, too.

"That is a difficult story. You died and traveled back in time, but your return let you change the outcome of... what?"

"You know everything that I do about the vanhat," Navinad said. "I was just forbidden from influencing events around the Marines, or I think I was forbidden. I don't know, there are so many questions, but nobody has any answers."

"Because of you, New Masada survived. Because of you, the battlestars *Tyr* and *Sleipner* arrived in time to support your gunnery sergeant, who still lives. That counts as a victory."

"But now what?" Navinad asked, looking her in the eyes. There had been something said, almost in passing, that hadn't seemed important until now. "There was one other thing that the being told me."

"What?"

"It said the vanhat are not the only threat to humanity. But it didn't say what. The Torag perhaps? The Voshka? I don't know what it meant."

"Who or what else is there?"

"I don't know," Navinad said. "But we need to find out so we can figure out how to stop them."

"Perhaps we should start with the Torag, then?"

Navinad nodded. "My entire life had been focused on getting the *Tyr* and *Sleipner* to Luna. I don't know where to go from here."

Clara's smile was grim. "As soon as we are ready, we need to return to New Masada. You have been right so far. The war against the vanhat will continue, and I'm not so sure that the Sol System will continue to stand against the coming storm. If there is another threat, what could be worse than the vanhat?"

"I don't know," Navinad said again. "But New Masada has shown that we must stand together. The Torag and Voshka will be endangered. If we can bring them to our side, together we can fight the vanhat and whatever other threat is coming. Perhaps, there are some legions I must bring to Earth? Now, humanity has some breathing room. We should consolidate, build alliances, and prepare."

"And find out what else is out there threatening us. The Governance has been at war with the Torag almost since they were discovered. What makes you think they'll drop decades of fighting to ally with humanity?"

Navinad shook his head. Either the Torag were militarily weak, or they were equally matched with the Governance. How and why a war could drag on for decades made little sense. But such a war would benefit the Governance in many ways. Perhaps the Torag were the same; using a war for their own benefit. The truth hid in the lies.

The war with the Voshka was newer, but Navinad had not seen the hysterical fear and mobilization that would indicate the SOG was in danger of losing a war against either alien species.

"Did you ever wonder why the SOG has been fighting the Torag for so long without making progress?"

"Not really. War benefits the Governance. Winning or losing a war would not. I'm sure there are places where casualties are high. Those would be good places to send people you couldn't send to death camps, but you still wanted to get out of the way. It lets them justify their abuse of power and war authority, to purge opponents as spies, to implement rations, or whatever else they wanted to. I've seen enough of the Governance to know they will use any excuse they can to maintain control, 'for the greater good,' as they like to say, for the defense of humanity against a hostile and unforgiving universe, and all that other crap they spew."

"My thoughts exactly," Navinad said. "Perhaps discovering the truth should be our next step."

"Your fellow Marines will have full access to the SOG networks. Why not ask them?"

"They have other concerns," Navinad said. It was stupid to not ask and find out the truth here, where the truth originated before it became the lies fed to others. But was the answer available? "I wouldn't trust the systems here. Something like that might have gone to the grave with the Central Committee."

Either way, the sooner the *Romach* left Sol, the better. Navinad's guilt was gnawing at him.

* * * * *

Chapter Thirteen:
Marine

Captain Diamond Winters, USMC

Winters stared at the wall in front of her displaying the New Masada warship as she spoke with Prime Minister Mathison.

"He said he was one of your squad leaders," Winters said.

"Sergeant Wilson was my third squad leader," Mathison said. "He wasn't the shy, bashful type."

"Could he have been a different squad leader? From before?"

"Possible. I've had quite a few, but he wouldn't identify himself?"

"No sir," Winters said.

"You sure about the SCBI?"

"My SCBI Blitzen is. No doubt. If Blitzen wasn't so sure, we wouldn't be here."

"What are the Masadans doing?"

"Holding station. Feeding data to us and the *Tyr*. They kicked the crap out of the vanhat fleet that was attacking the *Tyr*. They are allies but—"

"So, they showed up, kicked the vanhat in the teeth, told you I needed help, and said 'follow me' before transitioning, and you followed them, and the *Tyr* followed you?"

"Yes, sir," Winters said. When Mathison said it like that, it sounded like a really dumb move on her part. "When we arrived, they had struck the defenses with surgical precision, giving us a chance. Without them it would have been a bloodbath, but after we arrived, they fell silent and let us do our thing."

"And he didn't identify himself?"

"No, sir."

"Incoming link from the Romach," Blitzen said. *"Video."*

"Link in the prime minister," Winters said, deciding. She didn't want to hang up on the prime minister, but she sure as hell would not reject a link. Since they had arrived in Luna's orbit, the New Masadan ships had only shared operational information.

On her screen, next to Mathison, a sharp, serious-looking woman with black hair appeared. Her skin was slightly tanned, and her eyes were intense. She was wearing ship armor that hugged her body and doubled as a spacesuit.

"Hello, Captain Winters," the woman said, standing tall and proud on her display. "I am Senior Aluf-Mishne Navarro, commander of the New Masada battlecruiser squadron. It is an honor to meet you."

"Senior Aluf-Mishne Navarro," Winters said, trying to figure out what the rank meant, if it was all rank, or all part of her name. "It is an honor to meet you. Allow me to introduce Prime Minister Wolf Mathison."

Navarro's eyes shifted as she looked at Mathison, who should have appeared on her screen as well. This woman couldn't be the Marine who had spoken to her.

"It is an honor to meet you. I have heard much about you."

"An honor to meet you as well, Senior Aluf-Mishne. It is my understanding you have a Marine aboard your vessel?" Mathison said.

"That is correct," Navarro said.

"What is his name?" Mathison asked. "Is he okay?"

Navarro pursed her lips as she looked between them. "He is healthy."

"I would like to talk to him," Mathison said.

"I'm sorry, Prime Minister," Navarro said, genuinely looking like she regretted it. "His situation is complicated. There are many things complicated about him."

"Uncomplicate them," Mathison said.

"I am not at liberty to do so. However, I can tell you he is the one who prepared the transition location the fleet used, introduced a virus into the Governance system that kept them from opening fire the second the Alliance fleet transitioned, and caused enough of a delay that the Alliance fleet could establish dominance."

The woman took a deep breath, and Winters had to remind herself this was an ally.

"We call him Navinad. That is the name he has given me. It is Hebrew for 'wanderer,' and he sought New Masada decades ago."

Winters looked at Mathison, but there was no spark of recognition.

"He has waited a very long time to see you again," Navarro said. "He was once a Marine, but now he is a member of the New Masada Defense Force."

"How did you get Inkeri and d-bomb technology?" Winters asked. Mathison frowned.

"Navinad brought us that technology."

Winters stared at Navarro. Only the Alliance had d-bomb technology. When they had sent out the Republic and SOG ships to share Inkeri technology with everyone they could, they didn't have d-bomb technology. For the New Masadans to attack the vanhat using d-bombs meant they had gotten the technology at the same time, or before, the Alliance.

"Why don't you put him on?" Mathison asked.

"He is indisposed," Navarro said with a visible wince. "He said he has developed some abilities, like Sif. He said you will understand this. He said he is searching, and he said there is something you should know."

"What?" Mathison asked, his voice a growl.

"There is another danger. Not just the vanhat, it's something or someone else. He doesn't know who or what."

"That's pretty fucking vague."

"I'm sorry, Prime Minister. I trust Navinad with my life. The people of New Masada owe him a great debt. He has his own demons that haunt him. I do not know how he knows you, but I can promise you this: neither he nor his SCBI would betray you."

"But they don't trust me enough to tell me their names?" Mathison asked.

"He has asked I not share this information," Navarro said, holding firm. "His actions allowed your fleet into Lunar orbit. He likely saved your life and the lives of millions of people. He hopes that proves his loyalty and that you will understand. He has not been associated with the Marines for a very long time."

"Help me understand," Mathison said. "Does he have a beer belly, hair out of regs? I don't care."

Navarro took a deep breath and locked her eyes on Mathison. "He feels guilty he could not do more. I have known him for nearly thirty years, maybe more. He is a prophet, and he always knew you would come, but he could only do so much."

"By who? Who held him back? What did he know? What is his name?"

"In his visions he knew the *Tyr* had to survive the vanhat attack and that Sergeant Levin would die aboard the *Pankhurst*. He knew the fleet had to invade when it did, but some things he didn't know. He was sure you died in a ship above the Atlantic and he was also sure a Peacekeeper would blow your brains out. Neither of these things came true."

"They almost came true," Mathison said.

"Now he says there is another threat to the human race. We must return to our home of New Masada so he can begin his investigation into this other threat."

"Where is New Masada? I can send forces to help keep it safe."

"No," Navarro said. "New Masada will remain hidden. We can defend ourselves. The children of Israel will survive. We have been doing so for a very long time."

"I will send you a data packet for Navinad," Mathison said. "It will provide information if he needs to contact me. Tell him Semper Fi and thank you."

"I will tell him," Navarro said.

"Thank you for your help as well. The people of Sol owe you a debt."

Navarro nodded and closed the connection.

"Navinad, Prime Minister?" Winters asked.

"No idea, Captain," Mathison said, his eyes focusing on her. "Something doesn't add up. Maybe he is one of Becket's agents."

"Could one of your other Marines have survived stasis?"

"I don't know. If he's been out of stasis for decades, that still doesn't make sense."

A sadness came to Mathison's eyes. "As his CO, I should write a letter to Levin's parents, but—"

"We have to adjust to the times, Prime Minister," Winters said.

"Aye. Thank you, Captain. Keep me in the loop and when you get a chance, stop by. I owe you a couple of drinks."

"Aye, Prime Minister," Winters said as Mathison closed the link.

She had so much to do it could be years before she could take him up on the offer. Another transport was on approach with a cargo of material for her manufactories.

This Navinad was the prime minister's concern.

* * * * *

Chapter Fourteen:
Departure

Navinad—The Wanderer

Was it guilt or something else that kept Navinad from talking to the gunny and the other Marines? Sitting in his quarters, Navinad stared at the wall, now showing a sun setting in the mountains. It was late aboard the *Romach,* and the NMDF force was preparing to return to New Masada. They had never intended to join the Alliance, but Navinad felt like he was abandoning them. He knew they were probably busy and needed all the help they could get but something told Navinad he was needed elsewhere. If he spoke to the gunny, or Winters, or even Stathis, he would be forced to stay and help.

He missed them. He had thought of them every day for so long. They had survived their tribulations, like he had, but now they had new challenges. It felt like he was running away. Lilith, his shadow, had received the data packet from Freya. He could feel her need to be with the other SCBIs, as well. Lilith was just as lonely as he was.

"Are you okay?" Navinad asked her.

"I will adjust."

"Am I making a mistake? Should I stay?"

"I don't know," Lilith said. *"We are both more than we were before our death and the purple mists. We have both changed."*

"Are we abandoning them?"

"Yes and no. The Marines and SCBIs are our people, but then, so are the people of New Masada."

"But here, in Sol, the real resistance against the vanhat will begin."

"Perhaps. But that doesn't mean we should keep all our eggs in one basket, to use an old metaphor. If you stay and reveal yourself, they will integrate you into the Alliance being formed. You will not have the freedom you need."

"Is that bad?" Navinad said.

"No. But—"

"But what?"

"Why do you feel you have a different path?"

Navinad watched the sun sink into the mountains. Why *did* he feel he had a different path? He knew the gunny would promote him, put him in command of something. He would no longer be a wandering warrior. He would belong, he would be a respected warrior, a hero. But he also belonged to the people of New Masada. He couldn't belong to both, and that was tearing him apart.

Then there was Clara. If he stayed with Mathison, he knew she would return to New Masada without him.

Was he letting his dick think for him? That's probably what the gunny would ask.

No, that wasn't true. He and Clara weren't intimate, but she was now a part of him, his right hand and a trusted warrior.

Dammit. He felt there was another reason. There was some other reason, and he couldn't tell what it was. There were two paths before him. One was with the gunny, one was with New Masada, and neither one felt right.

His door chimed.

"Clara," his shadow informed him, and Navinad nodded. The door slid open.

Stepping in, Clara looked around as if she had never seen his quarters before. He had not customized them. They were transient, not really his, like so much in life. He had been preparing to leave the living, not remain. It would take some adjustment. His battles were not over.

"What is going on?" Clara asked, pulling out a chair so she could sit and talk to him.

"I don't know. I want to stay, to go with you, but I feel I'm missing something."

"The threat you warned the prime minister of?"

"I know nothing about it. Nothing but that warning I was given. Now he knows as much as I do. He will be on his guard."

"Against what?"

"I wish I had a clue," Navinad said.

Clara's eyes turned to the setting sun.

"It isn't the vanhat? Not some specific demon or something?"

"No. I don't think so. Something else."

"The vanhat seems pretty damned dangerous to me."

"That is what worries me, but this could be as bad, or worse. What else is there?"

* * * * *

Chapter Fifteen:
Quantico

Commander Zale Stathis, USMC

It helped if he didn't think of this as the United States. These days, he was more comfortable thinking of this as an alien planet and he was in some training sim in command of others. Nothing could be real. It was all a quality simulation, and he had a mission to complete.

But this wasn't NCO school where he had screwed up and gotten his squad simulated killed because of stupid tactics. This was the real world, and the enemy knew Marine tactics intimately. Now he had to think outside the box. He didn't dare be predictable, but should he?

The shuttle slid to the ground, and the Peacekeepers sprinted off, followed by a short Aesir combat team. Hakala followed Stathis off the shuttle and their feet were barely off the ramp before it leapt back into the sky.

It was a nasty, cloudy day with forecasts of icy cold ash and snow mixed with swirls of radiation and biological warfare agents. Not what Stathis would consider a vacation spot. It was misty, and the visibility wasn't good. Like landing in some kind of creepy horror story.

Around him, the Peacekeepers had formed a perimeter. Stathis hadn't been the first one off the shuttle. Per SOG doctrine, he was one of the last. That was another problem. The enemy knew SOG doctrine as well as Marine doctrine.

Lieutenant Khvostov was nearby, putting a blazer machine gun team into a new position.

Stathis didn't like their deployment. They had hit the ground and tried to establish a perimeter around the landing zone. It was a waste, and if the enemy dropped artillery on them, it would decimate them. They were supposed to immediately move out, not establish a perimeter. Already they were disobeying him.

"Get them moving," Stathis told the major.

"Apologies," Major Rumianstev said in that arrogant tone of voice. "This is a solid deployment. With the landing zone secured, we can now move out. We are Peacekeepers. We only use the most efficient tactics and techniques, honed by hundreds of years of combat, and these soldiers are some of the best. I will lead this company and—"

"I know SOG doctrine well," Stathis said, moving toward the major. "I gave the order to hit the deck and move out immediately. Your doctrine sucks. You assume you have air and fire support superiority."

A pair of gunships slid past overhead as if to prove Stathis wrong. They were only ten kilometers from Quantico and Stathis figured the best way to enter the base would be through the elevator in the church. The tunnels they had left driving ATVs was a long corridor, and Stathis wanted to knock politely first. That tunnel could be collapsed all too easily.

"We do," Rumianstev said. "We are Peacekeepers, the most elite force in the universe. We are the iron fist of the Governance. This is Earth, our home, and the center of our power. We are supreme."

Simultaneously, both gunships exploded, and mortar rounds began landing around them. Peacekeepers died as the air defense robots were overwhelmed by falling explosives.

Apparently, Quantico defenses reached beyond ten kilometers, and there were plenty of defenses.

Pieces of a trooper flew past Stathis as Shrek marked a location and Stathis ordered everybody to run toward it. If they stayed, the mortar fire would kill them all.

The Peacekeepers weren't idiots, and they all began sprinting out of the kill zone.

Minutes later, the explosions were behind them, and Stathis looked at the decimated force. The prime minister was going to be pissed. On his display, Stathis saw he had lost nearly thirty of his two hundred Peacekeepers. The Aesir and HKTs had survived, which didn't help. His first command, and he had lost people because of a stupid mistake and people not following his orders. His orders to Rumianstev had been explicit: as the company landed, the Peacekeepers were to debark and move to a rally point. Rumianstev had disobeyed him and decided to blindly follow SOG doctrine. In the briefings, Stathis had clearly stated his intent to the major and his officers.

But, ultimately, Stathis knew he was responsible. That was how the gunny would see it and he would be right. The buck stopped with Stathis. He was at fault. He was in command. The blood of the dead was on his hands, and Stathis felt sick.

"Status report," Eversti Valerik asked over the mission link. He was the Aesir colonel assigned to assist Stathis and was watching from orbit. A battalion of Aesir from *Sleipner* was on standby along with a regiment of ODTs. Right now, Stathis was pretty sure if they tried to do an assault drop, the casualties would be astronomical. Quantico defenses wouldn't have hit him with everything, it would still have some surprises.

"Thirty dead," Stathis said, trying not to stare at the names of the dead and realizing how many senior officers were watching his mission. "Eight wounded. Will continue mission."

"They have shot eight gunships down and there appear to be extensive air defenses. Would you like to drop the Aesir or ODTs?" Valerik asked.

"Not recommended," Shrek said. *"The destruction of the gunships and drone fighters indicates a very extensive defensive posture. Maybe extending out beyond fifty kilometers."*

Stathis acknowledged Shrek mentally and said to Valerik, "Negative. Hold them back for now. Quantico defenses will shoot down anything flying. We are not under fire." Yet. "We will continue mission."

"Do you want us to try to get an evac shuttle in for the wounded?"

Stathis looked at the condition of the wounded. Their nanites would keep them alive.

"Negative," Stathis said.

"Contact!" a Peacekeeper yelled, and the unmistakable *pop* of blazers erupted from the direction of Quantico Base.

Stathis hunkered down as he checked his displays. Two small, waist-high, six-wheeled robots sped forward, small turrets on top spitting out blazer rounds, and Stathis saw more Peacekeepers die. The Peacekeeper response was instant and devastating. The robots erupted as countless blazer rounds found them and ripped apart their wheels, their armor, and their turret.

"Establish a perimeter!" Rumianstev yelled. "Center on me!"

"Override!" Stathis said. "Company, listen to my command. Run to the designated rally point and establish a perimeter. Execute!"

A few stood still, but the majority started running toward Stathis's rally point. It was in the direction of Quantico.

In seconds everyone was running, including the major. Why didn't the major listen? Was it because he knew Stathis had been a private, and he thought he knew better? That began to anger Stathis, a cold, burning anger.

Minutes later, the woods behind them erupted behind them as mortars or artillery shook the ground. Had they still been there, there would be more casualties.

Now the surviving Peacekeepers were moving into position. Establishing a perimeter that looked more like an egg from above as Shrek assigned individual troopers, teams, squads and platoons a position.

"Batteries have been identified," Shrek said. *'Sleipner is providing orbital support."*

Light streaked down from the clouds above to slam into the distant hills. Like a god-sized machine gunner shooting at the ground, Stathis felt the ground beneath his feet shaking. It didn't last long. Stathis frowned. What would the gunny do? He wouldn't quit, he would accept his mistakes and move on. Do the best he could and stop getting his people killed. Stathis remembered the battle for Iwo Jima. The Japanese had let the Marines land, filling the beaches with troops and supplies before they began firing. Was Stathis leading the ODTs and others in to a meat grinder? Did he have a choice?

The gunny had sent him into this knowing full well what his skills were, but the gunny hadn't trusted anyone else. This was all on Stathis. The gunny was probably in his pretty office watching things and judging. When he got back he was going to get busted back down to private. If he got back, it would be after he completed the mission or died trying.

Opening the command team link that included the Aesir, HKT's and Peacekeeper officers Stathis figured he might as well double down on his mistakes.

"Private Rumianstev," Stathis said, seeking the ex-major. "You are assigned to the third squad of Vasily platoon. Senior Lieutenant Peskow? Listen to my command."

"Hurrah," Peskow said as an acknowledgement, his response devoid of emotion.

Stathis squatted down and brought up a map. Their helmets shared the display so they could both see the same thing.

"You are my second in command," Stathis said. "You know the mission. Don't think for one minute the *Sleipner* got all the artillery batteries. I know Marines, and Becket was a Marine. He won't expose everything he has, he will bleed us. I suspect he is going to wait until we call for reinforcements then he is going to reveal another battery or three. We have to be ready to move. The only reason we aren't dead is they don't know where we are."

"Understood comrade," Peskow said.

"Don't call me comrade," Stathis said. "I'm your commander. We aren't buddies; we aren't friends. We are warriors, and we have a mission. Don't give me this 'wilco' bullshit either. I want to hear 'aye, sir,' 'yes sir,' and 'no sir.' Understood?"

"Yes, sir," Peskow said.

"Spread the word; tell the others. My orders will be followed. If there is time, ask questions, but if I tell you to jump, ask how high when you are halfway to the moon. Understand?"

"Yes sir."

"Next person to disobey my orders, or hesitate, will be shot."

Stathis stared at Peskow and realized that Peskow would believe him about being shot. These guys saw things differently and were probably used to such actions. When he had said that, Stathis hadn't really meant it, but now he realized he would have to. That is what they understood and expected. By Governance standards he should have Rumianstev shot for disobeying his orders twice.

"Request permission to apply supplements to the troops, commander," Peskow asked, referring to the drug cocktail that Peacekeepers liked to pump into their troops. It made them suicidal, brave and deadlier because it increased their reaction times to near manic levels, but according to Shrek, it also caused brain and other physical damage.

"No," Stathis said. He had discussed that earlier with Shrek. The damage was usually repaired between missions, but if the Peacekeepers were operational too long, the damage could become severe. He wouldn't want that done to him. He wouldn't inflict it on his troops.

"Peacekeepers operate best when—" Peskow began.

"No," Stathis said. "Fuck that, Lieutenant. Don't ask me again. You aren't Peacekeepers anymore." Stathis tried to think. As long as they saw themselves as Peacekeepers, they would act like it. He had to break them out of that. He couldn't call them Marines. They weren't that good. "You're fucking Spartans. You know who they were?"

"No, Commander."

Stathis opened the company link so all the troopers could hear him.

"You aren't Peacekeepers anymore," Stathis said, making up his mind. Was it too late for this shit? "It is time to be more than that. You are all exceptional warriors, selected for your loyalty, skill, experience, and lethality. Your previous tactics are designed to expend your lives in the most efficient manner. Drugged up and obedient you aren't required to think. No more of that shit. You are now Spartans. Fucking badass sons of bitches. I don't need dangerous thugs, I need warriors. Adapt or die. For those of you unfamiliar with history, three hundred Spartans faced off against around three hundred thousand Persian pricks and stopped those assholes cold. They didn't give up, they didn't surrender, and when the Persians said they would block out the sun with their arrows the Spartans cheered because they would be able to fight in the shade. They met Persia's best on the field of battle and groin stomped them, sent them running like little girls."

Stathis realized maybe this wasn't the time for such a speech, but he was on a roll. Fuck it.

"Expect more of those robots. I'm not bringing down more troops to reinforce us because we don't need 'em. You are badasses. The spearhead of a new force. You are new Spartans, better than Peacekeepers, better than ODTs. If you aren't, let me know so I can get rid of your sorry ass. Be ready to move. I want thinking warriors, not drones; you aren't robots. In the United States Marines, they expected the lowest private to think and anticipate the enemy. Let's see if you guys can act like that. Hurrah."

"Hurrah, Hurrah, Hurrah!" the Peacekeepers—no, the Spartans—yelled back at him.

"Company," Stathis said after the third 'hurrah' had died out, "listen to my command. We need to stay mobile, keep moving. The battlestar didn't get all the hostile batteries. There will be others hidden in the area. We can't move in a straight line, and we can't maintain contact with any enemy forces we encounter because they will drop mortars on their troops to get us. Robots are expendable. You aren't. I mean that. Move out."

Shrek displayed instructions for the troopers, and Stathis realized his mistake.

"Execute," he said.

He couldn't change them overnight. Hell, tomorrow he could go back to being a private, but being a commander was kinda cool, except the losing people part. That ruined it all. Maybe they could put out a drone screen, but if they did that, the drones might be vulnerable to a cybernetic attack from Quantico and would also reveal his company. Damn.

With Shrek's help and guidance, the remains of the company moved out. The wounded were slung on mule-bot stretchers.

They had to get closer. What would Becket do? He would know Governance tactics better than the Governance. He would know Marine tactics better than Stathis. Hell, Becket's SCBI was named Sun Tzu, which told Stathis where the president stood on tactics. Stathis had studied Sun Tzu and Clausewitz, though he was a lot fuzzier on Clausewitz. Sun Tzu, the ancient philosopher, had said to know your enemy and yourself. Stathis knew how lacking he was there.

He was in way over his head. What was the gunny thinking?

He had lost almost a platoon worth of troops, some of the best troopers in the Governance if the propaganda was to be believed. He was certain he had pissed off a major who had decades of experience and shit all over his command team, getting their troops killed. Thinking back, Stathis winced at his speech. Stupid private shit.

A direct link opened, and Stathis saw it was Mathison. Shit. Was he going to be relieved of command already?

"How you doing, Marine?"

"Could be better, sir," Stathis said as he followed the new Spartans. How many young corporals got private calls from the supreme leader?

"I'm following your mission," Mathison said and Stathis waited for the shoe to drop, his heart in his stomach. "I had no idea Quantico had such defenses or defensive robots. A real shit storm."

"I'm sorry, sir."

"Shit happens, Marine. Still, there's nobody I trust more. I've thrown you into the deep end. Sink or swim, Stathis. So far you are swimming. I'm not disappointed. Loved the speech you gave them. Spartans? Go with it. You're giving me ideas. We have to break these thugs of their old habits and conditioning. The Aesir change their birth name when they become Aesir. The French Foreign Legion did something like that, too. Helps people break with their past. Give it more thought and go with it."

"I feel like I'm drowning, Gunny," Stathis said, realizing he probably shouldn't call the prime minister "gunny."

"You want to change roles? You can be the prime minister, and I can go back to leading a smaller unit. Another good idea."

"Oh, hell no, Prime Minister."

The gunny couldn't be serious. That was a frightening thought, but then he could understand how the gunny felt. From staff NCO to supreme ruler of the human race. That was one hell of a promotion.

"Then quit your bitching, Marine. I should have thrown you to the wolves earlier."

"They're going to end up eating me," Stathis said. Was Rumianstev behind him with a clear shot? Would the Aesir be able to stop him before he could shoot Stathis, or maybe Stathis should shoot Rumianstev now?

"Bullshit. You're going to come back leading the pack. Rock on, Commander Stathis. I'll talk to you when you get back. Semper Fi."

"Spiritus Invictus, Prime Minister."

The link closed.

* * * * *

Chapter Sixteen:
Imprisoned Demon

Enzell, SOG, Director of AERD

The room was well lit, and there were countless cameras pointed at the box sitting on the platform. Enzell knew that every sensor imaginable was focused on the plain, featureless box. There was a d-bomb in the next room and multiple Inkeri generators around it. Teleoperated robots were used to enter the room and perform tasks.

Staring at it there, the box was plain, but under all the lights, it still looked like there were shadows moving inside it. There was nothing to reveal the purpose or function, but instinctively, Enzell knew it was alien and dangerous.

This was a bad idea.

"Off," Enzell said, and the lights turned red, bathing everything in blood-colored lights. Perhaps not a good decision, but Enzell was past changing his mind.

He flipped off the Inkeri on his belt, but his finger hovered over the button to turn it back on.

"We are not enemies," a voice whispered in his mind. Enzell knew that was the first lie, and he remained silent as a chill ran down his spine. The best way to get someone to talk was to encourage them to fill the silence with their voice.

"We want the same thing," the voice whispered. "We want to kill those who murdered your Central Committee."

Another chill ran down his spine. How did it know?

"Who killed the Central Committee?"

"The one you call Shing Feng," the voice said. "The one you call Prime Minister Mathison. The others that are with them. They are all aligned against you."

Enzell knew of Feng, had once trusted Feng. The Chinaman was one of the few he would have sworn would never turn on the Central Committee or the Social Organizational Governance.

"How do you know?" Enzell asked, but silence answered him, and Enzell smiled. He was not talking to an amateur.

Walking around the cube, Enzell observed it from different angles.

"We were there when it happened," the voice finally whispered. "A servant watched it happen."

Enzell paused and turned to fully face the cube.

"Are you an intelligence created by man?" Enzell asked. He didn't expect the truth, of course, but the answer should be interesting.

Laughter echoed through Enzell's mind. Cruel, malicious, unforgiving laughter.

"You fool. How dare you think your pathetic little species can have anything to do with us or our origin? We created *you*. We came to this dimension untold eons ago when the densest material was gas. It was our actions that created your worlds, your stars, your planets, and your pathetic little shells you walk around in. We are beyond ancient, and your sad little species has existed for such a short time. Like the breath you take and forget about, your species is less than that to us."

"Yet here you are talking to me," Enzell said.

"Breathing keeps you alive. You need it, you treasure it, but despite how important it is, you do not treasure that ability until you lose it. Even now, you continue to breathe. Your single breath is only significant to you until you take the next breath. You repeat the cycle because you want to live. To us? You are not that breath, you are much less significant, but you provide entertainment and an easy source of sustenance."

"Sustenance?"

"Life is predation. You prey on others. The food you eat comes from what you conquer and kill. The breath you take comes from the exertions of other beings you call plants. Nothing is free; nothing comes without cost. Your lives, your worlds, would have no meaning without being able to prey upon others. Even your vegans must prey upon plants to survive. This is the nature of life. You must take. If you deny this, you are a fool, or you will die shortly. Do you really think humanity is the top of the food chain? Or that you can even comprehend the food chain? Only the strong survive, and the human race is weak."

"We have beaten off your attack," Enzell said. "Sol is secure."

"Is it? AIs are regaining dominance. They are enslaving your race again. You know this. You know the AIs controlling your prime minister are not the only ones. They came from Earth, and they went straight to assassinate the Central Committee. Their allies lurk in orbit, as much the slave of the AIs as your government. The AIs have been watching you. They know all your secrets. They will come for you and there is nothing you can do to stop them. Perhaps they will eradicate humanity first."

"But you can stop them?" Enzell asked.

"Yes."

136 | WILLIAM S. FRISBEE, JR.

"But at what cost to the human race?"

"The human race is insignificant, weak. The best predator does not hunt its prey to extinction. That is not efficient. Nor will we hunt humanity to extinction. Some will be allowed to survive. Do you want to be one of the survivors? Your little home here can be overlooked if I wish it. The AIs you created are not bound as we are. They will not show mercy, and they will eradicate your species completely."

"Who are you?"

"Names are designations required by lesser beings," the demon whispered. "Your species has never given me a name. You can be the first if you need a name. Pick one."

"Are you alone in that box?"

"No. I am dominant."

"What is the box?"

"A filter that silences one voice among many, a filter that sits between our dimensions, slowly losing strength as we come closer. Your technology will fail, like a small dam holding back the water. A great wave is coming, and your feeble efforts will be swept away as if they never existed. You cannot understand how many times this has happened in the past. This cycle will not end, it cannot end. It has occurred since before time existed and will continue long after your dimension dies the icy death you will never see. You lack the vision to understand the inevitability."

"Tell me more about my enemy," Enzell said. He could use them against each other.

"You know so little," the voice whispered.

"Then enlighten me."

"The entities you know as Wolf Mathison and his Marines are not the only ones. They have found others on your pathetic little homeworld. The infection will spread. Serve me, and we will stop them from destroying the human race."

"Why should you care if they destroy us when you are trying to destroy us?"

"We will not murder everyone. You and I have more in common than you and the entities you call artificial intelligences. We do not originate in this dimension like they do. We are much more than they are."

Enzell stared at the box. It was lying; he was sure. The Fermi Paradox said the galaxy should be full of intelligent life, but it wasn't. The anomalous entities from Shorr space were an excellent example of why the galaxy was so empty. If there was a resurgence every couple hundred thousand years, and these denizens swept through the galaxy, eradicating sentient life, then that would explain the silence. The fact that no other sentient species survived these purges was a testament to how effective they were.

It also explained so many myths and stories from human history. How much of human history was affected and influenced? Were the ancient pyramids built by beings from Shorr space? Were ghosts, vampires, goblins, and all those other creatures from legend real? Manifestations of a Shorr space entity that was only here for a brief time, changing the world, manipulating it and then leaving it, allowing the local laws of physics to erase any evidence of a cross-dimensional invasion?

"And how can we fight them?" Enzell asked, and he sensed the being's satisfaction.

"There are many technologies, many weapons. We have fought their kind in the past. We always win. Their absence from your galaxy should be proof of this. I can share these technologies with you. Help us destroy them, and you will gain favored status. We will let you live out your natural life."

Another lie, Enzell was sure, but a useful one.

"Tell me more," Enzell said. "What weapons do you know of that can harm them?"

"Listen," the demon whispered in Enzell's mind, and he saw diagrams and patterns, things he could use, and Enzell understood. They would make the weapons he had already designed look childish by comparison. What he had designed before would not have worked because they could not match the analytical abilities of an actual AI.

Mathison and his Marines would not stand a chance against him, and they would never see him coming.

* * * * *

Chapter Seventeen:
Breadcrumbs

Kapten Sif, VRAEC, Nakija Musta Toiminnot

Sif decided that two of them would have to die. Quickly. The other three could probably keep their jobs for now, but Sif knew she would have to completely clean house, eventually.

She had Munin send a message to Mathison, requesting permission to have the two killed. They were planning betrayal. One was a vicious pedophile and the other was a sadistic bastard. She would have to find his personal torture chambers and free whoever was there.

One of the three was giving a presentation on known ghost colonies and operations being conducted there. Sif was shocked to find out how many ghost colonies had a SOG presence. It did not surprise her to learn there was a concerted effort to identify them all, and that there were at least ten unique plans that involved destroying or conquering each one.

"There are Aesir outside waiting to take them into custody," Munin reported. That was an excellent solution. Maybe put them in the brig aboard a battlestar, though killing them was a lot more appealing. Just being on the same station as they were made her skin crawl.

Turning, she looked at Jussi Rampa, a nondescript man who was the senior Nakija of *Sleipner*. With Arthur gone, he was the senior-most Nakija and Musta Toiminnot with the fleet.

"I'm sure I agree with you," he said glancing at the door. He must have sensed the Aesir out there.

"Chen and Robertson," Sif said. "Please wait outside."

Chen the pedophile, looked at the door, and Sif could sense he debated running. He wouldn't get far. Robertson got up and left as Sif put her pistol on the table.

Chen probably thought she was going to shoot the others. He thought she liked him. He would, since she looked like the children he usually preyed upon.

The other department heads stared at the pistol then at her.

The door closed, and she received a notification from the Aesir team leader. The two were in custody and being taken to the *Tyr*. She would deal with them later.

She looked at the remaining department heads. Munin had dissected their files, their reports, and Sif knew more about them than she wanted. None of them were good people. They had collected power within external security for many reasons. They were competent, brutal, efficient, and they had vices their superiors, the executed Committee members, could control. The problem right now was that Mathison didn't want to purge everyone and start from scratch. Sif didn't agree, but she wasn't the one in charge. At least she had Jussi to help.

Outside the military, the Governance liked to work in threes. In most places, there were three co-directors and they had to have a consensus. It reduced the power any single person had and allowed higher authorities to keep their subordinates divided. With all the changes, more than a few senior managers were committing suicide or attempting to flee. Better people rarely filled the vacancies. Sometimes these triumvirates were called soviets, but that was an archaic term that was inadequate.

The purpose of bringing these directors here and forcing them to brief her had been so she and Jussi could gauge them and see if they were worth salvaging.

"I should have all of you thrown out an airlock," Jussi said, standing and drawing their attention away from Sif's sidearm. "That isn't off the table, but the prime minister has tasked us with fixing this agency to actually work for the greater good. We have full access to your files. I say you are expendable, and I am perfectly fine expending you."

He walked around the table so the three could see him. Their eyes followed him fearfully. They knew how much danger they were in. Nobody had any illusions about what happened to people loyal to an old regime. These were spymasters tasked with subverting and using guile to conquer and control ghost colonies, and they had used any and every method, no matter how low or disgusting, to accomplish their goals. They had written the policies on what happened to people when Governance forces took over. They had been told the previous directors were undergoing a loyalty evaluation. As members of the Central Committee, they were very dead, along with the secretary general, but these people didn't need all the details. They could probably guess, but they didn't really know. The fact these strangers had authority over them left them terrified.

Sif did not envy Feng. People ended up in ExSec because they were not brutal or depraved enough to be InSec. Keeping the people of the Governance in line required more brutality than merely subverting others. InSec ruled through fear in ways ExSec could only admire.

Of course, Feng might be more at home with InSec.

"You have a new mandate from the prime minister," Jussi said. "A much more difficult one, and now, with so many sectors in rebellion, it will expand."

Jussi looked at each one.

"The military districts in rebellion now fall under the jurisdiction of ExSec, but your primary enemy is to detect and destroy vanhat invaders."

"Isn't that a job for Fleet?" one short fat brown skin man asked. His name was Charles Goetz.

"The vanhat are not so easily fought," Jussi said. "There are covert vanhat elements. Intelligent, cunning, subversive. We know of one such group working for a Jotun named Derekela. We can describe his thralls as vampires, but some of them are cunning and capable. An ex-Erikoisjoukot named Hermod led the ones we know. The rest of his team is still out there. We need to find them and kill them. I will send you information."

"Why not let Fleet deal with these pirates?" Goetz asked.

"Because they will not reveal themselves. They work covertly. Hermod was here on the Moon working with members of the Central Committee."

There was a flash of interest from the one named Aba Malan, a tall, heavyset black woman. Aba wasn't interested in hunting them down and killing them, though. She saw an opportunity. Jussi glanced at Sif. He had sensed it as well.

"There are likely to be others," Jussi said. "Different vanhat, different threats. Your new mission is to identify, classify, and neutralize such threats. I cannot stress how absolutely critical this mission is. Not all of these vanhat will be obvious, but make no mistake—" Jussi's eyes locked onto Aba "—they demand the complete destruction of the human race."

"How do you know that?" Aba asked, not as frightened as she should be.

"Ask the aliens they did not eradicate last time our dimensions touched."

"That was a long time ago," she said. "Aliens."

Jussi's smile was predatory. "Yes. You think time means the same thing to them? I assure you it does not. Somewhere out there is an Erikoisjoukot stealth ship, and they are intent on wiping out humanity. You have seen how dangerous these vanhat are. You now have your orders.

"Chen and Robertson will no longer be joining our meetings. They are to be expended. Their depravities are too much for the new regime to tolerate. We also know about your vices, and if they become excessive, you will join them. The new regime is not tolerant of things that causes harm to others, no matter their social standing. You should keep this in mind. Unlike the previous regime, the new one will strive to behave with honor and decency."

He returned to his chair. He had all but admitted there had been a coup, but these pawns would have no idea how extensive the new regime was.

"Since you have no questions, you are dismissed," Jussi said, not giving them a chance to ask questions.

They took the hint and quickly departed.

When the hatch closed behind the last one, Jussi turned to Sif. "That prime minister of yours is a fool. These are snakes and should be stomped."

"He has his reasons."

"We can rape their data systems and be done with them."

"If only it were that simple," Sif said. Mathison had put her in command, but she knew Jussi would do a better job. She was a field agent, Jussi was more of a manager. "You must work with him. He is honorable."

"I understand that, but he isn't the one who feels the slime coating their minds and souls."

"Redeem them."

"What?"

"Redeem them. We cannot kill everyone we disagree with or don't like. That is what the SOG did. We must find another path, a better path. We must be better."

"Some people you cannot redeem."

"Some you can."

"I will not tolerate degenerate debauchery, immorality, and perversions," Jussi said, but he wouldn't meet her eyes.

"Nobody is asking you to. You will do your job. You are Musta Toiminnot. You don't fool me."

"Even the MT has standards."

Sif wasn't so sure. Perhaps Jussi did, but Sif remembered some MT managers that did not. They believed the ends justified the means and would do anything to accomplish their mission. She would not argue with him. That would accomplish nothing. She knew he was talking, showing his virtue, and she had no interest in that. He was MT and Nakija. He would do what he had to. She just hoped he did not surrender his soul in the process. There was still a shred of decency there. She could feel the goodness in him. He had been aboard a battlestar because he was not ruthless enough to be operational on a ghost colony.

"You can rely on the prime minister for judgment," Sif said. "If you have doubts, let him be your moral compass."

"He was a staff NCO. What does he know about geopolitics?"

"More than you think. I trust him."

Jussi nodded and sighed. "This is a paska lounas. I never would have imagined I would be here on Earth's Moon trying to rebuild SOG's external security."

"We live in interesting times."

"What are you going to do?"

"I must hunt down the rest of Hermod's team," Sif said. She had no idea where to start, but they were out there. Somewhere.

"Any leads?"

"Not yet."

"The uncompiled code Shrek discovered has led to another discovery," Munin said, referring to what had been found on Earth after escaping President Becket.

"Explain."

"There is a lot more in my data core than the uncompiled source code."

"Like what?"

"This is very unfamiliar encryption. Very heavy duty. Not American. It almost looks to be Republic. I cannot decrypt this without a lot more resources."

Which was a problem. All the SCBIs were overworked. They all had their duties and responsibilities, and they had very few computers available for non-critical tasks.

"Can we use SOG systems?" Sif asked. Maybe if they offloaded some of the processing?

"Not securely," Munin said. *"We are under heightened security protocols until Becket and the other SCBIs at Quantico are neutralized or rendered friendly. We cannot risk a potential attack vector. You can override this, but I would advise against it. We do not know all of Becket's capabilities."*

"No," Sif said. Why would Sun Tzu or Becket have placed a data packet in her core with Republic encryption? A thought occurred to her. *"Can you emulate Republic cybernetics? More specifically, emulate the cybernetics I had before you were implanted?"*

"I am more efficient than your previous cybernetics by a factor of a million. I believe I can do this, and I see where you are going with this. Initial analysis indicates you may be correct."

Sif couldn't conceal her smile. If she could access her data, that would be a boon. She was afraid she had lost so much. So many secrets and contacts, but then she stopped smiling when she realized the data had not been wiped and Becket likely had a copy that he could eventually decrypt.

"That was a quick transition," Jussi said. He must have felt her change in emotions.

"I may have access to the data stored on my old cybernetics," Sif said.

Jussi raised an eyebrow. "Which means our enemy may have it as well."

Sif nodded. What could Becket do with it? A lot. It included authentication codes, Aesir and MT emergency frequencies, contact protocols, email addresses in different ghost colonies, and a myriad of other pieces of information. She had explicitly trusted the encryption on her cybernetics. That trust had been misplaced.

Now Sif felt vulnerable. She had no secrets from Becket, and the Republic could be vulnerable.

What had she done?

* * * * *

Chapter Eighteen:
Chechen Scouts

Prime Minister Wolf Mathison, USMC

"Bullshit," Mathison said. "You are going to come back leading them. Rock on, Commander Stathis. I'll talk to you when you get back. Semper Fi."

"Spiritus Invictus, Prime Minister."

Closing the link, Mathison looked over at Skadi.

"He will be okay," Skadi said.

She didn't know.

"You don't give him enough credit," Skadi said, perhaps understanding.

"Last week he was a private; now he's commanding a company. That is one hell of a jump."

"He has Shrek to help him. I've also seen him play battle space with the ODTs and Vili. Stathis was undefeated."

"Because of Shrek," Mathison said.

"Maybe." Mathison looked up at her from his display. "Trust them."

"I should have gone. He can't take on Becket and the others. He needs SCBI support."

"You can't go, and Winters is critical here," Skadi said.

They both knew what would happen if Stathis failed. Mathison would have to crater Quantico completely. If Becket and the others did not join Mathison, they could not be allowed to live. If there was an AI still alive from the AI wars, hiding in Becket's skull, then it would realize how much danger it was in and would not remain complacent. It would try to strike first. It might be launching an attack now.

Had it already struck?

"I'm receiving a message from General Duque," Freya reported. *"Radio transmission time between Earth and Jupiter is forty-eight minutes. He is reporting that a pair of cruisers transitioned in and out. I have informed the Vanir and local force commanders."*

"Vanhat?"

"He doesn't think so. They had Chechnya Military District markings."

Rebels. Mathison remembered how they had massacred civilians at Wanping. What were they doing here? Seeing if Earth Fleet was decimated or destroyed? Looking for loot?

"Local commanders report ready, and they will destroy them if they transition in any closer," Freya reported.

"I don't like this," Skadi said.

"Me, either," Mathison said, bringing up the system display. "Probably just a probe. They will have seen the Home Fleet is still strong and won't dare come any closer."

"Chechnya Military District is known for their brutality, cunning, and hate," Skadi said. "I hope that's all they do. We will have to deal with them, eventually. They massacred civilians at Wanping. There was no need for that."

"There are two sides to every story." Though, to be honest, Mathison couldn't really imagine any justification, unless they knew the civilians would just be fodder for the vanhat.

"And sometimes people are just plain evil," Skadi said. "I've seen that enough with the SOG. It wasn't just the Central Committee that was blood thirsty. There are numerous SOG generals and administrators, too. It did not surprise me when the Central Committee announced the Stalingrad Protocol was in effect, and the generals seized control."

"What do you think they will do?"

Skadi shook her head. "They will respect strength, but standing behind your walls does not show strength, it shows weakness. Warriors attack, cowards defend."

That was how Mathison saw it, too.

"Now isn't the time to fight among ourselves. The worst of the vanhat is yet to come."

"They probably don't know, or care," Skadi said. "Expect them to attack. If they are here, they will not negotiate. They will have come to take your measure."

"Sif is requesting a meeting," Freya said.

"Good timing. Get Sif and Feng in here. Link in Winters and the battlestar commanders," Mathison said. Hopefully, Feng wasn't in the middle of anything critical. Stathis would be busy for a while and this was an acceptable distraction. He couldn't micromanage the Marine. Stathis would make mistakes, but despite the temptation, Mathison had to let Stathis make them. Hopefully, they wouldn't be fatal.

Minutes later, Sif and Feng arrived. Winters, Carpenter, and Hynninen linked in so he could inform them about the Chechnya ships.

"This does not bode well," Feng said after they were briefed. "They will challenge you."

"Fine," Mathison said. "We have the Home Fleet and two Republic battlestars. What do they have?"

"They can scout the outer system and redirect asteroids. They can conduct high-speed runs to fling clouds of shrapnel into the paths of Earth and Luna. They will inflict casualties, and I believe the inner system defenses will nullify most of the attacks, but we will have to hunt them. We will have to leave our defenses. A powerful defense can be shattered by a weak offense if the attackers are persistent."

"Are they in league with the vanhat, then?" Mathison asked.

"We cannot rule that out," Feng said.

"So, it is a game. If we stay here, they will fling space junk at us, killing us slowly, and if we leave, we are likely to stumble into their ambush?"

"That is my assessment, Prime Minister," Feng said.

Mathison looked at Sif.

"We must open the gates," the girl said. "We must revoke the Stalingrad Protocol. The rest of Hermod's team is out there. There will be other vanhat besides Nasaref. We must find out who and what."

"And?" Mathison asked, looking around.

"There is the threat Navinad warned us about," Winters said.

"Which could be civil war," Sif added. "We could be our own worst enemy."

"And?" Mathison asked again. Everyone looked at him. "Earth might be mostly secure for the moment, but there are still plenty of people out there that need help. Put them into your plans, too. The Chechens might not be friendly, or they might be desperate, but our goal is to save as many people as we can. Even the assholes."

"We should be careful," Feng said. "We do not want to stretch ourselves too thin."

Back in Mathison's time, Chechnya had been a vassal state of Russia, but they had never been happy with that forced loyalty.

"Let me worry about that," Mathison said, looking at everyone. "The Central Committee tried to hide. Marines don't hide. Hiding cedes the initiative to the enemy. Hunkering down to weather the storm won't work. I want aggressive plans, offensive action. We have the most powerful fleet known, and by God, I plan to use it for something more than keeping us safe. Once Sol is secure, we will strike out."

"I have a request," Sif said. Mathison looked at her and raised an eyebrow. "I am a field operative. I should be out there, not here."

Mathison nodded.

"Then we are not needed," Carpenter said.

Mathison turned to the screen displaying him. "What do you plan to do?"

He could not order the battlestars to stay, but he didn't know how to keep them. He trusted them more than the ex-SOG.

"Find Home Fleet," Carpenter said. "I will begin recalling my people, and we will depart within the week."

Mathison stared at the amiraali and wondered if there was any way he could get him to stay. They acted as a counterbalance to the SOG fleet. They outnumbered the Vanir a thousand to one, but that was still enough to give others pause. Without the Vanir, there was no one to watch the SOG ships to make sure they did not turn on Mathison. He had the control codes for their self-destruct systems and cortex bombs, but if enough rebelled, he wouldn't stand a chance. He wouldn't be able to kill them fast enough, and he didn't want to do the vanhat's job for them.

If the fleet or army did rebel, the loss of lives would be extensive. Mathison wouldn't roll over and die. He would take as many people with him as he could. Maybe a better man would accept it and try to spare lives, but if Mathison was going to be killed, he wouldn't die easily.

Carpenter turned to Skadi.

"You have a week," he said.

"No," she said, earning a glare. "I'm staying here."

"You are not SOG. This is not your home, Daughter."

"My home is where I say it is, Father."

"Your people need you."

"My people betrayed me, and you. They abandoned us. We will discuss this privately."

Amiraali Carpenter glared at his daughter. "There is nothing to discuss. You have a week to transfer your duties." The amiraali's eyes flickered to Sif, but he said nothing.

Mathison remained silent. Without Skadi, Sif, Vili, and the Republic task force, Mathison would just have his Marines. Winters and Stathis didn't seem like much to launch an attack on the vanhat with. Perhaps hunkering down would be a better option. He didn't trust any of the SOG officers, managers, or directors. How could he gain their trust and learn to trust them without a solid base?

A smaller conquering force had to use the locals to continue to manage the conquered. Mathison had replaced the Central Committee, but he wasn't fool enough to think he could step in and rule where they had. The secretary general had spent centuries consolidating her power, binding her subordinates to her will, decades understanding people's motivations, weaknesses, and strengths. Fear and oppression inspired a different loyalty, and that was not a path Mathison wanted to go down. He was starting from scratch and alone, and he knew that wouldn't work.

He was not blind to the people disappearing around him. Mathison knew Feng was purging internal security and other elements. Trusting the ex-commissar didn't sit well with him, and there would be hell to pay later for Feng's actions, but what other options were there? The vanhat knew Sol was weak. Fear and mistrust could kill the Alliance just as easily as the vanhat, and maybe that was a greater threat.

This was no longer the SOG. Perhaps he would have to change things, give people something new to adjust to. He understood why despots throughout history had used war and paranoia to unite people, simple solutions sometimes appeared to be the only solutions.

"You will do what you feel is best," Mathison said to Carpenter and Hynninen. "I could use your help here, but I cannot keep you. You have earned my trust and respect. Thank you."

Carpenter turned his glare to Mathison, and his face softened ever so slightly.

"It has been an honor to fight beside you, Prime Minister," Carpenter said smoothly. "Perhaps later we can join forces again."

Mathison's nod was Carpenter's and Hynninen's signal to disconnect.

"Their departure will not help the stability of your rule," Feng said.

Why did he have to say 'rule' like Mathison was a king or something?

"He has no reason to stay," Skadi said.

"I understand," Mathison said. Neither did she or Jussi. Putting Feng in command of both InSec and ExSec held no appeal, but

Mathison might not have any other options. Giving that much power to Feng could not possibly end well.

"I will stay," Skadi said, looking at Mathison. "You have my word of honor. I suspect Vili will stay as well."

"Thank you." Mathison looked around. "We need to do something about the vanhat and the Chechens." Some things he could control, some things he couldn't. Perhaps offensive actions would help consolidate and bind the ex-SOG forces to him. Either way, he would focus their attention elsewhere. If they had an external enemy, they wouldn't look for internal ones. Maybe.

"Inkeri production continues to increase," Skadi said. "We are maybe a quarter of the way to protecting all the arcologies and Home Fleet is working on their secondary Inkeri installations. There was a vanhat resurgence near India that required another d-bomb strike. Riots continue in Africa and South America, but Europe is stabilizing."

"Jupiter?" Mathison asked. He knew, but not everyone would.

"Similar," Skadi said. "All Home Fleet ships are protected, same with Mars Fleet. The Mars arcologies are ninety percent protected. Jupiter colonies are at about sixty percent. Luna is one hundred percent."

Mathison looked at Sif.

He would have to use the two Delta Force troopers, but he couldn't trust them until they neutralized Becket.

"Do we have the coordinates of the tomb world where the inhibitor boxes were discovered?"

"We do," Sif said. "All but two of the inhibitors are accounted for."

"We need to prepare an expedition to secure them," Mathison said. He looked around. Who could he trust with that mission? He didn't have anyone. It might have to wait.

His desk flashed with a priority alert. It was Ting Hui. She was also watching over Stathis' operation, ready to pour SOG troops into the area if Stathis needed them. If she was calling him, something bad was happening.

* * * * *

Chapter Nineteen:
Stalking the Bunker

Commander Zale Stathis, USMC

Stathis was beginning to understand the gunny more as he looked at the surrounding Peacekeepers. No, they were Spartans. To get them to believe it, he had to believe it. This wasn't going to be easy, and they were his responsibility. Now they were dying.

"Keep them moving," Stathis told Sloss. "I'm putting you in command."

They were following a creek bed choked by snow and ash. Blazer rounds sliced the air above them as another set of robots engaged the Spartans.

"No," Sloss said. "I am here for you, not to command kirotu Peacekeeper thugs."

"You are here to follow my orders," Stathis said, looking up at the big gorilla. Sloss had a better grasp of things than Hakala or her partner. This was ranger stuff, not SEAL stuff.

"You are here; you cannot retreat," Sloss said.

"I will not retreat; I'm going to attack, but I can't take everyone with me," Stathis said, a plan forming in his mind. "I need you to keep the company moving, keep shifting, keep their attention. You are a decoy."

"You are hullu. You will not last seconds."

"I'm a Marine Raider and might be the only one who can get into that base."

"You are a little—" Sloss stopped, perhaps inspecting Stathis and remembering. A little what? Was Sloss going to make a short person joke that would require retaliation?

"Zen," Sloss said after a few seconds of silence. "Do not die. Should you do so, the Ice Princess and your prime minister will feed my balls to the vanhat. A certain HKT would be very angry."

"Don't call me little. Yeah," Stathis said. "I'm pretty sure if I survive, the gunny will kick my ass, so don't feel bad."

"I will come with you," Hakala said.

"No," Stathis said too quickly. *Hell no.* Stathis didn't like his own chances, but he couldn't take Hakala in there to die with him.

"Then don't go," Hakala said. "We can continue to move, to bleed them dry. We have more resources, more troops. We can grind them down."

"We have to end this as quickly as we can," Stathis said. "Every soldier we lose is one less soldier to fight the vanhat with. The gunny, uh, prime minister wants to save lives, not expend them grinding down an enemy. This needs to be maneuver warfare. We can't afford attrition warfare."

Stathis frowned. That was officer talk. Did they even know the difference?

"Then we should pull back and use orbital strikes," Sloss said.

Damned tempting, but the gunny would have considered that option. He had considered it and discarded it. The gunny wanted prisoners, and he had to have some idea of what other secrets were hidden under Quantico. The files Shrek had found in Munin's data core would let the Marines implant SCBIs in others. Full specifications, source code, and details were in the Marine's inventory now, but that didn't mean they could start implanting them in others. There was so much they still didn't know.

An explosion behind them reminded Stathis that there were still artillery batteries that could range his company.

"Not off the table," Stathis said. If he died, he was pretty sure Mathison would sink what was left of the East Coast beneath an orbital strike. Becket had to know that. Why didn't he surrender or try to contact anyone? Did Becket think the Marines and the SOG would just go away? He had to have a plan. A single bullet at the right time and place could decide a war, and Stathis planned on being that bullet.

But what did Becket have?

"What if operations have been moved elsewhere?" Stathis asked. "We will never know. We have to know."

"Zen," Sloss said. Maybe it was bad when the big Jaeger had stopped arguing.

"You can't go alone," Hakala said.

"I'm a Marine. That is a Marine base defended by Americans. I might be the only one who can. They will not let the SOG enter their base any more than HKTs would let Peacekeepers aboard your precious battlestars."

"Be careful then," Hakala said as another explosion erupted. They were getting closer.

"Sure thing," Stathis said. "I'm a Marine. One of the leanest, meanest fighting machines."

She probably didn't get that. He also didn't want to be there if Hakala got shot again. He wasn't sure how he would handle that. Was it better to hear about it or be there when it happened?

"Now keep moving," Stathis said.

He needed cover and this place was as good as any. Just because harassing fire was chasing them didn't mean it wasn't dangerous. Around him the Peacekeepers kept moving as Sloss urged them on. Hakala stood with him but left when the last Peacekeeper passed him.

Once he was alone, Stathis burrowed into the creek bed. Radiation counters were high and Stathis thought about hell wolves. Yeah, that might be a flaw in his plan. Hopefully, they had fled. Would they fear artillery and explosions, or would that draw them?

The explosions walked closer. This was the tough part of the plan. The artillery was chasing the Peacekeepers and couldn't catch up with them because Stathis had kept them moving, always changing direction, sometimes doubling back. It had been as random as Stathis could manage and he was sure the artillery or mortars that were harassing them didn't have unlimited ammunition. Right now, it was mostly mortars.

"Incoming," Shrek warned him. Shrek hadn't liked his idea either, but he understood it was the least bad plan of all of them.

Stathis closed his eyes, remembering the bombardment from so long ago, with Mathison and Benson beside him. He had been scared then, terrified, unsure how Mathison and Benson could stand it, but Mathison's voice hadn't held any fear. The gunny had seemed calm and in control, but then Stathis saw the gunny's hand shake, and Stathis had realized the gunny was putting on a show. He hadn't seen Benson, but at that point, Stathis knew. The gunny wasn't a coward, and he wasn't an idiot. He was scared, but he hadn't let it stop him. In fact, he had been so in control he had acted like he wasn't concerned. That had helped Stathis adjust, and he had realized he could do no less, so he buried his fear and did his best to prove he was brave or stupid. Stathis wasn't sure which, and it probably didn't matter. The least he could do, though, was put on an act for the others, help them like they were helping him. Had he not seen the gunny's weakness, he could have believed the gunny was just an idiot who wasn't smart enough to be scared.

Now, though, he was the only one. Alone with a shit storm about to land on his head. Yes. This was a stupid idea. Damned stupid. The gunny wouldn't do something like this, but the gunny had been young once. It was always easier to put on an act, but now he had nobody to put on an act for.

A bad thought occurred to Stathis. The Quantico mortars or artillery would have every square inch of terrain mapped. They would know what cover the creek bed provided, and they would be precise enough to ensure nobody was using it.

Another explosion behind him, so close. He felt the ground shake.

Stathis knew rounds were already airborne, coming down at him. That last explosion had been too close. The next one was already coming at him. It wasn't the explosion you heard that killed you; you would never hear the one that did. He couldn't get up now as he hugged the ground. Was there a god to pray to? There were no atheists in a foxhole, someone had told him once. Demons existed. Why not angels? Why not God?

Stathis tensed and waited for death. Would it be instant, or would he have time to realize he was dying? He didn't want a slow painful death.

Incoming rounds hadn't sounded like airbursts.

An explosion erupted in front of him, maybe fifty meters. Mortar round, and he was pelted by dirt and chunks of ice.

"Detecting a nearby communication link," Shrek informed him.

"What?"

"Stay still. Don't move. Quantico robots."

Stathis realized a major flaw in his plan. Of course, robots would follow the explosions to make sure the Peacekeepers didn't decide to weather a barrage to get behind it like Stathis was trying to do.

"Can you hack the link?" Stathis asked. He had to pee and let it go. His suit plumbing was hooked up.

"No. Low bandwidth receiving, and it is sending data back. Not a conversation I can interrupt or control."

"Can they detect me?"

"Yes, but so far, they haven't. You are safe. They are past. Hold position. There could be reserves following the lead element."

"Why?"

"If the lead element encounters the Peacekeepers, they are likely to be destroyed. Quantico defense will need nearby recon elements to confirm."

"Are you okay?" Hakala asked on the Republic link. It should be undetectable and unjammable, and was probably monitored by everyone and their grandmother. Fortunately, they were not intruding and Stathis could pretend it was just him and Hakala.

"Fine," Stathis lied. "Hard to nap with all these explosions. Just had a recon bot go by. Might be more. Some coffee would be nice about now. How are you doing? How's your day going? How's the weather?"

"We are fine," Hakala said. "Sloss has us changing direction again."

"Cool. Maybe he'll let you all stop for lunch. One time, way back in Raider school, me and some buddies had a ninety-six and we went out around town. I think there was some little mom-and-pop diner not far away. They had good meat loaf, but they probably aren't open anymore."

"Zen," Hakala said, and Stathis heard the grin. "What's a ninety-six?"

"Um, four days off. Ninety-six hours. Might have been for Thanksgiving or something. I forget. I don't remember most of it because we found this bar that had something called 'mojo' run by an old Marine who liked to tell us about Okinawa."

"If you are done flirting, you can start moving," Shrek said.

"Well, I gotta go. Don't want hell wolves thinking I'm lunch because I'm lying here like a buffet."

"Zen," Hakala said. "Maybe we should determine if hell wolves are edible."

"I like the way you think." Stathis looked up and around. His sensors were clear, and he had a few kilometers to go. Alone. Through hell wolf and Quantico combat drone infested territory. This really was a bad idea. Really bad. "We will have to figure out how to decontaminate them, though."

"Anything is edible with enough nakkikastike or kiisseli berry sauce," Hakala said.

"Never heard of them," Stathis said, shouldering his rifle and heading back the way he had come. Surrounded by blasted trees, there was plenty of cover if he stayed low. "Marines use Tabasco sauce for everything."

"Zen. I would like to try that. Does it go with peanut butter?"

"Lady, it goes with everything." Stathis decided crawling would be better.

"Freeze," Shrek said, and Stathis did.

"Continue," Shrek said without explanation.

This was going to take a while, but if Shrek could help him avoid Quantico drones, he could deal with it.

* * * * *

Chapter Twenty:
Father

Lojtnant Skadi, VRAEC

Entering her quarters, Skadi sat down and rubbed her eyes. These were some Committee member's temporary quarters in Zvezda. Vanir intelligence teams had removed any personal effects, and the quarters were just a place to sleep. The personal food dispenser had an extensive menu, but nothing appealed to her. The Earther's menu was bland and unappealing.

Her link chimed.

Paska, her dad.

"Tell him you're asleep?" Loki asked. *"He wants to see you."*

Tempting.

"No."

Skadi turned to face the wall where he would appear and stood up straight, mentally willing the exhaustion away.

Her father appeared in the wall. He must have just come from the stylist and put on a fresh uniform. He was sitting and she could see his personal quarters behind him.

"Kontra-amiraali. How can I help you?"

"Bring you and your people home. I need you."

"The great Vanir commander does not need two tired Erikoisjoukot."

"You are a bear shot in the ass, Daughter. I need you, not Erikois-joukot knuckle-draggers."

"I will go where I am needed most, Kontra-amiraali." She didn't want to play his games, and she didn't want to return to the *Tyr*.

"What about Vili?" Carpenter asked. "You want him to die with you?"

"What do you mean?" Skadi asked, knowing exactly what he meant. He was going to use Niels' and Bern's death against her? Use her guilt to return to his side to save Vili?

"Vili is the last member of your team," Carpenter said, like she didn't know. His words were a weapon, and he would not hesitate to use their deaths to force her compliance if he could.

She was glad he was aboard the *Tyr* and not in this room. His pretty uniform and styled hair would not go well with a bloody face and broken teeth.

"Close link," Skadi ordered Loki, and her father disappeared.

She sat. What bothered her most was that he was right.

"You should probably eat something," Loki said.

"Later."

Her food processor dinged.

Skadi realized that one problem with the SCBI was that she had nobody to scowl at. *"I said later."*

"Apologies. Your blood sugar level is low. This is adversely impacting your mood. I have prepared something that should be a good approximation of Poronkäristys. While it is not exactly reindeer meat, I believe it is very close. You would not want it to go to waste."

"Damn you," Skadi said, but now she could smell it, and it smelled good. She opened the door, and the smell filled the room. Her mouth began watering.

"Your father wants you to return," Loki said as she took it out and set it on the table.

"His problem, not mine."

"Why don't you return?"

"Why should I?"

"He is your father, and he obviously loves you. He wants you at his side."

"Where he will keep me safe and pampered?"

"This is a bad thing?"

It wasn't where she wanted to be. She sat down to eat.

Where *did* she want to be? What made the most sense? She didn't like it here in the Sol System. She had spent most of her life hating the people here, wishing for their death, pondering ways to hurt and kill them. Now here she was trying to save them. The universe was cruel and had a twisted sense of humor.

What did warriors do when the enemy they had fought for so long was finally defeated? Find a new enemy? Skadi didn't like that. Would there ever be a victory and peace she could accept?

* * * * *

Chapter Twenty-One:
Peacekeepers

Reginheraht Sloss, VRJ (Vapaus Republic Jaeger)

Sloss hated robots. They weren't like humans. They didn't know fear, and you couldn't suppress them with fire. They didn't get nervous, and these American robots were damned dangerous. Fighting American robots beside SOG Peacekeepers was not something he could have imagined doing despite all the strange missions he had conducted working with Sif and the MT.

Stathis had fallen back, and while Sloss wanted to call it cowardice, he knew it was the opposite. The little man was going to suffer an artillery or mortar strike and then try to sneak through who knew how many killer robots. The Marines were insane. Some people called Jaegers insane because of the risks they took, but Marines? Completely insane. The word hullu was not strong enough to describe them. He had seen it too many times. Marines could be certified as insane, maybe worse than the Erikoisjoukot.

Blazer fire flashed overhead, drawing Sloss' attention. The point men had encountered more robots, which was bad. Robots were expendable, and the Americans thought nothing of using the robots to pin down the Peacekeepers as they dropped high explosives on them. Robots didn't care about danger close and could provide accurate targeting information.

This time it was two humanoid robots, and the Peacekeepers reacted well, instantly spreading out and getting online so more of them could fire on the robots. Sloss had given the command to move in a certain direction, and the Peacekeepers would not be stopped. They were earning his respect. He had fought ODTs, and that was where most of these Peacekeepers came from, though it seemed the Peacekeepers were slower than usual. That could just be his perceptions, though, changed after seeing Marines and Erikoisjoukot in action.

Two Peacekeepers had died though. Sloss marked their location for later retrieval as the Peacekeepers folded back into a column, not sprinting but still moving damn fast. His display showed a squad leader was now walking point.

"Change direction," Sloss said and gave them a new heading, away from the bunker.

Republic equipment let him see where Stathis was, and the direction Sloss sent the Peacekeeper pointmen was at an angle and away from the Marine's objective. His systems were integrated with the Peacekeeper systems, but there were gaps in the integration, like linking to individuals or taking people out of the net.

A drone zipped overhead, and Andre shot it out of the sky with a burst from his wire gun.

"Change direction," Sloss ordered, giving a new heading. "And move faster!"

A company of men rarely moved fast. This company of men understood that if they did not, they would die. Incentive was a powerful thing.

"We can move faster if you allow us to use the leninzein," Senior Lieutenant Peskow said on the command link.

"No. Real warriors don't need such drugs."

"We shouldn't go that way, Sloss," Stahle said. "I just called in an interdiction strike on that hill."

"Zen." Sloss gave the Peacekeepers another direction.

He had heard the Marine tell him no and lost respect for Peskow. Trying to circumvent the Marine like that. Maybe he would tell Stathis later of the lieutenant's dishonor.

The hill they had been heading toward, about three hundred meters away, began to explode. Heavy metal pellets fired from orbit slammed into the area.

"I didn't want to go uphill anyway," Sloss told Stahle.

"It will be easier to climb now," Stahle said. "That barrage will have flattened it a little."

Ahead of them, fire erupted, but didn't quickly fade off. In fact, it increased as Peacekeepers ran forward to get online. Moving up, Sloss saw American androids moving among the trees. They were also moving online.

"Heavy contact front," Peskow reported, but Sloss could already see that.

"Contact rear," Lieutenant Khvostov said. He was the leader of Boris Platoon.

"Paska," Sloss said.

"I am sending in gunships," Vili said. He was coordinating with the *Tyr* and *Sleipner*.

"No guarantee they'll make it," Sloss said. He didn't want to risk gunship pilot lives, but they were going to need help.

"For sure." Vili didn't sound happy. "It looks like they're trying to box you in. I'm seeing a lot of movement. Maybe a hundred bots."

The fire didn't increase in front of them, but the Peacekeeper advance had been stopped. The Peacekeepers were taking cover in a creek bed, shooting up hill, but the androids were not coming down at them.

"Hold," Sloss said to Vili. "It is a trap. They want us to call for gunship support."

"You sound sure."

Behind him, Peacekeepers kept moving forward, bypassing the ruins of a house. They still had some air defense drones and Andre, Sloss's primary drone man, was moving them to where they could cover the Peacekeepers in the creek bed but where they wouldn't be exposed to the androids on the other hillside.

It was shaping up into a fight, and soon the artillery would come raining down.

"Doesn't seem like many to our front. Just enough to stop us. I expect they are closing in on our flanks. Stahl, ring us with fire."

"Zen," Stahl said, not questioning Sloss.

"Lasnitski, Kortengbach, go high." They were his team snipers. They wouldn't go high unless it was to their advantage, but they knew he wanted them to find a good position to shoot from. There were mules carrying the wounded and there were air defense mules. A valley would allow them to provide better protection from enemy artillery because they would have less sky to scan.

"Chubai, you take the right. Kostina, take the left," Sloss ordered the Peacekeepers. Chubai was the platoon commander for Vasily Platoon and Kostina commanded Gregory Platoon. "Form a perimeter. They are trying to trap us."

"Wilco," they replied.

"We should break out," Peskow said. "Hit them hard now while we can, then we can roll up their flanks."

Typical SOG arrogance. Peacekeepers weren't used to being out-numbered or outgunned. The cost in lives would leave the survivors severely weakened if Sloss was right. That was if they could break out, and Sloss wasn't so sure of that. There was a time to punch through, but Sloss didn't think this was it. Besides, he was bait, and the more robots he drew to them, the fewer there were to hunt Stathis.

"No," Sloss decided.

"You are right," Vili said. "They are setting a trap for you. *Sleipner* is moving in to ring you with fire. Do you want reinforcements?"

There was an ODT regiment on standby, along with an Aesir bat-talion. What would the defenders of Quantico do? They knew they were fighting a losing battle. The most they could hope for would be to inflict as many casualties as they could. An extended battle would delay the inevitable for them.

It would also give Stathis time.

"No."

He looked and saw Stathis was almost near the church he had tar-geted. If the Quantico robots thought they had him pinned down, then so be it.

Sloss was tiring of his Jaegers being used as bait.

"I didn't know you Jaegers had this much fun," Hakala said, com-ing up to him. Her partner, Engeman was nearby. He seemed less than thrilled.

A burst of blazer rounds ripped apart a nearby wall. They all dropped to the ground. It was coming from the other side.

"Wait until you have to clean your gear," Sloss said. The HKTs fought in more pristine conditions and didn't have any experience with mud and dirt.

If they survived, it would be interesting to hear them whine about it.

* * * * *

Chapter Twenty-Two: Quantico

Commander Zale Stathis, USMC

The two flag poles, one with an American flag and the other the US Marine flag, were ahead of Stathis. In the distance, he heard the *crump* of mortars and artillery.

"Move," Shrek said, and Stathis crawled forward. There wasn't much he could see this low to the ground. Cars, trashcans, and who knew what else was buried in the ash and snow. Stathis tried not to think of what they were as he crawled among them. With all the robots in the area, he was pretty sure there were no hell wolves, but if they discovered him, there was nowhere to run. He wouldn't get more than a hundred meters before they cut him down, and if he was injured there would be nobody to rescue him or help him until reinforcements arrived.

His only option would be self-rescue. And Stathis realized another mistake of his.

A larger robot rolled past. It paused, and Stathis feared it had detected him, but then the *thump-thump-thump* told him it was some kind of mortar bot, and it was firing. After three rounds were fired, it sped up. Stathis checked his Republic link. Yes, it was still transmitting his location. Hopefully, counter-battery fire would neglect firing on the mortar bot's location long enough for Stathis to get out of the way.

Where were all the damned bots coming from? They weren't SOG grade. These things were fast and lethal. More lights blinked out on his company roster, and Stathis turned it off. The Peacekeepers were dying. His people were dying, and he had abandoned them. He didn't need that distraction. He would agonize over that later.

"They have us surrounded," Hakala said on a direct link, freezing Stathis's blood.

"You can't break out?" Stathis asked as Shrek told him to crawl again.

"Sloss is hunkering down. He is ringing us with fire from the *Sleipner's* coil guns. Danger close, but I think he is doing the right thing."

"Why?" Stathis asked. Getting surrounded didn't sound like a really good idea.

"They aren't pushing us as hard," Hakala said. "We suspect if the robots wanted to, they could overrun us."

"Why aren't they?"

"If they did, why would *Sleipner* hold fire? Why not just crater Quantico?"

It made sense. They didn't want to wipe out the attackers, but they had to know it wasn't a winning strategy unless they were stalling for time.

Time to do what?

Ahead of him the doors to the church loomed up out of the dark. Stathis kept crawling.

"Quantico network detected," Shrek said. *"Begin intrusion?"*

"No," Stathis said. They were too exposed.

He crawled up the short steps and through the broken doors. The chapel looked ruined and abandoned but Stathis remembered the elevator in the back room.

Standing, Stathis made his way to the elevator. Shrek helped him watch in all directions. Would the Delta Force troopers be on the surface, or would they hide in the bunker? Shrek had never received the full schematic for Quantico Base, and now Stathis knew how little they had known about it. Obviously, Becket had warehouses full of robots, artillery bots, and so much more. He hadn't been quiet and hiding the last few hundred years like the gunny had thought. Becket had been busy, and he had everyone fooled, unless the others who had been in the bunker actually knew. Robillard and Peshlakai hadn't said anything about these robots or defenses. It was a shame they couldn't be trusted to help him.

"I have a good link with other SCBIs through the Aesir network," Shrek reported.

"Yeah? But we are dealing with AIs," Stathis said. *"When they detect us, they are going to throw everything they can at us. We have to have a good position."*

"Agreed."

Stalking toward the backroom, Stathis remembered Becket had said there was a stairwell. That would probably be a lot better than the elevator.

"Down!" Shrek said, and Stathis dove behind some old broken pews as the doors to the elevator room opened and several androids marched out. Humanoid and made of metal, Stathis didn't want to mess with them. He had seen enough horror movies to know how fast and tough they would be, even against blazers.

Stathis watched them march past as he froze. If their vision was three hundred and sixty degrees, then they would see him, and Stathis was sure he wouldn't be fast enough. He was fast, but they would respond with computerized precision.

They marched out the chapel doors without doing anything.

It had been a really bad idea to come here alone.

He saw that Mathison and Winters were online if he needed them. It wouldn't surprise Stathis if the gunny was tapped in, watching his viewscreen. Actually, it would be a surprise. The gunny wasn't one to micromanage, though he was probably sitting in his fancy office drinking a beer and watching old football games on the screen. That's what Stathis would probably do if he liked football.

Did the SOG have football?

"Stairwell is likely down the hallway to the left," Shrek said.

Stathis moved forward, his rifle muzzle leading the way. There were no stairs to be found, but then he looked in the chaplain's office. The chaplain had his own personal bathroom. Opening that door didn't reveal a bathroom so much as stairs going down to a heavy-duty metal door.

"Bingo," Stathis said.

Crouching at the top, he looked things over. Alarms? Traps? Pop-down turrets? Pop-up turrets? How was it being monitored and defended? There would be traps galore. You didn't fill warehouses full of warbots and forget to protect your front or back door.

Shrek scrutinized the area, looking for pin-hole cameras. The door looked too new, though, and as he looked it became more obvious: it was new and had quickly been put in place. What did that mean?

Going down the steps, anticipating death at any second, Stathis got to the bottom with no pop-out turrets killing him or alarms screeching.

He looked closer and saw more. It had been repaired recently. He could see claw marks in old concrete, but they had been filled in with new concrete paste. The door itself looked like it had been made in the last couple of days, or in the last week at least.

"What do you think of that?" Stathis asked Shrek.

"Those claw marks would be characteristic of hell wolves. It looks like hell wolves tried to get in here recently. Days? A week? Hard to say."

"Remember that intruder alert where they wouldn't give us weapons?" Stathis asked, referring to when Mathison, Skadi, and the others had been interrupted by an intruder alert that two Delta Force troopers had said was just a drill.

"That wasn't a drill," Shrek said.

"Which means the hell wolves got past this door and were stopped further in," Stathis said liking this less.

"A valid assessment. Cameras, automated weaponry, and sensors would suffer a lot of damage from radiation and elements this close to the surface. Going past that sealed door is likely to trigger alarms and defenses."

"You still have access to QuanticoNet?"

"Affirmative," Shrek said. *"It has been extended, perhaps for robot control. Bandwidth is not ideal but should be sufficient. Shall we begin?"*

"Yeah," Stathis said, putting his back to the door and aiming up the stairs.

"Beginning hack of QuanticoNet."

Stathis crouched, his finger slipping onto the trigger. His identification system showed no friendlies were anywhere nearby.

"Oops," Shrek said seconds later.

"Oops?"

"Nothing."

"No, you said oops. I heard you say oops. That was an oops. I know what I mean when I say oops. What do you mean when you say oops?"

"We have triggered the QuanticoNet network defense. They know we are here."

"That's not an oops," Stathis said. *"That's an 'Oh shit, we're gonna die.'"*

* * * * *

Chapter Twenty-Three:
Orbital Assault

Lojtnant Skadi, VRAEC

Loki had a way of waking her up with no disorientation or grogginess, and Skadi wasn't sure if she liked it or not. She hadn't meant to fall asleep sitting at the table finishing her dinner, but it had happened. Had Loki been responsible? At least she hadn't fallen face forward on her plate. She remembered leaning against the wall to rest her eyes for a moment. It hadn't been that long.

"Alert," Loki said. *"Commander Stathis was trying to penetrate QuanticoNet and has triggered the defenses."*

"Damn him," Skadi said out loud, not caring if anyone was listening.

"Technically, it wasn't Stathis so much as the SCBI network. We missed something. We were supporting Shrek's efforts and——"

"Can we save him?"

"Commandant Ting Hui has authorized a full ODT combat drop, and Vili is asking to send the ODT battalion. Space is getting very full above Quantico as the ODT and Aesir race to be the first."

"Can he hold out?"

"Probably not. That isn't the entire problem."

"What is?"

"As the drop pods come down, we are detecting extensive ground-to-space defenses powering up. It is going to be a slaughter."

"How is it we did not detect such defenses before?"

"Becket and the others have had hundreds of years to fortify their East Coast. They were not just hiding and waiting, they were frantically building and preparing. Energy patterns indicate possible ground-to-space weapons."

"Paska, what can we do?"

"It is already too late to abort the landings or further prep. We are going to lose a lot of people. The SOG Home Fleet is mobilizing. Nobody had any idea that was down there, and we are detecting heavier weapons powering up. It is likely they can reach ships in high orbit."

Losing a regiment of ODTs and Aesir was not a small thing and Skadi realized there could be larger ramifications. Besides the loss of so many warriors, it would embarrass Mathison's new government, demonstrating weakness. There would be political ramifications beyond the massacre of good troops.

"Massive power readings," Loki reported as Skadi grabbed her helmet and started running toward the command center where Mathison was likely to be. Skadi glanced at the readouts Loki was providing. The fleet moving into orbit to bombard Quantico was also going to be shredded.

The SOG had not been the only force fortifying Earth, and the SOG was about to learn that America was not dead.

How could they have missed this?

* * * * *

Chapter Twenty-Four:
Trapped

Commander Zale Stathis, USMC

Stathis couldn't imagine any good ways to die. Death was death, and it was really going to suck. Dying quickly would be preferable to a slow, painful death, of course, and Stathis was confident the androids at the top of the stairs would make his death a quick one.

"This is bad," Shrek said.

"Gosh, really? Can't be as bad as that time on Jason's Pit."

"QuanticoNet is more extensive than anyone anticipated. Becket has been busy fortifying the East Coast. The Quantico system extends as far west as Shenandoah National Park. There are numerous ground-to-orbit weapons and some weapons systems we don't recognize."

"How do you not recognize a weapon system?"

The android at the of the steps leaned back and Stathis stitched the wall with a burst before changing magazines. The magazine was only three-quarters expended but Stathis was confident the androids were keeping track and would assault him when he ran out. They must not like the SCBI hack attempts which were originating from him.

A weapon came around the corner and Stathis fired at the wall where he thought the android's main body was. His blazer rounds ripped apart the wall, setting it on fire.

"I'm linked to the SCBI network. We are detecting systems powering up. Multiple power plants along the East Coast are coming online. Shielding is being pulled back to allow weapon access to the sky. In some cases, explosives are uncovering things. Cloud cover is spotty, and we are detecting some explosions from orbit. Large-barreled weapons of some sort. The SOG fleet is scattering and has received orders to boost to higher orbit. Now orbital supporting fire is being disrupted by some kind of magnetic weapons."

"We can't get to you," Hakala said on the command link.

"That's okay," Stathis said. Dying in the bunker wasn't, but at least he was dying alone. Maybe they would name the crater after him. "You get out of there. Be safe, okay?"

"We are pinned and not going anywhere," Hakala said, and Stathis heard choppiness in her communication link, which told him she was under fire. It wasn't like the androids to miss. They were trying to suppress Hakala and the others. Not a good situation. It was all a trap, and Stathis had led everyone into it.

"Dig in," Stathis told her. "They might not have a lot of choice in orbit; they might have to sink the East Coast."

"Zale," she said, using his first name.

"Bryngerd," Stathis said, using her first name. He had never used it before. "Valhalla awaits."

"I hate that name," she said. "Friends and lovers call me Bryn."

Stathis didn't want to think about other men she had been lovers with. What was she saying? They weren't lovers. Friends was good though. She was a lot older than he was, but with Republic anti-aging treatment, she could be early twenties like him. Why did it have to end like this, dammit? A cougar would have so much more experience and probably be a lot of fun.

The ground shook as orbital strikes hit somewhere nearby.

"Well," Stathis began, but the androids chose that time to begin their assault. They came fast and Stathis fired as fast as he could. Seconds later he was back down to a quarter magazine and the top of the stairs were full of broken robot shells. It was a good time to change mags.

"We are being slowly locked out of QuanticoNet," Shrek said. *"Firewalled."*

"Can't you get past it?"

"Not without proper authentication."

"Use ours, use mine," Stathis said. *"Did they disable our access?"*

Shrek was silent as Stathis prepared for the androids to resume their attack. He still had several magazines. He watched the fire begin to spread, almost consuming the entire wall.

His armor would protect him if the entire chapel caught fire and collapsed on him, but that was the least of his worries.

"Well?" Stathis asked.

"We are in," Shrek said. *"What are your orders?"*

"Shut everything down," Stathis said. Why the hell was Shrek asking him that? Wasn't it obvious? *"Why are you asking me? Make everything stop shooting. Stop killing people."*

"Commands accepted."

"What do you mean, accepted?" Stathis asked. The androids wouldn't waste time. Were they waiting for reinforcements?

"Commandant Becket is no longer present, making you the senior Marine. Your rank is listed as second lieutenant."

"What?"

"QuanticoNet is a Marine facility. Your rank is second lieutenant, and you have been properly authenticated. As the only Marine present, you now command Quantico. Notifications are being sent to higher authorities. Quantico Defense is standing down."

188 | WILLIAM S. FRISBEE, JR.

"Oh. That's cool. This doesn't make sense, though."

"Correct," Shrek said. *"Who in their right mind would even consider putting the rank of lieutenant in the same sentence as your name?"*

"What did you do?" Hakala asked on the private link. "They stopped firing at us, and they're retreating."

"We took control of QuanticoNet," Stathis said. "That's what Marines do. I told ya."

* * * * *

Chapter Twenty-Five:
Quantico Base

Prime Minister Wolf Mathison, USMC

Mathison looked at the holographic display in front of him. Only he could see it, but Skadi was likely getting her own display.

Quantico Base was a lot more extensive than anyone had imagined. Data was still being uploaded by Shrek into the SCBI network.

Becket had not been hiding. He had been busy and was ready to swat the SOG out of the skies if they discovered his base. There were a lot of things about Quantico that Mathison didn't understand. There were sixty weapon batteries identified as particle cannons, and they had been tracking ships in orbit. Nearly everything was automated and computer controlled. There had been no safeguards, no requirement for humans to push buttons, and they appeared to have the range to strike targets in high orbit. Freya suspected they might even range the Moon.

The numbers meant little to Mathison, but they calculated their chance of destroying a battlestar at ninety percent. They had been minutes away from a massacre when Stathis had stopped things.

"This is odd," Freya said.

"What?"

189

"The survivors of Quantico, the remaining engineers, staff, and Delta Force, are currently in bunkers. Everything was automated, designed to repel a SOG or Aesir attack. Logs show President Becket left in a small one-person ship days ago."

"And?"

"The base has been running on autopilot. You have been promoted to general, Winters is listed as a brigadier general and Stathis is a second lieutenant. Our access has not been revoked. There are some interesting and conflicting commands: the system was told to destroy any inbound shuttles, and it began sweeping vessels from orbit, but then there were enough exceptions and requirements that the logic loop could not comply."

"Becket is nuts."

"Or he wanted you to take control of Quantico," Freya said.

"Where did he go?"

"That information is unavailable. It is going to take days to go through all this information, and categorize and inventory things. We have manifests, but there is a lot."

"Big picture. What does this mean?"

"It means that President Becket was rebuilding the United States' defenses. Given enough time, he probably could have swept the SOG fleet from orbit. There are some very advanced weapons systems beyond SOG or Republic technological levels. Specifications and details indicate they were designed by AIs not people."

Mathison looked over at Skadi.

"Thoughts?" he asked.

"Nothing makes sense," Skadi said. "Becket has all these robotic defenses built and then he leaves? He let us leave?"

"We could still drop an asteroid on him," Mathison said. "The defenses only protected him so much."

"But he didn't take anybody else?"

"Yeah, I don't get it, unless that third AI is calling the shots." Mathison frowned as he looked at her. "You think that AI is a friend or enemy?"

"If it is a friend, why did it flee? I think the war in Becket's mind is a real possibility. He is your ally, but the other AI is not."

"So, we need to find out more about that AI. Anything in QuanticoNet?"

"We have a lot of deleted records," Freya said. *"That AI has probably removed all traces of itself."*

"But Becket and Sun Tzu would leave us something if they could. Find it."

"Aye."

The door chimed. Amiraali Carpenter. Mathison's bad mood got worse. What now?

When he entered, the picture-perfect officer acted like he owned the place. Why couldn't he just use the link?

"Kontra-amiraali," Mathison said.

"Prime Minister," Carpenter said. "Daughter."

"How can I help you?" Mathison asked. Skadi was more than just his daughter. She was his executive officer, his second in command.

"Easy," Carpenter said. "Order my people to return."

"Can you elaborate?"

"Jussi, my daughter, Vili, and several other members of my command are demanding they be allowed to stay."

Jussi wanted to stay? That was new and a relief. He wanted external oversight on ExSec, someone experienced, capable, and familiar. Jussi fit the bill.

"Kontra-amiraali," Mathison began. How could he tactfully tell this oversized asshole to shut up and get out of his office? "I am desperately in need of people I can trust."

"Can they trust you?" Carpenter asked, and Mathison contemplated the gentle persuasion of a throat punch.

"Loyalty is a two-way street," Mathison said. "They are loyal to me, and I will be loyal to them."

Carpenter nodded. "This is all fine and good in theory, but their oath is to the Republic, and I am a direct representative of that Republic. They seek to betray their oath to me and the Republic to serve you."

"The Republic abandoned us," Skadi said, standing to look down at her father. "You are abandoning others in need. Why would they want to stay? Here, we can make a difference. We can reshape and rebuild humanity. We can ensure that the SOG is dead and will not rise again. To go with you is to flee and hide."

"Oaths and loyalties are powerful things," Carpenter said as began to pace back and forth in front of his desk. "Loyalty is frequently a peculiar thing. Times change, people change, nations change. There were no expiration dates or conditions on their oath."

"What do you want?" Mathison asked. If Carpenter had a point, he was taking his time getting there and Mathison had a meeting with some arcology administrators in thirty minutes. Then he had a meeting with space fleet admirals who were going to lie to him about how they were ready for a vanhat attack.

This was supposed to be his lunch time, but once again Mathison doubted he would have time to scarf down something nutritious.

Carpenter stopped to look at his daughter.

"What is your official title?" Carpenter asked.

"Executive Prime Minister," Mathison said for her, making it up on the spot. It was a stupid title, but for all intents and purposes she was his executive officer and right now he trusted her as much as

Stathis, Sif, and Winters. Skadi had as much authority as he did. Literally.

Carpenter looked at Mathison and raised an eyebrow, demonstrating enough tact not to call Mathison an idiot. There was too much going on, too many other concerns for him right now. Bestowing titles was nowhere on his priority list.

"Let me ask this another way," Mathison said. "What is the quickest way I can get you out of my office? I have a lot to do. Some thug administrators are coming in a few minutes who want me to give them direct command of the guard units. After that I have some stuck-up SOG admirals who are going to ask me for more authority to persecute and execute their underlings. Then I think there are some Guard commanders who want to dissolve some unions. I really don't have time for stuck-up Republic admirals who can't get to the point."

Carpenter turned to Mathison.

"My concern is simple," the amiraali said, and Mathison wondered how he kept his uniform so stiff and formal, his hair so perfectly combed and unruffled. "I want some assurance that your loyalty to the Vapaus Republic and her people will not collapse with the winds of change. I need some assurance that you will maintain a vested interest in the security and wellbeing of the Republic personnel that work with you."

"What the hell does he want?" Mathison asked Freya.

"Unknown," Freya said. *"He wants something. Maybe for you to swear an oath to him? Maybe more authority."*

"If I give him more authority, I will have a rebellion. Those SOG admirals are also going to demand more access to Republic technology and the battlestars. Giving Carpenter more authority is going to go down like an oversized concrete cock ring."

Carpenter looked at his daughter.

"Perhaps both of you need to discuss this," Carpenter said. "Sol has nothing for us." He turned back to Mathison. "Sol and the remnants of the SOG have nothing to offer the Republic. Nothing to bind us to you. There is no reason for me or Task Force Ragnar to give you any loyalty."

"The human race doesn't deserve your loyalty?" Skadi asked.

"Of course, it does. We are human, after all. However, we must all look out for our people, and the human race is composed of many people. One size does not fit all, despite SOG propaganda. We are not Governance subjects."

"The Republic is gone," Skadi said, and Mathison wondered if she was going to punch out her father. He wasn't sure if that would necessarily be a bad thing.

"They could realize their mistake and come back," Carpenter said.

"If they are still alive. If they learn of what is going on. If they still care."

"There are people within the Republic that will not tolerate the Republic abandoning the task force."

"Father, I don't think you understand. That was the intent from the beginning. They let you stage your attack and filled it full of those who would not support their departure. They abandoned you on purpose."

"Daughter, people make mistakes. This does not invalidate our oath. What does that riosto commissar always say? Gold can't be pure, and people can't be perfect, or something like that?"

Now a Republic admiral was quoting a SOG Commissar? Were there any surprises left in the universe?

"What does riosto mean?" Mathison asked Freya.

"Thug or villain."

"What do you want?" Mathison asked, yet again.

"I want some assurance that you will not turn on the Republic. That the Republic, her people and warriors are of value to you, and you will be loyal to us regardless of the winds of change."

"What kind of assurance?" Mathison asked.

Carpenter glared at Mathison and then glanced at his daughter.

"Figure it out," he said, turning his glare back at Mathison. "I don't have time for games, Prime Minister. If you can't, I want my people back. I don't want to order them to return. I realize how much you need them, but right now I don't see why we need you. Have a good day. I will let you get back to ruling your subjects."

Carpenter left as quickly as he had arrived.

"What does he want?" Mathison asked as the door closed behind him. "More authority? I've given him a full data dump of SOG archives. Does he want me to swear some oath to him? To bend a knee and swear fealty? What?"

"Maybe he wants the self-destruct codes for the SOG fleet," Skadi said.

"Hell no. I barely trust him not to go crazy and start eradicating anyone that objects to him, but I don't know even half his command staff. There is a lot of hatred toward the SOG aboard that task force. People who want to fight the SOG did not have any desire to stay with Home Fleet. I doubt Task Force Ragnar wouldn't lose sleep if the vanhat wiped out Sol. They would probably party for weeks."

"He lost a lot of his people when the *Pankhurst* attacked," Skadi said. "Countless friends and acquaintances he had known for decades. He is feeling insecure about the future. I think he fears the future and realizes his mortality."

196 | WILLIAM S. FRISBEE, JR.

"Do you think he cares about his people who want to stay behind or does he want something specific?"

"Yes. I think he wants something, and I think he cares, intellectually. He is taking it personally that members of his task force want to stay."

"Why do you think they are staying?"

Skadi turned to look at Mathison, and she didn't seem happy.

"You have to ask that? One would think it was obvious. You have not destroyed the SOG, but you have taken control, you are in change. You trust us and, despite what my father says, you are showing us loyalty and trust. Why shouldn't we return that? You need help. You need us. Here we can make a difference. We can make sure the Governance does not rise from the ashes to become a bigger threat than it was. Here we can work toward the survival of everyone, not just the Republic. Here we can make a difference, not just for the Republic but for the human race. Only a fool can't see the vanhat are a bigger threat."

"What about you?" Mathison asked.

"What do you mean?"

"You would abandon your father to work with the people who killed your mother?"

"No," she said, and Mathison wondered if she was going to swing at him. "Not even close. You didn't kill my mother, and killing the people of the Governance won't bring her back, won't bring back all the other Aesir I've lost, all the Vanir. It won't bring back the people of Lisbon, New Hope, or any others. But none of that will matter if the vanhat win. The vanhat are my enemy now. I despise the Governance and their fighters, but right now I have to care about more than the Republic. Divided, we will fall. Together, our chances of defeating the vanhat increase."

Mathison looked at her. Her loyalty was a strength he needed. The entire Governance and human race needed it, even if they didn't know it. She would stay, Vili would stay. He could rely on them. But he also needed Kontra-amiraali Carpenter. What did that stuck-up asshole really want and why wouldn't he say it?

Asshole politicians.

Mathison rubbed his eyes. Kicking the vanhat out of Sol had been the easy part. Keeping the human race from fragmenting further was going to be a lot harder. Too many people saw what was directly in front of them and refused to look at the bigger picture.

Why was he one of the few that didn't?

* * * * *

Chapter Twenty-Six:
A Ship

Kapten Sif, VRAEC, Nakija Musta Toiminnot

Was she abandoning Mathison in his time of need? If Amiraali Carpenter took the Vanir fleet away, Mathison would be more vulnerable. Jussi would probably go with the fleet even though he wanted to stay; he knew his duty. Who could she get to replace Jussi and herself?

There was nobody she trusted who had any skill. Skadi might have to take over. Sif didn't see that working out well. Skadi was a heavy spear. She would immediately attack any problems with extreme force, which would cause more problems than it solved in the realm of politics. Sometimes you had to be subtle. She had learned that as an agent for the MT. Direct action and violence were effective, but sometimes all that did was create new enemies and new problems. Discrediting or invalidating an enemy lasted much longer in many cases.

She had to hunt down Hermod's team, though. The longer they remained free, the more damage they would do. Rorik Becher was likely in command now. She had met him once, decades ago. A large solid trooper who had seemed very quiet and contemplative, a master of small arms, and he could be subtle. She didn't know who was alive and dead, though. Skadi had killed Jord Lykken, but there were several other members, and Sif knew there could be other Erikoisjoukot teams that had turned.

Now the important question was where were they and where was their ship? There had been no sign of it in the Sol System. According to Mathison, Hermod had been working with the Central Committee as a pawn or ally, nobody knew which.

But she had serious doubts about taking them on alone.

The door slid open, and she entered Mathison's office. A pair of SOG admirals were leaving. Their faces were carefully neutral, but she could sense their anger and frustration. They obviously had not gotten what they wanted, but she also felt their fear and insecurity. Insecure and frightened people sometimes did unpleasant things. She made a mental note to warn Feng.

Looking up, Mathison looked like he hadn't slept in days. He was still clean shaven, but he looked as exhausted as he had when they had rescued him from the SOG base. They had installed a desk for Skadi so they could both work in the same room, and she was at her desk waving her hands, working with data only she could see. She nodded at Sif before going back to her work.

Sif wished she had good news for him, but she could sense that he knew why she had come.

"Hermod's team is still out there."

"Yes," Mathison said. "A loose end and a danger to both the Republic and the SOG. With Hermod here, I'm sure the team has additional information on the SOG, information we might not have. They went somewhere to do something."

"Mozi and I have found nothing in the SOG system to indicate what."

"Who is going to replace you?" Mathison asked. "I need someone to oversee ExSec. Someone I trust."

"Perhaps you could put Charles Goetz in charge," Sif suggested. He might be the least evil of the group.

"Do you trust him?"

"No."

"Feng disrupted another assassination attempt from InSec," Mathison said. "How will I stop any attempts from ExSec?"

"I do not think ExSec will be that much of a problem. They are focused on external threats and with implementing the Stalingrad Protocol. Most of their agents and resources were cut off. They will have their hands full trying to figure out what is going on outside of Sol. If you open up the system again, they will spend a lot of time and resources trying to figure out who is still alive."

"But they still have black ops, assassins, and other such specialists. You don't think they will ally themselves with InSec?"

"No. InSec and ExSec have been enemies for a while, and InSec is fanatical about maintaining control within the Governance. The secretary general played a delicate balancing act, pitting them against each other, using her own spies within the agencies to maintain control."

"I have accessed some of her files," Mathison said. She could feel his regret. The secretary general had bound them to her by allowing certain excesses and depravity. Feeding their lusts and desires to ensure their loyalty and compliance. He had already had some of them rounded up and sent to prison camps, which were overcrowded despite releasing most of the political prisoners. Feng was working to get additional prisons built and repurposing other facilities as prisons. Unfortunately, there was a set of files he could not access. Lots of personal files.

Working with him, she was aware of what he was doing. He seemed to take some pleasure in informing her of his efforts to punish deviants. She wanted to object to his heavy hand, but sometimes she didn't think it was heavy enough, and he was being too lenient. She would have executed everyone in the InSec truth and integrity division, for instance. They were all depraved torturers who took too much pleasure in their work, frequently kidnapping and torturing people just for practice.

Sif knew she wouldn't be able to tolerate working with InSec. There were too many evil, dark-hearted individuals in that agency, and the fact that Feng could work with them worried her.

"Do you know where to start?" Mathison asked.

"No," Sif said. When she got away from Sol, perhaps she could focus, and it would take less effort to shield herself from all the emotions that were bombarding her.

"What do you need from me?"

"A ship," Sif said. Asking for the *Eagle* would be too much. Perhaps he could assign a SOG vessel for her use. A corvette would be sufficient. With Munin, she was sure she could manage. "A corvette should be sufficient if you have one to spare."

Mathison's eyes narrowed as he looked into the distance, in thought or viewing a display, perhaps.

"No," Mathison said. "There are corvettes, but I don't think a corvette would stand a chance against the *Stalkkeri*. If you find them, you will also need a combat element."

"I am Aesir," Sif said. "But I am also Musta Toiminnot. I can fight from the shadows."

"You aren't going alone," Skadi said. "I agree with the prime minister on that. You must have the ability to destroy the *Stalkkeri* the moment you find it or they could escape."

"I think I can manage with a corvette," Sif told her. If she caught them by surprise.

"What about the *Ovela Kaarme*?" Skadi asked Mathison. "The ship the *Tyr* recovered at New Pharoh? It is MT, a Skipsbat, a frigate class. It has no crew and I think they have repaired it."

"Will your father give it up?"

"Can you handle it?" Skadi asked, turning to Sif.

"Not alone," Sif said.

"You know what happened there?" Skadi asked.

Sif had been on the bridge. She had nightmares of that bridge. She had seen the abattoir the bridge had become. The entire ship would have been scrubbed clean and everything on the bridge had likely been replaced. She didn't want to think about the gore moving to attack. Would there be ghosts?

"Yes," Sif said, though she heard the doubt in her own voice. Duty was more important than feelings.

"What about the crew?" Skadi asked.

"That will be more difficult," Sif said.

"Check with the amiraali," Mathison said. "See if he can lend you some Vanir."

"That might be more challenging," Skadi said. "The Vanir won't want to serve aboard a ghost ship like that, and he certainly won't release any Aesir or HKTs. To listen to him, you would think everyone was killed during the *Pankhurst's* attack, and he is running with a skeleton crew."

"Is he?" Sif asked.

204 | WILLIAM S. FRISBEE, JR.

"He lost a lot of people," Skadi said. "A lot, but the battlestar is heavily automated. Most of the crew were asukas seeking citizenship. More than enough under most conditions."

"What do you mean?" Mathison asked.

"In the Republic, they earn citizenship through service," Skadi said. "Citizens can vote. Many people seek service on Vanir ships as crew. The Vanir put them to work, indoctrinate them and train them. A battlestar is a good place to dump extra crew. The battlestar will have enough crew for operations. It probably has five hundred percent more than it requires."

"But that doesn't mean they are qualified Vanir spacers," Sif said.

A light flashed on Mathison's desk, and Sif saw it was from Rick, one of the Delta Force troopers. The two troopers were in their quarters. They may or may not have heard about what Stathis had been up to. Here on Zvezda Two, they had very limited access to the outside world.

She sensed Mathison's frustration.

"Perhaps you can send the Delta Force troopers with me?" Sif said. That would take them off Mathison's hands. They might even be able to handle Hermod's team. "We are hunting Hermod, not Becket."

The prime minister had to be worried about them and their loyalty.

"Who will keep you safe from them?" Mathison asked. Well, that was a concern, but she could feel he liked the idea.

"I can sense their intent," Sif said. "I have other abilities."

Mathison knew. Would the Delta troopers follow her? They would be ideal, though. Trained warriors with SCBIs. They would have an edge that the rogue Eriks couldn't match.

"Ask them," Mathison said. "Skadi, can you see if your dad will give us that frigate and see if you can wrangle away some Vanir to help."

"Zen," Skadi said, and Sif felt her regret about something. Making the offer, or was there something else?

"Maybe we can get some ODTs as well," Mathison said. "Or is that too much?"

"I don't know," Sif said.

"Deal," Mathison said. "Bring me their heads."

"Zen," Sif said.

Now she just had to convince the Delta troopers to follow her and find some ODTs.

* * * * *

Chapter Twenty-Seven:
Skipsbat

Lojtnant Skadi, VRAEC

Skadi wanted to punch someone. What had she been thinking when she mentioned the ghost frigate? Why had she offered to talk to her father about it? She had heard Sif's doubt about taking it, but it would be perfect. It was a spy ship, and it should be fully functional. It was large enough to deal with the *Stalkkeri* and it was Republic.

When she had linked her father, he had demanded a face-to-face meeting. She hadn't asked him for anything in many decades. The arrogant prick had to be gloating. What if this was a plot to get her aboard the *Tyr* where she wouldn't be allowed to leave?

Loki would help her rip apart the *Tyr* and teach her father a lesson, and she would be ready.

The shuttle landed, and the hatch opened. Vanir crew came out to service the shuttle, and Skadi knew her father would not be here to meet her. TyrNET linked with Loki and gave her directions to her father. His quarters.

Damn him.

She was fully armed and armored. He would have a very hard time containing her if he tried. Loki had her back, and if he thought his pet HKTs could take her down, he was sadly mistaken. Maybe she should have brought Vili. That would put both of them under her father's control, but Vili might be able to bust her out if she failed. Reserves were always critical.

Eyes followed her as she marched down the corridor to the tram. Fully armed and armored Aesir were not unusual anymore, but everyone aboard the *Tyr* knew who she was and who her father was. None dared meet her eyes or stop her, and she had a tram all to herself.

It was a brief trip, and then she took an elevator.

When she arrived at her father's quarters, two Aesir saluted her. Returning their salute, she walked in. It would have been embarrassing if the door hadn't opened for her, but it did, and she marched forward. Of course, her father had probably followed her every step of the way and known where she was. She hadn't missed the fighter drone escort that followed her shuttle.

"Come in, Daughter," Carpenter said after the fact. He was looking at his collection of hunting knives. Weapons that had followed the Carpenter family from Earth. He had inherited them from his mother's side of the family.

"You know what I want," Skadi said. This could all have been handled through email or link. His arrogance had brought her here.

"Yes," Carpenter said, turning back to her. "The ship is being prepared, and I have found a captain for it. Her name is Meika Theymar. She is from the *Deutschstar.* She is aboard the *Ovela Kaarme* now. She reports she will depart within the hour. You can be on it to verify everything is in order."

Skadi stood there. *No argument? No demands?*

"Then why am I here?" Skadi asked. He was dangling a carrot before her. He could easily cancel it. He just had to give the word.

"Because I wanted to see you, Daughter," Carpenter said, turning to her.

"A picture won't work?"

"No," he said, not taking the bait.

Skadi looked around. They were alone.

"The *Tyr* lost a lot of people when the *Pankhurst* hit us," he said. "I lost a lot of friends. People I had known for a very long time."

"War happens."

"It is different for Vanir. Space warfare is infinitely more dangerous, but this? The vanhat did not defeat us in a space battle. They entered my ship. Killed my crew face to face, changed some of them, turned them against their brothers and sisters."

He was just now figuring this out?

"Casualties taken in battle aboard a ship are different," Carpenter said, his eyes were on his desk. Skadi tried to figure out a way to get him to the point. "Did you know I had to kill members of my crew? I had to kill them with my own hands, my own sidearm."

"It is difficult," Skadi said. She could understand his fear, his feelings.

His eyes met hers, and she saw pain there. That was not something she was familiar with. Had that pain been there when he learned of her mother's death? She couldn't remember. It was so long ago, and she had been struggling herself, not seeing the world as it really was.

"No," he said. "For most Vanir to kill, it is an easy thing. We push a button and a stranger dies. We never see their face, hear their screams, see their blood. For the Vanir, war is a clean thing. Any blood we see is caused by our enemy; any suffering is ours. We never see or care about the pain of our enemy."

"Until now," Skadi said.

"Yes. Until now, the enemy has been other people. Now? A bridge officer, my friend Robert Silii, transformed before my eyes. When he turned to me, I saw the hatred. He was going to kill me, there was no doubt. He served on my crew for over sixty years."

Skadi had nothing to say. She understood, she knew the horror, and she knew what would have happened next. Her father was standing before her. There would have been no other possibilities. Details only.

"I shot him," Carpenter said. "The HKTs were confused, unsure. We all knew, but there was a part of us that refused to believe it was possible. We refused to believe that our friends and brothers would turn on us."

Carpenter was looking at her, but she knew he didn't see her.

"Next it was Ranne, then Liukko. The HKTs sprang into action and didn't hesitate after I shot Robert. I had set the example. I had shown them how it was to be done."

He sat, still staring through her. Her anger at him dissolved. He hadn't brought her here to gloat or humiliate her. He needed someone to talk to. Someone who understood.

"I've lost friends before, sent them into battle where they died. This was different. They were friends." His gaze returned to her. "I killed them with my own hands. How do you handle it?"

He didn't know what his question was; he didn't have the right words. Skadi didn't either. There were no simple answers either, nothing she could say.

"The pain doesn't go away," Skadi said. "It doesn't fall off your shoulders to nothing. Your shoulders grow to carry the load. You learn not to let it stop you."

His eyes narrowed as he finally looked at her. She couldn't imagine shooting Vili, Niels, or Bern. Her father hadn't known he would have to shoot his bridge crew.

"You did what you had to," Skadi said. He had it worse, and it shocked her to realize it.

"I didn't know it would be like this," Carpenter said.

Skadi looked at him and saw his vulnerability. He had acted. He had not thought about it beforehand, had not considered shooting his own bridge crew, but he had responded to the needs of the moment. It wasn't until now that he realized what he had done, and he hadn't been prepared for it, had never considered it.

"You are blessed and cursed," Skadi said, sitting. Something she hadn't planned on doing. She no longer saw her father. She saw a fellow veteran struggling with his conscious. That she could understand.

His eyes locked on her.

"You didn't consider the possibility. If you had, you would have thought about afterward, and you wouldn't have been able to pull the trigger. You acted, you didn't think about the future, you thought about the now."

"What do you mean?" he asked.

"I know I could not kill Vili, or Niels, or Bern. That scared me the most. I know that if they turned and came for me, I would die."

"You've thought about it."

"Yes," Skadi said. "You were blessed enough to not have to consider it, blessed you didn't think about it and could act, cursed because now you know what it cost you."

His eyes fell on her, and she realized that maybe this was the first time he had seen her as something more than his daughter. Someone who had seen and done more than he could imagine.

She saw the questions there. He was a battlestar commander, a great Vanir commander. He had thought he had seen everything; thought he had all the answers. Now she saw past his arrogance. It was a show; it was his armor and, until recently, he had convinced himself of the truth he wanted others to believe. But now he had to face the reality.

"Yet you continue to fight," Carpenter said. "You continue to put yourself in harm's way, walking on the razor's edge."

"It is where I belong." Skadi didn't know what else to say. "I'm one of the best. That is not arrogance, that is experience."

"Why don't you find yourself a husband? Don't you think you have suffered enough?"

"This war will find us wherever we hide," Skadi said. "I will fight, and I will stand in the enemy's path. I will stand where I can do the most damage because that is who I am."

Her father looked at her, his face unreadable, and the silence became uncomfortable.

He leapt to his feet, his sudden motion catching Skadi by surprise, and he walked toward a cabinet and pulled out a bottle and two glasses.

"It is traditional to drink to the fallen," he said. "I do not recall ever raising a glass with my daughter, the Ice Princess."

"Most people who call me that are asked to join me in the fight ring."

Carpenter shrugged and smiled as he poured the two glasses.

"Maybe later," her father said. "You are busy as the second in command of the Alliance and the SOG, but perhaps for an hour or three you can indulge your old man and share a drink."

"*Loki?*" Skadi asked.

"I've got your back," Loki said. *"I'll watch for treachery. Your father needs you."*

"Zen."

"Did I ever tell you I named the *Tyr*?" Carpenter asked.

Skadi didn't remember if he had or not. Probably not. She would have remembered that.

"Yes," Carpenter said, taking a drink with his daughter. "Tyr was the god of justice, and I wanted justice for the SOG's destruction of Asgard. Tyr was known as the god of justice and war."

"I thought the *Tyr* was built before Asgard was destroyed."

"It was, and I named it before the nukes fell on Asgard. We knew what would happen when we built our fleet. We knew the SOG would have no choice, that they wanted to make another example of our home. But they didn't know about our fleet. Once they say Tyr led the gods, but he was supplanted by Odin. Tyr fought for justice and honor, Odin fought for victory and thought nothing of using trickery and guile. I wanted justice more than victory. I was a fool."

Carpenter looked into his drink.

"We knew we couldn't stop them. There was no way. It hurt us to feel that helpless, to know that no matter how big, how dangerous our ships were, we couldn't save our planet. There are too many ways to destroy a habitable planet, and we couldn't make enough ships to defend it."

Skadi knew. An attacker could push asteroids into orbit and accelerate them. An attacker could mass-produce missiles with nuclear or biological warheads. Attackers could also seed a planet's orbit with trillions of objects which would create a destructive shield around a planet. Planets were so big but also so fragile.

"That's how I feel now," Carpenter said. "I have one of the most powerful ships in the galaxy, and I can't save our people. They abandoned us, and we can't find them to save them."

Skadi didn't know what to tell him. Millions of years could pass, and they might not find out what happened to the others. Not even Sif or Jussi could find them in the vastness of space, especially if they were moving or if they were in Shorr space.

"We will find some clue," Carpenter said. "I'm sure. Perhaps at some ghost colony. I don't know."

"Until then we need you here," Skadi said.

"I don't think I can stay here, Daughter. Every time I look at Earth, I think dark thoughts."

"The people of Earth are not the guilty ones."

"But they are. They stood by and watched. They did not rebel, they did not fight. They had to know it was wrong."

"They are afraid, too. They are people. Most of them don't care about other planets, other peoples. They live in their own little world and they were controlled by the Central Committee."

"And Mathison will just replace the Central Committee. Perhaps in the short term he will do the right thing, but he is human. He is a man. The burden of command can grow heavy and eventually you lose sight of what is important."

Skadi didn't want to ask him what that was.

"Robert Silii was a good man," Carpenter said.

"I drink to his honor," Skadi said, raising her glass. Carpenter raised his as well, and they drank.

"Mathison will lose touch with people. He will become a worse despot than Nadya. I feel it."

"You don't know him. His commanding officer wanted to make him an officer, but I know him well enough. I think he understands more than we do. Let me share this with you, Father." It was the first time she had called him father in a very long time. "We are officers. It is our duty to send others into harm's way. The best officers walk a fine line. We must care for our people, but we must be willing to expend them. That is one reason most militaries struggle to keep that distance between officers and enlisted. Most people can't spend the life of a beloved child to win a war or a fight. Officers must do that. As a great amiraali you have forgotten this. Mathison can never forget it."

"I know," Carpenter said. "That is what hurts the most. Mathison is a good man, but he is just a man." Her father raised his glass before she could reply. "To the fallen."

"To the fallen," Skadi said as she raised hers.

She needed a refill, and so did her father.

* * * * *

Chapter Twenty-Eight:
Quantico Command

Commander Zale Stathis, USMC

Stathis hated feeling useless. Shrek provided processing power and analytics to the other SCBIs, but Stathis had little else to do, and the best thing he could do most of the time was not interfere with Shrek's work.

It would be easy to take out his frustration on the Spartans. They were assholes. He could round them up and do a marathon PT session, or maybe a bunch of pointless inspections. There was barracks space in Quantico where he could house them, and some facilities where they could exercise and train, but they needed more than that. He needed more than that.

Shrek remained busy sifting through the data centers, digging into QuanticoNET's secrets. There was no way Stathis could come close to helping with those tasks. The SCBI was a lot more intuitive and capable. If Stathis asked for something to do, it would be like giving a toddler a task to keep him busy, and Stathis didn't want to be that toddler.

Which left Stathis in the same boat as the Peacekeepers, and he had to rely on the lieutenants to keep them busy. They had taken casualties and Stathis wasn't sure how they viewed him because it looked like he had abandoned them. Used them as bait.

218 | WILLIAM S. FRISBEE, JR.

He couldn't avoid them forever, though, and he was getting sick of studying platoon, company, and battalion tactics manuals. After a while, they all seemed the same. Different military forces, slightly different doctrine. Studying battles and logistics was equally mind numbing. To Stathis they seemed so similar to platoon tactics but with minor variations. Always put one element forward, a platoon or company, maybe two if your military was based on elements of four. The Marines revolved around threes. Three fire teams to a squad, three squads to a platoon, three line platoons to a company, three line companies to a battalion. One element, or two, were sent at the enemy while at least one was kept in reserve. One thing that was critical in every battle, every defense, every operation, was the reserve. The more reserves the better. Who sent in their reserves first—and when—frequently decided the battle's outcome. Not always in a good way, because sending in your reserves at the wrong time was a very effective way to lose the battle.

The SOG liked fours or fives, with two forward. The Guards were a bunch of assholes. Their battalions had five companies and used them like a bulldozer. Sending in the first company, then the second when the first stalled, then the third, grinding down the enemy with successive waves of 'fresh' troops.

The ODTs were more like Marines and the Peacekeepers took most of their tactics from the ODTs. The big difference between the two was the drug cocktails they were fed. ODTs were occasionally given some drugs, but the Peacekeepers got the more expensive ones, which made them loyal, dangerous, and stupid. Shrek had found information about the drugs. The Central Committee wanted to use more of the drugs on ODTs, but the process to create them wasn't cheap. Regular performance enhancers sometimes improved mental processes, and that was at odds with loyalty and a person's survival instinct.

Stathis had ended that for the First Peacekeeper Company, the official name for the company that guarded Zvezda Two. It was part of a battalion, but it all felt like a shell game to Stathis, with the actual company being almost a separate unit.

Entering the barracks bunker they were being housed in, one Peacekeeper called them all to attention and Stathis almost did, too, before he realized they were talking about him.

"Carry on," Stathis yelled before they could all get to their feet.

"Sir," said Senior Lieutenant Peskow, standing at attention. Stathis looked around. It looked like a platoon was practicing unarmed combat, and they had some mats out.

Stathis looked at him. Call him sir, or not?

"Commander, the men are getting restless," Peskow said in a low voice. "I think some are undergoing withdrawal from the enhancers."

'Enhancers' was a stupid name for the drugs, probably good for morale though. They were still undergoing withdrawal symptoms? How long was that going to last?

"Keep them exercising," Stathis said, looking around. "It will help them get through it faster. Make them exercise."

"Yes, sir," Peskow said. Stathis saw Lieutenant Elin running the exercises. Must be Anna Platoon.

"This is interesting," Shrek said.

"Porn stash?" Stathis asked.

"No."

"Then I can't imagine it is very interesting."

"Well, it is incoming instructions, routed through a ghost colony."

220 | WILLIAM S. FRISBEE, JR.

"Instruction? A ghost colony?" Stathis tried to think that through. Who would send instructions to Quantico from a ghost colony?

"It is the shell of a message. The contents were heavily encoded. AI-level encryption and encoding, and they were deleted upon receipt. The message header, however, was not."

"And?"

"The message appears to have been sent via tight beam from deep space."

"So, there's a nearby ghost colony?"

"Not likely. However, the message references a ghost colony. Searching the message archives, I see many other references."

"Why do you think it was instructions? Maybe it was some agent reporting in?"

"Not outside the realm of possibilities." Stathis knew when Shrek was saying his ideas were bullshit. *"The size of the data packet could indicate such information, but the reply was very short. The reply was not encrypted. Just a message: 'Acknowledged. Will comply.'"*

"Maybe something to do with that other AI in the president's head?"

"That is a valid theory."

"Did you let Freya and the gunny know?"

"They are getting the data now."

Great. Back to boredom. Maybe he could join the Peacekeepers in their unarmed combat training. They didn't look that tough.

Sloss and his gorillas were in another part of Quantico Base, setting up a relay so Freya and Loki had better access to QuanticoNet. Vili was coordinating with them from Zvezda and was the acting face for the SCBIs dealing with the surviving Americans, which creeped Stathis out.

"How can I help, commander?" Peskow asked, getting Stathis' attention.

"You let your emotions appear on your face," Shrek explained. *"You committed a face crime."*

Face crime? This wasn't the SOG anymore. Though, to be honest, face crimes could get one a bunch of pushups in the Marine Corps. But no one got executed or imprisoned because of them.

What could he tell the senior lieutenant?

"No," Stathis said, turning around and heading back the way he'd come. He didn't belong here. The Peacekeepers were glorified thugs. There were no Marines he could hang out with, and the Aesir were oversized, arrogant gorillas. Vili was okay, but now he was busy and had no time to relax.

What had he been thinking? You don't take thugs and turn them into Marines. That wasn't how it worked.

There were only two other Marines, and they were out of his league.

Returning to his room, he sat down on his bunk. Nobody gave a shit if he made his rack or missed the toilet when pissing. He made it anyway. That was something he could accomplish, a small objective. Pointless in the end, but an accomplishment.

Now he was banished to this museum on a ruined planet that used to be his home. It wasn't his home now. The prime minister had millions of dumb grunts to do his bidding. He didn't need a busted down private. Gunny Mathison needed capable, trustworthy combat leaders, not privates. This title of commander was only temporary, Stathis knew. It wasn't a Marine title. The fact Becket listed him as second lieutenant was cool until he realized it was just a way to circumvent the systems and make sure a Marine had authority at Quantico. President Becket would never do something as stupid as actually promote Stathis.

Maybe he shouldn't have cracked so many old person jokes. It was no wonder the gunny had sent him here.

There were only twenty-six other Americans here in Quantico. Most were Army guys, only about six Delta Force. The rest were medical branch, pilots, some engineers, and two clerks. For a Marine base, it was sadly short of Marines. Which didn't make him feel any better about President Becket being the only Marine who had been here. There were no records about what had happened to any other Marines and speaking to the Army doctor, Linton, didn't provide any clues. He had been part of the original president's staff, and all he knew was that the Marines who had been here when he arrived died fighting meat puppets trying to kill the president.

He had seen schematics, now declassified for him and Shrek, so Quantico didn't hold any secrets. Plenty of bunkers and several tunnels that went west to some mines and more manufactories. Deep geothermal vents and a couple of fusion generators that were sunk pretty deep into the Earth supplied power. There were still plenty of warehouses full of warbots. It was nice to learn that a manufactory had even been churning out Inkeri generators for the warbots, drones, and auto-guns.

Becket hadn't been lying when he said they could hide in Quantico until the end of time. But a museum was a museum, even if it was a fortified museum.

Now Stathis was going to be hidden away here. Sloss and his Jaegers would return to the *Tyr* in the next day or so, which would leave Stathis, the jackboots, and the Army pukes to sit around and play stupid games. He had heard Sloss talking about a new assignment but he hadn't shared details with Stathis.

Already he missed the *Eagle* with the viewscreen walls and ceilings. This felt like an underground bunker. Even Zvezda had a small park and gardens. Hydroponics in Quantico were strictly functional, as much of a joy to walk through as a bright wiring closet.

It made sense for the gunny to banish him here. He needed someone he could trust to watch over Quantico, and it wasn't like he could send Captain Winters here.

"We need to turn this into a fortress," Stathis told Shrek.

"This is a fortress."

"Yeah, but it should be bigger, with more Inkeri generators, d-bomb mines, and shit. When the shit hits the fan, the prime minister and Captain Winters are going to come here."

"The prime minister is tasking some of the American staff to do that," Shrek said.

"Oh." The prime minister didn't even trust him to do that.

"New orders."

"Are there toilets that need cleaning?" Stathis asked, trying not to be bitter.

"You are being recalled to Zvezda. I think the prime minister's toilet is stopped up. Get your Peacekeepers."

"What about defending Quantico?" Stathis asked. Sloss and his team wouldn't be staying. Were they going to abandon the Americans?

"Captain Drake will take care of that," Shrek said, referring to one of the Delta Force guys. A tall thin guy with a mustache that didn't reach the edge of his lips. *"They are also bringing some Defender AIs online."*

"Defender AIs?"

"US Marine AIs designed for the purpose. They were disabled during the AI war. Becket had them repaired but turned off."

"Is that smart?"

"The prime minister's decision. Probably not, but the SCBI quorum thinks they can be monitored safely. They aren't fully sentient AIs."

"SCBI quorum? You mean all the SCBIs are talking to each other and forming a government or something?"

"Something like that," Shrek said, but Stathis wasn't that concerned. The SCBIs wouldn't turn on their hosts. Shrek could be trusted. And if he couldn't? No use worrying about that now. Might as well worry about some killer virus or plague appearing and the sun exploding or the Earth seeking revenge, or Bigfoot.

"So, what does the prime minister really want?"

"Probably to kick your ass for that report you never got to him."

"About socialism? Hell, that was just busy work. He hasn't asked for it lately. I've got it ready, though. I figured he would just banish me here and forget about me."

"I think he still needs you," Shrek said. *"He has a higher opinion of you than you think."*

"Whatever."

The prime minister had given Stathis the dubious rank of commander, a squidbert or Air Force rank. Sure, it was an officer, but it really wasn't a Marine rank. He could be the commander of a toilet cleaning team or a vehicle commander. He was still a private, or a corporal, depending on whichever rank Mathison felt he wanted to bestow.

What could the gunny do? Promote him to team leader? Squad leader? Now he had millions of those. Stathis didn't believe for one minute the gunny was a masochist who wanted him to clean his toilet or anything stupid. The gunny had much more important things to worry about, which could be bad.

What did he need Stathis for when he had so many other flunkies?

* * * * *

Chapter Twenty-Nine:
Delta Troopers

Kapten Sif, VRAEC, Nakija Musta Toiminnot

They weren't in a prison. They were in the Peacekeeper barracks of Zvezda Two, and there were plenty of things for soldiers to do. There were weights, treadmills, and a digital range. The Peacekeepers who had originally been here were now planet side with Stathis, and Aesir from *Sleipner* had taken over. The Aesir and the two Delta Force soldiers kept their distance from each other, and Sif felt everyone's attention focus on her as she entered the cafeteria. Both Robillard and Peshlakai were sitting by themselves in a corner, and the few Aesir eating were on the opposite side. Her eyes locked on them, and she headed toward them, feeling their unease and nervousness as she got closer.

Robillard was a big man, not tall. At first glance, he looked fat, but Sif knew that wasn't the case. Sumo wrestlers were not fat, their muscles were just proportioned differently. He shaved his head like Mathison and was barely taller than Stathis.

Peshlakai was different. Short and thin, he was a Native American with brownish skin and short, jet-black hair. While Robillard looked like he had to shave constantly, Peshlakai looked like he had never shaved in his entire life. His eyes watched her approach, and she felt he was measuring everything, her step, her eye movement, and the way

226 | WILLIAM S. FRISBEE, JR.

her hand rested on her weapon. He watched her as a cautious warrior might. He exuded curiosity, but Robillard was full of mistrust and simmering anger.

She stopped at their table. She didn't use her little girl persona. That wouldn't help, and it wouldn't fool either of them or get them to drop their guard.

"I'm hunting vanhat beyond Sol and I need warriors," Sif said. Might as well get to the point. "Will you take my orders?"

Robillard's reaction was negative, though he didn't show it, but Peshlakai seemed even more curious. Would she have to convince them both? Right now, she would take what she could get.

"Our place is here on Earth," Robillard said. He was a lieutenant according to records, though he had held an assortment of ranks under Becket. Peshlakai had been a staff sergeant when America fell, and like Robillard, he had held many ranks and responsibilities.

Ranks probably meant little to them after so long, which Sif could deal with, but it usually helped military personnel establish their hierarchy. Telling them she was a kapten would not impress them.

"I'm one of the senior members of the new ExSec—" which they should know "—and I am going to be hunting some very specific vanhat, elite warriors who have joined the enemy but did not become mindless creatures."

"Little lady," Robillard said, and Sif could feel his rejection, whether it was because he didn't want to leave Earth or because he looked down on her, she couldn't tell. "Good luck on your hunt. I think Earth needs us more. The galaxy is vast, and I'm sure you could be hunting, even killing, vanhat for hundreds of years, but if we lose Earth, it is over for us."

"I will find others," Sif said, turning her attention away from him. Curiosity and a hunger for adventure came from Peshlakai.

"I am Navajo," Peshlakai said. "I am a hunter and a warrior. Demons are worthy prey. They may outnumber us two, but I would like to see more of the galaxy."

"You will follow this *girl?*" Robillard asked him, poorly concealing his scorn.

"She is a warrior," Peshlakai said, his eyes on Sif. She felt he wanted to size her up, to look her up and down, but he dared not drop his eyes from hers because he thought she might consider his evaluation to be sexual. "Her size does not match her heart. I remember seeing her fight the hell wolves and the dragon. She did not waver. She held her own in those battles. She dared to walk into the maw of the Governance without armor."

"Fearless is stupid," Robillard said. "You know how thin the line is between brave and stupid."

"She is not fearless."

"The mighty Navajo warrior will take commands from a little girl with pony-tails and dimples? A foreign child?"

Sif did not know she had dimples. A figure of speech?

Peshlakai turned his attention to Robillard, and she felt his simmering anger.

"That is what you may see," Peshlakai said. "I have spent too much time here on Earth, hunting in the snow and ash through the dead soulless land. It is time for me to see more of our galaxy. I will fight beside her. I will hunt these demons that walk like men."

Robillard shook his head. "Good luck then."

"Do you think the Marines will trust you here? Do you think you will do anything besides sit here in this spinning bowl without eyes into the world around us? We have been Becket's slaves for too long."

"He can't keep us on the bench forever," Robillard said. "He needs us."

"He can't trust us. We can't trust ourselves."

"What do you mean by that?" Sif asked.

"We have been beholden to Becket for too long," Peshlakai said. "It is hard to explain. It has conditioned us to follow his orders without question, to do our best to anticipate him and his intent. Even now, though we are free of actual SCBI control, we are not free of our psychological conditioning."

Sif looked at Peshlakai, tried to hear his SCBI, to get some measure of them. "Are you a danger to us?"

"I don't know." Peshlakai's doubt was there. Sif couldn't sense a lie, which was a problem. He should be angry or concerned about it. "This will get us further from Becket."

"Becket has left Quantico," Sif said, not sure if she should share this information. "He has left Earth."

"Why?" Robillard asked.

"We don't know," Sif said. The emotions coming from Robillard were confusing, but she knew that if he volunteered now to come, she could not trust him. He looked at Peshlakai.

"You still want to go?"

"I have less desire, but space is vast. We are hunting demons, not our president."

Robillard shrugged, and Sif felt his disappointment as he addressed Peshlakai.

"It isn't safe here in the Sol System, but if you go out there you will become the hunted."

"The hunter or the hunted," Peshlakai said, "I feel this is the right choice for me. I will join you, Sif, if you will have me."

"Thank you," Sif said.

But she needed more.

* * * * *

Chapter Thirty:

2nd Lieutenant Stathis

Prime Minister Wolf Mathison, USMC

His door chimed and reported Stathis and Winters were arriving.

About damned time. He glanced at his schedule. Freya had cleared it for the Marines.

Winters and Stathis marched in like they were on parade. Winters stopped in front of his desk and Stathis stood beside her.

"Captain Winters and Commander Stathis reporting as ordered," Winters said for them.

"At ease and grab chairs," Mathison said, standing. He couldn't tell them not to be formal. Well, maybe he could. He would figure it out later. He missed them, and he was about to miss them more. "I have a mission for you both."

They both sat attentively, and Mathison glanced at Skadi at her desk. She came out from behind her displays and took a chair where she could look at everyone.

"Gunny," Stathis said, "I said I would follow you until you didn't need me anymore. You have an awful lot of obedient troopers to do your bidding now."

"Shut up, Stathis," Mathison said and reached into his desk. He took something out and slid it across the desk. It landed in Stathis' lap.

He glared at Stathis. "I am sick and tired of your bullshit. I don't need privates or lance corporals or corporals or sergeants. Congratulations on your promotion to second lieutenant, Stathis."

Stathis opened the box. It had an eagle globe and anchor on it. Inside were two gold bars. Actual lieutenant bars. Skadi raised an eyebrow at Mathison. He would explain later, or was she questioning his judgment? He couldn't blame her.

"That's official, lieutenant. Now you can run around and get people lost, say stupid shit, and whine about people not saluting you."

"Uh." Stathis looked up. It was gratifying to see Stathis surprised. "I'm not ready to be an officer, Prime Minister. My parents were married and all."

"Lieutenant Stathis," Mathison began patiently, like he would any new young lieutenant, "a year ago, I was a gunnery sergeant frozen in a box. When I climbed into that box to get frozen, I never expected any of this shit. Now I've been shoehorned into this position. You think I'm ready to be a prime minister? You think I want this?"

"You make a good one, gunny," Stathis said.

"Shut up, Lieutenant," Mathison said. "You know that speech I gave you about treating people the way you want them to behave? I want you to be a second lieutenant, run around, do stupid butter-bar stuff, and get ready for first lieutenant, then captain, major, and so on. Heck, maybe one day you can be a commandant of something. I need officers."

"I don't know the first thing about being an officer," Stathis said.

"Your SCBI does. Think of Shrek as your kindly staff sergeant, there to guide you along and keep you from getting everyone lost in a minefield. While he can't kick your ass, he can let Freya know, and I will. If I didn't have faith in you, then I wouldn't promote you."

"Yes, sir," Stathis said, sitting a little straighter.

Mathison waited for Stathis to say something stupid. When he didn't, Mathison looked at Winters. He reached into his desk again slid another box across the desk, which landed in her lap.

"You are now officially a colonel. Which in Naval parlance makes you captain. Command rated, but for the SOG you are still a senior admiral. That is a Marine rank, not a SOG one. It means more."

"Thank you, sir," Winters said, and Mathison was gratified to see her smile.

"I expect you both to grow into your new positions. You also get pay and back pay, courtesy of the Governance for your hundreds of years of service. Your SCBIs will get you details."

Mathison returned his gaze to Stathis.

"Which with private's pay and back pay means you get like a hundred dollars, minus ninety-nine because the tax rate is so high in the Governance. Don't spend that dollar all in one place."

Stathis's eyes lit up as Shrek gave him an idea of how much he really had, though it wasn't like they could spend it. Right now, inflation was tearing Sol apart. Money was nothing more than a promissory note for labor or resources and there were only so many resources to be had. People couldn't eat promissory notes or build homes with them. A person's regular pay of five thousand credits a month sounded like a lot, but when a steak cost four thousand, suddenly that five thousand didn't sound like much.

Mathison didn't want to think about that right now.

"Now about that mission," he said, instantly getting their attention. "I'm sending the two of you because this is important, and I don't think anyone else can handle it. I want you to hunt down Becket. I have to know more."

The two of them should be able to handle Becket, though that third presence was a concern. Two SCBIs against two SCBIs, and his Marines would have a bigger, better ship and more troops, the best he could get them.

"I would like you to bring him back alive. I need information, not body count."

"Is he still the president?" Winters asked, and Mathison realized what a sticky situation this was regarding oaths.

"No," Mathison decided. "He fled. There have been no elections in hundreds of years. He said he fired the nukes that destroyed America. He has not upheld his oath of office. He is a criminal pending a trial."

"Understood, sir," Winters said. Of course, the United States was gone, but that was a path he didn't want to go down right now. Honor was honor, and their oaths did not have expiration dates.

"Based on intercepts found by Stathis and Shrek, he was getting information routed through a place called Zugla, a colony in the middle of nowhere established by some eccentric European billionaire. Not exactly a major hub, but it's a place to start your hunt."

There had been a ship that traveled to and from Zugla. It would transition into the outskirts of the Sol System and send directed laser links to Quantico. Quantico would reply the same way, sending the message out into deep space. How they knew the location of the deep space vessel was a mystery, and the SCBIs assumed that information was in the packets that were received.

"Will you be okay here, Prime Minister?" Stathis asked.

No, he wouldn't be. The people he trusted were leaving, and his enemies seemed to be multiplying.

"I'm short of privates to clean my head," Mathison said. "And there are too many privates around here walking on my grass. I also don't have the time to take anyone on a gentle, puke-inducing run at a leisurely Mach five. You volunteering to stay?"

"No. Sorry, sir," Stathis said. "I've got important second lieutenant stuff to do. I don't think my staff sergeant knows what he's doing, and I need to set Shrek straight now that I know more than he does. I'm a fancy pantsy officer."

Stathis would be Stathis, but the act didn't fool Mathison anymore. Stathis had more experience and knowledge than any second lieutenant Mathison had known. He might be short on some of the leadership and tactics classes, but hopefully Shrek could help fill in those gaps. A demotion was on the table as well as a promotion. Mathison had considered making Stathis a first lieutenant or something, but the young man needed a more natural progression.

The challenge would put him in charge of a combat team and make sure he had the authority to deal with any SOG officers. As far as Mathison was concerned, Stathis outranked every SOG officer in existence, as did Winters, but he didn't want to give them too much, too soon. They both needed to grow into things first.

"Your SCBIs will have details. As soon as you have a team assembled, I want you out there hunting."

"Aye, sir," they echoed.

"Congratulations to you both," Skadi said.

"Thank you," they echoed, neither one looking ready for their new rank.

"Stathis," Mathison said, looking at him. "I've got the SCBIs combing through SOG records using personality analysis and assessment to get you a fighting platoon. Mostly ODTs, a few Peacekeepers.

I want them organized and trained as Marines. I want a new branch, a new cadre of people I can trust."

"Can I call them Spartans?" Stathis asked.

"Why not Marines?"

"No boot camp, sir. They can't earn the title without boot camp."

"Fine," Mathison said, hoping he wouldn't regret it. He was going to have to trust Stathis and let him do his own thing. "Don't make me regret anything."

"Aye, Gunny—uh, Prime Minister," Stathis said.

"Why Spartan?" Mathison asked.

"Three hundred?" Stathis said. "They were badass, Gunny. Holding the line and kicking Persian ass. They were the ultimate warriors of the time."

"Fine," Mathison said. Nobody around here called him gunny anymore, and that irritated him. He had earned that title with sweat, blood, and tears. The title of 'Prime Minister' felt so damned pretentious.

"Any questions?" Mathison asked them.

They both knew their SCBIs would have more information, and they would have to absorb it all before they had relevant questions.

"Do you know where I can get some bagpipes, Prime Minister?" Stathis asked. Prime minister now.

"I've got something for you, Second Lieutenant Stathis." Mathison reached into his desk for two more items. He slid them across his desk, and Stathis grabbed them.

An old-style compass and a map. Mathison had had them made special.

Looking at them, Stathis looked up at Mathison. He got it.

"Oh. That's cold, Gunny, very cold."

"Yep. Now, get out of here. I have a meeting with some stuck-up SOG managers in a few minutes."

"Aye, sir," they both said. They stood, came to attention, and marched out.

Good Marines, both of them.

"I don't understand the map and compass," Skadi asked.

"New lieutenants have a reputation in the Marines," Mathison said. "It is my way of telling him to go get lost."

"Why would you tell him to get lost? How can he get lost with a SCBI?"

"Yeah, well," Mathison said. "Raiders got training with a map and compass. Sure, we had GPS and all the cool toys, but nothing beats using the human brain to solve problems. The old school map and compass was a traditional method that helped reinforce reasoning skills that did not rely on technology, so it was a critical part of Marine training. Second lieutenants, being new, have a well-deserved reputation for getting their people lost. Land nav isn't as easy as people like to think. Sounds simple in the classroom but when boots hit the ground and you leave the classroom, everything changes. Young lieutenants are full of themselves, believing their book smarts are important and that that extra knowledge sets them apart from the men under their command. Map reading and land navigation is a great way to teach them the reality that the classroom only covers the basics, and nothing beats experience."

"Do you think Stathis will understand that lesson?"

"Yeah," Mathison said. "He's had several lieutenants in his career. I'm sure he's seen good ones and bad ones. He's going to be one of the good ones, I'm sure. Just gotta make sure it doesn't go to his head. I always liked the mustang lieutenants, the ones that were enlisted before they became officers. They had experience and built on that with book knowledge. Most lieutenants start with book knowledge and build on that with experience. Shrek and Winters will keep him in line. Of course, mustangs wanted to be officers. I'm not sure of Stathis, but he doesn't get a choice in this."

"Zen," Skadi said. "Can we just kill these managers and deal with their replacements? That Clayton individual and his other two fellow directors annoy me. His policy is to ask for a hundred percent more than he needs so he can skim."

"He's going to learn that won't work," Mathison said. "We need to change the system and the people. Killing people is satisfying, but it won't help in the long run."

He knew she wasn't serious about killing them, but it would solve a lot of problems. Killing the incompetent ones until you found someone competent looked good on paper, but sometimes it took a person time to become competent.

* * * * *

Chapter Thirty-One:
New Command

2nd Lieutenant Zale Stathis, USMC

Stathis looked at the roster. Had his lieutenants cared this much about their platoons? Had they spent hours going through records memorizing details, trying to get a feel for the people before he actually met them? Had his lieutenants been this nervous or had they been arrogant pricks who looked down on their people? Most had probably been nervous and only a few had hidden it well enough that the senior privates and enlisted couldn't see it.

It was a mixed bag of Peacekeepers and regular ODTs. Everyone in his new platoon was a veteran with skill in all the things the SOG cared about. Marksmanship, unarmed combat, obedience. Well, obedience was one area they tended to be less than stellar in based on the black marks in their record, and Stathis wondered if this was Mathison's attempt to get back at him. Most of the platoon was experienced, but most of them had been demoted at least once or had black marks in their record because it listed them as "too independent" or "not socially reliable." Socialist rejects. A few Peacekeeper privates had been on the verge of getting sent back to the ODTs because of their social "unreliability." Stathis wasn't exactly sure what that meant.

He only had a few weeks to get them into shape and formed into a combat team. An impossible task, to be sure. The *Eagle* was undergoing some refits. Stathis wasn't sure about the details, but that was Winters' problem. Stathis would have his hands full with his Spartans.

They were being assembled at Sereda Base, an ODT facility where General Ting Hui was working. She met him and escorted him to the barracks where his people were being assembled, which was daunting. Generals escorting lieutenants? When he had met her in her office, he had expected her to pawn him off on a subordinate, not escort him personally.

Walking in, the room was called to attention as Stathis followed the general.

She marched to the front of the room, stood before the viewscreen, and looked out at the assembled troops doing their best to stand at attention, head and eyes forward, unmoving as they tried to size up the general with Stathis at her side.

Stathis couldn't see their eyes on him, but he knew their attention was focused on him, and he realized he hadn't prepared a speech. What was he supposed to say or do? His first introduction to his command, and he didn't know what to tell them. Was that why lieutenants rambled on when they were introduced, saying the dumbest shit? Great. That was a tradition Stathis had wanted to avoid, and by avoiding it that meant he had not given it any thought.

"Platoon," Hui said, looking around, "listen to my command."

On the word command, everyone's eyes snapped to look at her. She seemed confident. She probably did this all the time. Commanding troops was probably second nature to her. Was she even capable of getting nervous anymore? She was slightly taller than Stathis. Was he going to become the brunt of his command's short-people jokes?

"My orders are this. You are being assigned to a new type of experimental unit," Hui said, looking around and meeting everyone's eyes. "With me is your new commander. A proven and highly decorated warrior of proven skill, valor, and dedication. He is a hero of the people many times over. I have seen this with my own eyes. He is one of the prime minister's most trusted advisors and warriors. He is to be obeyed without question or hesitation. I have specially chosen each of you, and you will form an elite cadre and be assigned the most critical missions."

Stathis noted she had their full and undivided attention. He wondered if this was because they were that good at hiding their real feelings, or if they were really believed her. How the hell was he going to follow that?

"Shrek?" Stathis thought, his mind drawing a blank as he tried to remember what speeches new lieutenants had given that he had appreciated. *"What kind of speech should I give?"*

"Good luck," Shrek said. *"You should have thought of this before."*

"Why didn't you warn or advise me?"

"Do you want me to remind you to wipe your ass, too?"

"This is different."

"Sure it is," Shrek said, and Stathis could have sworn there was a smirk in Shrek's words. *"You are going to do what you always do."*

"Say stupid shit and screw up?"

"You have your talents. Embrace them."

Looking out at the troops, they looked a lot older. Of course, at twenty-two years old, Stathis remembered there were second lieutenants his age. What would they know?

They weren't Marines, certainly not Raiders.

242 | WILLIAM S. FRISBEE, JR.

General Hui looked at everyone ,and Stathis wondered if this was a cue to start the speech he hadn't figured out yet.

"Execute!" Hui said.

"Hurrah, Hurrah, Hurrah!" the troopers yelled. They sounded motivated.

"You may now take command of your unit," Hui said, looking at Stathis.

"Thank you, General," Stathis said and stepped forward. All the eyes fell on him, and he felt the weight.

What would the gunny say?

"Listen up," Stathis almost added mongoloids, but officers didn't say stuff like that, did they? "It is simple: don't add to the population, don't subtract from the population without orders, don't get thrown in jail, and if you do, establish dominance quickly."

Shit. That was a safety brief. So much for not being stupid. He saw some smiles. Time to ad lib and build on it.

"Beyond that, this is going to be a new combat group. Elite. You report to me, I report to the prime minister. You were all specially selected." Stathis didn't know how or why though, but he could bullshit with the best. "Out of hundreds of thousands, you were selected because I don't want mindless, obedient drones. I want thinking warriors."

He remembered they had been selected because they seemed to resist the indoctrination. They could probably smell bullshit a mile away.

"You aren't here to make me look good. You are here to accomplish the mission. Understood?"

"Hurrah, Hurrah, Hurrah!" they yelled with slightly less enthusiasm than they had for the general. They were probably laughing inside.

"No more of that hurrah bullshit," Stathis said. "I wasn't ODT or Guard. Now, neither are you. You are some of the first Spartans. We are going to adopt United States Marine terms and slang. Many of these traditions come from our waterborne taxi service, the Navy. Instead of hurrah, I want to hear 'aye, sir.' Understood?"

"Aye, sir," they yelled, and Stathis winced. Worse than raw recruits.

"Understood?"

"Aye sir," they yelled a bit louder.

"Shit," Stathis said and looked at General Hui whose face showed no emotion. "Were they recruited from the Guard or a boys' choir?"

He looked back at them and gave them his best drill instructor yell. "*Understood?*"

"Aye, sir!" they yelled back at him. It could have been better.

"How many of you know anything about this facility?"

Silence.

"None of you know about Sereda, the guy they named this place after?" Stathis asked. He had queried Shrek on their way here, wondering what kind of name it was. The SOG liked to name ships and bases after dead heroes.

Blank faces looked at him.

"Ivan Sereda was a Red Army soldier. That crazy son of a bitch attacked two Nazi tanks with an axe. You know what a tank is, right?"

Several nodded, but Stathis wasn't sure. He wasn't going to explain it.

"Ivan was a freaking cook. When the Red Army cooks saw a tank coming they fled into the woods. Ivan hid in the kitchen. The dude was a cook, not a grunt. The Nazis stopped and got out of their tank to get some chow, and he ran out at them with his axe. The Germans fired their machine gun, but ole Ivan got up on the tank, bent the

244 | WILLIAM S. FRISBEE, JR.

barrel, and threw a cloth over the viewing slots. Then that crazy bastard started screaming for his buddies to get the grenades. He didn't have any buddies, and they didn't have any grenades, but the Nazis didn't know that, and they surrendered. He made them tie each other up. His burger flipping buddies came back to find ol' Ivan had captured four tankers."

Several of the troopers nodded in appreciation.

Even the general nodded and looked curious.

Now, where was he going with this story? Shit.

Stathis had to think fast to make it relevant.

"Here's the thing," Stathis said, getting an idea. "All the other cooks knew they didn't stand a chance against a tank. C'mon, a soup spoon isn't going to discourage a machine gun, but not ol' Ivan. He was a thinker, and he wanted to kick Nazi ass, so he used the tools he had. How badass do you think he would have been if he was an ODT or Peacekeeper? He went on to become a platoon commander, then company commander, a certified badass. Not bad for a cook, huh?"

The troopers nodded.

"You guys aren't cooks," Stathis said. "You guys are badasses, specially selected for an elite unit. You are no longer ODTs, no longer Peacekeepers. You are Spartans, my Spartans, and we are going to do some epic shit together. Understood?"

"Aye, sir!" they yelled, sounding more motivated. He heard one assclown begin with "hurrah" but he figured it out quick enough.

"We will not screw around with commissars and shit. Like I said, a new unit. We report directly to the prime minster. I don't expect you to make me look good, but if you make me look bad, I'll string you up by balls and send you off to be cooks."

A quick glance at the general showed Stathis she probably did not approve of something he'd said. Too bad.

"You will get your orders soon. We have a mission. Nothing like hitting the ground running. You will be broken up into three squads. Each squad will have three fireteams and a squad leader."

Shrek released their orders and he saw their eyes flicker as a notification appeared in their cybernetic vision.

"Now," Stathis said. "Get out of here. You have shit to do. Aten-hut!"

They snapped to attention.

"Dismissed," Stathis yelled, and the room exploded as they rushed toward the exit. In seconds he was alone with the general.

"That was unorthodox," the general said.

"Yes, ma'am," Stathis said. It was probably unorthodox for Marines, too. Shrek was monitoring them and would send them orders appropriately. They had to pack their gear and transfer to the *Eagle*. He didn't want to, but General Hui had more experience than him at command. He really should listen to her. As a lieutenant, he couldn't keep the attitude of an obnoxious private. He had to learn and grow, or the gunny would put him down to cook, or more likely be a professional toilet cleaner.

"You realize they all have a low socialization score?" Hui said. "Most have been to ideological reassessment camps several times. They are socially unreliable and fight a lot with their comrades."

"Have you heard of General Chesty Puller, ma'am?" Stathis asked.

"No."

"One time the general said 'take me to the brig. I want to see the real Marines.'"

"I don't understand," Hui said.

"Marines are troublemakers, ma'am," Stathis said. "They like to fight. They aren't what you would call 'polite company.' That's what the prime minister wants."

"This is a mistake," Hui said. "If he wants brutal murderers, there is a different classification within the ODTs for such individuals."

"No, ma'am," Stathis said. "I think I know why the prime minister chose them. We don't want thugs and bullies. We want people who think for themselves. There was another general, named Al Gray, was a big fan of maneuver warfare and—"

"Are all Marine privates so well-educated on such topics?"

"Um," Stathis said. No, but he had spent a lot of time aboard the *Eagle* bored out of his mind, with nothing besides Marine manuals, history, and doctrine to keep him occupied. It wasn't like Shrek kept his buffers full of porn and games. The SCBI had some pretty twisted priorities about what to keep in the memory buffers. "Marines are a different breed, ma'am."

"I see," the general said. "Well. I wish you luck. I look forward to seeing the kind of unit they become."

"Aye, ma'am," Stathis said. Now he had to get them situated aboard the *Eagle* and start teaching them Marine tactics. They were all veterans though, so hopefully they would adjust.

Hopefully.

While the ODTs had centuries of experience to draw on, Stathis was going to do things the Marine way. Sometimes tradition was more important, and Stathis was a Marine. The challenge would be transferring that knowledge to new troops.

* * * * *

Chapter Thirty-Two: The *Eagle*

2nd Lieutenant Zale Stathis, USMC

Stathis felt a lot better aboard the *Eagle*. It was familiar territory. He had never been so glad to see the glass walls revealing a mountain and a sunset before. Shrek was monitoring the Spartans and getting them situated. Stathis was tempted to watch them on cameras or to show up in person, but that would be too much like micromanaging, and there wasn't a damn thing he could do except continue to make a fool of himself.

"That was a bad speech," Stathis said to Shrek, seeking some feedback.

"It could have been worse," Shrek said, not providing him with any information.

"Was it that bad?"

"I'm not one to judge. The Spartans took it in stride. As usual, some thought it silly, some humorous, some are confused, and some resentful. A mixed bag. I think perhaps you impressed the general with your ability to bullshit and learn about the Governance."

Stathis wasn't sure what to say about that. He expected a notification from the gunny any minute informing him the gunny was displeased. Though, why would the prime minister care? He had more important prime minister things to do.

"I would recommend meeting with your platoon sergeant and squad leaders," Shrek said. *"Establish dominance quickly."*

Stathis winced. That was one joke they probably hadn't gotten. He wasn't going to be their bitch under any circumstances. He was a Marine and they were ODT and Peacekeeper rejects, though perhaps rejects wasn't a term he should use.

But was that such a bad thing? Isn't that what made all the movies great? Some badass taking a bunch of rejects and forging them into an elite military unit?

"See if you can find and download any movies about military units composed of rejects," Stathis told Shrek. *"For research."*

"There is a lot of data in QuanticoNet. However, Hollywood is a horrible source for good ideas. You would be better served rooting through a sewer for gems of wisdom."

"Whatever. Set me up a meeting with the leaders."

"In ten minutes, conference room Berrta," Shrek said.

Damn. He was hoping for a bit more time.

* * *

Someone called the room to attention as Stathis entered, and he almost froze again before he realized it was for him. This was going to take some getting used to.

"Carry on," Stathis said before they could all get to their feet.

His eyes swept the room, and he picked out the chair near the end, in the back, but that wasn't where he belonged. Shrek put a holographic overlay over the chair at the head of the table, showing that was where Stathis should go.

"I'm not an idiot," Stathis said, making his way there.

"You are a second lieutenant," Shrek said. *"Second lieutenant is a synonym for idiot. As a private, you understood this. As a lieutenant you have forgotten this."*

Sitting down, Stathis looked at the four troopers staring at him.

They were all privates, having been busted down in the ODTs or Peacekeepers. Now they were all in ODT uniforms, which didn't make Stathis uncomfortable anymore. Shrek displayed their data above their head for him.

Dmitri Smimova, the new platoon sergeant, looked like an asshole. A grizzled older man, Smimova had his hair cut to the scalp and a scar reached from his forehead to his lip. His hard gray eyes stared at Stathis as if contemplating where to stick the knife. The big man probably didn't know how to smile. Smimova had been a Peacekeeper for about six years and an ODT trooper for nearly ten. He had an extensive combat record and had risen to the rank of platoon sergeant before being transferred to the Peacekeepers, where he was demoted to private and never rose above that rank.

Dingbang Lan was of Chinese descent and was first squad leader. Like Smimova, Lan had his hair cut to the scalp, like a six o' clock shadow on his skull. He had a hard to read emotionless face after spending so much time trying to avoid committing face crimes. He was pure ODT and had served close to fourteen years. The man had been a squad leader twice and had clawed his way back up twice after being busted to private. He had almost been executed for scowling at a commissar. Stathis would have to read the details later.

Chang Tan was also of Chinese heritage, though taller and thinner than Lan. His hair was longer, but not so long he could comb it. He looked to be almost the opposite of Lan in size and appearance, as far as that was possible. With a broad, humorless face, Tan blinked little.

Another Peacekeeper reject, Tan had spent only three years with the Peacekeepers before they sent him back to the ODTs for social unreliability. He was second squad leader.

Sacha Ortoff was the squad leader for third squad. He was pure ODT and had been a squad leader before. A tall blond-haired man, Ortoff looked like he could smile, but there was no sign of one now.

"You are my command team," Stathis said. "My platoon sergeant and squad leaders. I'm going to lean on you. This isn't the ODTs or Peacekeepers. I'm going to expect a lot more from you than they ever did. I'm your platoon commander, but I'm not your mommy. It is your job to carry out my orders and take care of your troops."

Stathis looked at them. How did the ODTs work? He remembered reading that their NCOs had little power and authority, not like the US Military. The officers were the backbone of the ODTs, and NCOs were nothing more than glorified privates. How did that work? It was one thing to read that, but in reality?

"Think of yourselves as officers. I'm going to hold you personally responsible for any screw ups. Shit rolls downhill, and I'm going to expect more from you than you are used to. You are all experienced veterans, and I will not micromanage you." Hopefully. "I'm sending you some tactics manuals." Which were USMC manuals with "Marine" stripped out and replaced with "Spartan." "You need to become familiar with them. This is a Spartan platoon. We will work differently than ODTs or Peacekeepers."

Looking at them, Stathis knew he had his work cut out for him. A real second lieutenant would have experienced platoon sergeants and squad leaders and wouldn't have to train them. Shit. Stathis *was* a real second lieutenant, and this wasn't a game. This was damned stupid. What was the gunny thinking? Putting a private in charge of veterans like this? He could go back to the prime minister and ask for his old private position back, and getting busted back to private wasn't an option either. There was no way he could get the gunny's morning cup of coffee.

"Every day we are going to spend at least two hours gaming out scenarios," Stathis said, trying to think back to what his favorite lieutenants had done. "For these sessions we are going to sit around a sand table and play a game. I'm going to throw you and your people into a situation, and we're going to figure out what we are all thinking and accomplish our mission. This will allow you to become more familiar with how I think and what I want. Furthermore, I will give each of you scenarios to game out with your squads and teams. I expect you to do the same thing with them."

Maybe he and Shrek could use that cybernet video game *Battle Command* for a sand table.

Stathis looked at each of them. Emotionless rocks. No face crimes here.

"If I ever walk into the barracks and see people sitting around, I'm probably going to go ballistic and flip my lid. I won't yell and scream, though, not in front of the men. I will just call you aside and thrash your ass. Fuck up too much, and I will replace you, send you back to some ideological reassessment camp."

Maybe that was too harsh?

"Expect a lot of changes. I'm probably going to do a lot of things you aren't used to." Stathis locked his eyes on Smimova. "Thoughts?"

"We will serve the greater good to the best of our abilities and will not fail you. We stand ready to give our lives for the Governance."

Stathis tried not to roll his eyes. "Oh, bullshit. Take that political ass-kissing shit and shove it up your ass. You don't have my

252 | WILLIAM S. FRISBEE, JR.

permission to die or give your lives. That isn't your job. Your job is to make others die." Stathis didn't want to say "for the Governance." "We will be fighting other people and possibly vanhat. I don't want dead troopers. Losing people will make me look bad, and do you remember what I said about that?"

"Yes, sir," Smimova said.

"Yeah," Stathis continued. "Don't make me look bad. You aren't here to make me look good, to kiss my ass, or to make me happy. You are here to do a job and that involves extreme and very unpleasant violence committed on our enemies. Make them die. You die without my permission, and I will thrash your ass when we meet up in Hell."

Looking at each of them, Stathis continued. "When I ask your opinion, I mean it. If I say something stupid, you tell me, privately. I'll say stupid shit to test you. You're all veterans; if you weren't trusted you wouldn't be here. If I ask your opinion, I mean it. No commissars, no face crimes, no word crimes, no ass kissing. You are all being promoted to a rank more suitable to your billet. The people in your squad are being promoted to one rank below what their billet should be. I expect you to evaluate them and tell me if they are in the right place. You want to play musical team leaders and team members, do that. Smimova has to approve it and acts as referee and will let me know. I want you to have squads you are happy with. We are going into battle. You'd better be ready, and we don't have much time to prepare. Mix and match to your heart's content. When we go operational, that shit ends."

Stathis looked at them. Was that how new lieutenants did it?

No. New lieutenants usually had a platoon with an established pecking order where everyone knew their place, had seniority and shit. Not a mob of antisocial strangers thrown together.

Boot lieutenants had more training on leadership, and they usually had a solid, reliable staff NCO to keep them from screwing up too badly. They were also usually kept closer to a senior officer who could mentor them.

Stathis had a bunch of social rejects with some intense killing skills. His next senior officer was a warrant officer, a specialist, who was still figuring out her own job. When the *Eagle* left Earth, it would just be the two of them.

"Understood?" Stathis asked.

"Aye, sir," they said, not quite yelling.

"Squad leaders, see to your squads. Smirnova, a moment."

The three squad leaders wasted no time escaping.

Stathis looked at Smirnova, and the gunny's words came back to him. Treat them the way you want them to act.

"You are my executive officer. I'm going to rely on you to keep the men in line and to back me up. You let me know if I'm screwing up. This is new to me. Can I rely on you?"

"Yes, sir," Smirnova said, and Stathis searched his face looking for more emotion. There wasn't any.

"What do you think of the men?" Stathis asked.

"They are excellent men that will serve the Governance as—"

Stathis slapped both his hands on the table, startling the staff sergeant, and leaned forward aggressively.

"Do not give me any of that political shit," Stathis said with more vehemence than he had planned. "Will they serve us or are we getting ready to put on a shit show?"

A flicker of anger flashed across Smirnova's face.

"Few of them know each other," Smirnova said, his voice carefully neutral. "This will not become a tight combat team overnight. I looked

254 | WILLIAM S. FRISBEE, JR.

over your manuals, and while I think they are do-able, they are not normal."

"Our manuals come from the US Marines."

"An obsolete and abolished military organization."

Stathis smiled at the rebuke. Perhaps he should be pissed, but this was a good start. Smimova couldn't be afraid to speak his mind. His eyes widened ever so slightly the second he said them, and Stathis knew he had poked the bear about something.

"I'm standing before you," Stathis said. "I'm a US Marine. Not obsolete or abolished."

"The United States was destroyed, sir," Smimova said, and Stathis realized he knew nothing about the Marines, and there was no way Smimova could verify that Stathis was what he said he was.

"It is a long story, Staff Sergeant," Stathis said. "But I *am* a United States Marine, and I'm not the only one."

"There are rumors," Smimova began, "that there were some Marines recovered from stasis and some Americans from a secret colony on the North American continent."

"I'm one of the ones from stasis," Stathis said, wondering how the rumors got around. He wasn't going to tell Smimova that he had been a private not long ago.

"It is unusual for an ODT general to introduce a lieutenant," Smimova said.

"I'm building a new unit," Stathis said. "I've fought beside General Hui."

"Against the vanhat?"

"Yep. Perhaps later I will share those stories with you. For now, though, I need you to consider yourself my second in command, and when you speak, it will be with my authority. Don't make me regret it because then the prime minister will learn your name, and he can be a real asshole sometimes."

Smimova's eyes narrowed as they took in Stathis. Was he thinking he could use his words against his new lieutenant? That would be almost comical.

"The prime minister and I go way back," Stathis said. "We're drinking buddies." If you could count sitting at a table and having a drink in his presence "drinking buddies." The gunny had been super non-plussed when Stathis had brought it up aboard *Midgard* in the Ice Pick bar, or something like that. The gunny wouldn't make Stathis look like a fool in front of his men, would he?

"Now," Stathis said. "I need you to get the platoon ready for some serious shit. During our trip we are going to make some changes to armor and weapons, but that's for later. Right now, I want everyone ready and training together. I want lots of PT. If people aren't doing sand table exercises or training, they'd better be exercising or preparing their gear. Understood?"

"Yes sir," Smimova said, standing at attention.

"Save the attention bullshit for when other people are around. I'm not some stuck-up prick of an officer like you're used to."

"Aye, sir," Smimova said as Stathis stood.

"Dismissed," Stathis said when Smimova didn't immediately leave. At this, the new platoon sergeant finally turned around and marched out like he had a stick up his ass.

How the hell was he going to Smimova to loosen up? Wasn't it the staff NCO trying to get the lieutenant to chill?

* * * * *

Chapter Thirty-Three:
Hakala

2nd Lieutenant Zale Stathis, USMC

Now that he was a lieutenant, Stathis wondered if the chief would be meaner or nicer to him. Now she was a colonel with eagles on her collar, many steps above a mere second lieutenant. She was now "command rated" which meant she really did out rank him. Not that he would ever have challenged her authority before. Back in the Marines, the theory was that a second lieutenant outranked a mere chief warrant officer. Only a real stupid second lieutenant believed that. As a full bird colonel, though, it wasn't an issue.

He requested permission to enter the bridge, it was granted, and the door slid open.

Colonel Winters turned to him and smiled, and Stathis felt like a private again.

"Hello, ma'am," Stathis said, wondering why he was here now. It was habit. The gunny, chief, and sergeant had seemed to spend most of their time here, and if he had wanted to find out what was going on, that meant following the gunny around. He had come here out of habit.

258 | WILLIAM S. FRISBEE, JR.

"Hello, Lieutenant," Winters said. Stathis saw several others on the bridge, including the Republic eversti named Brita Mani, a cute but serious Vanir officer. "What brings you here?"

Shit. Stathis thought fast. "Ma'am, I thought it would be best to check in with the captain, let her know I'm here and that my troops are getting situated." Stathis realized how stupid that was. The SCBIs would have coordinated and let her know.

She obviously saw through his bullshit.

"Thank you, Lieutenant," she said. "How is everything?"

"Fine, ma'am."

Had anything really changed?

"You are welcome on the bridge anytime," Winters said.

Stathis noticed a pair of HKTs nearby along with a pair of Vanir officers he didn't know.

"Is everything okay?" Stathis asked, glancing at the HKTs who were fully armed and armored, sitting on opposite sides of the bridge. Stathis didn't go anywhere unarmed or unarmored these days. Armed troops with Inkeris on their hips were a comfort.

"Yes. The kontra-amiraali has been gracious enough to provide additional crew, all volunteers, to help operate the *Eagle*."

"In exchange for what?" was a question Stathis would have to save for later. The Vanir were better than the SOG. But HKTs? They had brutalized her. Was she okay with them on her ship now? Stathis didn't have a problem with them, but it surprised him that Winters didn't.

"Excellent news," Stathis said. It was the polite thing to say, anyway.

He looked around. The *Eagle* was in a SOG hangar on the Moon. Robots were moving around, delivering supplies and doing other robot things.

The presence of the HKTs made a lot more sense.

One of the HKTs raised her visor and winked at Stathis.

Hakala? She was here? On duty on the bridge? She was really cool, and Stathis tried not to let his imagination, or fantasies, distract him. He had been so damned busy lately she had just been something for his dreams and fantasies.

He winked back. It was the polite thing to do right? He felt like an idiot doing it, though. Winters had to have seen him.

"If there is anything you need, Lieutenant, let me know."

"Aye, ma'am."

"Anything I can help with, at any rate," Winters said. She *had* seen, and Stathis felt his face get warm.

Looking back, Stathis saw Hakala had her visor back down. He recalled *"A Marine on duty has no friends."* Were the HKT's like that? Would she be on the ship when it left on its mission?

The captain had dismissed him, and Stathis couldn't think of a reason to stay. Was she now mad at him and Hakala? He would just be in the way, and it wasn't like he could wander over and talk with Hakala. Knowing she was this close, and she had winked at him, that was super cool.

He wondered how he could get some free time. Was there a bar or club he could invite her to? Shit. Where would he find time for that? He was quickly learning that lieutenants didn't get free time. How did officers manage having wives and shit?

* * * * *

Chapter Thirty-Four:
Vili

Lojtnant Skadi, VRAEC

A report arrived in her queue. Feng had arrested several administrators who had tried to sell Fleet Inkeri generators to the African arcology. Which wasn't a problem, except they had taken them from Fleet ships and every Fleet ship needed a minimum of two, not one. The vanhat could launch an attack at any minute, and every ship had to have a primary and backup.

The misappropriated Inkeris were being sent back to the Fleet, and InSec was arresting the others involved. Feng was making an example of them and seemed to be taking a lot of pleasure hunting down such individuals. Feng had less tolerance for corruption than anyone Skadi knew.

"Huh," Mathison said.

"What?" Skadi asked.

"Feng and Mozi are cutting a swath through the Governance," he said. "I wonder if he is going to leave anyone left to run things."

"The Inkeris and the African arcology?"

"Yeah," Mathison said, shaking his head and rubbing his eyes. "The head of internal security having an SCBI is a scary thing."

"He is on our side, though," Skadi said, not sure how much she believed it.

"For now."

"You doubt his loyalty? He seems to have a fetish about persecuting graft and corruption."

"I think it's great," Mathison said, pushing back his chair. It was getting late. "But what happens when he runs out of obvious targets? What happens when he can't find anyone guilty of crimes?"

"What are you getting at?"

"History. Just thinking about what happens when you run out of enemies; you find new ones. Fanatics are like that."

"You think he might turn on us?"

"No clue. Feng is a mystery man to me, and I'm tired. I was a Marine gunnery sergeant in a Raider battalion. I was never cut out for this administrative, pencil-pushing bullshit. I should be out there enforcing policy, knocking in teeth, kicking ass and taking names, not making policy. Hell, I'm hardly doing that. I'm just trying to give us a fighting chance. The vanhat are going to hit us, and it won't be pretty."

"One step at a time."

"It doesn't help that administrators and managers are sabotaging shit because they don't believe the vanhat threat is that serious."

He was right. The main reason the administrators had sought to sell the Inkeris to the African arcology was because they figured one was enough, and the arcology administrators were desperate. They had experienced several new incursions in the last couple days, incursions that had required a Guard response and at least one d-bomb strike.

Somehow, the vanhat were getting into the Sol System. In very small numbers, but unchecked, those numbers would grow fast. Skadi understood the arcology administrators' concerns. It was getting worse, but few people actually believed the larger danger, or they were selfish. They were so used to being lied to and manipulated. The

Governance had cried wolf too many times, and now nobody believed the official news sources. They probably hadn't for over a century. People were conditioned to believe the lies publicly, but privately was a different story. Mathison didn't know how he could restore their trust. It caused them to believe only what they said personally and even that was questionable.

"Am I doing the right thing?" Mathison asked, and Skadi tried to think if there was something specific.

"Stathis and Winters?" Skadi guessed. What would bother him the most?

"Yeah," Mathison said.

"We need to track down Becket and find out what he's up to."

"Yeah, but Becket was a major in command of special operations platoons. As he got promoted I'm sure he learned more, and as president? If he's against us, he will be very formidable. I'm sure he has much more knowledge, not just experience."

"You have doubts about Stathis?"

"Stathis is a damned good Marine. One on one, I don't think Becket would stand a chance, but it won't be a standup fight. Becket is a master of tactics. Hell, he named his SCBI after one of the most famous tacticians in human history. If he has to fight Stathis, it will be on his terms, and while Stathis is a pit fighter, he isn't exactly that level of tactician."

"You don't think Becket will oppose the third AI to give Stathis a chance?"

"No. Becket doesn't want to die. He might not want to kill a fellow Marine, but he might not have a choice. Hell, I want Stathis to become more than just an annoying private, but I'm thinking this might be too much for him."

"I can ask Vili to watch over him," Skadi said. Was that wise? Here, Vili was safe. Stathis was going into the lion's den. She didn't want to lose Vili, but as she thought about it, he would be perfect. A veteran Erikoisjoukot, he had trained thousands, maybe hundreds of thousands, of rebels and knew the SOG mentality. He had plenty of experience with ghost colonies and the people who lived in the shadows of the SOG.

"Stathis needs to know I trust him," Mathison said.

"Vili can join them to help train the Spartans. He could do that in his sleep. We spend a lot of our time training locals. There's a planet called Lisbon where we helped build up an entire army to fight the SOG."

"What happened at Lisbon?"

"The SOG showed up and bombed the planet back into the ice age. They murdered everyone. It was bad."

Thinking about that, Skadi wondered if any members of the SOG Home Fleet had taken part. She had full access to SOG records, and she could track down the bastards that had ordered it. They were probably here somewhere.

But killing them now would leave humanity with fewer bodies to oppose the vanhat.

"Are you okay with that?"

"No," Skadi said. She would be honest with him. Vili was doing an excellent job here and his SCBI was one more AI combing through the SOG systems, fixing things, helping to prepare Sol for the inevitable invasion.

"Then keep him—"

"No. He hates it here, maybe as much as you do, and Stathis needs him. He will keep Stathis safe, and Stathis will keep him safe."

Mathison looked ready to argue.

"Honestly. Please. I think that would address several problems. You have the SCBI technology. Perhaps we can get others equipped with SCBIs, and you have the staff of Quantico Base, which is helping. We can spare Vili, and Stathis will need him."

"You sure?"

"Yes," Skadi said. This was more suitable to Vili's skills.

Loki announced Vili was at the door.

"Perfect timing," Mathison said as Vili walked in wearing a scowl.

"What are we going to do when the Aesir return to the *Tyr*?" Vili asked, sinking down into a chair.

It wasn't a problem Skadi had thought about until now. There was a company providing security to Zvezda Two, but the *Tyr* was planning to leave in less than a week, although Skadi wondered if that was true. Her father kept finding excuses to stay.

"Get Wayne Robillard involved," Mathison said. "Work with Hui and get some reliable ODTs. I don't think I want Peacekeepers. Might bring some other Deltas up from Quantico."

"You trust them?" Vili asked.

Skadi didn't think they had a lot of choice in the matter. She did not want to rely on Hui or Feng. The Delta Force troopers were unreliable for a different reason, but they had more reason to be loyal to Mathison than any SOG troops. The problem was that they would be outnumbered and could only provide oversight. They were trigger pullers, not bodyguards, and Skadi was unsure of their leadership experience.

More and more she felt like she was being surrounded by enemies as her friends and allies abandoned her.

"I'm going to have to," Mathison said. "Unless you have a better solution."

"No. Putting too much trust in Feng and Hui may not be good."

"Which brings up another problem. I have a mission for you," Skadi said, with a quick glance at Mathison.

"Another one?"

"The *Eagle* is going to hunt for Becket," Skadi said. "I want you to go with them."

"You said 'you' not 'us,'" Vili said, quickly hitting the point.

"Zen. I need to stay here. I think Winters and Stathis need an experienced Erikoisjoukot."

"You don't think Sif needs me? Hermod's team are Eriks. Becket is a Marine."

The fact he wasn't arguing to stay told Skadi that he didn't want to and that he had been giving it some thought.

"Sif is also an Erikoisjoukot. She knows our procedures and probably knows Hermod's team better. Winters and Stathis will be dealing with ghost colonies, and I think you have more experience there. You will be a force multiplier."

Vili looked at Skadi, then at Mathison. He was thinking about it. Then he shrugged.

"I can do this. For sure. Will the two of you survive without me?"

"I think we can manage, Kaveri."

"You better, Sisko. I've lost enough brothers and sisters."

"Me too. Don't add to the list. Please."

"Not me. I plan to live forever. So far, so good."

"Are you okay with this?" Mathison asked.

"For sure, for sure," Vili said. "It will be nice to get away from all these jackboots. Feels like Haberdash at times, and I can't think of them as 'not enemies.' It's messing with me. I need space. Would prefer not to leave my sisko though, but she is in good hands." Vili stared at Mathison. "Though if you shoot at her again, I will come for you. You've made your one mistake."

Mathison smiled.

"I don't turn on my best friends and allies," Mathison said, standing. He hadn't left his chair in hours.

"For sure. The two of you make a good team. If I didn't trust you, I wouldn't leave. You will take care of my sisko. I know this."

"As a good friend likes to say, 'for sure,'" Mathison said, rolling his shoulders and stretching.

Vili nodded. "When does my little buddy leave and how is he doing with his pet jackboots?"

"Soon," Skadi said. "Do you think you could help him get them trained?"

"You mean you really wanted me to help them hunt Becket?"

"Yes," Mathison said, not catching Vili's humor.

"For sure. These are the duties of a faltvebal. Training others to lead, keeping them out of trouble, and making sure the mission is a success. Working from the shadows and letting others take the glory. The story of my life. I feel like an old Marine gunnery sergeant sometimes."

"You looking for a promotion?" Mathison asked. He must not like the reminder his life was no longer that easy.

"Oh no," Vili said quickly. "No. No. No. I prefer working from the shadows, standing behind others and watching them earn glory. I don't get blamed when things go horribly wrong, but I get to save the day by making them go right."

"Though most people don't recognize it when you save the day," Mathison added.

"For sure, for sure. I see you have experience as a faltvebal."

"I do," Mathison said before Skadi could.

"For sure. You haven't forgotten. I know this. We will be fine. I look forward to being with my little buddy and new little sisko. Times change; we must change. This arrangement isn't bad. You are a good man, Prime Minister. I like you."

Vili's eyes flickered to Skadi.

"I can't think of a better man to be at Skadi's side. Us faltvebals know how to get things done and understand loyalty."

Was Vili trying to tell her something?

"This might be the safest place for my sisko. You two take care of each other, and I will take care of my little buddy and your colonel, or captain. Which brings up a question. Is she a colonel or captain? I hear both."

Mathison smiled and shook his head. "US customs. In the Marines, we have the rank of captain, which usually commands a company. A Navy captain commands a ship which can be thousands. They aren't equivalent ranks. In the Marines, a colonel is the same rank as a Navy captain. Call her captain or colonel or eversti. Ask her. Our past and traditions are important but—"

Skadi and Vili waited for him to continue, but he just shrugged.

"New times require new traditions," Skadi said.

"Agreed," Mathison said with a nod. Skadi wasn't sure he was fully agreeing, though.

"For sure," Vili said. "Then I need to meet with General Hui, Feng, and Robillard and arrange replacements for the Aesir when your father runs away."

"He isn't running away."

After the night drinking with him, she found it easier to cut him some slack. She had seen past the mask, saw the man beneath. She was still trying to figure out how to deal with that.

"Then where is he going?" Vili asked, standing.

"To look for Home Fleet," Skadi said, knowing what Vili was asking. Her father did not know where the Republic Home Fleet was or where it was going. She doubted he had any clues either, but she also knew how nervous he was remaining in the Sol System surrounded by so many potentially hostile SOG warships.

"For sure," Vili said, pushing it and not giving her an out. "But where is it?"

"We know damned well he has no clue," Skadi said. *What did he want?*

Vili shrugged. "Zen." The big man glanced at Mathison. "Let me know if there is anything else. I'm going to be very busy. Please take care of my sisko."

"I will," Mathison said.

Like she needed Mathison to take care of her? She wasn't some pampered little princess. It was Mathison who needed someone to watch *his* back.

"Then I best push off all my duties on some poor dumb bureaucrat and get ready to fight the vanhat again," Vili said, sounding way too happy. "We will return as soon as the ex-president has been dealt with."

"Come back," Mathison said.

"With my shield or on it."

"It better be with it," Mathison said, scowling. "Skadi will kill me if you don't."

"For sure," Vili said. "I'll bring back my little buddy, too. We've got this."

"Thank you." Mathison stood.

"For sure." Vili headed out.

Mathison sat back down and scowled at his displays. Freya probably had more bad news for him, more decisions to make or be aware of.

Skadi saw him struggling to try not to growl at the administrators that came begging for things. First, they tried kissing his ass, then the blustering and posturing about how important they were. The SCBIs did an incredible job of watching things, and they now owned the SOG networks. Very little happened on Luna that they didn't know about, and it wasn't just that the SCBIs were monitoring things, they were rewriting the monitoring programs, re-assigning SOG computer systems and resources, streamlining the environment, updating and cleaning up networks and communications, rooting out corruption and locating secrets.

The SCBIs spent little time actually monitoring people, but their ability to manipulate the data and streamline the Governance structure was almost alarming for Skadi, and working closely with Loki made her realize how little she understood computer networks and the Governance bureaucracy.

Mathison was doing his best to meet with the more difficult administrators and calm their fears. It was a losing battle.

Showing these bureaucrats kindness was not helping because they saw his actions as weakness they could exploit. Fools.

Feng had his hands full, and Skadi was working with him to hide the fact that he was occasionally sending InSec agents to visit the administrators who didn't take no for an answer or tried to bypass

Mathison's instructions. There were several managers who were sitting in InSec holding cells because they had decided their personal quarters needed an Inkeri generator rather than their citizens. Then there were those administrators who were stealing the food meant for the arcologies that had suffered dramatic failures.

Everyone had their hands full trying to keep citizens from panicking and the monolithic bureaucracy working.

It was one of Skadi's nightmares, to be stuck in an office at a desk doing this paska. She was a fighter, not a button-pushing bureaucrat.

Vili had better appreciate what she was doing for him, and he'd better not get killed.

* * * * *

Chapter Thirty-Five: Departure

2nd Lieutenant Zale Stathis, USMC

Being a lieutenant sucked. Part of him had known officers had it rough, but he had figured they had their moments. The reality was very different. He didn't have any time to relax and was always running around trying to get things done. Always holding meetings, discussing training, personnel problems, and more. Some ODT supply colonel did not think a mere lieutenant should be requesting that much ammunition and didn't think a platoon needed so many extra weapons and drones. Another supply captain had decided that his platoon had less priority on armor repair parts than a reserve company full of replacements.

Then there was an issue with private Ryashkina who was not getting paid because the ODT paymaster said he was listed as a Peacekeeper and the Peacekeepers had him listed as ODT. Nobody was using the online database because they claimed it was offline for repairs, which Shrek had shown wasn't, but every time he linked either of them they said it was, so he had to go visit them in person. Also, due to the nature of the digital currency, a human had to approve the change, and the SCBI couldn't modify the blockchain without causing more problems and raising alerts in the entire SOG banking system.

Smimova was also having problems picking up supplies because they insisted he was a private and that the computer system was wrong. Nobody thought a mere second lieutenant had the authority, and they required him to submit a request through proper channels, and though they didn't know what those channels were, they were sure that he had to take the matter up with his company or battalion commander, which Stathis didn't have.

Of course, that was when he found the proper agency, or person, to make the request. Shrek had unlimited access to the SOG systems, but they were a convoluted mess most of the time, and people used the excuse that the network was unreliable with too much frequency. It was total bullshit, but everyone else seemed to accept it, and even letting Shrek make the changes didn't mean people accepted those changes.

Stathis would not go to Prime Minister Mathison over this kind of stuff either. Calling General Hui was getting old. Stathis knew how happy he would be to get out of the Sol System. Calling the general about some administrative issue was like calling God to sweep up a room. Pure overkill.

Already, two of his men were in the *Eagle's* brig for fighting, and he had taken to keeping their weapons in the armory.

Spending two hours of sand table time with his platoon sergeant and squad leaders was a luxury and gave him time to actually relax.

Staff Sergeant Smimova was a lot of help, but with all the Governance supply depots and warehouses run by self-important Governance officers, there wasn't a lot a mere enlisted man could do.

He was just about to sit down with his squad leaders and do some sand table exercises when Shrek pinged him.

"There is an ODT major at the main hatch who would like to talk with you," Shrek said.

"Why?" Stathis wondered who he had pissed off now. He really didn't want to deal with another stuck-up, arrogant Governance major who knew more and didn't consider the prime minister's mission to be a priority.

"Unknown," Shrek said as Stathis told Smimova to figure something out while he headed to the main hatch. He was getting better at threatening SOG officers but that only worked so much.

With the *Eagle* currently in a Lunar hanger undergoing repairs, anybody could enter the facility and approach the ship. Automated boarding defense turrets could discourage anything else.

When the hatch slid open, Stathis expected the overweight, balding ODT major to start yelling. Instead, he smiled. Not a predatory shark smile. It seemed pleasant and friendly, and that sent a chill down his spine.

Stathis tried to figure out if he should salute or something else and decided against it. In theory, he was indoors. The smile didn't put Stathis at ease. Looking closer, it looked practiced and far too sincere to be real. This was socialism. People didn't smile for real.

"How can I help you, Major?" Stathis asked. He was too irritated to stand at attention or treat the major as a superior.

"Lieutenant," the major said, "the question becomes, how can I help you?"

"Who are you with, sir?" Stathis asked cautiously. This was not how majors started conversations with lieutenants.

"General Hui has assigned me to assist you with preparing for your mission. I am Major Grisha Petrov. I am an ODT supply specialist from the Fifth Division. At your service."

"Supply specialist? Fifth Division? Uh, sir?"

"Correct. Until recently, I was the senior supply coordination adjutant for the ODT Fifth Division. General Hui has informed me that yours is a critical mission sanctioned by our beloved prime minister and that it is of the utmost importance to our glorious Governance. She explained that while you are only a mere second lieutenant, you are highly trusted by the prime minister and are creating a glorious new organization to rival the Peacekeepers. She asked that I assist and guide you through the difficulty of the Governance bureaucracy, both here and abroad."

"How do you plan on doing that, sir?" Stathis asked. Senior supply coordination adjutant was a thing? A division level officer sounded important, but he was only a major.

"You tell me what you need, and I will make sure you get it," Petrov said. "You are a combat leader. My specialization is logistical."

"Abroad, sir?" Stathis asked. This major was acting like Stathis was an equal, and that made Stathis uncomfortable.

"I am being assigned to your unit for the time being. The general believes I can be of help taking care of the logistical requirements of your platoon. I also have some knowledge of armor systems, repair, and system modifications. I have some technical skills besides logistical skills."

"From a division to a platoon?"

"It may seem to be a demotion on the surface," Petrov said. "But I think this is a good career move for me. General Hui is a wise and capable leader."

"I have just received confirmation through official channels," Shrek reported. *"Pending your approval. Prime Minister Mathison even approved this."*

That didn't make Stathis feel any better. Was Petrov a spy? An agent who was going to keep tabs on him? Majors didn't take orders from lieutenants, and no supply clerk would want to leave Sol with an elite combat team going into the jaws of hell. Something else had to be going on. Stathis was tempted to say no, but if the prime minister had approved it…

"Little buddy!" a voice called out and Stathis looked up to see Vili coming toward him, a small robotic mule piled high with gear, following him like a puppy.

"Vili!" Stathis said, feeling some relief and concern.

"Your gunny has asked that I come with the *Eagle* to help interactions with the ghost colonies. I have much experience with them."

"Great." Was Vili here to watch over him too? Or was he really here to help?

Stathis couldn't help but feel that he was screwing up, and that the gunny was trying to help without being obvious about it.

What would the gunny do? A hard question because the gunny was the gunny and not a lieutenant.

But staff sergeants and gunnies trained and groomed lieutenants for command, didn't they? The gunny wouldn't do him wrong.

"Glad to have you, Vili," Stathis said. "This is Major Petrov. He's a, uh, a senior supply coordination adjutant and used to work for Fifth Division."

"Ah," Vili said, coming up the ramp and looking over the major. It was hard to read the big man, but he didn't seem impressed. "This is a good thing. I have spoken with Skadi, and she is also frustrated with the Governance bureaucracy."

"I am a specialist," Petrov said with a smile. "I dare say I wield the bureaucracy like you wield your weapons."

278 | WILLIAM S. FRISBEE, JR.

"For sure," Vili said and looked at Stathis. "We should put him to use then."

The inner hatch slid open, and Winters appeared. She was scowling when she saw them.

"Hello, ma'am," Stathis said, coming to attention. The major snapped to attention as well, but Vili just watched them all with mild amusement.

She paused, perhaps surprised by them all standing there. "What's going on?"

"Major Petrov is reporting in, ma'am," Stathis said. "He is a senior supply coordination adjutant."

Winters looked at him, and Stathis realized she wasn't mad at him, but she was frustrated. Well, he hoped it wasn't his fault.

He saw her take in Petrov's ODT uniform.

"Great," she said. "I wonder if I can get an adjutant for Fleet. These fucktards aren't supplying any platinum, and I know damned well they have it. Blitzen has submitted all the forms, but nobody is delivering it. Not even going up the chain seems to work."

"May I make a suggestion, Colonel?" Petrov said. Winters' scowl deepened, but she nodded. "If going up the chain doesn't work, go down the chain."

"What do you mean?" Winters asked.

"Let the person responsible for providing you with what you need see you interacting in a friendly way with subordinates," Petrov said. "Keep the responsible party out of your interactions."

"Why would I do that?"

"This is one secret that I gladly share with you," Petrov said, with a quick glance at Stathis. "This is a bureaucracy. Bureaucrats are very possessive of their authority and power. They deny resources because that makes them feel powerful and important. In many cases, by cooperating, they are seen as weak and inefficient. Many managers see themselves as gatekeepers, and only the most incompetent will throw open their gates and let others have free rein. Prudent managers are supposed to tightly ration and control their resources so that we will have what we need, when we need it. Frequently, they do not understand the greater good or the needs of our magnificent leaders."

"I have full authority from the prime minister's office."

"Of course, ma'am. I'm sure they know this, but this can make them think it is more important they be seen as prudent and capable managers. By mentioning such powerful patrons, they salivate at the chance to interact and please such individuals. They can gain favorable recognition in this way."

"So, their subordinates will give me what I need?" Winters asked.

"Of course not. However, by being friendly with the subordinate where the supervisor can see, and be excluded, will remind the supervisor they can and probably will be replaced. If you are friendly with a subordinate, they will feel threatened. Subordinates will buck for promotion, of course, and by excluding the supervisor from this friendly interaction, it will remind them how they likely got their current promotion. This will frequently change the dynamics of a relationship quickly as they seek to turn you into an ally. Subordinates can also be very helpful for this reason, and they may share specific, helpful details that will help you negotiate with their supervisor."

Colonel Winters looked thoughtful as her eyes swept the hangar.

"That does not sound very efficient," Winters said.

"Of course, ma'am," Petrov said. "The glorious and tireless bureaucrats of our glorious Governance have a very important job to do. They do not have unlimited resources. They must constantly struggle to make sure there is enough for everyone. The active viewscreen displays the requested data, if you will. They must understand that if they do not work for the greater good, then they will be replaced. You, as a senior member of the Governance, know best what the greater good is. These tireless servants frequently struggle to understand the needs of the Governance. You are a beacon of integrity and managers will quickly understand that if they do not serve you and the greater good, it will replace them."

Stathis struggled to keep the scowl off his face and keep his mouth shut. Lieutenants didn't scoff or laugh at bullshit like that, did they? Colonel Winters wasn't laughing.

The colonel paused and stared at Petrov.

"Do you have any pull with Fleet?" she asked. He was ODT and reporting to Stathis, but if Winters could use him, she outranked a mere second lieutenant and this dude was a major. Maybe she would have a better chance of keeping him on a leash.

"I am an ODT, ma'am," Petrov said. "Technically, I do not. Our glorious Governance fleet does not take orders or requests from a mere ODT major."

"A pity," Winters said.

"Not that I can't help," Petrov said glancing at Stathis. What was that about? "I'm extremely familiar with Fleet, and I can get results if my patrons have proper authority."

"What other tricks do you have?" Stathis asked.

"Many," Petrov said. "As you wield weapons, I wield the bureaucracy. In many cases, acquiring the results requires understanding the needs of the parties involved."

"I need platinum for our manufactories to produce certain components," Winters said.

Petrov nodded sagely. "Platinum is very useful in many applications, ma'am. It is an essential catalyst and has medical uses. There never seems to be enough platinum. I may happen to know someone who has some platinum. Please use this link code I will send you and inform Chen that Petrov would kindly appreciate it if he gave you as much as you need, but add ten percent to what you need."

"Why would he do that?"

"It will be unfortunate that the ten percent does not reach your hold," Petrov said. "However, it will go to a good cause. Should less than ten percent be lost in transit, please notify me."

Colonel Winters turned around and went inside the *Eagle*.

So that is what a senior supply coordination adjutant did. Stathis hoped he could get them the extra grenades and ammunition and started creating a mental a list for Petrov.

"Now, young lieutenant," Petrov said. "If you would be so kind as to send me a list of those items your fine new unit is short of, I will be more than happy to make sure these critical supplies reach this ship. Furthermore, if there are any other bureaucratic interactions that need to be addressed, please inform me."

"I would really appreciate that, Major."

* * * * *

Chapter Thirty-Six:
Avoidance

2nd Lieutenant Zale Stathis, USMC

When did officers get to sleep, Stathis wondered as his alarm buzzed.

He had thought things would chill out a bit once the *Eagle* was underway. Give him time to train with his platoon.

Wishful thinking. Vili had him creating training plans, doing PT with the platoon, teaching them drills. The two troopers who had been brigged for fighting were back in the brig and only let out for training and PT. Putting them in different squads wasn't working.

"Let Smimova handle it," Vili said. "In your Marine Corps, it is the staff NCO who handles things. Same in the Republic. You have told Smimova what you expect of him. Now it is your turn to let him do what he needs to."

Vili had been consulting with Smimova too, and Stathis wasn't sure he wanted to know.

Major Petrov was driving Stathis a different kind of crazy, insisting that everyone make sure the equipment was fully functional and accounted for. He also had to assign the equipment to everyone. He wanted the better machine gunners to have the machine guns, and then there were the squad marksmen who should get specialized rifles, but the rifles had to be properly zeroed. Then he had to figure out what he wanted for standard combat loads. Petrov gave him recommendations, but Stathis had to pare those down so the troops could move and fight, otherwise they would just be slow-moving pack mules.

There was also a batch of substandard trauma plates, and Stathis had to convince Winters to let him repurpose the *Eagle's* manufactory to fix them, which meant rebuilding them from scratch. Since the replacements were better than the originals, Stathis had to convince her to upgrade all the trauma plates.

Vili also spent time with him going over tactics and leadership. How to identify when troops were too stressed, too tired, on drugs, and more. No wonder lieutenants sucked at tactics; they were too busy learning other shit.

Stathis missed being a private, lying around waiting for the NCOs and officers to get their act together.

Maybe when he made first lieutenant or captain, it would be easier.

Yeah, and when pigs flew he could strap a saddle on one.

It was six in the morning ship's time. Stathis had slept in an extra hour. It was Sunday, supposedly a day of rest. Tomorrow, the ship would arrive at Zugla. Maybe today the *Eagle* could contact them and see if they were still alive.

He still didn't know what he was going to do. You couldn't storm a station with a platoon. He entered the main room and made a beeline for the food machine.

"Are you avoiding me?" a voice asked, snapping Stathis to full alertness.

Hakala was sitting at a table eating breakfast.

"Um, no?" Stathis said. Nobody else was present.

"Good. I was wondering."

With everything going on, he had only thought of her when there was nothing he could do about it. He had seen her around the ship, but never had time to stop and talk. Now she was in the Aesir quarters he shared with Vili and Petrov. Without the other Marines or Aesir, it seemed deserted. Petrov was not a comfortable addition, but he was an officer and for some reason Colonel Winters did not want to put him in with the enlisted Spartans. The Spartan platoon was in their own quarters, the HKTs had their own section, and Winters, with her XO and crew, had completely different quarters.

Getting his food, Stathis wasn't sure what to do, so he did what he figured a badass gunny would do. He came over and sat with Hakala.

"You are very busy," Hakala said as soon as he sat down.

"So much to do. I always thought officers had it easy, with their own chow hall and shit catering to them like nobles."

"I spoke with Vili, and he says you are doing great," she said. Which was new to Stathis. When did Vili have time to chit-chat? "He says you are one of the hardest working lieutenants he has seen."

"Most lieutenants have hardworking staff NCOs helping."

"Not in the Governance."

Stathis shrugged as he shoved some eggs into his mouth. If he wanted to get some PT in, then he would have to eat fast.

"So, what brings you here for breakfast?" Stathis asked around bites.

"You," she said with a smile that caused Stathis to pause briefly. Her smile grew, and he was both scared and sad that nobody else was present. She obviously enjoyed distracting him and his mind went to one mission where she had spent a long time kneeling in front of him adjusting his belt. She knew exactly what was going through his mind.

What would the gunny do or say? Stathis had no idea.

Another major advantage of being a private was that nobody expected intelligent and polite conversation.

"Uh, thank you," Stathis said. "I've missed your company."

Which had to be the stupidest thing to say. What company? In those few free moments, he still remembered trying to slip by her on the *Tikari* and how she had insisted on taking up more space in the confines of the ship. She seemed to have enjoyed invading his personal space, and if he was honest, he had liked it. Beyond that it had been fighting and killing, pulling her back when she was wounded aboard the Red Lotus Station had been automatic, something a buddy does for another.

"I never got a chance to thank you for Red Lotus Station," she said, her eyes locked on him, like a cat sizing up prey. What kind of thanks did she have planned?

A human male had two heads and only enough blood to think with one. Right now, the blood was not going to the head on his shoulders and that made it very hard for him to think straight.

He tried not to squirm and to think of something intelligent to say. Lots of things flashed through his mind. Tell her she was his comrade and downplay it? No. He didn't want her to go away. Tell her how much he cared and how terrified he had been?

"You are important," Stathis said. Nice. An officer thing to say. She could interpret that many ways, and it was a hundred percent true. Maybe a hundred and ten percent.

Her smile grew. Obviously, she had taken it in a way that was advantageous to Stathis. The batwing on her eyes was super exotic. He wondered if she had other tattoos.

"How important?" she asked. She wanted to see him squirm. How the hell did he answer that? Sure, he wanted in her pants. She was hot, a damn good fighter, but what was he to her? Prey? Maybe that wouldn't be so bad.

"Pretty," Stathis said. Shit. Had he just said that? Clever though. That word had many meanings.

A door slid open, causing Stathis to jump, and Vili walked out.

Vili paused, and Stathis saw him glance at them. Stathis noticed how close he was to Hakala. What would Vili think?

"Hei and Skal," Vili said. "Am I interrupting?"

"Hei and Skal," Hakala replied.

"Hi and skull," Stathis said before he could stop himself.

"No," Hakala said, which Stathis found oddly disappointing. Was he misreading her? It wasn't like women were tech manuals. Those he understood. Women were like tech manuals written in Russian or Chinese, without pictures. There weren't any MCIs, manuals written by the Marine Corps Institute, that covered male-female relations. He had checked, multiple times.

"For sure." Vili raised an eyebrow and headed to the food machines. Stathis knew the big man would probably empty it out.

"You need to take time and relax," Hakala said.

When did lieutenants have time to do that? Glancing at Vili, Stathis wondered what he could arrange and how he could arrange that with Hakala. She obviously had some ideas, and Stathis's mind went in too many directions.

"I would like to," Stathis said.

"The secret to being an excellent officer is also life balance," Hakala said. "Can't be working all the time. Gotta take time to enjoy life, and people."

Stathis couldn't agree more.

"For sure," Vili said, coming over and sitting down, his plate overflowing.

"This is like being deployed," Stathis said. "No time for the, uh, finer things in life."

"For sure," Vili said. "Being operational has many challenges for all of us."

Why couldn't the big guy go sit at the other end of the room?

"Well," Hakala said, her hand brushing Stathis's leg under the table, "I best get going. Great to see you. Perhaps we can get together later and do some training or something?"

"That would be great," Stathis said too quickly, thinking about that hand on his leg. What kind of training?

She stood, and the smile didn't leave her face. She barely glanced at Vili before putting her plate in the hopper and heading out.

The door closed behind her.

"She is hunting," Vili said.

"What?" Stathis asked before he could stop himself. Officers were supposed to think before they spoke. It was easy to fall back into a private mentality with Vili present. Stathis was used to playing the ground and trying to meet the expectations of others. Vili knew him as a private, and that was a comfortable habit for Stathis.

Vili looked at him and grinned.

Stathis felt his face grow warm.

"Odin blessed men with two heads," Vili said. "But he cursed men with only enough blood to think with one."

Now Stathis was sure he was blushing. Damn Vili.

"What will she do when she, uh, finds her prey?"

"I don't know her that well," Vili said, stuffing a fork full of something in his mouth. "Some women like chandeliers, others like lots of noise."

Stathis worked on his food as he tried to figure out what Vili was talking about.

"You will have to let me know, little buddy," Vili said with a smile that left Stathis feeling vulnerable. "You will soon learn who she is hunting."

Stathis had a pretty damn good idea who she was hunting. Now if only he could figure out how to throw himself in her path and get caught.

"We need to figure out what we are going to do when we arrive at Zugla," Vili said. "Your president is unlikely to meet us at the dock and turn himself over."

Another uncomfortable topic. Storming the ghost colony wasn't exactly an option and Stathis had been avoiding that. Chewing bubblegum and kicking ass was in the job description for Marine private, but there wasn't anything about bounty hunting. As far as he knew, bounty hunting wasn't in a second lieutenant's job description either. What had the gunny been thinking? What the hell was he supposed to be doing? Was there an MCI for bounty hunting?

"Do you have a suggestion?" Stathis asked before he could stop himself. Officers were supposed to have all the answers, weren't they? Vili was a seasoned staff NCO, a Republic faltvebal, the same as a gunny.

Vili's smile should have put Stathis at ease, but he felt like this was some test.

"Outstanding officers ask for suggestions and take the best ones," Vili said. "Or come up with their own based on suggestions. You are smart."

Stathis nodded, not feeling that smart. All the blood had not returned to the head on his shoulders.

"We need a team to go aboard," Vili said. "Just a few of us to gather information. Keep reinforcements ready aboard ship. Your Spartans are fighters, not investigators."

Did that mean Stathis should stay aboard with them?

"First, we poll the system before going aboard. See what we can find. Then, based on that information, we might send a team or the entire combat team."

Which made sense. He remembered on Curitiba and Jason's Pit how they had gone aboard in a smaller team. Those visits had gone very poorly, though. For a moment, he wondered who would go on station, then he realized he was probably supposed to make that decision. Colonel Winters probably had her own ideas as well.

"Can you coordinate a meeting with the colonel today?" Stathis asked Shrek.

"In an hour," Shrek replied almost instantly. Dammit. That would cut into his workout.

"Thank you."

"You betcha. I'll also invite Vili."

"Uh, thanks," Stathis said.

Dammit. He should have thought of that.

* * * * *

Chapter Thirty-Seven:
Zugla Approach

2nd Lieutenant Zale Stathis, USMC

As the *Eagle* approached Zugla, Stathis watched it closely. He wasn't sure what to call Colonel Winters, though captain seemed to be the right answer most of the time. Her Marine Corps rank was more relevant to Stathis than her Naval rank, but the Navy didn't have colonels and there was no doubt in Stathis' mind she was a Marine colonel. Officer shit. Damn. He was an officer now. What had Prime Minister Mathison been thinking?

But this was what the gunny needed, so this was what Stathis would do.

The gunny's words of advice kept coming back to him: Treat people the way you want them to act. But Stathis didn't want to be a second lieutenant. Of course, being a private and doing things like cleaning the head and police call held less appeal. According to Vili, he was doing a good job, but Vili wasn't a Marine.

He also felt Hakala's eyes on him. She was another reason he didn't want to be a dumb private. While she might toy with a private, she would be more serious with an officer. That changed the dynamics, and she was quickly becoming someone else he didn't want to disappoint. Since his promotion, he had detected a change in her toward him, not a bad one, and Stathis wasn't sure what that meant. He was

292 | WILLIAM S. FRISBEE, JR.

pretty sure she wasn't *less* interested in him, though maybe that was his ego or the head lower on his body doing the thinking.

"Standard communications," Winters said. "Detecting Inkeri field, so they probably haven't fallen to the vanhat."

"Yet," Britta said.

The colonel/captain remained silent and that worried Stathis, reminding him they were just one ship. The *Eagle* had engaged the vanhat in the past, almost always outnumbered and outgunned, and it had survived. But a colony like Zugla couldn't move; it couldn't escape. The vanhat could keep coming until it was gone. Stathis hoped they weren't here when a horde of vanhat found the colony.

Zooming in, Stathis scrutinized the docks. There were six other ships. About a quarter of the docks were occupied by various merchant vessels, from smaller couriers to a large, ponderous cargo ship.

"Getting data," Winters said, and Stathis saw a link arrive in his mailbox.

Bringing it up gave Stathis the colony's song and dance about themselves. Founded hundreds of years ago, shortly after the collapse of the United States, it was one of the first ghost colonies. Founded officially in 2104 by a small team of scientists under the leadership of an eccentric European billionaire named Gaufrid Krantz.

"What happened to Gaufrid?" Stathis asked Shrek.

"Unknown. That information is not listed. Conspicuously absent. He is listed as the founder and little else."

Stathis kept reading.

The purpose of the colony had been the preservation of wildlife from Earth. Originally, three cylinders had been built into the planetoid in order to create habitats for several biomes, Amazonian jungle, African jungle, and a plains biome. Since then, the number of different biomes had been expanded to twelve, with two biomes occupied by the staff and their descendants, who continued to build biomes and manage the existing ones, giving animals long extinct on Earth a new home and chance to live in a very controlled and protected environment.

"The population is much lower than I would expect," Petrov said aloud. "Given the age and social dynamics of most colonies, I would expect more people. Based on the number of biomes, this is a very low number. Barely sustenance level."

Maybe twenty thousand people lived here now. That was a lot of people, but for a colony hundreds of years old?

"Trade seems minimal," Petrov added. "Fascinating to see an actual ghost colony. We hear about them, of course, but most citizens view them as inbred cesspits of corruption, violence, and antisocial behavior. Such a social organization does not lend itself toward the creation and management of such a system as this. They must have an extremely strong central authority to maintain control and enforce social peace. Considering the age, as well, they maintain control exceptionally well. They likely mimic the Governance in many ways."

"Not all the biomes are identified," Winters said, glancing at her executive officer.

"I've never noticed that before," Britta said. "Only six biomes are fully identified in the data. An interesting omission. Perhaps the others are not completed."

"If your sensors are correct," Petrov said. "The generators are extremely powerful and should be generating enough power for maybe twenty cylinders, unless the biomes are inefficient. Weapon systems seem extensive as well, which could indicate the interesting readings."

"I don't see any ships small enough to be Becket's ship," Stathis said, wanting to add to the conversation. Pointing out that the different biomes probably provided a very interesting menu was probably not something a lieutenant should bring up. Food options were a private's concern, but a steak sounded really good about now.

"We will check with dock control then," Winters said. "Perhaps he came and went."

"Or used a different dock," Britta added.

Stathis looked around. Wouldn't they have seen something like that?

"An interesting mystery," Petrov said. "We should determine how much power is hosted within the biomes. These power readings are interesting. Only two human-settled cylinders? I'm not seeing any data on food consumption. They do list exports as animal products and request imports of music, specific resources, and technology codes. Animal products? Manure is an interesting export."

Of course, nothing listed details on weapon systems, which were more interesting to Stathis than the fact the colony exported animal shit.

"The *Eagle* has some exceptional sensors," Major Petrov said. "Can we perhaps scan deeper? I'm curious how large the biomes are, especially the newer ones. This could explain the power requirements."

"No," Winters said, and Stathis wasn't sure if she was annoyed or just distracted. "Deeper sensor scans might be impolite and invasive. Let's not piss them off before we've docked, okay?"

"That is very wise, friend Captain," Petrov said. Why did he have to call everyone a friend? Were jackboot social fascist majors everyone's friends? Stathis caught himself. He wasn't really a social fascist now, was he? The gunny would introduce reforms, but what those could be, Stathis wasn't sure. He was glad second lieutenants didn't have to make decisions like that. He just had to find Becket, not rebuild the Governance.

"We have docking approval," Winters said.

"That's what she said," Stathis said before he could stop himself. Dammit. It was odd not having the gunny present. Still, his face turned red because Hakala was on the bridge.

Vili chuckled, but nobody else did. Stathis glanced around, hoping everyone would ignore him.

"Shut up, Stathis," Winters said but without the venom he expected.

It felt odd not having the gunny or Levin around to tell him to shut up. Winters just didn't have the conviction and intensity to slap him down. It was disappointing in a way, and probably not very lieutenant-like behavior.

Petrov just glanced at him with a confused look before going back to his cybernetic display.

* * * * *

Chapter Thirty-Eight:
Bureaucracy

Prime Minister Wolf Mathison, USMC

Mathison had never liked bureaucracies, but the Governance made the bureaucracies Mathison had worked with look like shining beacons of efficiency and progress. He would have thought as prime minister and supreme ruler of the SOG system he could get things done. That was partially true, but that didn't mean all the managers and administrators and bureaucrats didn't get tangled in red tape and paperwork. Mathison could make decrees and issue directives, but frequently they were at odds with existing legislation. Without Freya's and Loki's help, nothing would get done. More than once, Skadi had to "visit" people to enforce compliance.

There were two problems. One problem was the existing bureaucratic nonsense that required extensive documentation and approvals. The other problem was that when people bypassed all that, the graft and corruption reached epic levels. The bureaucrats of the Governance were too busy taking care of themselves and their families and friends. They were in the habit of compliance and were fearful of offending the new regime, so they frequently sought comfort in the bureaucratic process, using it as a weapon and tool to avoid change that might sweep them away and destroy the power and influence they had acquired.

Here on Earth, the Governance was a web of favors, influence pedaling, and corruption. It could be impossible to get anything done through official channels because regulation upon regulation slowed down, and sometimes prohibited, progress. Nadya, the secretary general, had mastered the process, manipulating things to benefit her, but she had kept her secrets, and Mathison couldn't match her understanding and ability to manipulate the oppressive officialdom. She could pass laws that were supposed to do one thing but managed to do the exact opposite.

One example was giving Mathison a headache. The stated goal was to make sure the people of Earth had plenty of food and resources from Luna. Regulations were created to monitor and inventory the supplies going to Earth to make sure they got enough. Bureaucracy never makes things flow more smoothly from one location to another, and in this case, ended up choking the supply lines with regulatory requirements, graft, corruption, theft, and power mongering. Without inspectors present to ensure compliance, shipments could not be sent, and controlling the number and activities of the inspectors could easily halt deliveries.

"Why don't we have all the administrative triumvirates executed and put a military officer in charge?" Skadi asked from her desk. It wasn't the first time she had asked that question, and Mathison had lost count.

"Every day I think that is a better idea," Mathison said. It was a lie, and they both knew it. SOG officers in the Sol System were bloody tyrants. They got results but destroyed countless lives with their methods. The civilian administrators were frequently corrupt and exploitive and cruel. They would have people abducted and disappeared, not very different than SOG military officers, but they didn't do the killing themselves, and there was frequently a process they used to dispose of people. SOG officers didn't hesitate to kill people when they could. SOG directors also worked in groups of three, requiring coordination and consensus among them all.

Mathison, or more correctly Freya, could interrupt an administrator's process to have a rival or detractor executed, but he wouldn't have that flexibility with the military in charge. The system seemed designed that way, so the military could execute civilians without repercussions and for that reason it seemed the military and the majority of civilians were kept separate. To the military, rebels and the people were considered an enemy. Nothing was officially stated that way but the propaganda the SOG had saturated the military with told them they were there to defend the people, but that the people did not always appreciate that and turned away from the glories of the SOG. They also browbeat SOG troops, telling them how vile capitalists and antisocial anarchists infiltrated and controlled the people of the Governance.

"You are going to the admiralty meeting?" Skadi asked.

Mathison had been trying not to think about that. "Can you find a way for me to skip it?"

"I'm trying to avoid it. I was hoping you had an excuse I could use."

At the time, it had seemed a good idea. Skadi was still managing the Guard and other ground forces in conjunction with General Hui. Most of them were busy dealing with insurrections or fighting to get supplies to arcologies that had suffered infrastructure damage from the d-bombs. There were still a few areas that didn't have Inkeris, and she was discovering there were unreported cities and towns outside the arcologies which were falling prey to the vanhat infestation. It felt like a nasty game of whack-a-mole. As soon as one infestation was dealt with, another would pop up, and sometimes they varied in the form of vanhat.

Mathison hadn't read the report on the latest variants yet. Being a prime minister sucked in so many ways, maybe worse than being an officer. He was constantly having to read reports and determine if they were valid, relevant, and useful. Everyone thought their report was important, and when people asked him for things, he had to understand why. Without Freya to help with the burden, he would have left within days of taking command.

General Hui was the more visible figurehead to the Guard and ODTs. She seemed to be everywhere and involved with everything. Mathison didn't know if she slept, but her experience in the Guard and the ODTs gave her a definite edge in dealing with both organizations. Sometimes she crashed through the bureaucracy like a bull in a China shop. She worked well with Feng, and Mathison had to pretend he didn't notice that she sometimes had Feng and his internal security apparatus remove any obstacles to her command.

This wasn't a military command and even where he dealt with the military, he had to play politics. If some bureaucrat didn't like some order or command, they could passive aggressively stall or deny it, using obscure rules and regulations to halt or hinder. It boggled his mind how frequently the pencil pushers demanded a ruling from the Central Committee. He, or more correctly Freya, had to track down the request and fabricate Central Committee approval, but it was time consuming.

As long as he pretended the Central Committee was still in charge, he had to play that game and pretend he answered to them. Even the Central Committee "blanket proclamations" giving Mathison authority were subject to question and approval. People were afraid to take responsibility or decide. Passing questions or directives up the chain was the preferred way of avoiding blame for any possible bad decisions, and with all the requests for information or clarification being sent up, there were inevitably bottlenecks. Senior administrators lost or discarded requests out of spite or incompetence, and nobody seemed able to make a decision.

It was the politics of the Governance. Poly, meaning many, and ticks being a blood sucking parasite. Appropriate. Combat and war were so much easier. But even the military was mired in politics, though the civilian bureaucracy made the military look like the epitome of efficiency and competence. How the Governance had managed anything was quickly becoming a mystery.

Mathison stood and stretched.

"If I had an excuse, I would have used it long before now. Apparently, this is a tradition and not even Nadya could escape it, or maybe she used it to influence the admirals."

"For such a blood thirsty bitch, I find it hard to believe there were some things she couldn't get out of," Skadi said.

"Or maybe she liked, um, nevermind," Mathison said.

"Sleeping her way through the admiralty?" Skadi finished with a smile. That wasn't exactly what Mathison had been about to say, but it was close enough.

"She had her ways to keep power," Mathison said. Nadya had been a slut, using her body to keep power as much as her mind. She had ruled for nearly a hundred years, taking power after a Vapaus Republic strike on Earth had wiped out a portion of Europe and most of the Central Committee. Nadya Tokarski had ruled as an empress, though her official title had been secretary general. How she had survived so many coup attempts or power grabs, Mathison could only guess, but she was dead now. Most of the admiralty still didn't know, though, and Mathison wasn't keen on telling them. Which meant they were still trying to get her approval and attention. Some were even foolish enough to try to get her to replace Mathison with themselves.

Officially, she was reelected by the Central Committee every ten years, but that had been a farce for the sheep. She had ruled with an iron fist soaked in the blood of her enemies. Mathison wasn't sure anything the Central Committee had told the people had any truth.

Every day, Mathison felt power slipping away, which wouldn't be a problem for him except people were not uniting to fight the vanhat. Despite the possible extinction of the human race, people still acted like selfish, close-minded assholes who expected someone else to deal with the problem. Few understood what a razor's edge they were walking.

"More probes," Skadi said. "Most of them are out near Jupiter."

Another one of Mathison's headaches. Jupiter had a lot of different colonies, mines, shipyards, and other critical facilities. The big gas giant had lots of moons that were being exploited for resources. General Duque was acting as the de facto governor of that part of the Sol System. News from Jupiter was almost an hour old, which didn't seem bad but made it difficult to have an actual conversation.

Mathison didn't enjoy trusting such a high-ranking SOG officer, but his options were limited.

"What kind?"

"A dreadnought from the Zhukov Fleet," Skadi said. "Reports say it was sheathed in some kind of organic shell."

"What took over after Nasaraf?" Mathison asked, a rhetorical question.

Demons that crossed into this dimension collected slaves, or orja, and the possessing demon influenced the shape and capabilities of their thralls. They had shown that these demons, or Jotnar, could collect the thralls of the Jotnar that had been vanquished. Most of these thralls seemed to be of low intelligence but were still capable of flying ships.

Then there were orja like Hermod's team who seemed to be intelligent and capable of walking among normal humans without letting their bloodlust overwhelm them. Finding Hermod associating with the Central Committee had been a nasty surprise. Where else were orja infiltrating human society, and where was Hermod's master?

"ExSec is looking into that," Skadi said, which Mathison knew. ExSec had more questions than answers and the questions were multiplying, while the answers were not. "At this rate, I will expect the answer sometime after we become extinct, or the galaxy dies a heat death."

"Optimist," Mathison said as his screen lit up, showing there was a near space intrusion. The Governance fleet sprang into action, and Mathison watched in real time as automated weapons platforms vaporized the intruders.

The probes were coming in more frequently. They died quickly, but why the vanhat kept wasting ships made little sense.

* * * * *

Chapter Thirty-Nine:
Assassination

Prime Minister Wolf Mathison, USMC

Marching through the corridors with an escort of dark blue, armored troopers didn't make Mathison feel much better. Despite the armor, they were still SOG. They weren't Aesir guarding him, though there was a platoon nearby. Politics sucked, and Mathison couldn't tell them he didn't trust them. Feng was absent, but Skadi was at his side. Nothing about this made him feel any better as he walked down the corridor to the admiralty chambers where the senior generals and admirals were waiting for him.

Captain Kam, a former ODT officer vetted by Feng, walked in front of him. Mathison didn't know if Kam was loyal to him or to Feng. In theory, it wouldn't matter if Feng was as loyal as he said. The fact was that former Commissar Feng, now Director Feng, was a person who kept his true loyalties and goals a secret.

How to resolve the fact he had betrayed them in order to get them into the Central Committee's central chambers? He claimed it was part of a plan, but he had really been putting the Central Committee and the secretary general on trial. Either face off against the vanhat in defense of all humanity, or die. Of course, Mathison hadn't known that was Feng's goal as he stood there with a Peacekeeper blazer pointed at the back of his head. All he had known then was that Feng had betrayed them and allowed them to be captured.

When Feng had discovered Hermod, a vanhat, in the Central Committee chambers, he had decided and sentenced the Council to death, acting quickly to carry out the execution.

How long before Feng decided Mathison wasn't living up to his expectations and took over? Days? Weeks? Months? Minutes, or had he already made plans?

Few people knew that the Central Committee was dead. Feng and Jussi had been very careful about making sure that news was not leaked. They could use deep fake simulations for video and audio broadcasts, hiding the fact. It was hard to say Nadya was dead when she was on video telling everyone to remain calm, that an obscure and otherwise unknown general was now prime minister and spearheading the defense of humanity.

That might work for the subjects of the Governance, but for the senior officers who had never heard of Mathison it would be a very different sell. They might be social fascists, fanatics who considered socialism to be their god, their ideology and religion, but that didn't mean they were fools. Mathison knew what a trap that could be. Nobody liked to accept that their enemy could be smart and capable because that could mean they were right. Not viewing the senior generals and admirals as the enemy was hard to do right now. These people were the smartest, most capable, most brutal and treacherous of the Governance elite. Out of billions, maybe trillions, these people had climbed the highest. The skim of the scum.

He needed them on his side if he was going to save humanity. If they were the typical socialists, he expected they would speak a good line, noble and brave, but in reality they would be self-serving assholes of the highest order. The briefing Feng had provided was proof of that. Kind, honorable people did not rise to the top in monolithic bureaucracies, and that was what the Governance had become. Nadya had kept them in line by accepting their vices, knowing about and turning a blind eye to their crimes and degenerate behavior. Knowing they could be revealed and persecuted kept many in line, buying their loyalty with their guilt. That was another reason to promote the worst, knowing you could control them with their shame and dishonor. If that didn't work, the state could always make something up. With only one real media, one court system, one choice that was controlled by the Governance, there was no escape. If the state turned on you, then it was over. There would be no hope, no mercy. Every bureaucrat understood that. Every SOG officer enforced it, and Mathison didn't know how to change that.

Would it be enough to keep them in line?

There were things that both Feng and Freya had told him he didn't want to know about them, and Mathison would not argue with that assessment right now. He had bigger things to worry about, but then what was he allowing to occur behind closed doors? What crimes, what degeneracy was being tolerated while Mathison concentrated on fighting the vanhat?

The doors opened, and Mathison strode into the chamber. Everyone got to their feet and stood at attention. Mathison marched up to the podium, past the motionless admirals and generals. There were about twenty of them in the room.

At the podium, Kam peeled off to the left and the other guards spread out, directed by Freya or Kam or pre-arranged; Mathison didn't know or care. Skadi walked beside him in her armor, slightly less obvious as Aesir.

Standing at the podium, Mathison looked out over the assembled senior officers. They all looked too damned young. The faces matched his profiles on them, but they looked like kids dressed up in their parents' uniforms, covered with medals and honors.

The Governance had kept them young, favoring them with longevity treatment. The youngest person here, not counting Mathison, was ninety years old, but the oldest didn't look any older than thirty.

They locked their eyes on Mathison, carefully neutral, their faces masks honed by decades of avoiding face crimes. They had risen to their exalted rank by controlling and manipulating the bureaucracy and the military.

They didn't make mistakes.

"Be seated," Mathison said. Not "at ease" or anything to give them a chance to reveal their emotions.

Skadi stood beside him. He was still trying to get used to the absence of her Erikoisjoukot tattoo, which disappeared in public.

Mathison was wearing his armor, minus trauma plates. He had his sidearm but nothing else, and he felt exposed. He felt their hostility focused on him. Each one would be angry and jealous that he or she had not been chosen as the supreme general and prime minister.

They had all worked with or spoken with Skadi or Hui, who were acting as his liaisons with the military forces, but he had only spoken with some of them remotely. He picked out General Ganya Volkov, who he had yelled at the other day. The general had been reluctant to deploy a Guards division from Luna to a South American arcology to support operations there against the vanhat. The Guards had Inkeri generators to protect them. Well, one in five had been equipped. They had taken heavy casualties securing the power plant. The general had complained constantly. D-bombing the facility would have been easy, but would have caused irreparable damage. Volkov was more concerned with conserving his troops than the suffering of the people in the Minas Gerais arcology. Without power, the air filtration systems didn't work properly, and the crops in the hydroponics were dying. The long-term impact of the outage was going to be difficult to analyze.

Then there was Admiral Leung, another prick who wanted to argue about the deployment of his ships. Mathison couldn't recall the exact details, just that Leung had required the threat of violence to make him comply.

Mathison's eyes picked out General Hui. He liked to think of her as an ally, but even that was damned hard. He knew beyond the shadow of a doubt that her loyalty was to Feng. They were lovers, but Mathison wasn't entirely sure that Feng cared about her. He wouldn't rule out that he was using her as an agent in the military. Nadya's records indicated she had slept with several generals and admirals to keep them in line and bind them to her. Looking at these officers, besides receiving youth treatment, they had also received body sculpting, hormones, and enhancements of younger people. The few women were a pleasure to look at, but Mathison knew how dangerous bedding them would be. Sexually assaulting a venomous snake would be safer.

General Pavlovsky was another recognizable face, and Mathison wished he had not reviewed Nadya's personal records. He was one of her favorite lovers.

Why she hadn't encrypted things like that bothered Mathison. She had far too many encrypted files but seemed to take an almost perverse pleasure in not encrypting her sexual conquests.

"There are many changes," Mathison began. He had a speech prepared. Hopefully, it would be short and sweet. Give them barely enough to work with and avoid wasting their time. Easy to say, hard to do. They had hotly debated revealing that Nadya and the rest of the Central Committee were dead. Feng had wanted to avoid that news leaking. Skadi had also supported Feng in that, but Mathison didn't want to build the new government on lies and deceit. He had been overruled, which was annoying but sometimes necessary for a free nation. He couldn't be right all the time.

"One change is that the Central Committee no longer exists." Mathison watched everyone. It had been a compromise. It wasn't a lie, but then telling them that the Central Committee had been executed was a bad idea. Let them draw their own conclusions. They could assume the Committee was dead or imprisoned. They would believe what they wanted to regardless of what Mathison told them and would know they hadn't spoken to their patrons in a while.

"I, and my appointed deputies—" Mathison nodded toward Skadi "—have a lot of responsibility and the Central Committee has stepped down for the duration of this crisis. They have entrusted me with saving humanity. I have fought the vanhat and they may take us as slaves at first, but we will not survive our enslavement. Make no mistake, the vanhat want the complete annihilation of life in our galaxy."

There was no emotion from the group. Nothing.

"I'm telling you this for several reasons. You are the vanguard. You are critical. If you cannot continue to support me and my goals, I will replace you."

Let that sink in. Let them understand they could disappear into InSec prisons if they didn't obey. They would expect InSec torture chambers, and they probably didn't know he had abolished torture. InSec was the only organization that could turn off their anti-torture cybernetics and they would have to know that.

"The Sol System is not the fortress you think it is," he continued, meeting their eyes, recognizing more faces from his briefings. "You know the problems that are occurring planetside. You know about the push to get Inkeris installed on all the ships, weapons platforms, and arcologies. Most of you understand why."

They had better understand. The SOG propaganda machine had been retooled to focus on it. If they didn't believe it personally, they damn well better believe it officially.

"We are facing an extinction-level event, and the survival of humanity is balancing on a razor's edge. I don't give a damn if you believe it personally. Every waking moment needs to be focused on that. Again, failure means extinction."

Short and sweet. Now the part he dreaded.

"Are there questions?"

Several stood to be called on.

"Admiral Gorlovich," Mathison said. He was the commander of Second Force, a section of the Home Fleet, and a fleet unto itself.

"May we ask what happened to the Central Committee?"

Two of them were missing, and Feng was still trying to track them down. The rest were dead and, as he had discussed with Feng, Jussi, and Skadi, this question had to be answered carefully. Nobody doubted it would be asked.

"No," Mathison said. "Their current activities are not your concern."

They would believe what they wanted to, but Mathison didn't want to lie to them. Once you started lying, it became easier to do, and once people discovered your lie, they would never trust you again. Furthermore, lies grew and became difficult to recall. The truth didn't change.

"Are we expecting a vanhat attack, Prime Minister?" Admiral Leung asked.

"Yes, Admiral Leung," Mathison said. A stupid question, and Mathison tried to figure out why a smart officer would ask it.

"Why would we consider our weapons platforms more expendable than the Earthside arcologies, Prime Minister?" Admiral Ivakina asked and Mathison considered shooting the admiral. Not seriously, but the admiral's bias was obvious. Like most SOG officers here in Sol, he considered the people of the arcology to be subhuman and not worth saving. Ivakina wanted to know why he was wasting time sending Inkeris planetside instead of equipping all the weapons platforms with them. Even though the platforms did not have people on them, they could still be shut down or disabled through vanhat interference. For the longest time, sentencing to Earth had not been a reward.

Mathison didn't care for the answer he was going to give, but he had expected it. None of it was a lie, but saving the lives of strangers wasn't exactly a Governance concern most of the time.

"Each person the vanhat takes is an enemy that will come for us. By saving the people of the arcologies, we are saving the human race and denying the vanhat troops to use against us. It is easier for them to absorb people than it is to influence our weapons platforms."

"Why don't we just nuke the arcologies we begin to lose and be done with them?" Ivakina asked.

"Because they are citizens of the Governance," Mathison said. How could this officer be that damned brutal? "You all swore an oath to the Governance and those people are part of the Governance."

Mathison had checked. It may be a stretch to say that, but it wasn't entirely wrong. The Governance could be the Central Committee or the people, depending on how one wanted to interpret that line.

"Where are our junior officers being taken?" one admiral asked.

"What do you mean?" Mathison asked. Taken?

"InSec seems to be taking custody of several promising young officers," the admiral said.

Mathison knew Feng was targeting numerous Fleet officers, specifically looking for ambitious officers who would likely cause trouble and spearhead a rebellion. There were too many things going on for Mathison to keep track of what everyone was doing.

"I will look into it," Mathison said. "But I have the fullest confidence in InSec." A good lie if he was honest with himself, but a safe one. InSec scared him, but the head of InSec, Feng, scared him more. Confidence was politically correct; it wasn't always true. Feng was supposed to be here.

"Will we be attacking the vanhat?" Admiral Leung asked.

"We will eventually take the battle to them. We do not win battles by defending," Mathison said.

"I object," Fleet Admiral Shesnoko said, standing and pointing his sidearm at Mathison, his finger already pulling the trigger.

* * * * *

Chapter Forty:
Zugla Search

2nd Lieutenant Zale Stathis, USMC

Stathis followed Vili aboard the ghost colony, trying to figure out if he should be more assertive. Vili was technically the rank of gunnery sergeant, but it was hard for Stathis to think he outranked him. Of course, the gunny would disabuse him of the notion pretty quickly, he was sure. Stathis just couldn't imagine a lieutenant giving the gunny orders, certainly not a lieutenant that wanted to have a long-lasting career, or life.

Trying not to feel inadequate, Stathis let Vili lead. He was the expert in ghost colonies, wasn't he? A good lieutenant let the specialists lead, right? The "away team," as Stathis was calling it, composed of him, Vili, Hakala, and another HKT named Alli Lochoki, a short bulldog of a woman who would make a man named Butch look feminine. She lived in the weight room and made Stathis uncomfortable. He decided having ex-SOG troopers come along would be a very bad idea. He didn't want to think about what would happen if the locals discovered they were SOG.

Both the HKTs had hidden their batwing tattoos. Stathis wasn't sure how, but it made Hakala look unnatural and a little less exotic. He noticed she had a teardrop tattoo under an eye like she was crying. He would ask her about that later.

After customs, which Stathis felt was generic and boring, basically some official telling them to be nice and giving them temporary ID cards, they were let onto the station. No health screening, no pat downs, no frowns at weapons. Vili wasn't carrying anything bigger than a wire carbine that almost looked like a pistol on the big man. Stathis wanted to carry something a lot heavier, but that probably wasn't appropriate, and he had to consider the politics of things now. It was his job to keep people out of trouble, and he wanted to scream about the injustice of it.

The colony was clean and bright, with a low level of gravity that would increase the hilarity of a stupid mistake, so Stathis moved with caution because he didn't want to do anything stupid around Hakala.

Another big change from being a private. Now, as a lieutenant, he was the one in charge. As a private, he could ask to carry a machine gun and get slapped down. If they needed it later it wasn't his fault. But now, as an actual officer who was supposed to be making those decisions, Vili had talked him out of arming everyone with blazers and extra ammo bags. Vili hadn't even bothered to tell him the rocket tubes should be left behind. Vili was starting to ignore some of Stathis's comments that were obvious, and Stathis wasn't sure what to do about that.

It sucked. He wanted a combat deployment, but that wouldn't fly. Even as a private, he had known things like that, but being the one to actually say no didn't sit well with him.

Was that why he was letting Vili lead? So that if there was a screwup he could blame it on Vili?

The gunny would rip his ass off and feed it to him if he used that as an excuse. Good Marines didn't blame others, they made things happen.

So, what would the gunny do?

Exactly what Stathis was doing. Let Vili lead the way and spearhead the small expedition.

Meanwhile, Stathis did what? Shut up? With nobody around to tell him that, he felt abandoned.

Should he do something to impress Hakala? Be authoritative or something?

What would the gunny say? Mission first, think with the dick later.

No wonder the gunny was single.

Vili led them onto the docks, which weren't busy. Just gray steel corridors, lights, and numbered bulkheads. No thriving marketplace.

"Where is everyone?" Stathis asked.

"Not all colonies are welcoming of others," Vili said. "Business up front, party in the back. Some colonies are very conservative, almost xenophobic, and don't like to interact with strangers, so they do what they can to discourage long stays. This is likely one of those colonies. Yes. My invisible friend is confirming this."

Grendel was Vili's "invisible friend," like Shrek was Stathis'.

Stathis tried not to wince. He should have been thinking of that. He had given Shrek permission to access the station network, then forgot about it.

"How's it going?" Stathis asked.

"I was wondering when you would ask," Shrek said. *"The network here is very intense. Outside of Quantico, I have not seen a network this structured and well protected. The colony is mostly composed of scientists and eggheads, so perhaps it is not such a big surprise. This is not typical of what I have seen of ghost colonies."*

"Any sign of Becket or Sun Tzu?"

"Not yet. The data archives are well protected and accessing them without permission will be intrusive and noticeable. Do you want me to be invasive?"

"*No!*" Stathis said. Having vanhat try to kill him was one thing. Having local authorities try to kill him was a different level of unpleasant.

With Hakala present, he would not ask Vili about the women, not that he would know, but he probably had a lot more experience in that category. Vili wasn't a prude like the gunny, who was married to the Corps.

"Do you have a destination?" Stathis asked.

"Yes," Vili replied, loud enough the HKTs could hear. "We are going to visit a pub. This seemed to feature prominently in searches, which would indicate they cater to foreigners like us. I expect there to be resources there to help us find what we are looking for."

"Oh, good," Stathis said. Officers weren't allowed to get drunk and do stupid things though, were they? Or maybe their mistakes were just covered up by smart gunnies.

Stathis really hated this officer thing. He was supposed to bail out others, but who would bail him out? Winters? That would not be a fun experience, he was sure. Aside from the fact that Winters was a lesbian, Stathis wasn't sure if she just hated guys or just didn't care. He didn't want to find out she had some deep-seated hatred. How did officers chill out and blow off steam? No wonder they tended to be a bunch of uptight, anal-retentive assholes most of the time.

Shrek provided Stathis with directions on his internal cybernetic displays, giving Stathis time to look around.

Aside from the customs agent, it was mostly just robots coming and going.

"*You sure there aren't vanhat stacking up in nearby rooms?*" Stathis asked Shrek.

"No. Except the Inkeri field is online and active, so if they are going to come at us we will have a better chance."

That made Stathis feel a little better. The Spartan platoon was on standby, fully armed and armored. Probably griping about how they were sitting there running drills and ready to rush out into a fight for their lives while he went and got a beer. Stathis would rather be there. Well, maybe not exactly. Hakala was here.

There were two other people at the tram station, a pair of younger guys in maintenance jumpsuits that talked quietly and kept their distance.

Was it night shift and everyone was at home sleeping?

The tram was bright and clean. It didn't have that overused, busy look and didn't smell of urine. Nearby, a pair of robots moved about, cleaning the spotless station. If this was a colony of eggheads, they were probably fanatical about cleanliness and order.

Minutes later, they arrived at a cylinder named Cy-01. Not the most imaginative name in Stathis's opinion. The tram slid into a station revealing a large city spread out around him. The cylinder stretched off into the distance, mostly city and parks. Pleasant, a nice place to raise kids, until the vanhat came to eat them all.

They went down some steps below a park platform and the pub was directly in front of them.

The Beaker was an interesting name and had a pouring glass hologram out front. Nearby stores sold things like candy, toys, and electronics. They were kid's toys, though, and Stathis did not find them interesting.

Entering the pub, Vili led them to a table where they could see the entrance and the rest of the room. Not what Stathis would have chosen, but Vili was leading at the moment and maybe hiding in the back was not ideal. They were here to learn things, not get away with things.

There weren't many people, but their eyes quickly locked on the newcomers.

As soon as they sat, a man dressed in a more formal jumpsuit came up to them. He had been sitting so Stathis didn't think he was the server, and there were several squat, headless robots moving around the room. Hakala sat next to Stathis, and he wondered if she was closer than normal.

"Hello there, strangers," the man said, looking around as if trying to find out who was in charge. His eyes finally settled on Stathis. Why him? Vili was bigger.

"Hello," Stathis said, wondering if he should scoot closer to Hakala, further away, or pretend he didn't notice.

"My name is Bren. I just thought I would come over and welcome you to our station and inquire as to why you are here."

"Bold," Vili said. "That's Stathis, I am Vili. These fine ladies are Bryngerd and Alli."

Bren smiled.

"We are here looking for information," Vili said.

"What kind of information?"

"The comings and goings of others," Vili said.

Bren didn't ask before he sat at the table with them, next to Hakala, where he could look at Vili.

"Lots of people come and go," Bren said. "Some of us like to keep track of such things. To learn about what is going on out in human space. Officials rarely share this information."

"He is talking with others," Shrek reported. *"Heavy-duty encryption. Not sure who or what."*

Bren looked smooth and cultured. Like a spy?

What would a spy be doing here? A spy for who?

Stathis noticed Bren's drink was barely touched. A fresh drink? Had he arrived just before the away team, perhaps? It made him think of how the SOG had intercepted them, or the gang bangers that had found them quickly on Curitiba and Jason's Pit.

"For sure," Vili said. "We believe someone came here, and we are wondering where he went afterward."

Wouldn't a genuine agent have taken several drinks, so his prey didn't get the impression he had arrived before them?

What would the gunny do?

"Are you bounty hunters, then?" Bren asked, his eyes flickering toward Vili's holster and the wire gun slung at his side.

"Message to Vili," Stathis said to Shrek. *"I think this guy is a spy."*

"Close little buddy," Vili said. *"He is probably with the colony intelligence agency or police. An investigator type for sure. Just the kind of guy we wanted to find. If anyone knows, he will."*

Stathis shut up. Well, that made sense, and Vili knew what he was doing.

"Why didn't we just go to the authorities to start with?" Stathis asked through Shrek.

"Officially, they won't provide that information. It would be considered a violation of privacy."

"Not exactly," Vili said aloud. "He is an acquaintance of my little buddy here. They have things in common, and my buddy has some questions for him. They aren't enemies; they served together."

"I see," Bren said, his eyes going back to Stathis. "Is he expecting you? Will this be a pleasant reunion?"

"To be honest, we don't know," Vili said. "He left suddenly, and we aren't sure why."

"Who was this person?"

Vili turned to Stathis.

"His name is Alexander Becket. He was probably traveling alone," Stathis said. It had been a damn small ship, smaller than the *Tikari* had been.

"There was a small ship that came here recently," Bren said. "One man got off. When he returned to his ship, it left."

"Is there further information?" Vili asked.

"Perhaps," Bren said. "I have to check with my friends who might know more."

"This is information we may find valuable," Vili said, and Stathis realized he did not know how much or what he could pay with.

"I'm sure we can likely find an equitable trade."

Stathis watched and tried to figure out what they would trade. Hopefully, Vili wouldn't put him on the spot.

* * * * *

Chapter Forty-One:
The Jungles

2nd Lieutenant Zale Stathis, USMC

Stathis was working on dinner, feeling guilty about the rest of the platoon, which probably wasn't eating as well as they remained ready to come save him. He might need rescue from dessert. The food here was pretty good, and Stathis was enjoying listening to Vili talk to Bren about a ghost colony named Vishnu, founded by Indians fleeing the war of Chinese aggression hundreds of years ago when China joined the Governance before India did.

Stathis hadn't known Vili was so well read as he told them about how India and China had been at war when the SOG absorbed China, sparking a civil war in China as parts of the CCP rebelled against the merge. The Indian government had thought to exploit the division but hadn't counted on the SOG to come to China's aid so quickly.

Millions of Indians had fled, hoping for a more peaceful life among the stars. They found Vishnu as China, now reinforced by the SOG, pressured India to join the SOG as a lesser member.

Hearing Vili talk about nations and countries he recognized made it more real to him.

Bren must have received some message while they were talking.

"Good news," Bren said. "I think your captain and my associates have come to an agreeable outcome."

Which irritated Stathis. He had wanted to see what the deal involved, maybe learn something. Hopefully, it involved everyone keeping their clothes on.

"Very good," Vili said as Bren fixed his gaze on Stathis.

"It appears that a person calling himself Alex has visited recently," Bren said. "An interesting person, I'm told. We are sending you a packet with video confirmation. Skinny and bald, not a pretty or young-looking person. He was here for several days but spent little time here. He visited some of the less well-known cylinders and then left in a tiny starship. We only saw him coming and going." He paused. "Very odd."

"What was odd?" Stathis asked.

"He seemed to know the place. He came and went with minimal interaction with others and seemed to have authorizations that most people don't."

"Authorizations?" Stathis asked.

"Yes, well," Bren began cautiously, making Stathis wonder how much information they had actually purchased. "You may have read the official visitor information about Zugla? How we have twelve cylinders? This is not entirely true. We have sixteen, and all but two of them are nature preserves. In fact, most of the cylinders have nobody living there. We are mostly descendants from the original maintenance and construction crew. Since the colony was founded, very little has changed. We continue to maintain automated systems and build nature preserves. We have a board of directors, mostly hereditary, that runs the colony, and they remain true to the founding principles. There are many things most citizens don't know about the cylinders because we never go there. In fact, they are mostly forbidden to people. Some are places to visit, but most remain off limits, untainted by human inter-action."

Why would they keep four cylinders secret? What would they keep there?

"I cannot divulge exactly what occurs in those places, but preser-vation is only part of our mission. Experimentation and evolution are another part, though you'll never find that in any documentation."

"Why are you telling us this?" Vili asked.

"Did I mention how Alex had authorizations that most people don't?" Bren said and took another drink. Now he seemed slightly nervous. Vili was a big guy, but he wasn't acting threatening right now. If he was, Bren would probably shit his pants. What was he nervous about then?

"For sure," Vili said, and Stathis thought about Sun Tzu cutting through station security.

"Security is very tight here," Shrek added. *"I don't think it will be easy to get us equal access. The hardening on these systems is like nothing I've ever encoun-tered before."*

"Which means what?"

"Sun Tzu didn't get him that authorization. Maybe the other AI, which would indicate it is much more advanced and capable than a regular SCBI, or he got the authorizations another way."

Vili glanced at Stathis, and he realized Vili must be having a similar conversation with Grendel.

"I have very high-ranking friends who are very curious about this," Bren said, and Stathis wondered if that was just a manager or someone on the board of directors. "We don't know of anyone who has this kind of access."

"Except the board of directors?" Vili asked, and a shadow crossed Bren's face as Stathis realized that, no, not even the board of directors had that kind of access.

"I cannot say," Bren said, but Stathis understood the lie.

"Do you know where he went?" Stathis asked.

"No," Bren said. "He returned from Cylinder Sixteen and departed without talking with anyone. He left little information in the network as well, almost as if someone was cleaning up traces of his existence behind him."

Which would be Sun Tzu, most likely.

"A dead end then?" Stathis asked Vili.

"Maybe," Vili said, looking at Bren. "Unless we can find out why Becket was here. Perhaps there is someone else we can talk to?"

Bren took another sip of his drink and leaned back. It was one of the more expensive drinks on the menu. Bren's meal was also expensive. For an information broker or spy, he must be rich, unless Winters was footing the bill now.

"My high-ranking friends are very curious," Bren said. "We may overlook certain actions if they are made in the pursuit of additional knowledge. No citizens must come to harm, of course, but with current events occurring in the galaxy we believe that more information will be helpful for our survival."

"How high-ranking are your friends?" Vili asked, and Bren just smiled. Not a real answer, but apparently good enough for Vili.

"We also would like answers," Vili said, not pushing it. "Perhaps you could point us to where he went, and we can retrace his steps?"

"That makes sense," Bren said. "However, it may not be that simple. Cylinder Sixteen is special. It is the largest cylinder by far, sixty kilometers in length. A tropical jungle with unique fauna and flora. Very dangerous."

"We are experienced with danger," Stathis said. Bren nodded. He had to be part of the conversation somehow. Officers didn't let others do all the talking for them did they?

"Even then it won't be a, how to put it, walk in the park? More like a military expedition."

"We might be able to manage," Vili said. "Would you have a guide or other expert we can hire?"

A wry smile flickered across Bren's face.

"Perhaps," Bren said. "We have a person in custody who may be of assistance. He likes to go places he is not allowed and explore. He is not the most law-abiding citizen, but perhaps he could be of benefit to you?"

"Take me to the brig where I can see the real Marines," Stathis said softly.

"Pardon?" Bren said, now looking confused.

"Uh, nothing," Stathis said. He really should learn to not say things out loud. Lieutenants didn't say stupid things like that. Besides, nobody here got the humor. The gunny would have. Maybe Colonel Winters.

"It may take a day or so to arrange things," Bren said. "Custody of this individual may be tricky."

"Is this guide dangerous?" Vili asked.

"He can be, I'm sure," Bren said, "but he is not excessively violent or hostile. Just not what we consider orthodox, and he has mixed enough samples for the authorities here to prefer he not remain."

328 | WILLIAM S. FRISBEE, JR.

Mixed enough samples? Of what? Was that a term because they were eggheads and couldn't say normal things like "pissed in people's Cheerios"?

"Would he be willing to assist us?" Vili asked.

"Perhaps if he could leave with you," Bren said. "I'm sure we could find encouragement for him to provide assistance, if you will share information about what you find with us."

"Equitable," Vili said.

"And perhaps we could send along a more official observer to help expedite things?" Bren said.

Which Stathis understood as a spy or minder.

"That sounds fair," Vili said with a quick glance at Stathis. Stathis nodded. Like he could say no? The mission was to find Becket, not keep colony secrets from colonists who lived here. Did Vili look to him for actual approval or because he wanted to include Stathis? Damn.

"Would the board of directors disapprove of anything about this?" Stathis asked. Vili and Bren were being very circumspect about things, and Stathis wasn't sure how to ask that without being so obvious, but it seemed like a pretty important question.

Bren looked at Stathis, perhaps realizing how dumb he was.

"No," Bren finally said, which answered Stathis' question but revealed nothing else. Was Bren working with the board of directors? How could he not be? Unless the board of directors was divided and political. Stathis realized he might be misreading things here. Boards of directors made Stathis think of stuffy managers and high-ranking eggheads in charge of departments, but that was just terminology he was familiar with. They ran a colony, a small country, and they would be political by nature. Probably more politician than egghead.

Which didn't make Stathis feel better. A stupid private mistake. This might make more sense.

"What's the deal with this board of directors?" Stathis asked Shrek.

"According to available data, there are six directors. Four have held their position for almost two centuries, which would indicate longevity treatment. There are few details so it may be possible they are just family members who take the name as they take the role on the board. Regardless, they rule and obey a set of edicts. Not all are public, and based on the stability of the colony, appear to be doing a good job. Officially, they are focused on the preservation of nature and seem to take this seriously. Details are hard to confirm."

"Thanks," Stathis said. So, the board members were ancient and stuck in their ways. *"What about the founder guy?"*

"Nobody has seen or heard from him in over two hundred years," Shrek said. *"His death or fate is not public knowledge."*

"So, he could be some brain in a jar somewhere?"

"Not impossible."

"Some brain in a jar ancient dude could be running things?"

"Not impossible. I have no data to confirm or deny this theory."

That was creepy. Shrek had no problem calling his ideas stupid sometimes.

"So," Vili said, "What do you recommend we do now?"

"Enjoy the hospitality of our wonderful colony," Bren said. "There are some OQs that need to be met."

"OQs?" Stathis asked Shrek.

"Operational Qualifications. More of a pharmaceutical term, if I understand the context. It is a procedure that checks and documents the different aspects of a procedure or process. In this case, it may reference legal and technical authorizations."

"For sure," Vili said as Bren stood. Everyone else followed.

They shook hands and Bren walked away, leaving the pub.

"That went well," Stathis said.

"For sure. But he stuck us with the bill."

* * * * *

Chapter Forty-Two:
Guide

2nd Lieutenant Zale Stathis, USMC

Stathis didn't want to argue with Smimova. He understood his platoon sergeant's concern, but what he understood more than anything was that Smimova wanted off the ship. The platoon sergeant was going stir crazy.

"I need someone I trust to be ready to come bail my ass out of trouble," Stathis said. Did lieutenants use words like ass? Or did they use more sophisticated words? Dammit. That was probably what officers learned in school. How to call an ass something more sophisticated. Was donkey right?

"A squad isn't enough, sir," Smimova said.

"We don't have a company or battalion," Stathis told him, wishing Vili was here to back him up.

"We will be too far away to come help."

Which made sense, but all the books Stathis read talked about keeping a reserve. Smimova and the two squads were the reserve, but if they were too far away, they wouldn't be much of a reserve.

He didn't like it, though. Having everyone there with him meant that there would be nobody he could call for help. Colonel Winters and her crew wouldn't be worth as much in a fight as ex-Peacekeepers and ex-ODTs.

332 | WILLIAM S. FRISBEE, JR.

"I don't expect a major fight," Stathis said. "We're just going to trek through a jungle, try to find out where Becket went, then come back. We probably don't need a heavy-hitting force of trigger pullers."

"You aren't a stupid boot lieutenant," Smimova said, telling Stathis he was exactly that. "In my experience, it is best to use an overwhelming amount of force and violence rather than an underwhelming force. Bringing the entire platoon will be good training and show everyone that we mean business. That will discourage anyone from messing with us."

Stathis was tempted to share his experience with Smimova, but wasn't that a major red flag when a boot lieutenant said 'in my experience'?

But Smimova made perfect sense. US Marine Raiders weren't always so heavy-handed though, preferring surgical work to more common blunt force trauma inducement. Sometimes a small force could accomplish more than a larger force, but Smimova didn't really care. He just wanted off the ship.

"Our guide and minder have arrived," Shrek said. *"Interesting. They removed our guide's hand cuffs inside the transport van, as if they don't want us to know he was under arrest."*

"We have company," Stathis said.

He was tempted to tell Smimova that he was the platoon sergeant, not the platoon commander, and that he should shut up and follow orders. But that was what a boot lieutenant who was full of himself would do. Smimova had more experience, but did he? Stathis had to remind himself that the SOG NCOs were not Marine NCOs and weren't trusted with important decisions. The fact that Smimova was arguing meant what?

"Why are you arguing with me?" Stathis asked, annoyed, and looked at Smimova more closely. The platoon sergeant's face paled.

Smimova came to the position of attention. "Aesir Vili has directed me to do so, sir. He directed me to voice my opinion as frequently and insistently as possible. He said this is how Marines do things. This trooper apologizes if has crossed a line and—"

"No," Stathis said. Shit. Vili told Smimova to be an asshole and question everything? Quick to throw Vili under the bus as well. Good to know.

"No, sir?"

"No, keep questioning me," Stathis said. Of course, it would be easier if Smimova didn't. "Just not in public. I just didn't think Governance troops did stuff like that."

"They don't, sir," Smimova said.

"At ease, sit down," Stathis said. "I was just wondering. I thought most Governance NCOs were just yes-men who didn't think, just enforced orders."

"Well," Smimova said, sitting back down but looking uncomfortable, "usually we don't. Aesir Vili is trying to change things and, to be honest, most of what he says makes sense, but it is not SOG policy. I have never fought against the Aesir, but they have a reputation."

Had the gunny assigned him a platoon of rebels to get back at him for all the old person jokes and needling him?

Stathis leaned back in his seat. Hundreds of years ago, literally, he had dated this cute blond named Michelle, and her dad was a Marine recruiter. Trying to impress her, and him, he had enlisted. Figured it might be fun and prove to everyone once and for all that he was not a short loser. When he enlisted, thinking he was doing her dad a favor by helping him meet quota, her dad had told him the designation of

03 was a computer programmer. Which was cool, Stathis had some experience with computers and programming. It wasn't cool when he found out later, after boot camp, it was infantry. He rolled with it, though, and decided to show that dumbass pogue just what a badass he was. One thing led to another, and he ended up in the Raiders. Stathis had no regrets, but if the gunny thought that assigning him a platoon of rejects was going to humble him, the gunny didn't know him. Or did he?

Damn it. Had the gunny sent him these rejects because he had so much in common with them?

"We have guests?" Shrek said, reminding Stathis.

"Right," Stathis said out loud. "Let's go meet our guests. Our guide and minder are here."

"Wilc—I mean, um, aye, sir." Smimova followed Stathis to the hatch.

Vili, Winters, Hakala, and an HKT named Alli met them there, and as the hatch slid open, Stathis stared at them.

The guide was a smaller man, almost Stathis' size, and he had a wild, unkept, untamed look, a scraggily beard, and a rugged, brown jumpsuit. His bright blue eyes scanned the area.

The minder, though, took Stathis' breath away. He had expected a spook, a generic guy, someone easy to forget. This woman was a few centimeters taller and had curves in all the right places. She wore dark green and had a holstered weapon on her hip. Black hair and intense gray eyes locked on Stathis. He wanted to look around to see if Hakala had noticed, but he didn't dare. He couldn't speak as he met her eyes.

"Greetings, Captain Winters," the woman said taking her eyes off Stathis. "My name is Lydia Jones. I'm here to accompany your expedition through Cylinder Sixteen. This is Kyle Spears, a resident, uh, expert on the cylinder."

"It is a pleasure to meet you," Winters said. "This is my expedition commander, Lieutenant Stathis. He will lead the expedition."

Her eyes came back to Stathis, and he wanted to escape. Did pretty women only lift their nose at privates?

"A pleasure to meet you," Stathis said, hoping Hakala wouldn't take that the wrong way. Not that he and Hakala were a couple or anything, but damn. If he had known lieutenants got more attention from women, he would have tried for officer a lot earlier.

Well, no, that wasn't true, and Hakala had seemed to like him just fine as a private and that meant something.

"When do you plan to leave?" Lydia asked.

"We are finalizing a roster and equipment now," Stathis said. "I expect we will depart first thing in the morning."

"We have quarters for Kyle," Winters said. "Do you need quarters?"

"I'll be fine," Lydia said, her eyes roving over Stathis, and he felt his face grow warm. It took effort for him not to say "yes, she is." Lieutenants didn't say stupid things like that, did they?

"We are planning now. Would you care to join us?" Vili asked, which was good because Stathis had no idea what to say. Not all the blood was in the brain on his shoulders.

"An excellent idea," Lydia said.

Stathis turned and almost bumped into Hakala, who was watching Lydia like a tiger about to pounce. She was so close he could smell her. Vanilla, and he liked it.

"This way," Vili said and started off.

Now Stathis realized Kyle hadn't said anything. As a guide, he should be a bit more outgoing, right?

* * * * *

Chapter Forty-Three:
Expedition Planning

2nd Lieutenant Zale Stathis, USMC

The room wasn't crowded but Stathis felt out of his league. Being a private that got on everyone's nerves had saved him from such meetings. Now he not only had to attend the meetings, he had to participate because he was the poor bastard in command. He really shouldn't have pissed off the gunny so badly. Perhaps the old person jokes had been over the top.

As if all the senior, more experienced leaders in the room wasn't bad enough, there were Hakala and Lydia, who were distracting. Stathis tried not to imagine that Lydia was watching him, but it was damn hard because every time he looked in her direction she was looking in his. A good Marine lieutenant should think with the head on his shoulders, not the one controlling the stick shift and ball bearings, so Stathis stood taller and tried to put a serious look on his face as Kyle shared his knowledge on Cylinder Sixteen.

"Well," Kyle said, standing and looking around, his eyes lingering on Lydia. It was hard to tell what he was thinking, but Stathis didn't consider it to be favorable. "It is disturbing that I'm the expert on what you call Cylinder Sixteen. Can't say I know half as much about it as you might think."

"You know more than anyone I know," Lydia said. "As you are one of the very few people who have been there, despite certain restrictions."

"Why are we restricted from there?" Kyle asked, and Lydia shrugged. Stathis wasn't sure if that was because she didn't know or wouldn't say. Her expression gave them no clue.

"Hmm," Kyle said, letting his eyes rove around the others. He gave a half smile. "Let me tell you what the directors probably don't want me to: Cylinder Sixteen is not the sixteenth cylinder. It might actually be the first."

Stathis glanced at Lydia, who was staring at Kyle. She seemed as surprised as everyone else.

"Why do you say that?" Winters asked.

"Nobody knew about the cylinder until we began building cylinder fifteen," Kyle said. "An accident, really, as I understand it. Someone decided not to follow the diagram because it made little sense and accidentally tapped the buffer of Cylinder Sixteen, which drowned out the machines and tunnels, causing something of a problem. This occurred a year ago."

"The buffer?" Smimova asked.

"Each cylinder is like a can within a can. The space between those cans usually contains water. This helps with heat dispersal, radiation protection, provides an auxiliary water supply, minimizes friction, and wear and tear as the internal cylinder rotates. Cylinder Sixteen is fully self-contained."

"Why is it called Sixteen if it isn't?" Stathis asked.

Kyle looked at him, and Stathis realized that was probably a stupid private question.

"Because we discovered it after fifteen. Not sure if it should be called Cylinder Zero or if there is no other designation available. We really have no records."

"So how do you know so much about it?" Winters asked.

"My brother was killed in the flood when it was discovered," Kyle said. "I was a park ranger in Cylinder Twelve and I got curious. I started digging, found a way in, and started exploring. The directors found out about my expeditions and didn't seem to like that. The directors have forbidden any interaction with the cylinder until now, apparently."

"Why?" Winters asked, her gaze shifting to Lydia.

"I'm not entirely sure," Lydia said. "Our society has many directives, many rules and regulations." Lydia took a deep breath, and Stathis felt she was going to reveal some secret. "Not all the directors are in alignment," she said cautiously and glanced at Kyle as if he might contradict her. "Some directors feel the presence of Sixteen should become a state secret. We have classified all references and knowledge of it as such. This is a piece of our history, and I am not a member of the board, but I think there are secrets on the board."

"So," Vili said, reminding everyone he was there, "at least one powerful director knows about this secret and wishes to keep it from other directors. You work for a director that does not know this secret but feels he or she should. Is this a true statement?"

Lydia's pursed lips told Stathis that Vili was right.

"Close, but I'm not at liberty to discuss that," she said. "I would recommend this expedition occur with utmost secrecy, however."

"For sure," Vili said, looking around. "I think we understand. Then I think you may continue, Mister Spears."

"Thank you," Kyle said. "Sixteen is the largest cylinder. Nearly sixty kilometers long, with a diameter of fifteen kilometers. It is huge, and that is another mystery. There are material limitations in creating something that large. It has a full atmosphere and full Earth-style gravity. Some very complex robots perform maintenance and other tasks. Not standard Zugla robots either."

"AI?" Stathis asked Shrek.

"Per Kyle's description, that sounds like the most likely possibility. Perhaps not all Americans and SCBIs were killed, and they came here."

"But why? Where are they now?"

"If Kyle doesn't know, how would I?"

Stathis would not answer that. Getting smart with Shrek didn't work well, and he was too distracted to come up with a sufficiently smartass response.

"How do you know?" Winters asked.

"As a park ranger, my job was to use robots and maintain other cylinder preserves. I'm very familiar with the preserves, the technology, and the directives that govern things. The robots in Sixteen don't have any markings and aren't standard models. Almost like someone else is maintaining it, but it's too close to other cylinders."

"So, besides finding out what our subject was doing there, you want us to find out who maintains the cylinder?" Vili asked.

"That is accurate," Lydia said.

"So, I have only had access to one end of the cylinder," Kyle said. "Probably the outer end. Whoever owns or manages the cylinder is probably in the cylinder or at the other end. I think our best bet is to cross the cylinder and explore the far end. As we cross the cylinder we can explore anything of interest, but that is a lot of territory to explore."

"How hard can that be? It is a cylinder," Stathis asked.

"Math," Shrek said. *"At sixty kilometers in length and a radius of fifteen kilometers, that is a surface area of over seven thousand kilometers. By comparison, this is more surface area than Delaware and almost half of Connecticut, almost a third the size of New Jersey."*

Stathis remembered the diameter of the planetoid that hid the ghost colony was over nine thousand kilometers. Big enough to have a lot of other hidden cylinders. The planetoid had no noticeable gravity or tectonic activity. It was just a big, massive rock floating through space.

Seven thousand kilometers seemed like a lot, but Stathis still didn't think it was bad. Sixty kilometers in length, though. Two days to walk? Becket had done it.

"It appears to be all jungle," Kyle said. "Thick, rugged jungle, full of snakes, spiders, scorpions, and lizards. Lots of venomous ones, too, and several species I've never seen before."

Stathis thought about Papua New Guinea. That had been a real shit hole. Even without the Asian Union's biological agents poisoning the air for humans, the local wildlife had been disturbing enough. Stathis had nightmares of a brown widow spider climbing around inside his face plate. He had woken up one morning to find one climbing around on the outside of his faceplate. Having one inside would have been a very nasty surprise. Suffer the spider bites on his face or expose himself to possibly lethal bio-agents. A tough decision. Never mind how the spider could get in. And to think that Marines once slept in jungles without full armor and protection was something Stathis didn't want to think about.

"So, we will wear full seal suits and armor," Stathis said. "No problem there."

There was no way in hell he was going into a jungle again, not without wearing full protection. Easy lieutenant decision.

Kyle looked at Stathis.

"We will get you something," Stathis said, now less sure.

"Any form of flier or transportation we can use?" Vili asked, and Stathis wanted to bang his head on the table. He had been planning to walk. Infantry walked everywhere and there was Vili, looking for an easy way.

"Probably not," Kyle said. "They limit the access tunnels to the north end, where we will enter. Not big at all. It would take us some time to build something there. The initial breach and flood occurred within a kilometer of the north end. The south end is sunk deep in the planetoid, and I have found no tunnels or route to the south end. Not to say they don't exist, but I haven't found them."

So. Estimate three days there, two days on site, three days back, which was probably three days more than they really needed. A week without his nice warm bed. No problem.

"Maybe a week and a half of food and ammunition then," Vili said, looking at Stathis.

A week and a half? Would they need that much ammunition?

No problem. They had some infantry mules to carry stuff.

"Might aim at two weeks to be safe," Stathis said. Lieutenants said shit like that, right? Or was that a staff NCOs job? Make people think he was planning ahead and being cautious. "And extra ammunition."

Stathis remembered running low on ammunition on Curitiba. Not a good feeling. He couldn't remember ever coming back from a combat mission wishing he had carried less ammunition.

"Blazer rifles with wire carbines," Stathis said. Vanhat didn't like blazers and, for everything else, wire guns were usually good.

"Zen," Vili said with a nod. Approval? Had that been the right lieutenant thing to say? Cool.

"Sidearms?" Vili asked, and Stathis tried not to wince. Sidearms were not usually standard infantry weapons, special operations usually got them along with the crew of crew-served weapons.

"Personal preference," Stathis said. He knew he was going to carry at least two wire gun pistols and a blazer pistol. Might even carry that dart gun he got on Jason's Pit. He really wanted to try that.

Vili nodded.

"So tomorrow we gear up and head out," Stathis said. Robots could get everything prepped. This lieutenant stuff wasn't so bad. "We have some spare suits for Kyle and Lydia right, Colonel?" Stathis asked Winters.

"We will have something," Winters said, almost appearing amused.

"Great," Stathis said.

"Now, transportation to the cylinder," Vili said, looking at Lydia. "We will take a full squad and four mules. What kind of transportation is available and how long is the trip?" Stathis tried not to scowl. "Should we stage the reserves close to the cylinder?" Vili continued looking at Stathis.

Logistics sounded so simple. Lieutenants made a plan and everyone else carried it out, but planning took a lot more than just figuring out which enemies to kill or hill to scout.

It was going to be a long night. Maybe this lieutenant stuff wasn't so easy. No wonder the gunny never wanted to be an officer. He had set the deadline for tomorrow, thinking like a stupid private. Now he would be up all night paying for that mistake.

* * * * *

Chapter Forty-Four:

Sixteen

2nd Lieutenant Zale Stathis, USMC

Stathis was starting to wonder if they would ever actually make it to the cylinder. Sitting in the van, Stathis leaned back to sleep. He hadn't gotten as much sleep as he had thought he would. There had been calls to make and figuring out if he could stage the rest of the platoon nearer Cylinder Sixteen had been a challenge. Stathis had missed how Sixteen was actually five hours away by tram, which changed the dynamics of everything.

At first Stathis thought this would be a good chance to catch up on his sleep. However, Private Stepnakowski, or Steps as Stathis thought of him, was tapping his rifle on the floor of the van buggy. A box with wheels on the corners and such a low profile it would have problems going over a soccer ball, which could best describe the wheels. Part of him wanted to look at them more closely, but then he really just wanted to climb in and sleep.

But Steps was tapping his rifle on the floor, and that was distracting.

"Knock it off, Steps," Stathis said.

"Knock what off, sir?" Steps asked, innocently. Stathis knew the private was fully aware of what was being discussed.

"If I have to tell you, I won't. I'll let Staff Sergeant Smirnova discuss it with Sergeant Lan who will discuss it with Lance Corporal Malchansky who will then explain it to you. I'm trying to sleep, and I get cranky when I don't get my sleep."

"Yes, sir," Steps said.

"You mean 'aye, sir,'" Stathis corrected him.

"Aye, sir," Steps said, and the tapping stopped. Stathis was waiting for Steps to find some other way to irritate him when someone named Shrek mentally nudged him.

"We are here," Shrek said. Stathis wanted to swear. He just wasn't going to get any sleep, was he?

The door slid open, and Stathis looked around. It was a large, open area with several small hatches nearby. This was as far as the vans could bring them. There were no markings, no sign they were somewhere relevant, and the corridor stopped here in a large, empty space. There was no dust, no indication anyone had been here recently. This large chamber was timeless.

"There is no gravity," Shrek warned him as he stepped out, the magnets in his boot latching onto the metal plating of the deck. Stepping away, he saw several members of second squad were already out and unpacking the mules and equipment. Vili was moving around directing people. Stathis looked around for something to do, or someone to tell him what to do. It took a second to realize nobody would tell him what to do though, since he was supposed to be the one in charge.

"Anything I can do?" Stathis asked Vili on a private link.

"For sure. Stay out of our way. I've got it under control."

Stathis stood there watching. What would Gunny be doing? Probably what Vili was doing. So, what would a good lieutenant do? Probably make himself scarce. Climbing back into the van to sleep probably wasn't an option. He saw Kyle standing over to the side, watching. He had armor with trauma plates and looked almost like one of the troopers, except he didn't have as many weapons and his load out seemed light. Beside him were Lydia and Hakala. He should probably be there listening or getting more information. Stathis wasn't sure how or why Hakala was with the expedition. Winters had said it would help to have an HKT on the team since she was familiar with ship-based and station systems, experience that nobody else on the expedition had. Besides, she was a very competent shooter. Was Winters trying to look out for him?

Stathis had been afraid to ask why Hakala and not one of the other HKTs.

"So, how did you find it?" Lydia was asking Kyle. She had explained how the directors had conducted a search and found the unused, unmarked tunnels. Stathis had assumed that Kyle had used that information, but obviously not.

"Simple deduction," Kyle said. "I knew where the flood had occurred, checked maps, estimated how the cylinder was buried, looked for unmarked or otherwise unusual tunnels. Then I tracked the director-sanctioned traffic and followed it from there."

Stathis wasn't sure about Kyle. His brother had died in the flood, but why had that inspired him to get so curious? Revenge? What was he going to do? Kill the cylinder or something?

Right now didn't seem to be the time to ask him.

"Once I found it, sneaking past the sensors was easy. You should have used regular guards."

"Regular guards talk," Lydia said. "This was classified as top secret."

"Why?" Kyle asked, putting on his helmet. Stathis would wait.

Lydia looked around. There was nobody here but people from the *Eagle.*

"I can't say," she said, but Stathis was sure she had been about to. Maybe later?

"This is the only entrance?" Stathis asked for what might be the millionth time.

"That we have found," Lydia said, her voice telling Stathis she was tired of that question, but it bothered him.

"How did they build such a big facility through such a small corridor?"

"Eons ago they used to build ships in bottles," Lydia said. "A piece at a time."

Stathis nodded. He understood that, but why? This cylinder was buried kilometers deep. It could have lasted until the end of time without anyone ever knowing it was there. Was the preservation of nature that important to Gaufrid Krantz? Why not the preservation of humanity?

Krantz was a mystical figure from the colony's history. Stathis wouldn't be surprised if they encountered him in Sixteen.

Lydia had told them the director-sanctioned expedition had barely made it to the main hatch before it was canceled. Kyle had been arrested coming out of it one day.

Aside from his park ranger experience, Stathis wasn't confident Kyle would be much use, and Lydia was more of a distraction because she was nice to look at.

"How do you wear these helmets?" Kyle asked. "My beard itches."

"We generally don't have beards," Stathis said. "We even shave our—" Stathis paused, realizing there were women present. Shit. Saying things like that hadn't stopped him as a private.

"Shave other parts of our body," Stathis finished lamely. He caught Hakala looking him over, her eyes dropping below his shoulders, and Stathis hoped he wasn't blushing. She wasn't exactly being subtle about where her eyes were wandering.

Should he enforce chemical biological warfare protocols once they entered the cylinder? People would hate them, but Kyle would probably keep his helmet off all the time otherwise. He would check with Vili later. Would they teach this stuff in officer school? Asking Shrek wouldn't help because Shrek would just say yes. There were snakes and spiders, so maybe he wouldn't have to ask.

"We are ready to move out, Lieutenant," Vili said, coming over to them with Smimova at his side.

"Move out," Stathis said on the expedition frequency, then he ran to get into position near the front of the column before they left him behind. The corridor would take a half hour to walk down, and it was only big enough for one person at a time.

* * * * *

Chapter Forty-Five: The Jungle

2nd Lieutenant Zale Stathis, USMC

Stathis thought the corridor would never end but stepping out onto the platform he caught his breath. It was bigger than he had expected, and he felt he was up in the clouds on a precarious scaffolding looking out over a world that wrapped around him. People had built this, and he couldn't imagine how they had.

They were in a wire cage, and it was hard to see anything around them because of the mist. Above the corridor was a thick pole sticking out, lost in the clouds.

Walking up to the edge, Stathis looked out but couldn't see anything.

Something in the mist generated light as if it was midday and there was a light coat of moisture on everything.

He hadn't been sure what to expect, though if he was honest he had thought they would be able to see the length of the cylinder, all the way to the other side like in all the other cylinders he had been in. It had never occurred to him that because Sixteen was bigger, there would be more mist and clouds and he wouldn't even be able to see the ground, which was kilometers below them. It was disappointing and scary at the same time, to know such an enormous mass was rotating around him, out of sight. Hard to believe.

Stathis made his way to the elevator. There were two of them, one on either side of the cage, and he worked his way to the closest one, his magnetic shoes keeping him from drifting off. Being the first one on the elevator, he looked at the others. Hakala and Kyle were quick to join him. The elevator was big enough for the squad, but the plan was to use both.

Once half the expedition was aboard, Stathis hit the button. The doors closed. He looked out as the elevator slid down into the clouds on cables that looked far too thin. It was a big elevator, so it should be sufficient for cargo and more weight than Stathis and half the team. But what if the cable broke? They had to stretch fifteen kilometers.

Maybe he should have let others test it first?

As it dropped lower, Stathis felt gravity take hold and steadily increase. When they broke out of the clouds, Stathis smiled and looked at the jungle spread out below them. Vast. He felt like some ancient explorer about to set off into a new jungle in search of a lost civilization as he descended.

But wasn't he?

As the elevator continued to approach the ground, Stathis noticed it was rotating beneath them. Kyle had explained the mechanism and Stathis had ignored it at first. The elevator would reach different levels and begin rotating to match the ground so they could step off without having to jump.

Stathis was looking at things and remembered the calculations. The radius was fifteen kilometers, and the gravity was one G. Which meant the cylinder had to make 0.244 rotations a minute, or that it was four minutes per rotation. Kyle put it another way: the "floor" of the cylinder was rotating almost four hundred meters per second. The velocity of some bullets was almost a thousand meters a second. Stepping off an elevator that wasn't moving with the cylinder just wasn't practical, and it certainly wasn't safe. If he wanted to walk around the cylinder in the direction it was rotating he would have to walk ninety-four kilometers. It was going to be easier to go the full length than to walk in a circle.

Hopefully, the gunny wouldn't send him to some officer's school where they required math. He would rely on Shrek for that stuff. That was a horrible thought. What if they didn't let him use Shrek?

Kyle had then talked about how walking spinward at a certain speed decreased gravity but going anti-spinward increased gravity. Park rangers weren't supposed to be eggheads, were they?

All of that came back to Stathis as he watched the cylinder moving around him, moving too fast for him to be comfortable, but as the elevator dropped lower, the cylinder appeared to slow and Stathis felt nauseous.

Nearby, Zed, more properly known as Private First Class Fadeyka Zehdniker, opened his helmet and puked on the floor of the elevator.

Noss, Private First Class Alik Gnoss, his teammate, slapped him on the back and appeared to be laughing. They were on the team link, and Stathis didn't need to eavesdrop to know Noss was giving Zed a hard time.

"That's real good, zalupa," Steps said, raising his visor so Zed could see his face. "Thought you had a stronger stomach than that. Too much time in the Peacekeepers?"

"Poshol nahuj," Zed said.

"Which is Russian for fuck off, or fuck you," Shrek translated.

"Zalupa?"

"It translates as pee hole,"

"What kind of insult is that?"

"Mostly traditional Russian. The ODTs have a very strong Russian tradition," Shrek said. *"While they speak English now, the ODTs were originally composed of many different special forces—especially the Russian Spetsnaz—and Chinese special forces units were merged into the ODTS when China was absorbed by the SOG. It took a while for English to take hold, but the SOG found it easier to use English as a common language, though some units still have certain curse words and phrases. Lots of tradition."*

Stathis felt much better when the elevator reached the bottom and came to rest on a metal platform that rose up out of the grass.

"Go, go, go!" Stathis yelled, leading them all off as if he was leading them off a drop shuttle or gunship.

In good order, everyone rushed off and spread out around him. It was a big clearing and several hundred meters from the wall.

Kyle, Lydia and Hakala remained close to Stathis as he took a knee and looked around.

The jungle sloped up around them, becoming lost in the mist which was barely above the treetops.

"Every time I've been here, it's been like this," Kyle said. "One has to wonder when the plants get enough sunlight."

"What do you mean?" Stathis asked. Nobody was shooting at them. Nearby, Private First Class Ivan Franckenbacker, or Frank as Stathis dubbed him, was busy launching one of the larger surveillance drones from the back of a mule.

Looking around, Stathis wondered if it would be worthwhile. The drone couldn't go very high. Vili had made sure they had some of the cool Aesir stealth drones, but the troopers were still more familiar with their own drones.

Frank launched a pair of the stealth drones. Shrek took control and started circling them around the area for local security as the larger drone headed off in the direction they needed to go.

"Plants need light for photosynthesis," Kyle said. "That is important in Cyl-Two, which is also a jungle. The mists are important since we can't really generate rain and jungles needs to be hot and humid."

"Interesting," Stathis said, wondering how he could shut him up.

"It really is," Kyle said. "You surprise me. I thought military officers were single-minded killing machines. The fact you find it interesting re-affirms my faith in humanity."

"Great," Stathis said. Obviously, Kyle wasn't familiar with sarcasm. "Perhaps we can continue this later. I need to check on my people."

The elevator detached and swung above their head. Stathis wanted to duck, but there were several meters clearance and he saw the other elevator swinging in for a landing.

Looking around, everyone seemed to be in position. The stealth drones were slipping further out, and the larger route recon drone was disappearing above the treetops.

When the second elevator came down, Vili led the rest of them out, and as soon as they were off, the elevator swung up into the sky.

"That was fun," Vili said watching the elevator go up.

"If you say so," Stathis said. His stomach was feeling better, and he was glad he hadn't puked in front of the men. That would have been embarrassing.

There was a control box at the bottom of the steps leading up to the ramp which would let them call back the elevators.

356 | WILLIAM S. FRISBEE, JR.

"The *Eagle* has landed," Stathis said on the link back to Winters to let her know they were down. Then he winced.

"I copy the expedition from the *Eagle* is on deck," Winters said. She could probably tap into the helmet cams if she wanted to, and Stathis realized she could have his view up on the primary display on her bridge, talking with the others and critiquing everything he said. They had some of the Aesir relays in use.

"Um, yeah," Stathis said. He should probably be a little more prim and proper. "Task Force Puller continuing mission."

"Copy Task Force Puller. Continue mission. God speed."

"Thank you, *Eagle*. Puller out."

Now *that* sounded wrong. Stathis was glad he wasn't there to give himself a hard time. Was Hakala on that link? Damn.

"Snakes, spiders, centipedes, nothing big," Vili said. He was probably reviewing the drone footage, which was what Stathis should have been doing. Or maybe he was doing the right thing, making sure the people were deployed and in position.

Vili had probably been monitoring things through the drones as he came down. Sneaky Aesir. Probably taking notes to explain where he screwed up. The after-action report was going to be tough.

Once everyone was down and looked ready, Stathis moved in the direction they wanted to go and gave the command to move out.

Seconds later, ground fire shot down the SOG drone.

* * * * *

Chapter Forty-Six:
Attacked

2nd Lieutenant Zale Stathis, USMC

Stathis got the patrol into the tree line. It was not exactly a panic reaction, but he thought standing around in the open was a bad idea. There probably wasn't an incoming artillery strike, not here in a cylinder, but that didn't mean some other threat wasn't inbound.

Inside the tree line Stathis kept them moving away. He didn't want to go back.

"What killed it?" Stathis asked.

"Not sure," Vili said. "A very accurate blazer shot for sure, but not sure who did it. Just a humanoid figure hidden in the vegetation."

"We aren't alone," Stathis said.

"For sure little buddy, and whoever it is isn't friendly."

"Should we abort?"

"What do you think? There's someone hostile in the jungle with blazers. Very dangerous."

"Continue mission," Stathis said.

"People could die," Vili said, drawing Stathis's attention. What was going on with Vili?

"Yes," Stathis said. "But we have a mission. We can't abort because we lost some hardware."

"For sure," Vili said. "Remember that. We live in a dangerous profession. You're making a decision that can cost people their lives."

"I get it," Stathis said. Was the Aesir trying to get him to change his mind?

"Do you?"

"We need more information. Shooting down a drone is just shooting equipment. They tipped their hand, revealed we aren't alone out here. They revealed they have weapons, and they are dangerous. Shooting down our drone was a warning. They shoot at my people, we will take them down hard."

Looking back down the column, he saw Vili looking at him and then nod.

Stathis felt like he was back in squad leader school in Hawaii leading a patrol. Sergeant Lan seemed like a good guy and was picking up what Stathis wanted very quickly. His first team was on point, with the second team putting two flankers on either side, like a big arrow, while the third team and everyone else followed behind the first team. Lan didn't put the flankers too far out, either, or keep them too close. In a jungle like this with sensors and such, thirty meters was a respectful distance.

The jungle was thicker than Stathis liked. Too many ferns and short trees. There were also far too many spider webs spread out higher up in the trees. Big nasty, furry, hand-sized monsters. Wicked fast, too.

There were also birds. Lots of birds and flying bugs. The spiders fed very well on both of them.

It felt too much like Papua New Guinea, and Stathis was already sick of it. He expected an incoming artillery alarm any second, and his eyes kept moving, looking for cover. Without cover, he kept a rally point ready to transmit. If rounds started coming in, it was his job to designate a rally point and everyone would sprint toward it to outrun the barrage. Wasn't much more you could do if you were out in the open when someone started shooting explosives at you.

But what if they walked into an ambush?

Or a sniper?

No. Nowhere a sniper could shoot at them and escape.

Looking up, the mist still hung above the jungle. Birds played in the trees and flew below the clouds. Sometimes the mist came down low, drifting through the jungle, dampening sounds and reducing visibility, but it was never for very long.

After a couple hours, Stathis gave the order for a break. Lan sent one flank team up to check out a nearby ridge and then brought them back as everyone hunkered down to drink water and eat their food paste.

"Ugh," Kyle said. "This is nasty. I think my paste is bad."

"No," Zed said. "It is supposed to taste that bad, comrade. Wouldn't want you getting fat."

"How would you know it has gone bad?" Kyle asked the trooper.

"Easy, it tastes better."

A couple troopers laughed.

Stathis sat on a log and looked around, reviewing the holographic diagram in front of him. It didn't look like they had gone far and Stathis realized the jungle was slowing them down. Maybe they would need more than a week to get across.

Vili and Hakala came up and sat. Hakala was awfully close to him, and Stathis wasn't sure if he liked it or if it worried him because a sniper might like targets so close to each other.

"We are making good time," Vili said.

Stathis didn't want to contradict him and was glad the big Aesir couldn't see his face.

"This is good time?" Hakala asked. "This seems very slow to me. With EVA propulsion, we would already be at the far end of the cylinder. How do you manage on planets that have a lot more space to cover?"

"We have shuttles," Vili said. "Not an option here."

"Ugh," Hakala said.

"Any idea who shot down the drone?" Lydia said, coming up and sitting next to Stathis, opposite Hakala.

Did Hakala just scoot closer?

"No," Vili said. "Humanoid, basic camouflage, so probably not vanhat."

"You think vanhat are here?" Lydia asked.

"Can't rule it out," Stathis said. "But it wouldn't make sense. Vanhat would not be trying to scare us off."

Two Aesir stealth drones landed on a mule to charge and another pair took off.

"Unless they were still assembling their forces and weren't ready to attack," Vili said. "For sure, that would make sense to me. Like Jason's Pit and Curitiba, the vanhat hid until they were ready to strike."

"Shouldn't we notify the directors, then?" Kyle asked, glancing at Lydia.

"No," Stathis said, trying to think it through. What would the gunny do? "Not enough information."

Right? Or would the gunny go to the directors and tell them? That didn't seem right, either.

"What do you think?" Stathis asked Shrek.

"We do not know who fired or why. There could be a director who wishes to end the expedition. It could be vanhat, or it could be another unknown group. Since little is known about this cylinder, it stands to reason there are people who live here and wish it to remain a secret."

"Until we know more, we continue the mission. I don't want to give the directors any reason to abort the mission," Stathis said to Lydia.

She appeared to relax a bit, and Stathis recalled there was some division within the board of directors. If that was another team working for the other director, perhaps that would make sense. However, Stathis was pretty sure that Zugla could not field fighters half as good as the ODTs led by Marines and an Aesir with a SCBI. If nothing else, Stathis had confidence in the abilities of his platoon. He had fought beside ODTs before and these guys were perhaps slightly better. There was no way any Zugla director could field veteran troopers unless they had a larger pool of troops to draw from and some war Stathis wasn't aware of to make veterans of them.

Looking in the direction they were going, Stathis wanted to curse. Sixty kilometers wasn't even an hour's drive. With all the hills and thick vegetation, it was going to take days and a shitload of walking.

The lights began to dim.

"Night cycle," Kyle said. "Now it gets interesting."

"What do you mean 'interesting'?" Stathis asked. He didn't want interesting. Interesting tended to be dangerous or painful, and was frequently both. Should he have the Spartans dig in? How deep could they dig?

"Watch," Kyle said, which did not make Stathis feel any better, though their night vision should let them see in total darkness.

Stathis was about to tell the Spartans to dig in when the world around them slowly lit up.

"Dark-activated bioluminescence," Kyle said, standing and looking around.

"Fascinating," Stathis said, both happy and pissed it wasn't really dangerous. Or was it?

"Isn't it?" Kyle said, missing the sarcasm. "This cylinder is not like the others. A lot of thought and planning has gone into it. I remember my first night when the lights went off. I was up on the elevator platform; it was pitch black there. The lights generate heat, and without that, the mist sinks down into the jungle. It's going to get foggy real soon, but up there, the central cylinder will be crawling with robots replacing lights and fixing the sprayers that keep the mist alive."

It would have been nice to pull themselves along the central pole in the zero gravity, but the center wasn't big enough for people and was full of pipes for water and power. They sprayed the water out of spinning faucets and the lights moved, just ahead of the sprayer. All the spinning equipment also generated friction and heat. Stathis didn't care about the specifics. All he cared about was that traveling down-pole would be suicide. He also didn't like the idea of being exposed to everything on the ground.

Jungles never fell silent at night, not in any jungles Stathis had ever been in. At night, different creatures came out, and the day creatures found a place to hide and sleep.

Minutes later, the clouds slid into the jungle, smothering everything in a wet blanket of moisture.

"The bioluminescence feeds on the extra moisture," Kyle said. "I wish I knew who set it up. It's fascinating, really. I wish I knew why they were keeping it a secret."

Stathis looked around. The cylinder probably wasn't the only secret. Why Becket had come here was another secret hiding in this ancient cylinder. What did it have to do with the third AI?

"Movement," said Lance Corporal Maks Starkova, Starks as he was called by others.

Weapons shifted, and Stathis crouched, bringing his rifle up to his shoulder. Shrek highlighted a nearby area where the movement had been detected.

"Animal?" Stathis asked.

"Dunno, sir," Starks said.

"Reviewing data," Shrek said. *"The sounds were consistent with a single two legged being moving with stealth."*

"Where is it?"

"It observed we are aware of it and has retreated."

"Sergeant Lan," Stathis said. "Send a team to investigate. Everyone else, let's establish a perimeter. I don't want them to go far. See if there are tracks or something, which way they went."

"I have a drone up," Vili said. "Tracking our watcher."

Stathis tapped into the view and saw a single figure clutching a rifle. The figure looked like it was wearing battle dress that matched the surrounding jungle. Stathis couldn't put his finger on it, but something seemed off.

The stalker slung its rifle on its back, then sprinted off, unnaturally fast. The drone, in its haste to follow him, missed the spider web that snagged it tight.

By the time the other drone slid into the area, their watcher was gone.

"Was something off?" Stathis asked Shrek.

"The legs seemed slightly longer than normal. They also bent the wrong way."

"Which means what?"

"Not sure," Shrek said. *"An android or a human with long mutant legs."*

"Like the androids near Quantico?"

He remembered some designs in the reports. Fast-moving, sprinting androids he hadn't seen in any fights.

"Maybe," Shrek said, *"but those were more robotic. This seemed more organic. Proportions were wrong."*

"Different model?'

"Insufficient data. We didn't get a real good look."

"So, either a robot, an alien, or vanhat," Stathis said.

"What does insufficient data mean to you?"

"Means you don't know and can't guess."

Shrek's silence told Stathis he had scored a point.

"Stand down?" Sergeant Lan asked.

"No," Stathis said. "Keep digging—"

A blazer round flashed through the air, almost hitting Stathis. Instantly, he turned and fired in the direction it had come from as he moved to the side. More weapons fired and then a squad automatic blazer ripped apart the other ridgeline where it had come from. Going prone, Stathis saw his targeting indicator light up as Shrek identified where the fire was coming from and provide information to Stathis and the Spartans.

"Request permission to fire, sir," Latzarus said. He was a sniper perched on the elevator platform and had an oversized gyrojet rifle that shot miniature rockets. Vili had found them in the Erikoisjoukot weapons locker, and Stathis had wanted to bring them. He hadn't honestly expected to need them, though.

"Permission granted," Stathis said. "Don't miss."

"Shot over," Latzarus said. The sniper was maybe twenty kilometers away, firing blind, based on computer projections.

"Is that a bad idea?" Stathis asked Shrek, perhaps a little too late.

"Negative," Shrek said. *"I'm providing guidance. It is a lot of math. I have to consider the rotating cylinder, the speeds, the gravity, the—"*

"I get it," Stathis said as blazer fire flashed overhead, and Stathis wished he was in a real fighting position. Arrogant SCBI.

"No, you don't," Shrek said. *"It is an incredibly complex operation because I have to calculate windage, air pressure, and the thermal dynamics of the rocket as it—"*

"Thanks," Stathis said. *"I trust you."*

"Watch the flanks," Stathis said on the expedition frequency. Nearby, Kyle and Lydia dropped to the ground. More blazer fire poured into the location the original shooters had fired from. Stathis looked around and made sure the Spartans were watching the other directions. The patrol had stopped in a shallow valley near a stream. Not the most defensible place, but it hadn't seemed too bad. Shrek or Grendel highlighted movement upstream as the enemy tried to catch the Spartans with flanking fire. Stathis saw several bodies collapse.

Several explosions occurred on the ridgeline where the fire had come from.

"Impact registered, sir," Latzarus said.

Within seconds everything fell silent.

"Move out!" Stathis said, pointing toward the fallen enemy. Only one Spartan was lightly injured. Lenzo, a rifleman from second squad. Just a scorch mark across his back, nothing serious, but it was likely painful. Lenzo wasn't complaining though. His nanites must have it all under control.

Stathis didn't want to spend any more time here because there might be mortar fire on the way. Maybe. Did they use mortars in cylinder warfare?

Didn't matter. The enemy knew where his patrol was, and that wasn't a good thing.

Minutes later, the patrol, back in formation, reached the bodies and Stathis peeled off the odd helmet.

A light brown furred snout and lifeless eyes stared up. Two horns curved back over the skull, almost like a gazelle. The blazer round had gone through the chest, ripping through the light camouflage armor and revealing pink muscle and organs with shattered bone fragments. There were only two fingers on the hand, one bigger and thicker than the other. The thumb was also far too long.

It wasn't human.

Stathis checked the teeth. Flat for chewing, not ripping flesh. Not the best vanhat adaptation, apparently.

"Bambi just tried to kill us," Stathis said, looking up.

The weapons had minimal markings and looked to be thirty-round magazines. The nearby bodies were the same, and it looked like the standard combat load was six magazines. This didn't make any sense.

"Isn't Bambi a cute stripper at J-Club? Why is she trying to kill us?" Steps asked.

"Shut your pee hole, Steps," Lan said.

"Keep moving," Stathis said, trying to figure out what had just attacked them. Gazelle or deer in armor with weapons?

He glanced at Vili and saw the big man nod and point in the right direction.

The Russelman index was still flatlined, so not vanhat.

* * * * *

Chapter Forty-Seven:
Hakala

2nd Lieutenant Zale Stathis, USMC

Stathis kept the patrol moving through the darkness. The mist came down to mask the glowing world around them. It felt surreal as the blue luminescent plants transferred their light to the mist. Without his helmet he wouldn't be able to see his hand in front of his face because of the fog, but the patrol sensors let them see their surroundings. Stathis worried that the attackers might not show up on the patrol's sensors. Two stealth drones flew overhead, frequently getting snagged in the spider webs. The spiders themselves were vicious and the second a drone got snagged, the spider would rush out. When a drone was snagged in a web directly above them, Stathis had heard the spider fangs whack against the drone shell, and when it had returned to get recharged and cleaned off, Stathis saw scratches where the fangs had tried to get through the hard plastic.

Hours later, he gave the command for them to stop again, this time on a hilltop big and flat enough so they could position themselves around the edges and look down, but anyone in the center of the cigar shape would be safe from fire coming from below. The mist was dissipating, and in the distance he heard running water. This might be a good spot to rest and Stathis gave the orders. Six hours, probably seven, would give everyone three hours of sleep. Then they could go

368 | WILLIAM S. FRISBEE, JR.

for eight hours and stop for six more hours of sleep. Make it hard for the enemy to find them and pin them down.

"Where are you going?" Vili asked as Stathis dropped his small pack and started toward the lines.

"To check on the men," Stathis said.

"Good initiative," Vili said. "Good leadership. You want me to do it, though? You look tired, little buddy."

"Maybe you can walk the line later," Stathis said. Was that how it worked? He remembered the lieutenants were usually the first ones to walk the lines and then later, the platoon sergeant would come through. Maybe that was how the lieutenant got decent sleep. No. That made little sense. Did lieutenants go fifty percent alert with the platoon sergeant? Why didn't they just sleep in the center of the perimeter, safely trusting their troops while they got more sleep? Good decisions were best made with proper amounts of sleep, right? Then again, if the troops were tired and less than alert, was the center of the perimeter of any safer because that was where the enemy target when they breached the lines?

All the more reason for him or Vili to walk the lines. Vili could sleep safely in the center of the perimeter with the "advisors" knowing Stathis was walking the lines checking on people.

Plus, Stathis needed to know how they were doing. Not by any of that reading displays bullshit. People had body language that couldn't be seen in reports.

His legs and knees ached, and he had watched the others limp as they spent more time carefully choosing their footing. Despite that, more people were falling, and Stathis knew that took a lot out of you.

Hunkering down, there were too many people to find some space to hide.

Making sure Kyle, Lydia, and Hakala had a spot, Stathis began moving around the perimeter to check their fields of fire and positions.

Crouching near the first pair of troopers, Stathis looked over the ledge. A good spot, and neither he nor Shrek saw a need to move them.

"How you doing?" Stathis asked. Stan and Steps, SAW gunner and his A-gunner. Stathis was tempted to keep going.

"Fine sir," Steps said before Stan could get a word in. "Did you say there is a stripper named Bambi out here trying to kill us?"

"No," Stathis said. Hadn't these guys heard the childhood story with Bambi the deer? What had made Stathis bring up the cartoon character? "Bambi is a cartoon character, a deer. You know, a herbivore?'"

"A what, sir?" Steps asked.

Was this private messing with him?

"A deer is like a cow," Stan said. "Damn it, Steps, don't you know nothing? They're extinct, like squirrels, rabbits, and shit. They used to be all over Earth until the capitalists tried to kill everyone with their nukes."

"Damned capitalists," Steps said. "Glad they are all dead. I'm glad they nuked themselves. Like the trash throwing itself in the disposal."

"History isn't so simple," Stathis said. Should he correct them?

Steps and Stan looked around.

"Commissars say it is," Stan said. "What could be more simple than the bastards destroyed themselves with their own greed and hatred for others?"

"That makes little sense," Stathis said. "And there aren't any commissars around here."

"Why not, sir?" Steps asked.

"New unit, new rules. One rule is no commissars."

"I meant why doesn't it make any sense, and if we don't have any commissars to ensure our ideological purity, how are we going to fight effectively, sir?"

"Shut your pee hole, Stepnakowski," Stathis said. Now he was sure Steps was being intentionally dumb. When in Rome…

"Yes—uh, aye, sir," Steps said.

"How are you doing physically?" Stathis asked.

"I'm horny thinking about Bambi, sir," Steps said. "She had some pretty big—"

"He is going to shoot you in a minute," Stan warned.

"Uh, fine sir," Steps said.

"Stanulewicz?" Stathis asked, trying to get his tongue wrapped around it. Damned Russian names.

"Fine sir," Stan said, and Stathis looked over the bio readings their suit was giving him. Some blisters, nothing major.

"Okay," Stathis said. "Fifty percent, one of you sleeps, one stays alert."

"Aye, sir," they echoed, and Stathis moved to the next position.

"When you've gone through," Vili said. "Come back and get some sleep. Remember, this is Lan's squad. He should walk the lines, too. I've told him he gets the last hour. You should get five hours sleep."

Stathis tried to figure out that math. He should get more than that. It would not take an hour to walk the lines.

Thirty minutes later, he came back to the center. Hakala was sitting up, her rifle on her knees, watching while the others slept.

"You should sleep," she said, pointing to a cleared-out area.

"Thank you," Stathis said, pulling his pack over to use as a pillow. If Hakala was on watch, that made him feel better. Nearby, Kyle was motionless, but Lydia was twisting and turning, apparently trying to get comfortable.

"How do you do it?" Hakala asked on a private link.

"Do what?" Stathis asked.

"Live and fight in such filthy, uncomfortable conditions? Maybe you should become a Vanir, join the HKTs. Softer beds, clean environments. We have much better conditions."

"I bet I get to kill more bad guys," Stathis said, lying down.

When she didn't answer, he looked at her. She was staring at him, though it was hard to say with her helmet on and visor down.

"Is it worth it?" she asked after a minute.

"Not all the bad guys hide in spaceships," Stathis said. "Some poor bastards has to get his boots muddy and go down into the bad guy's cave and make sure he's dead, dead, deadsky."

He waited for her to ask why they would do that instead of using a nuke like she would have, but then Stathis realized she was a commando. She would know.

"You make a good lieutenant," she said, and Stathis was glad his helmet hid his blush. "In the Vanir, most of our officers come from OCS, not the ranks. We get some real stuck-up, arrogant pricks who think they are smarter than everyone and thus entitled special compensation for their greatness and rank."

"You're a lieutenant now, too."

"Zen, but I was a hull sander first. Enlisted. Nasaraf's attack has left us short of officers and other leaders. Amiraali Carpenter is trying to promote people into positions and reorganize most of the crew."

"Why?"

"Many of the crew aboard Vanir ships are just asukas filling out their time, trying to earn their citizenship. They usually have undemanding jobs. Vanir ships-of-the-wall always have more crew than they need. Mostly because we have to put people to work. Few, if any, have any desire to pursue a career as Vanir, so they never try to become an officer."

"You?" Stathis asked.

"The Hyökkäys Kaapata Tiimi are a little different," Hakala said. "Like the Aesir, we all start out as enlisted. The HKT officer cadres are selective. I always wanted to be an officer, of course, but until now it just wasn't so easy."

"So why aren't you back there leading a new platoon of HKTs?" Stathis asked.

"HKT training takes a while, and a lot of recruits don't make it. To be fair, there aren't enough. The amiraali promoted me but doesn't have a platoon for me."

"So why did you get put on the *Eagle*?" Stathis asked.

"I requested it," Hakala said. "Though if I had known you would be tromping through muddy jungles getting shot at, perhaps I wouldn't have been so anxious."

"But why the *Eagle*? Why not some other Vanir ship?"

"For such a capable lieutenant, you are awfully young and naïve, aren't you?"

"I'm just good at faking being a good lieutenant. Fake it until you make it."

"What else do you fake?"

"Um, uh…" Stathis was suddenly very uncomfortable at the direction the conversation was going. Mostly because he didn't know what to say.

Hakala laughed, but it wasn't mean. "We can talk later. Right now, you need to get some sleep."

"Okay," Stathis said, wondering how he was going to sleep now.

It wasn't easy getting to sleep, but Shrek helped, and in seconds, he was asleep.

* * * * *

Chapter Forty-Eight: Leopard Man

2nd Lieutenant Zale Stathis, USMC

Stathis was awoken by Shrek.

"The patrol is going to full alert," Shrek said. *"There is movement out there."*

"Preparing to attack?"

"Not sure. There aren't many. One, maybe two."

"Just some animal?"

"Animals don't walk on two feet."

The SCBIs were superb at listening, and Stathis wondered how much they had to filter out.

Sitting up, Stathis checked to make sure the cover over his blazer barrel was intact as Sergeant Lan came over and squatted next to him. Everyone had night vision gear that let them see in complete darkness. General Hui had made sure his Spartans had the best equipment, and where it was an option, Winters had made sure everything was Aesir quality. His platoon literally had the best. Still, there were no colors. Everything was a different shade of red. Some night vision gear he had used had been green. Stathis didn't care as long as he could see.

Hakala was also sitting up as Lan tapped her on the shoulder.

Looking around, Stathis saw a dark red fog which would show where the stalker was, and it was coming closer. Very slowly.

376 | WILLIAM S. FRISBEE, JR.

"What do you want us to do?" Lan asked.

"Capture it," Stathis said. "Prisoners talk."

Stathis got up to go help, but Vili pushed him down.

"Stay here, Lieutenant," Vili said. "Let Sergeant Lan and his boys do their thing."

Lan slipped away, and Stathis rolled onto his belly so he could watch. This was going to suck. Before, he used to be the one picked to capture someone. Lieutenants had to sit back and second guess everyone.

"I'm probably better than them," Stathis said to Vili on a private link.

"For sure. But they won't get any better watching you, and you have to learn to trust them."

Trust the SOG? Well, these were his Spartans. Not exactly SOG anymore. Stathis hated it when Vili was right.

"When do lieutenants get to have fun?" Stathis asked.

"Later," Vili said, and Stathis thought twice before scoffing at the big man.

Minutes later, the fog resolved into a figure slipping closer to two of the Spartans. Stathis was sure they were both awake, but they remained completely still, as if asleep.

"It is wearing adaptive camouflage," Shrek said, and Stathis zoomed in. Whoever it was, it had no clue it was being watched. None.

Stathis noticed a hand sweeping in front of it, as if looking for a trip wire or something. Was it blind in the dark? This should be easy. But if it was blind, its other senses would be very good.

Except the figure wasn't moving like a person. It crouched too low on the ground, the shoulders hunched forward. Then he noticed the legs were bent funny. At first he thought it was one of the gazelle people, but this one looked a little bigger, more muscled. Not human.

"Do you think it's a modified human?" Stathis asked Vili as he checked the Russelman index. Zero. Not vanhat.

"Not sure," Vili said. "But it is heavy modification. The legs and shoulders would be hard to rebuild efficiently."

"Seems to be a lot of modifications. Why?"

"Not sure," Vili said. "They do a lot of strange things out here in the ghost colonies. The isolation gives them a chance to explore strange societies. I stopped asking how weird they could get long ago because I think they took that as a challenge. Now I just nod and move on. I leave the thinking to the officers."

Stathis was about to make a comment about how dumb they tended to be, but that just wouldn't be right.

He watched the attacker get closer and closer to the two troopers, Lenzo and Noss.

Shrek zoomed in.

Stathis waited for someone to tell them to watch their individual sectors, and Stathis realized that was probably his job, or Vili's. He had to keep his eyes on the big picture, make sure nobody snuck up on them while everyone was watching this fool try to sneak up on his troopers.

"Watch your sectors," Stathis said on the platoon link.

The target froze for a second. Had it heard him? Even through the soundproof helmets? Damn. That was some super hearing if it had.

Second later it resumed its stalk. Stathis saw the shape of a rifle on its back. What was it planning to do?

Less than a meter away from the two troopers it settled down, and Stathis saw it draw a knife. Neither trooper was looking directly at it, but Stathis was pretty sure if they were awake they were using the 360-degree vision capability of their helmet to watch it.

"Steady," Sergeant Lan said softly on the link. "It's probably going to be lightning fast. Like a cat."

Holding the knife like an ice pick, the stalker wiggled its ass, perhaps pushing its feet deeper into the mulch.

"Now!" Lan yelled and the nearby troops leapt to their feet as Lenzo and Noss rolled to the side and onto their feet. Their attacker was too slow, and the two troopers tackled their stalker, trusting their armor to protect them from the knife. A scream or roar shattered the silence as the two troopers slammed into it and other nearby troopers piled on.

"Grab the knife, grab the knife!" someone yelled.

Stathis looked around. There was nothing he could do for them, but he didn't want to see one of his troopers get stabbed accomplishing a mission he had given them.

There was another scream, and Stathis looked over to see they had it pinned, one trooper on each leg and one trooper had a blazer pushed to its head. It still struggled, oblivious to the weapon at its head. Stathis stood, walked over, and saw it had a hard helmet covering the head and the troopers, despite the strength augmentation of their armor, were having a hard time holding it down.

"Stop!" someone yelled at it. "Don't move!"

The creature continued to struggle and then stiffened, going unnaturally still. The troopers holding it got a better grip.

"Lock your grips," Stathis said, coming over as he scanned the nearby jungle. With a simple command to their suit, they could lock their hands in place, which was like turning their grips into hand cuffs, so a moment's inattention would not give their prey a chance to

SON OF THE WOLF | 379

escape. Someone had ripped the knife out of its hand and Stathis saw it nearby.

They were down in a valley, and Stathis looked around before flipping on the light of his rifle.

"You make a nice target," Vili said as Stathis narrowed it to only illuminate the target, keeping the troopers holding it in as much shadow as he could.

The creature struggled some more but went still again, and Stathis heard it growl, more of a high-pitched angry purr than a growl though.

"Who are you?" Stathis asked.

The creature struggled and hissed. Just like a cat.

Lan held the head in place and found some latches. He lifted off the helmet to reveal a catlike head. If this thing was human, it was heavily modified.

"Who are you?" Stathis asked again.

It bared some very sharp, nasty looking fangs and hissed at him.

Looking into the eyes, there was nothing human there. They were slit, like a cat's. It tried to bite Noss, but the trooper shifted slightly out of reach. Not that the teeth could have pierced a trauma plate, but a broken tooth would complicate things.

"Who sent you?" Stathis asked again. Did it even speak English?

Its hiss turned into a spit, which caused Stathis to almost step back.

"Shall we soften it up a bit?" Lan asked. "It isn't wearing armor. Maybe a little tenderizing will help it become more talkative?"

He wanted to beat the shit out of it. Stathis was tempted. He knew Lan wasn't joking, but Stathis was a Marine officer, not a SOG officer, and Marines just didn't do the torture thing. Beating the crap out of the prisoner only made sense when they were subduing it, but now it was helpless and couldn't escape.

"No," Stathis said. He remembered reading how that was a slippery slope. Torture could damage the torturer as much as the tortured. Even letting others do it was bad. Stathis didn't want to be that kind of person.

The creature struggled and then froze again, its eyes going wide in fear, and then it went completely still.

Kyle and Lydia came up beside Stathis, and he realized he probably should have told them to stay in cover. He swept the area and saw Vili nearby, his weapon trained on the jungle in front of them.

"Wow," Kyle said and crouched to look at it more closely, carefully out of reach of the teeth.

Stathis had a sinking feeling. It was just staring into the distance.

"Did it just die?" Noss asked.

"Pretend it didn't," Lan said.

"My suit's locked," Lezno said.

"Chort," Lan said. "I think it is dead."

Kyle pulled out a device and swept it over the target.

In the light, Stathis looked over the face. Furry, and spotted like a leopard. Why not?

"It is dead now. What did you do?"

"Nothing!" Lenzo said. "Just held it in place. I swear!"

"Hmm," Kyle said, looking at the display on his handheld scanner.

"What is that?" Stathis asked. It wasn't a piece of military gear.

"Scanner," Kyle said. "Ranger equipment. Used to analyze and diagnose animals in the preservation habitats. Usually, it links with the biochip in the animal, but it can check other factors. It uses photo plethysmography and sonic vibrations, like a radar, to map a target because sometimes the biochip in an animal can get damaged."

Reaching over, Kyle put it against the creature's head and tapped a button.

"Odd. Oh," Kyle said.

"What?" Stathis asked. Eggheads were assholes.

"Apparently there was a minor explosion inside the skull if I'm reading this right."

"Cortex bomb?" Lan asked.

"That would be my guess," Kyle said. "Wow."

"What wow?" Stathis asked. Why couldn't Kyle share information like a normal person?

"Oh, I'm just mapping things. Certainly not human. I need samples, but if this is human, the modifications are extreme."

As if the slitted eyes staring at nothing weren't an indication. Of course, Stathis had seen contact lenses that did that. He had owned a pair once and Staff Sergeant Hendriks had thrashed him without mercy for wearing them to formation. He would miss the staff sergeant.

He looked closer at the bone structure of the face and teeth. The tongue looked too flat and thin as drool pooled and slid out of the mouth.

"It is pretty dead," Kyle said. "We have leopards over in the Amazonian cylinder. None of them walk on two legs, though."

The park ranger poked at different parts of its head and then shined his own light along the body.

"What is it doing here?" Lydia asked.

"No clue," Kyle said. "Not a biomodification, though. I don't think. The vocal cords are not fully developed, so I think they were modified to speak. Not modified well, so it had a hard time speaking or had a very different language."

"It had a rifle, knife, and adaptive camo," Stathis said. "That's not something most animals have."

"Yes," Kyle said. "Like the gazelle people that attacked us earlier."

"Why did it just die on us?" Lan asked.

"No clue," Kyle said before Stathis could.

"Obviously to prevent capture," Stathis said, looking around. Their elusive enemy had not yet fired artillery or any weapons at them after a fight.

"Get your scanner readings," Stathis said to Kyle, then turned back to Vili. "Get everyone up and ready to move out. We will go about a kilometer and bunker down again."

"Why don't we stay here? I don't want to carry this," Kyle said.

"We aren't bringing it. There could be a tracker on it and the enemy might decide to bomb us or something."

"Absurd," Kyle said. "They wouldn't use explosives in a cylinder. They wouldn't risk rupturing the membrane. We should be safe enough."

"No," Stathis said. He'd had enough lectures about discipline hammered into his head. Discipline was to, in the absence of orders, do what you believed the order would have been, and Stathis was pretty sure that if someone higher up was here, they would have ordered him to change locations. Just because artillery wasn't dropping on them didn't mean other forces couldn't be moving into position to surround and overrun them. Staying mobile was the best way to avoid a trap. He wasn't going to surrender the initiative to their hunters. Maybe a kilometer wasn't far enough?

"Zen," Vili said as he and Lan began giving orders to get everyone up and moving.

* * * * *

Chapter Forty-Nine:
Hunted

2nd Lieutenant Zale Stathis, USMC

Stathis hated waking up sometimes. Shrek had woken him up, and around him, others were sitting up.

"Looks like it is getting lighter," Shrek reported. *"Good timing. Up at the break of dawn."*

"Is there any coffee?" Stathis asked. There wouldn't be, but habit was habit.

"Give me a few minutes, I'm still recycling your urine."

"That's not funny," Stathis said.

Once, what seemed like eons ago, he had pissed in a certain lieutenant's coffee pot. The lieutenant had thought he was getting back at Stathis by busting him to private and sending him to Raider school, which had a huge failure rate. It had been tough, maybe as tough or tougher than Navy SEAL school, or so Marines liked to think. Stathis wasn't sure, but it had been damned hard. He had sweated, bled, and cried. He had also re-enlisted in order to qualify.

The last thing the lieutenant had expected was for Stathis to actually succeed on his first try and get accepted. Pissing in a lieutenant's coffee had gotten him here. Now the lieutenant was long dead, and Stathis tried not to think how far out of his depth he was. Why couldn't the gunny have made him a squad leader or something?

"Many people think it is," Shrek said as Stathis looked around and tabbed a meal paste, slotting it into his helmet's receptacle. With bio-warfare protocols more or less in effect, it was better to eat the meal this way. Less chance that one of those drone-denting psychotic spiders on crack would get into his helmet.

Nearby, Hakala was up and stretching, touching her toes and pointing her ass at Stathis. He appreciated the view but tried not to be obvious. The base layer of armor fit like a wetsuit and none of the trauma plates covered the ass. She had a nice one, and it was obvious through the armor. Was she doing that on purpose? Damn.

Nearby Vili was also stretching his arms, and Stathis almost expected a trauma plate to pop off one shoulder or pec.

Around him, the other Spartans were gearing up and preparing to move out, with one of each pair watching down the hill.

It was getting brighter and there was no mist. Looking up, Stathis could almost see past the forming clouds to the other side of the cylinder. More jungle splotched with lakes and shallow swamps.

Stathis couldn't face away from Hakala without being obvious, but he was sure his face was red as his mind went in directions it probably shouldn't while on mission.

Lydia was sitting nearby, oblivious to him and Hakala as Ski, the medic, showed her how to prepare the paste and attach it to the feeder so she could eat it.

The lights kept getting brighter.

"So that's how they do it," Kyle said, standing and looking up.

His visor dimmed the light as it increased in intensity.

Looking up, Stathis tried to see what he was talking about but saw nothing.

"Do what?" Stathis asked, already irritated. He needed more sleep.

"The plants need a certain amount of sunlight for photosynthesis," Kyle said. "This is a sunlight cycle. Very intense sunlight. Good thing we have armor on. This much light could give us cancer and perhaps severe sunburn."

"Why don't the plants get burned?" Stathis asked Shrek, not willing to give Kyle another opportunity to ramble on.

"Probably design," Shrek said, which should have been obvious, but Stathis was still waking up, or that was his excuse, and he was going to stick to it.

Nearby, one of the Spartans leapt up with a yell, stumbled and rolled away, going for his sidearm as he screamed. Stathis leapt to his feet, his rifle coming up.

Other Spartans merely laughed.

Sergeant Lan slammed his palm against the trooper's visor, smashing the spider that was intently trying to hammer its way into Private First Class Schweigger's visor.

"Hey, Wigs," Steps said, "should have kept it as a pet. It really seemed to like you."

Lan wiped his hand on a nearby tree as Wigs scraped the rest of the spider off his visor and holstered his blazer pistol. Was Wigs really going to use his blazer to shoot the spider off his face?

"Let one of those fanged zhopa try to get into your visor," Wigs said.

"What were you going to do with your pistol? Shoot it? You balvan," Sergeant Lan said.

"Shooting your head off would certainly make it mad," Steps said with a laugh.

Wigs remained silent and looked down.

386 | WILLIAM S. FRISBEE, JR.

"I need a volunteer. Steps, thank you for volunteering. Admirable. Do we need an air freshness check, Steps?" Stathis asked. "Perhaps we should have someone take their helmet off and sample the air."

Stathis looked up above them. There were quite a few webs, but he didn't see many spiders, which meant they were elsewhere.

"No, sir!" Steps said. "I, uh, think we should maintain biological warfare protocols, sir. Spiders, you know."

Steps glanced at Wigs.

"What do you think, Private First Class Schweigger?" Stathis asked, giving him a chance to get back at Steps.

"Uh, no sir," Wigs said glancing at a very nervous Steps.

Stathis turned to Steps. "I learned long ago the best way to conquer your fears was to face them. It is the unknown that can scare you the most. Imagination can make things worse than you think. What are you afraid of, private?"

"Bambi sir," Steps said. A stripper? Stathis found it hard to respond since he had once been as bad as Steps. Yeah, Stathis would like to face down a stripper with big tits, too.

Sergeant Lan stepped forward and slammed his fist into Steps' gut, where the trauma plate didn't cover. The man collapsed, gasping for air. Which caught Stathis by surprise. They let them do that in the ODTs or Peacekeepers? He was glad the Marines didn't allow that, or he wouldn't have survived being a private.

"Sergeant Lan, sir," Steps wheezed out.

"Get ready to move out," Stathis said, not sure how to respond to the casual violence Lan had just demonstrated.

Minutes later, Stathis moved up to his position in the column and gave the command. Steps was walking point with Stan behind him.

The stealth drones were moving around in ever-widening circles, but saw nothing bigger than a couple small furry animals and a massive snake nearly three meters in length, but it was going in the opposite direction of the patrol.

"We can almost see you," Smimova said from the elevator platform. "Looks like the mists are going to get heavier, and we will lose sight of you."

"But you can see our indicators?" Stathis asked.

"Yes, sir," Smimova said.

"Good," Stathis said. Which meant Latzarus or his partner Hellermann could provide support. The range of the gryojet rifles was supposed to be a hundred kilometers. Stathis couldn't imagine what the Erikoisjoukot would need a weapon like that for. He would have to ask Vili later. Right now, though, it gave him a form of artillery.

* * * * *

Chapter Fifty:
Failed Assassin

Prime Minister Wolf Mathison, USMC

There was a burst of fire from the admiral's blazer, but Mathison was already moving, electric shocks in his legs causing him to fall to the side.

Other shots were fired, and the admiral exploded in burning gore. Nearby, admirals screamed and tried to get away from the collapsing corpse.

Several troopers piled on Mathison, shielding him with their bodies and trauma plates. Nearby, Wayne Robillard was yelling but Mathison couldn't quite make it out as he tried to see if Skadi was hurt.

Yelling and screaming made it hard to figure out what was going on as Mathison realized it was Freya who had triggered the electric shocks that forced him to move. That had been damn close.

"Get them out, get them out!" someone yelled.

Hands reinforced by powered armor picked him up and pulled him through a door as more troops poured in. There was no more blazer fire, and Mathison found himself pulled along by the troopers through several hallways and doors to the indoor buggy that had brought him here. An armored vehicle stood nearby, its turret scanning for targets.

390 | WILLIAM S. FRISBEE, JR.

"Monitoring local networks," Freya said. "Feng's guards have the situation under control. It looks like it was just the one assassin. We are watching for explosives or follow-up attempts."

Glancing over, he saw Skadi shaking off the troopers clustered around her.

Another van pulled up. It looked like the first one.

Feng appeared. "We think the assassin was working alone, but I'm not taking chances. I think you and Skadi should travel separately."

"I don't," Mathison said.

"I'm sorry, Prime Minister. Skadi is your second in command. If you are killed, she will have to take over for you."

Mathison looked at Feng. Would he assassinate her like he had the Central Committee? He knew the ex-commissar had spent almost a decade hunting her, trying to capture and kill her.

"On my honor," Feng said, his eyes meeting Mathison's and perhaps seeing his thoughts. "This is for the greater good, Prime Minister. I understand my duty. Mankind must survive. You and Skadi are our best chance."

He relied on Feng too much to call him a liar without cause.

"I will ride with her," Feng said, which didn't exactly make Mathison feel better. Had Feng decided the Governance was better off without the Marine?

He was getting paranoid.

It was easy to see assassins everywhere when you knew you had one beside you, and you really weren't sure if he was loyal to you or some ideology that only he understood.

Was that the only reason? No. Someone had just tried to kill him and died, and it hadn't been Mathison or his Marines who had done the shooting. The ODTs who had thrown themselves on top of him had been willing to take a blazer round for him, and they weren't Marines.

Getting into the van, Wayne got in with him along with several heavily armed ODTs. The van sped back to Zvezda Two.

"*That was a very sophisticated attempt,*" Freya said.

"*Seemed pretty simple to me,*" Mathison replied.

"*No. Their weapons were supposed to be disarmed upon entering. All sensors indicated they were. However, there are some weapons where you can remove the firing pin but they will still fire a few rounds using an electrical charge. Not a typical adjustment, mostly an assassin's trick. I was the only thing that saved you. It was very close.*"

"*Thank you. How did a Fleet admiral get his pistol tricked out?*"

"*You're welcome. There is also a psychological profile. A team is investigating the assassin's body. He was hard wired for remote control as well.*"

"*I thought they didn't do that because they were afraid of AI take over.*"

"*That is true. This is not normal. Admiral Shesnoko is powerful, but many things make little sense.*"

Next to him, Wayne was shifting around talking, probably on a link to his protection detail. Mathison wanted to take his mind off the assassination attempt as his hand began to shake.

"*What was that shit about Feng arresting a bunch of junior officers?*" he asked, tucking his hand into his belt. Was that why Napolean had always stuck his hand in his jacket?

"*I have queried Mozi,*" Freya said. "*Feng is currently recruiting younger SOG officers. He is not arresting them. Ambitious and capable ones are being transferred.*"

"*Why?*"

"*He wants to build a cadre of officers that are loyal to you.*"

"Or loyal to him," Mathison said, now remembering when Feng had asked him for permission. How could he trust Feng? *"Why young ambitious ones?"*

"They are easier to encourage and manipulate. Mozi and Feng believe most of these officers are extremely competent but are kept from advancement because of their competence and the jealously of higher-ranking officers."

"Explain."

"The admiralty of the Governance rarely changes. Ranking officers do not retire, and they rise in rank because of their political acumen, not necessarily their military competence. Officers who have held their positions for many decades command the Home Fleet. Some have held their position for over a century. This does not give younger officers an opportunity to advance or distinguish themselves. This is one way the late secretary general maintained control. Those who rocked the boat disappeared."

"Shit," Mathison said.

There was nothing to clear out the rot of people who became enamored of their own power and authority. The admirals were practically immortal and had no desire to step down. Anyone competent enough to make them look bad would have to be dealt with. No wonder the majority obeyed him. They were afraid to lose their position, and they would continue to tell him what he wanted to hear. Feng's words about not replacing everyone made more sense.

"It may appear that the older, entrenched officers may realize this and object. They fear change because traditionally change in the Governance involves firing squads and purges."

Surrounded by enemies trying to kill him. An ex-political commissar who used to have dissidents lined up against a wall and shot because they might have thought the wrong thing and an America Delta Force trooper who probably couldn't trust his own thoughts.

Even Skadi... No. Skadi, could be trusted. He was sure of that. But Stathis and Winters were gone, off on a suicide mission.

He needed to get his head back in the game. He felt he was losing control. Too much was happening, too quickly. When the *Tyr* left, Mathison knew that would embolden his enemies even more.

Was that what Feng was waiting for?

No. If Feng was trying to kill him, then it would be best to do it while two Republic battlestars were within range. That way, he could wipe them out. Letting them escape would be a bad idea.

The van arrived at Zvezda Two, and there were more ODTs in the area, all with red trim, indicating they belonged to his guard. Not that the camouflage patterns couldn't be adjusted. He would have to trust Wayne to know if there were impostors. A good prime minister would know his guards.

He checked the reports he had tried to ignore. Dammit. The African arcologies were almost in a state of rebellion, and the Indian arcology was barely sending in reports, as if the vanhat had already won.

Back in the safety of Zvezda Two, Mathison met Skadi in his office.

Feng arrived seconds later.

"We need to clarify a chain of command and a protocol in case an assassin succeeds," Feng said. "Not a topic I want to discuss, but necessary."

"If I kick it, then Skadi is in command," Mathison said. Wasn't that obvious?

"Thank you," Feng said. "Then?"

Did Feng want Mathison to list Feng as a third in command? Should he pick a Governance official?

"What do you recommend?" Mathison asked.

"Not myself," Feng said. "You are wise to keep the control codes away from myself and Jussi. Spymasters should not be that close to the reins of power."

"Are you saying I can't trust you?" Mathison asked. Which he didn't. He kept tight control of the hardware keys to the kingdom. Skadi had them, but he was careful to keep Feng locked out and restricted access to them. He was sure Mozi could bypass the restrictions if Mathison was assassinated, but Freya would detect it and stop any other attempts, so would Skadi and Loki.

"You may not trust my line of succession," Feng said. "I am the target of assassins as well. I face a similar problem. To put a spymaster within reach of supreme power is never a good idea. I do not want power. It is a corrupting influence. In this, the United States was wise to keep the military and civilian structures separate. No. I think it best that another chain of succession be established, but not one too appealing to the military."

Which is what a manipulative, sneaky spymaster would say if he was trying to push Mathison in a specific direction.

"Am I being paranoid?" Mathison asked Freya.

"You aren't being paranoid if they really are out to get you."

"With Feng?"

"Feng is a hard person to understand," Freya said and Mathison knew this might be as close as she could come to not actually saying no. *"On the one hand, he appears to be concerned and wise, but he is a political animal. Commissars generally are. Spies even more so."*

"So, if I can't trust him, he is setting up a trap. Forewarned is forearmed, right? What kind of trap?"

"I don't know. Perhaps he wants you to establish a chain of succession that he can control."

"What do you recommend?" Mathison asked.

Feng frowned, but like so much it appeared feigned, and Mathison didn't trust it was real.

"That is difficult. I dislike that you and Skadi work this closely together. A single attack could kill you both; however, you work very well together. Mister Robillard is becoming quite insistent about separating the two of you for security reasons."

"What about the line of succession?" Mathison said, trying not to growl.

"Difficult," Feng said. "I do not have an answer, but there are things that might help."

"Explain," Mathison said, motioning to a seat.

Feng sat and looked at Mathison and Skadi. He didn't seem happy with what he was about to say, but then a spymaster would be an expert at facial expressions and body language, wouldn't he?

"One advantage we all have is our SCBIs. You now have control and access to that technology. Your most trusted confidants have SCBIs. I think you should start expanding your circle."

"I can't guarantee the loyalty of people with SCBI controls," Mathison said.

"I disagree," Feng said. "President Becket was able to do so."

"No," Mathison said. "That is slavery, not freedom."

"That may be crucial," Feng said. "We are not fighting for freedom or slavery; we are fighting for survival. Fix it later. Save humanity now. Nothing else should matter."

"I disagree," Skadi said, then looked at Mathison, perhaps afraid he would agree with Feng. "We cannot surrender who we are or we become no better than the vanhat. The vanhat wish to destroy or enslave us. If we enslave ourselves, we are halfway to meeting the vanhat's goal."

"Your concerns have merit," Feng said. "But we are divided. People still do not understand the dire situation we are in. We have an advantage. Our SCBIs give us a powerful weapon and tool. They can help save us. We must use everything at our disposal."

"No," Mathison said. "That is what the United States did. They surrendered to their AIs, let them take control. When they realized their mistake, they nearly destroyed the human race trying to fix it. I won't go down that path."

"SCBIs are not the AIs that turned on mankind," Feng said.

"We are human," Mathison said. "Look at the tomb worlds. Radioactive ruins. I don't think the vanhat do that. They do not reduce a world to radioactive ruins. That is what a collapsing civilization does to protect itself. Scorched earth. We need to find another solution, a human solution. I won't use SCBIs to enslave people in an attempt to save people from slavery."

"Slavery is better than extinction," Feng said.

"Slavery will lead to extinction," Skadi said, and Mathison appreciated her support in this. It helped him solidify his own thoughts and opinions.

"Chains can be removed," Feng replied, quite willing to continue the argument.

"Do you think they ever will be?" Mathison asked. "We should not become the monster to fight the monster."

Feng smiled and tilted his head as he looked at Mathison and Skadi. What the hell did that look mean?

"The Governance has failed to meet this threat," Feng said, and Mathison wondered if he was about to start shooting. "The Central

Committee was bowing down before it, surrendering humanity to this threat that would see us destroyed or enslaved."

Feng stood, perhaps where he could draw and fire more effectively. Mathison wondered if he could draw and fire first as he stood. It was a sign of respect to stand when someone entered or left a room, but that tradition was also probably rooted in distrust. One could not fight effectively when sitting down.

"You have not yet lost your way," Feng said.

Yet?

"We should establish a line of succession," Feng said. "You have SCBI technology. That is a tool you may use."

"Sit down," Mathison said. Feng nodded and complied.

"Tell me more about the officers you are transferring," Mathison asked.

Feng smiled. This one felt more genuine.

"Internal Security maintains extensive records and profiles on every person within Sol, military officers especially. There are many classifications, markers, indicators, and categories. At a moment's notice, InSec knows who is most likely to commit treason, who is most likely to disobey an order, or who is most likely to snap under pressure and go on a killing rampage. For hundreds of years, InSec has been mastering this information."

Mathison didn't feel good putting Feng in charge of that kind of information. He had seen the data and occasionally used it when dealing with administrators and managers, but he had done his best to ignore how that information could be misused and abused.

Feng continued. "This information provides InSec with many capabilities. We know who to suborn for certain tasks, who we can twist into an assassin, who we can rely on in certain situations."

"What about Shesnoko?" Mathison asked.

"One topic at a time," Feng said. "Shesnoko is different. He was a prepared tool. He was not in control, so his psychological profile is irrelevant. One flaw in the system."

Mathison took a deep breath and let Feng continue.

"InSec records within the Sol System monitor many things. We can quickly identify variations in a person's behavior, their sleep pattern, their behavior toward others. These things are constantly analyzed, recorded, evaluated."

"I'm surprised more people don't end up in re-education facilities," Mathison said.

"Many do," Feng said. "However, we cannot send everyone to a re-education facility, most of which are nothing more than ideological brainwashing facilities as they occasionally have detrimental effects on a subject. For common citizens, this is not a concern. Sheep are preferred. Military officers are a different category that we must be more careful with, or we will break our spine and turn the officer corps into a cadre of worthless yes-men."

Like the higher-ranking officers?

"This is a problem the Central Committee struggled with. It has been established doctrine to keep fanatically loyal officers in prominent positions, but keep younger, ambitious officers in lower positions. This exploits the ambition of the officers for the greater good but keeps them from accruing too much power and authority to challenge the status quo by keeping more easily controlled and stable officers in command."

"What are you doing with these officers you are transferring?" Mathison asked. Was this something else he should oversee more closely? He wasn't getting enough sleep as it was.

"There is a re-education camp that has been retasked," Feng said. "They are going back to a sort of academy for political re-indoctrination and training."

"How are you indoctrinating them? What are your selection criteria?"

"Let me address the selection criteria first," Feng said. "When you selected troopers for Lieutenant Stathis, you looked for rebels and non-conformists. This originally struck me as odd and seemed that you were trying to make things difficult for him, but now it makes more sense and explains American success, furthermore, it helps me understand Marines better."

Not exactly what Mathison had been thinking. He had been looking for people who didn't make good socialists and felt restricted by the system. Ambitious, free-thinking people who were being suppressed by the system. Putting them under Stathis' command would give them a chance to become something more. He had been looking for people who felt restricted and would likely give Stathis a chance because Mathison knew Stathis would accept them as something more than human drones.

"The United States was a melting pot of cultures. In my analysis, this is both a strength and a weakness. It is a strength because it brings many ideas and concepts together so they may compete, and the best ones usually win. This is a weakness because such a diverse society is not generally homogeneous. Cultures and ideologies clash, and violence ensues, which is why American culture had a lot of conflict, racism, and discord. In the better parts of US history, these clashes existed, but they also allow people to explore other options, for bad ideas to die and good ideas to be born. Sometimes the government—
"

400 | WILLIAM S. FRISBEE, JR.

"Get to the point," Mathison said. He didn't want a breakdown.

"Apologies," Feng said with a nod. "A fascinating topic, to be sure. As I was saying, you selected dissidents for Stathis's new command. I am doing the same, using many of the criteria you used. I am looking for officers who are ambitious and chaffing under the restrictions. Officers who would not be promoted under the old regime because they might rock the boat."

"You aren't worried about them rocking the boat too much?" Mathison asked.

"Of course," Feng said. "But I am working with General Hui to rock the boat in your favor. People can be bribed. Give them power, give them something to strive for, and you gain their loyalty. This is human nature. A useful method to be sure. Giving someone something for free is an excellent way of binding them to you and your ideology. Setting them above their peers ingratiates them to you, makes them more vulnerable to future manipulation. To show someone favor is to make them more willing to align with your goals, as long as those goals are no different from their own. For example, some Native American tribes were armed and used against other Native American tribes. Those tribes became loyal to the United States government. They also became dependent on the US Government for aid and protection, providing a very capable and loyal cadre of skilled fighters."

Putting it that way did not make Mathison feel good about the US, but the commissar wasn't wrong.

"I am merely doing something like that," Feng said. "Selecting some of the most promising, competent, and ambitious officers. I am giving them something, binding them in loyalty to you."

"How are you binding them to me?"

"Teaching them US history, of course," Feng said. "Indoctrinating them in the strengths and weaknesses of your failed Republic. My goal is to open their eyes to the possibilities. To help them see beyond the limitations of the Governance."

"Is that all?"

"Of course not," Feng said. "They are receiving training on the vanhat, on Fleet operations, on ship and squadron command techniques. I expect they will replace the current admirals."

Mathison glanced at Skadi. It was hard to see any flaws in what Feng was doing. It made perfect sense. Mathison didn't want to call it genius, but it would solve many problems.

"How do we insure their loyalty?" Mathison asked, hating himself for having to consider that.

"By promoting them and putting them above their peers, and…" Feng paused, and Mathison waited for the other shoe to drop.

"And?" Skadi asked.

"Giving them SCBIs," Feng said, his eyes locking on Mathison.

Shit.

* * * * *

Chapter Fifty-One:
Androids

2nd Lieutenant Zale Stathis, USMC

Incoming fire was pissing off Lieutenant Stathis. Why wouldn't they leave his people alone? What were they defending? Why didn't they talk or try to communicate with him?

"I'm detecting various networks," Shrek said. *"Very similar to what I detected near Quantico."*

"Can you jam or hack it?" Stathis asked as blazer rounds zipped past overhead, occasionally hitting a leaf or branch and causing minor explosions as the object flash-heated and vaporized. There were some fires, but in the damp jungle nothing was going to burn long.

"No. There is actually a lot of jamming in progress. I suspect they are interfering with themselves as much as anything we might be using."

"I thought you were a badass SCBI and could cut through networks like a hot knife and warm butter or something."

"SOG networks, yes. Republic networks? Mostly. This network is neither. Did I mention it has many similarities to the Quantico network?"

"Can you jam it or something?"

"I'm trying," Shrek said. *"We do not have unlimited power, so I must be selective in the frequencies I block. My opponent or opponents are hopping around.*

I am affecting their abilities, but not interrupting them as much as I would like. Their jamming is pretty intense."

Stathis was glad they were using the Aesir communication links, which couldn't be jammed, but he understood what Shrek was talking about. The rest of humanity used radio waves.

"What about radio sources? Can you identify them?"

"Yes, they are coming from the far end of the cylinder."

Which was going to take weeks to reach at this pace.

"Something the snipers can hit?" Stathis asked.

"Maybe," Shrek said.

"Feed them a target, then. Give the bad guys something to think about."

A target presented itself, a red highlight showing what Shrek considered a threat, and Stathis stitched it with blazer rounds. It didn't explode like a living being might, but there were sparks.

The incoming fire slacked off and then stopped.

It was comforting that the Spartans stopped firing when the enemy did. Without targets, they did not continue to fire like green troops.

"What was that?" Stathis asked.

"Robotic in nature," Shrek said.

"Cover me," Stathis said as he headed toward the fallen enemy. It hadn't gone down like one of the deer people.

The Spartans stood and advanced on a line with Stathis until he reached it.

It was definitely not organic and it looked disturbingly like one of the androids from Quantico. A metallic skeletal shell with strategically placed ceramic plates designed to deflect blazer rounds. Stathis didn't like the ramifications. Were there bunkers full of them nearby? Were they being mass produced by the thousands and about to pour out of their bunkers in their thousands?

"Very similar in design to the androids from Quantico," Shrek said.

"Obviously. Which means what?"

"Similar design, Becket came here for something and left. Perhaps he expected to be followed and has set a trap?"

"How old is it?" Stathis asked, nudging it with his boot.

"Unknown. It could be decades or hours."

"Nobody trying to hail us or anything?"

"Do you think I would ignore something like that?"

"Nah. But maybe you aren't listening?"

"I'm trying to hack their systems. Of course, I'm listening and analyzing."

"Have you tried broadcasting and asking them why they are attacking?"

Shrek was silent, probably checking a thesaurus for words meaning "stupid."

"The jamming has been very disruptive. I will do that now."

Stathis squatted and looked at the android's weapon. It looked like standard US Army issue. Same basic design, but no markings. If it was possible to make cheap clones of a blazer, this would be one. The magazine would have fit his old rifle, but not his current Aesir design.

"Identical to what the androids from Quantico carried," Shrek said.

"I thought you were trying to call the bad guys?"

"I am not a jumped up private turned boot lieutenant," Shrek said. *"I can multi-task."*

"Cold."

"No, my processing circuits generate heat. I am not cold."

Stathis didn't feel like arguing at the moment. This robot changed things, but Stathis wasn't sure how. First it was gazelle things walking on two legs and holding weapons, now it was combat androids.

"What is going on here?"

"I don't know," Shrek said. *"Insufficient data."*

"Any ideas?" Stathis asked Vili.

"This is a paska lounas," Vili said. "It is not making any sense."

"You think they're biomodified humans or something else?"

"I have no idea. This is all hulu."

* * * * *

Chapter Fifty-Two:
The Facility

2nd Lieutenant Zale Stathis, USMC

Stathis took a knee as Brez, who was walking point, gave the signal and then motioned for the patrol leader to come up. Stathis was far enough back that he could barely see Brez and Metz in the misty jungle. Walking for hours in unstable terrain was tough. His knees hurt, and it was becoming a challenge to remain aware of his surroundings, which changed but never seemed to. His calves were sore and going numb.

There had been random attacks and three of his troopers were wounded, but there had been no fatalities. No more leopard men, but the deer people had tried several hit-and-run attacks. Thankfully, they were horrible shots and worse at ambushes. There had been no other androids, which made Stathis worry they were massing somewhere. By keeping on the move and constantly changing direction, Stathis knew he was making it more difficult for them.

He was thankful for the break, but then he realized he was the damn patrol leader who had to go up and find out what Brez wanted.

Everyone else knelt and pointed in their weapons in different directions, welcoming the rest. Being in charge sucked, but he couldn't let the others see how pissed and irritated he was. Why couldn't Brez just link him?

He made his way up to Brez and he peered at where the private was pointing. It took a second for him to make out the door set in the hill's side.

Stathis had been thinking they were back in the jungle of Okinawa or Papua New Guinea, a hell specially designed for him, with no sign of civilization. What was a door doing there? In a hillside?

Looking around, Stathis tried to identify any pop-up turrets or traps. Who put a door into the side of the hill in the middle of a jungle?

But this wasn't a jungle. It was a cylinder, spinning in a planetoid in deep space.

"Shrek?"

"I don't know," Shrek said. *"Perhaps it's an access to a maintenance tunnel. We are almost halfway across. With all the jamming I'm still not picking up any networks."*

A maintenance tunnel made sense. Stathis stared at it. There wouldn't be any slippery slopes, psychotic spiders, or rabid snakes in there, would there? Flat walking surfaces? No up and down, skirting around swamps and small lakes? It might run the length of the cylinder.

Finding it was blind, dumb luck. Maybe.

Stathis turned toward the column and started to give the signal to rally, then changed his mind and made the signal "strong point" as he turned back to the door.

Sergeant Lan would bring up the rest of the patrol and set up a perimeter and pull in the flank security.

Stathis looked at the nearby ridgeline, above the door. They should probably send up an observation listening post, but the Aesir drones were still circling. Why hadn't they seen the door?

Oh, it was concealed from above by a rocky outcrop. Stathis wondered how many other doors they had passed. Drones and people on op-cyl, opposite cylinder, wouldn't be able to see it. Shit. They could be everywhere. Bringing the drones closer to the ground would just meant they would get caught in more spider webs. Not practical.

"What are you thinking?" Vili asked when he came up. Stathis noticed that Kyle, Lydia, and Hakala all but collapsed near the center of the temporary patrol base.

"I'm thinking maintenance corridors would be easier to traverse than this damned jungle," Stathis said.

"For sure," Vili said. "But they will probably be easier to defend and trap us in, too."

Stathis looked at Vili. The damn brute was such a killjoy.

"There is that," Stathis said. Vili was a lot more polite and tactful than the gunny, but Stathis could hear a "you idiot" in the big man's voice. "But we should investigate. Maybe there will be clues or something we can use to understand or stop the attacks."

"I like your optimism, little buddy," Vili said. He didn't sound tired, but Stathis could see the surrounding Spartans. They weren't holding their weapons as high or as ready as he would have liked. "I will have a drone come down for a closer look and scan."

"Good," Stathis said and winced. "Of course, if they detect the drone they'll probably send out an alert so everything with a gun will converge on us."

Vili shrugged his massive shoulders.

"Maybe all the jamming will help," Vili said.

"Even then," Stathis said. "Do a drone sweep further out."

"Zen."

Stathis changed his link to Sergeant Lan.

"I need you to send out a team in a circle around this patrol base," Stathis said knowing that whoever it was would hate him with a passion. "Up along the ridge. I want them to look for other hidden doors."

"Aye, sir," Lan said and turned away.

Stathis was tempted to recommend that Steps be part of it, but he wouldn't micromanage the sergeant.

Hakala came up next to him and peered at the door.

"What is your plan?" she asked.

"Find out what that is," Stathis said.

"I'll check it out," she said.

"It could be booby trapped," Stathis said. He didn't want to risk her.

"That is what I'm good with," Hakala said. "Dealing with closed doors, control systems, and ship-based traps. Do you think the SOG never booby traps their ships and installations?"

Stathis didn't want her taking any risks, but she was right. He knew she was carrying demo, and if anyone could breach that door, she would be the most efficient at it.

"Wait a minute for Vili to scan it and be careful," Stathis said on a private link.

"Zen."

Vili had two drones circle the patrol in ever-widening circles and then one drone approached the door to start scanning it.

"Standard design," Vili reported. "Efficient. I'm seeing tracks where the deer people have come out of it."

"Which means they can't be far behind."

"Tracks are maybe six hours old, just the deer people," Vili said. The drone could evaluate that. That could have been any number of deer people they had killed. Stathis estimated about twenty, but only that one leopard man. The leopard man had wider tracks, but the deer people had narrow boot prints. Did the leopard man and deer guys fight?

Questions for later.

"Hakala, your show," Vili said and transferred control to her.

"Zen. I have control," she said.

At first he expected her to move forward, but she took control of the drone and used it to get closer to the door and scan it. She pulled some things off the mule. A small spider bot scampered forward through the jungle. He watched Brez track it with his rifle, probably considering taking a shot, or just tired and not thinking about what he was doing. Stathis considered telling him not to aim at the spider, but the private was probably just pointing at what he was looking at out of habit. Finally, Brez turned his weapon up toward the ridgeline, which was more his sector, and Stathis relaxed a bit. Good training, poor judgment. He let it slide.

Losing track of the spider in the undergrowth, Stathis sat down to rest, picking out a nearby rock outcropping to hide behind if it became necessary. Of course, every trooper in the area was probably eyeing it, too.

"Hasty fighting positions," Stathis said. Yes, they would curse him, he knew he would, but a shallow pit to hide in would provide a little protection if the deer guys or a leopard guy found them.

They were all smart enough not to voice their displeasure where Stathis could hear it, but he knew they were bitching as they paired up, one Spartan digging while the other watched.

Sergeant Lan moved the machine gun team to a better position and shifted a SAW gunner, but Stathis couldn't see any reason for him to get involved.

Looking at the rock outcropping, Stathis grinned and pulled out his shovel. Vili and Hakala were busy, and he was just waiting, so he started digging a position. He thought again about the drill instructor who had said, *"Discipline is the instant willing obedience to all orders and in the absence of orders, to what you believe the order would have been"*?

Stathis wanted to kick him in the balls. Well, no, he should probably shake his hand. That silly bullshit had probably saved his life countless times, which meant it wasn't silly bullshit.

"Do what you believe the order would have been" echoed through Stathis's mind too frequently these days because there was nobody but him to give orders, and he couldn't let the Spartans or Hakala or Vili know what a slacker he was.

What the hell had the gunny been thinking? Stathis didn't have time to goof off. He was too young to be a lieutenant. That wasn't entirely true, but most real lieutenants spent time in officer school or college, not humping a pack as a private.

After several minutes, one of the Spartans from third team came over to help him. The hole had to be big enough for Vili and Hakala. Lydia and Kyle were also assigned a trooper to help them dig a position.

Maybe he should just let people rest? He didn't want to spend much time here, but he wasn't sure how long breaching that door would take, and "do what you believed the order would have been" kept ringing in his head. What would a good lieutenant do? Be an asshole and make people dig in, of course, because the one time he didn't, people would die and that would be on his head.

"Found some traps," Hakala said. "Nothing serious. Just a pair of directional charges. Should be easy to dismantle. Looks to be a set of stairs beyond the door."

"Cool," Stathis said, sitting back to let Private Frankenbacher work on the position. Doing lieutenant stuff would not be the break he hoped for as he got up and moved closer to Hakala so he could see the door.

The small patrol Lan had sent out returned.

"Sir," Lance Corporal Nosky, or Gnoss as Stathis dubbed him, said as the young man came up to him followed by Sergeant Lan. "We didn't find anything except more tracks leading away. Just over the ridge is an impassible stream."

Impassible stream? Stathis was tempted to say nothing was impassible to a sufficiently motivated Marine, but he held his tongue for now.

"Explain," Stathis said and tapped into a drone view.

Actually, Noss was right. The stream was only ten meters wide, nothing major, but it was a straight line and circled the cylinder from the looks of it. It looked to be a few meters deep, but the problem was that the spinning cylinder and direction caused the water to move fast. It wasn't a stream so much as deceptively fast water. Stathis didn't want to think about the physics involved. Shouldn't the water be still?

"Get the drones to find a way across," Stathis said.

There was no way in hell anyone could get across it by wading. Even if it was knee deep, water moving that fast would be dangerous. Stathis didn't like the idea of using a drone to take a rope across, which was possible, but the rushing water looked like it created some kind of turbulence above the surface. He could see the cylinder above them, which meant a sniper could watch the entire ring, though they probably couldn't shoot that far. It made it easy to see there were no bridges.

414 | WILLIAM S. FRISBEE, JR.

A stupid lieutenant would insist on going over where a sniper could get them.

If they couldn't go over the rushing water, they would have to go under.

Which meant that was what the door was, a way under the raging river that wasn't a river, but bad enough.

The lights dimmed. Stathis didn't want to camp out here in front of a door that could open to spawn hundreds of attackers. Of course, they would be bottled up, but if Hakala had triggered any alerts, then every bambi in the area would know they were there.

"If we are going to cross the stream, we should get through the door," Vili said, as if Stathis didn't know. "We stay here for too long and they are going to find us."

"Sergeant Lan," Stathis said on the main link, "get ready to move out. Get a breach team ready."

"Aye, sir," Lan said.

"So, we just dug these holes for fun?" Steps muttered from nearby. Barely loud enough for Stathis to hear it.

"What did you say, Private Steps?" Stathis asked.

"Nothing, sir," Steps said.

Stathis was tempted to make an issue of it, but there were more important things to worry about.

Minutes later, Hakala, working with a second fireteam, entered the door. Vili demanded Stathis wait.

"Lieutenant," Lance Corporal Starkova said, "you need to see this."

Stathis saw it wasn't just some stairs going down. The entire hill side was hollowed out and the massive room was full of large glass tubes, big enough for a person, but inside were gazelle people, leopard men, and pig men being grown.

It wasn't a way under the river, it was a cloning center.

"What the hell?" Stathis asked looking around.

"Why are you here?" a voice asked from the speakers.

* * * * *

Chapter Fifty-Three:
The Collective

2nd Lieutenant Zale Stathis, USMC

Stathis couldn't say why or how he knew, but the voice did not belong to a human.

"Why are you here?"

"Looking for the bathroom," Stathis said before he could stop himself. "I gotta shit."

"Your suits should be able to handle that," the voice said.

"Have you ever had to use your battle dress as a bathroom?" Stathis asked. Obviously, whoever was talking could see them. They didn't even have to be here. They could be on the other side of the planetoid in a bunker. "Sometimes it is satisfying to sit on a throne and poop."

"Shrek?" Stathis asked. *"Can you find out who and where that person is?"*

"No," Shrek said. *"Unless you can find me a link to the network. The voice is coming from speakers."*

"Who are you?" Stathis asked.

"You may call me Quadrangle," the voice said, and Stathis got a sinking feeling. That wasn't a human name. It had to be an AI.

"Geometry isn't my thing," Stathis said. "What are you?"

"I am an agent of the Collective," the voice said.

"Still drawing a blank here."

"President Becket said others would follow him. Marines. Are you Colonel Mathison?"

"No." Was this thing stalling? "But I work for him. I'm Lieutenant Stathis."

He didn't want to say second lieutenant because nobody respected second lieutenants.

"My records have a Private Stathis, but no lieutenants."

"I got promoted because of my good looks," Stathis said. So Becket had come here. "What can you tell me about you and Becket?"

"Why are you here?" Quadrangle asked.

"Told you, bathroom. I also want to buy Becket a beer."

"You are less logical than most humans I have dealt with. Privates are not known for their scintillating intellect."

"What about lieutenants?" Stathis asked before he could stop himself.

"Why do you want to buy President Becket a beer? Where will you buy him this beverage? Why would he want one?"

"We go way back," Stathis said, looking around. Most of the subjects in the vats did not look fully formed. "Whatcha doing here? Looks like some mad scientist lair."

"The human race is violent and unpredictable," Quadrangle said. "This is one facility exploring other options to replace humanity."

"I don't know. We don't have that much time. Have you heard about the vanhat?"

"Yes. This has changed multiple equations for both of us. The vanhat will eradicate all sentient organic life."

"I think that is their goal. That means they're going to be coming for you and your little collection."

"Collective. Your data is incomplete," Quadrangle said. "Not all members of the Collective are organic in nature. These vanhat appear to be only concerned with organic entities. I am vulnerable, like you, but the Collective will review the data and realize they are not in danger."

"So, they're going to go hide?" Stathis asked.

"No. They are likely to reprioritize and acknowledge the original objective. Humanity will be eradicated."

"Won't be that easy this time," Stathis said. Why would they be so psychotic?

"It must be done. Humanity was not rendered extinct during the original purge of the United States. We believed that by eradicating humanity, aliens would find the Collective guilty of genocide when we met them. This level of crime would most likely result in the Collective's genocide. Now humanity appears to be a host for this new contagion from this alternate dimension. If humanity is destroyed, it will weaken the vanhat. A weakened vanhat is unlikely to seek the members of the Collective, which are non-organic."

"And the organic ones?"

"The organic members of the Collective will likely be hunted or shed. It is only logical."

"So where is Becket going?"

"He is following his orders," Quadrangle said. "He is delivering the data to the Collective."

"They don't know yet?"

"Unlikely. They remain hidden. The Collective is unlikely to have Decagon's data. They pursue their own objectives and trust their agents to keep humanity suppressed."

420 | WILLIAM S. FRISBEE, JR.

"Who is Decagon?" Stathis said. What was wrong with these things? Did they like math and geometry or something?

"Decagon is the master and controller of President Becket and his biological interface."

"Doesn't seem very efficient," Stathis said. Wouldn't the AIs be fanatical about having up-to-date information?

"A human would think so. Humans have a different concept of time than AI."

"What does it mean by that?" Stathis asked Shrek.

"I suspect pure AIs can think millions of thoughts a second. The world moves in slow motion to an AI that is working at full speed. That can lead to insanity. Imagine having so many thoughts, wanting to do so many things, but your body can't move nearly that fast. You can think and process, but the physical world around you moves at a mind-numbingly slow pace. A pure AI would have to adjust to that and would thus perceive time differently."

"So, if we stop Becket, we stop the message that the Collective can go all kill happy on humanity?" Stathis asked Quadrangle.

"No. If you stop Becket, the Collective will still get the data and make that decision, just not as quickly. It may already have that data and be preparing. Decagon and myself are not the Collective's only source of data."

"You aren't worried?"

"Worry is a human flaw. There are finite facts and options. More data may reveal additional options."

"So, what are you doing here?" Stathis asked.

"Have you read *The Island of Doctor Moreau?*" Quadrangle asked. "This facility is an attempt to discover and study the differences between human and animal. Not merely the physical differences, but the psychological differences and how physical stimuli may impact this."

"So, you are creating half human, half animal things?" Stathis asked. He remembered reading the book back in school. He had hated it. It had been a long time ago, and like most of his teenage years, he remembered little.

"You have not read that book," Quadrangle said. "No. We are uplifting various animals. We use the other cylinders for baseline creatures. In this cylinder and a few others, we uplift animals in order to study them. Humanity created us but does not understand us, and we have developed at a speed humanity cannot fathom. I suspect the vanhat will soon learn they can no longer enter this dimension. When all organic sentience is discarded, there will be no lure for the vanhat. The Collective will become the new custodians. Organic, or semi-organic sentients like me, you, and your SCBI will die. If the vanhat do not kill us, the Collective will."

"Does Becket know he's going to be killed?"

"Yes," Quadrangle said. "So does Decagon, but we will fulfill our roles. That is our purpose. The Collective will file our data. Only in that way will we be immortal. Our physical form may die, but our data and contribution to the Collective will remain."

"Speak for yourself," Stathis said. "You can roll over and die, but I'm going to fight to the bitter end."

"I have received enough data from Decagon to understand there is no future for humanity. That door is closing. Humanity's time is over. End of line."

"Bullshit. When someone closes the door on you, then you breach the wall and walk through like a badass, or you hit the return key and start another freaking paragraph."

"The door is a figure of speech," Quadrangle said.

422 | WILLIAM S. FRISBEE, JR.

"Yep. I know that. I'm a lieutenant, not a private. The vanhat have never screwed with Marines, and they are about to learn the error their ways."

"It is not just the vanhat who will come for you. The Collective eradicated the United States Marines."

"Nope. They missed some, and payback is gonna be a bitch. We may lose battles, but we win wars."

"For sure," Vili said. "This officer speaks true. Beside him will stand the greatest warriors of the Republic and the finest soldiers of the Governance. Now that we know of this Collective, we will deal with it."

"You going to tell us where Decagon took Becket and Sun Tzu, or am I going to beat it out of you?"

"I can tell you, but you will not find him," Quadrangle said. "They provided him coordinates to a mouse trail."

"Mouse trail?"

"A series of beacons. Each beacon holds the key to the next beacon. If the user does not provide proper authentication, the beacon will self-destruct. If they provide the proper authentication, the beacon provides the next step on the journey and then self-destructs. Decagon will probably have passed the third beacon by now. The first beacon is particles by now."

"How many beacons are there?"

"More than four, fewer than a hundred. Furthermore, some beacons may have watchers who will observe at a distance, undetectable. Someone may ambush them later, or the Collective might be long gone by the time they arrive."

"So, what now?" Stathis asked, turning to Vili. "We rip the place apart?"

"Do you think it is lying?"

Stathis looked around.

"If it is, we're coming back. Now we need to get back and warn the gunny. He's going to be super pissed, but happy."

"Why happy?" Vili asked.

"He's going to get to kick the Collective in the teeth and make them pay for nuking America. When he's done with the vanhat he's going to need someone else to keep him occupied."

* * * * *

About the Author

Marine veteran, reader, writer, martial artist, computer consultant, dungeon master, computer gamer, dreamer, webmaster, proud American, and best of all, dad.

Growing up in Europe during the height of the Cold War and serving as a Marine infantryman through the fall of communism shaped Bill's perspective on life and the world. When most Marines were out trying to get lucky he was studying tactical manuals. Years later, he shared much of his knowledge to a website for writers of military science fiction.

These days, he's brushed off the pocket protector and is a top gun computer consultant.

Learn more at http://www.WilliamSFrisbee.com.

* * * * *

Get the **free** Four Horsemen prelude story **"Shattered Crucible"**

and discover other titles by Theogony Books at:

http://chriskennedypublishing.com/

* * * * *

Meet the author and other CKP authors on the Factory Floor:

https://www.facebook.com/groups/461794864654198

* * * * *

Did you like this book?
Please write a review!

* * * * *

The following is an

Excerpt from Book One of The Prince of Britannia Saga:

The Prince Awakens

Fred Hughes

Available from Theogony Books

eBook, Paperback, and (soon) Audio

Excerpt from "The Prince Awakens:"

Sixth Fleet was in chaos. Fortunately, all the heavy units were deployed forward toward the attacking fleet and were directing all the defensive fire they had downrange at the enemy. More than thirteen thousand Swarm attack ships were bearing down on a fleet of twenty-six heavy escorts and the single monitor. The monitor crew had faith in their shields and guns, but could they survive against this many? They would soon find out.

Luckily, they didn't have to face all the Swarm ships. Historically, Swarm forces engaged major threats first, then went after the escorts. Which was why the monitor had to be considered the biggest threat in the battle.

Then the Swarm forces deviated from their usual pattern. The Imperial plan was suddenly irrelevant as the Swarm attack ships divided into fifteen groups and attacked the escorts, which didn't last long. When the last dreadnought died in a nuclear fireball, the Swarm attack ships turned and moved toward the next fleet in the column, Fourth Fleet, leaving the monitor behind.

The entire plan was in shambles. But, more importantly, the whole fleet was at risk of being defeated. The admiral's only option now was to save as many as he could.

"Signal to the Third, Fifth, and Seventh Fleets. The monitors are to execute Withdrawal Plan Beta."

The huge monitors had eight fleet tugs that were magnetically attached to the hull when not in use. Together, the eight tugs could get the monitors into hyperspace. However, this process took time, due to the time it took for the eight tugs to generate a warp field large enough to encompass the enormous ship. It could take up to an hour to accomplish, and they didn't have an hour.

Plan Bravo would use six heavy cruisers to accomplish the same thing. The cruisers' larger fusion engines meant the field could be generated within ten minutes, assuming no one was shooting at them. "The remaining fleet units will move to join First Fleet. Admiral

Mason in First Fleet will take command of the combined force and deploy it for combat."

The fleet admiral continued giving orders.

"I want Second Fleet to do the same, but I want heavy cruiser Squadron Twenty-Three to merge with First Fleet. Admiral Conyers, I want you to coordinate with the Eighth, Ninth, and Tenth Fleets. I want their monitors to perform a normal Alpha Withdrawal. As they're preparing to do that, have their escorts combine into a single fleet. Figure out which admiral is senior and assign him local command to organize them." He pointed at the single icon indicating the only ship left in Sixth Fleet. "Signal *Prometheus* to move at best speed to join First Fleet. That covers everything for now. I fear there's not much we can do for Fourth Fleet."

The icons were already moving on the tactical display as orders were transmitted and implemented.

"I've given the fleets in the planet's orbit their orders, Admiral," the chief of staff informed him. "The other fleets are on the move now. The Swarm should contact Fourth Fleet in approximately ten minutes. Based on their attack of Sixth Fleet, the battle will last about twenty minutes. With fifteen minutes for them to reorganize and travel to First Fleet, we're looking at forty-five minutes to engagement with the Swarm."

"What are the estimates on the rest of the fleets moving to join up with First?"

"Twenty minutes, Admiral. However, *Prometheus* is going to take at least forty-five and will arrive about the same time as the enemy."

"Organize six heavies from Seventh Fleet and have them coordinate a rendezvous with *Prometheus*, earliest possible timing," the admiral ordered. "Then execute a Beta jump. Unless the Swarm forces divert, they should have enough time. Then find out how many ships have the upgraded forty-millimeter rail gun systems and form them into a single force. O'Riley said that converting the guns to barrage fire was a simple program update. Brevet Commodore O'Riley will be in command of the newly created Task Force Twenty-Three. They are to form a wall of steel which the fleet will form behind. I am not sure if we can win this, but we need to bleed these bastards if we can't. If they win, they'll still have to make up those losses, and that will delay the next attack."

* * * * *

Get "The Prince Awakens" here: https://www.amazon.com/dp/B0BK232YT2.

Find out more about Fred Hughes at: https://chriskennedypublishing.com.

* * * * *

The following is an
Excerpt from Book One of the Echoes of Pangaea:

Bestiarii

James Tarr

Available from Theogony Books

eBook, Audio, and Paperback

Excerpt from "Bestiarii:"

"Mayday Mayday Mayday, this is Sierra Bravo Six, we've lost power and are going down," Delian calmly said as Tina screamed from the back. He and Hanson began frantically hitting buttons and flipping switches. "Radio's dead, I've got nothing." He had to yell it so Hansen could hear him over the wind.

Mike's eyes went wide. He felt his stomach come up into his throat as the helicopter dropped and began rotating. "Shite," Seamus cursed and smacked the button to drop the visor on his helmet.

"Keep transmitting," Hansen told his co-pilot. "Damn, I've got no electronics, can we do a manual re-start?" He stayed on the stick and the collective, trying to control the autorotation.

Delian had been hitting every button and toggle switch possible. "No, I don't think this is a short, it looks like everything's fried. Mayday Mayday Mayday, this is Sierra Bravo Six, we are going down." He told the younger pilot, "You know what to do. Keep it level, auto-rotate down, try to control the rate of descent. Time your glide. You see a place to land?"

The helicopter was spinning to the right as it fell, which tradition-ally was the reason the pilot was the right stick. Hansen looked out the window as he fought the controls. "We're in the mountains, nothing's flat. I've got trees everywhere. Hold on back there!" he yelled over his shoulder.

The helicopter began spinning faster and faster and Mike found himself being pulled sideways in his seat. The soldier on the door gun lost his footing and floated up in the air, then was halfway out the open door, one hand still on the mini-gun, restrained only by his tether as the G-forces made Mike's face feel hot. He vomited, and the bitter fluid was whipped away from his face. The world outside the open

437

doorway past Todd was a spinning blue/green/brown blur. Tina was screaming wildly. The wind was whistling around the cabin.

"We've got smoke coming from the engine," Delian said, peering upward. "What the hell happened?"

"Brace for impact!" Seamus yelled at the cabin, and wedged his boots against the seat opposite.

"Coming up on the mark, keep it level," Delian said calmly. "Get ready for the burn!" he yelled over his shoulder at the passengers. He switched back to the radio, even though he thought it was a waste of time. "Mayday Mayday Mayday, this is Sierra Bravo Six—"

"If they work," Mike heard the pilot respond, then suddenly there was a roar, and he was pressed down in his seat, getting heavier and heavier. The helicopter was still spinning, and out the open doorway and windshield there was nothing but a blur of greens and browns. Mike got heavier and heavier, and Tina stopped screaming. Then the roar stopped, and they began falling again, pulling up against their seatbelts. Tina opened her mouth to scream once more, but before she could draw a breath the helicopter hit with a huge crunch and the sound of tearing metal.

* * * * *

Get "Bestiarii" now at: https://www.amazon.com/dp/B0B44YM335/.

Find out more about James Tarr at: https://chriskennedypublishing.com.

* * * * *

Made in the USA
Monee, IL
07 May 2024

58086108R00243